The War Of Women
Vol. I

by

Alexandre Dumas

The War Of Women
Vol. I
by Alexandre Dumas

ISBN: 978-93-62200-89-1

Published by

DOUBLE 9 BOOKS
2/13-B, Ansari Road
Daryaganj, New Delhi – 110002
info@double9books.com
www.double9books.com
Tel. 011-40042856

ABOUT THE AUTHOR

French author and playwright Alexandre Dumas fils is best known for his romantic novel La Dame aux Camélias (The Lady of the Camellias), published in 1848. Giuseppe Verdi adapted it into his opera La traviata (The Fallen Woman), which debuted in 1853. Other notable works by Dumas fils include a number of stage and film adaptations, which are usually titled Camille in English-language adaptations. The playwright Alexandre Dumas père ("father"), the author of classic works including The Three Musketeers and The Count of Monte Cristo, was the father of Dumas fils (French for "son"). Dumas fils received the Légion d'honneur (Legion of Honour) in 1894 after being accepted into the Académie française (French Academy) in 1874. The illegitimate child of tailor Marie-Laure-Catherine Labay (1794–1868) and novelist Alexandre Dumas, Dumas was born in Paris, France. His father gave him official recognition in 1831 and made sure the young Dumas attended the Collège Bourbon and the Institution Goubaux for the greatest education available. The elder Dumas was then permitted by law to remove the child from his mother. The younger Dumas was driven to write about sad female characters by her anguish.

CONTENTS

NANON DE LARTIGUES

I

At a short distance from Libourne, the bright and bustling city mirrored in the swift waters of the Dordogne, between Fronsac and Saint-Michel-la-Rivière, once stood a pretty little white-walled, red-roofed village, half-hidden by sycamores, lindens, and beeches. The high-road from Libourne to Saint-André-de-Cubzac passed through the midst of its symmetrically arranged houses, and formed the only landscape that they possessed. Behind one of the rows of houses, distant about a hundred yards, wound the river, its width and swiftness at this point indicating the proximity of the sea.

But the civil war passed that way; first of all it up-rooted the trees, then depopulated the houses, which, being exposed to all its capricious fury, and being unable to fly like their occupants, simply crumbled and fell to pieces by the roadside, protesting in their way against the savagery of intestine warfare. But little by little the earth, which seems to have been created for the express purpose of serving as the grave of everything upon it, covered the dead bodies of these houses, which were once filled with joyous life; lastly, the grass sprang up in this artificial soil, and the traveller who to-day wends his way along the solitary road is far from suspecting, as he sees one of the vast flocks which one encounters at every turn in the South cropping the grass upon the uneven surface, that sheep and shepherd are walking over the burial-place of a whole village. But, at the time of which we are speaking, that is to say about the month of May, 1650, the village in question lay along both sides of the road, which, like a mammoth artery, nourished it with luxuriant vegetation and overflowing life. The stranger who happened to pass along the road at that epoch would have taken pleasure in watching the peasants harness and unharness the horses from their carts, the fishermen along the hank pulling in their nets wherein the white and red fish of the Dordogne were dancing about, and the smiths striking sturdy blows upon the anvil, and sending forth at every stroke of the hammer a shower of sparks which lighted up the forge. However, the thing which would most have delighted his soul, especially if his journeying had given him that appetite which has become a proverbial attribute of travellers, would have been a long, low building, about five hundred yards outside the village, a building consisting of a ground-floor and first floor only, exhaling a certain vapor through its chimney, and through its windows certain odors which indicated, even more surely than the figure of a golden calf painted upon a piece of red iron, which creaked upon an iron rod set at the level of the first floor, that he had finally reached one of those hospitable establishments whose proprietors, in consideration of a certain modest recompense, undertake to restore the vigor of the tired wayfarer.

Will some one tell me why this hostelry of the Golden Calf was located five hundred yards from the village, instead of taking up its natural position amid the smiling houses grouped on either side of the road?

In the first place, because the landlord, notwithstanding the fact that his talents were hidden in this out-of-the-way corner of the world, was in culinary matters an artist of the first rank. Now, if he displayed his sign at any point between the beginning and the end of the two long lines of houses which formed the village, he ran the risk of being confounded with one of the wretched pot-house keepers whom he was forced to acknowledge as his confrères, but whom he could not bring himself to regard as his equals; while, on the contrary, by isolating himself he more easily attracted the notice of connoisseurs, who, having once tasted the delicacies that came from his kitchen, would say to others:—

"When you are going from Libourne to Saint-André-de-Cubzac, or from Saint-André-de-Cubzac to Libourne, do not fail to stop, for breakfast, dinner, or supper, at the Golden Calf, just outside the little village of Matifou."

And the connoisseurs would follow this counsel, would leave the inn well-content, and send other connoisseurs thither; so that the knowing Boniface gradually made his fortune, nor did that prevent him, strange to say, from continuing to maintain the high gastronomic reputation of his establishment; all of which goes to prove, as we have already said, that Master Biscarros was a true artist.

On one of those lovely evenings in the month of May, when Nature, already awakened from her winter's sleep in the South, is beginning to awake in the North, a denser vapor and more savory odor than usual was escaping from the chimneys and windows of the Golden Calf, while Master Biscarros in person, dressed in white, according to the immemorial custom of sacrificers of all times and of all countries, was standing in the doorway, plucking with his august hands partridges and quail, destined to grace the festive hoard at one of those dainty repasts which he was so skilful in preparing, and which he was accustomed, as a result of his love for his art, to superintend personally to the smallest detail.

The day was drawing to a close; the waters of the Dordogne, which, in one of the tortuous windings wherein its course abounds, turned aside from the road at this point, and washed the base of the little fort of Vayres, a fourth of a league away, were beginning to turn white beneath the dark foliage. A sense of tranquil melancholy overspread the landscape with the upspringing of the evening breeze; the laborers were toiling to their homes beside their horses, and the fishers with their dripping nets; the noises in the village died away; the hammer having struck its final stroke upon the anvil, bringing to its close another day, the nightingale began to raise his voice among the trees hard by.

At the first notes which escaped from the throat of the feathered warbler, Master Biscarros too began to sing,—to accompany him no doubt; the result of this rivalry and of the interest of Master Biscarros in the work he had in hand was that he did not perceive a small party of six horsemen, who appeared upon the outskirts of the village of Matifou, and rode toward his inn.

But an exclamation at one of the windows of the first floor, and the sudden noisy closing of that window caused the worthy inn-keeper to raise his head; thereupon he saw that the horseman at the head of the party was riding directly toward him.

"Directly" is not altogether the appropriate word, and we hasten to correct ourselves; for the man halted every few steps, darting keen glances to right and left, scrutinizing by-paths, trees, and bushes, holding a carbine upon his knee with one hand, to be ready for attack or defence, and from time to time motioning to his companions, who followed his movements in every point, to come on. Then he would venture forward a few steps, and the same manœuvres would be repeated.

Biscarros followed the horseman with his eyes, so deeply engrossed in his extraordinary mode of progression that he entirely forgot to detach from the fowl's body the bunch of feathers which he held between his thumb and forefinger.

"That gentleman is looking for my house," said Biscarros to himself. "He is short-sighted doubtless, for my *golden calf* is freshly painted, and the sign projects a good way. However, I'll place myself where he'll see me."

And Master Biscarros planted himself in the middle of the road, where he continued to pluck his partridge with much freedom and majesty of gesture.

This step produced the anticipated result; the cavalier no sooner spied the worthy inn-keeper than he rode up to him, and said, with a courteous salutation:—

"Your pardon, Master Biscarros, but have you not seen hereabout a party of soldiers, who are friends of mine, and should be looking for me? 'Soldiers' is perhaps too strong a word; 'gentlemen of the sword' is better, or best of all, 'armed men,'—yes, armed men, that expresses my meaning. Have you seen a small party of armed men?"

Biscarros, flattered beyond measure to be called by his name, affably returned the salutation; he had not noticed that the stranger, with a single glance at the inn, had read the name and profession of the proprietor upon the sign, as he now read his identity upon his features.

"As to armed men," he replied, after a moment's reflection, "I have seen only one gentleman and his squire, who stopped at my house about an hour ago."

"Oho!" exclaimed the stranger, caressing his chin, which was almost beardless, although his face was already instinct with virility; "oho! there is a gentleman and his squire here in your inn, and both armed, you say?"

"*Mon Dieu!* yes, monsieur; shall I send word to him that you wish to speak to him?"

"Would it be altogether becoming?" rejoined the stranger. "To disturb a person whom one doesn't know is somewhat too familiar usage, perhaps, especially if the unknown is a person of rank. No, no, Master Biscarros, be good enough to describe him to me, and let it go at that; or, better still, show him to me without letting him see me."

"It would be difficult to show him to you, monsieur, for he seems anxious to keep out of sight; he closed his window the moment you and your companions appeared upon the road. To describe him to you is a simpler matter: he is a slender youth, fair-haired and delicate, hardly more than sixteen; he seems to have just about enough strength to carry the little parlor sword which hangs at his baldric."

The stranger knit his brow as if searching his memory.

"Ah, yes!" said he, "I know whom you mean,—a light-haired, effeminate young dandy, riding a Barbary horse, and followed by an old squire, stiff as the knave of spades: he's not the man I seek."

"Ah! he's not the man monsieur seeks?" Biscarros repeated.

"No."

"Very good: pending his arrival whom monsieur seeks, as he cannot fail to pass this way, there being no other road, I trust that monsieur and his friends will enter my humble inn, and take some refreshment."

"No. I have simply to thank you, and to ask what time it might be."

"Six o'clock is just striking on the village clock, monsieur; don't you hear the loud tones of the bell"?"

"Tis well. Now, Monsieur Biscarros, one last service."

"With pleasure."

"Tell me, please, how I can procure a boat and boatman."

"To cross the river?"

"No, to take a sail upon the river."

"Nothing easier: the fisherman who supplies me with fish—Are you fond of fish, monsieur?" queried Biscarros, parenthetically, returning to his first idea of persuading the stranger to sup beneath his roof.

"It's not the most toothsome of delicacies, monsieur; however, when properly seasoned it's not to be despised."

"I always have excellent fish, monsieur."

"I congratulate you, Master Biscarros; but let us return to the man who supplies you."

"To be sure; at this hour his day's work is at an end, and he is probably dining. You can see his boat from here, moored to the willows yonder just below the large elm. His house is hidden in the osier-bed. You will surely find him at table."

"Thanks, Master Biscarros, thanks," said the stranger.

Motioning to his companions to follow him, he rode rapidly away toward the clump of trees and knocked at the door of the little cabin. The door was opened by the fisherman's wife.

As Master Biscarros had said, the fisherman was at table.

"Take your oars," said the horseman, "and follow me; there's a crown to be earned."

The fisherman rose with a degree of precipitation that was most eloquent of the hard bargains mine host of the Golden Calf was wont to drive.

"Do you wish to go down the river to Vayres?" he asked.

"No; simply to go out into midstream, and remain there a few moments."

The fisherman stared at his customer's exposition of this strange whim; but, as there was a crown at the end of it, and as he could see, some twenty yards away, the dark forms of the other horsemen, he made no objection, thinking that any indication of unwillingness on his part might lead to the use of force, and that, in the struggle, he would lose the proffered recompense.

He therefore made haste to say to the stranger that he was at his service, with his boat and his oars.

The little troop thereupon at once guided their horses toward the river, and, while their leader kept on to the water's edge, halted at the top of the bank, in such a position, as if they feared to be taken by surprise, that they could see in all directions. They had an uninterrupted view of the plain behind them, and could also cover the embarkation about to take place at their feet.

Thereupon the stranger, who was a tall, light-haired young man, pale and rather thin, nervous in his movements, and with a bright, intelligent face, although there were dark rings around his blue eyes, and a cynical expression played about his lips, —the stranger, we say, examined his pistols with particular attention, slung his carbine over his shoulder, made sure that his long rapier moved easily in its sheath, and then gazed attentively at the opposite shore, —a broad expanse of plain, intersected by a path which ran in a straight line from the bank to the hamlet of Isson; the dark church-spire and the smoke from the houses could be distinguished through the golden evening haze.

Also on the other bank, scarcely an eighth of a league distant, stood the little fort of Vayres.

"Well," said the stranger, beginning to lose patience, and addressing his companions on the bank, "is he coming; can you see him anywhere, to right or left, before or behind?"

"I think," said one of the men, "that I can make out a dark group on the Isson road; but I am not quite sure, for the sun's in my eyes. Wait! Yes, yes, there are one, two, three, four, five men, led by a laced hat and blue cloak. It must be the man we expect, attended by an escort for greater safety."

"He has the right to bring an escort," rejoined the stranger, phlegmatically. "Come and take my horse, Ferguzon."

The man to whom this command was addressed, in a half-familiar, half-imperative tone, obeyed at once, and rode down the bank. Meanwhile the stranger alighted, and when the other joined him, threw his bridle over his arm, and prepared to go aboard the boat.

"Look you," said Ferguzon, laying his hand upon his arm, "no useless foolhardiness, Cauvignac; if you see the slightest suspicious movement on your man's part, begin by putting a bullet through his brain; you see that the crafty villain has brought a whole squadron with him."

"True, but not so strong as ours. So we have the advantage in numbers as well as in courage, and need fear nothing. Ah! their heads are beginning to show."

"Gad! what are they going to do?" said Ferguzon. "They can't procure a boat. Ah! faith, there is one there as by magic."

"It's my cousin, the Isson ferry-man," said the fisherman, who evinced a keen interest in these preliminaries, and was in terror lest a naval battle was about to take place between his own craft and his cousin's.

"Good! there the blue-coat steps aboard," said Ferguzon; "and alone, by my soul!—strictly according to the terms of the treaty."

"Let us not keep him waiting," said the stranger; and leaping into the skiff he motioned to the fisherman to take his station.

"Be careful, Roland," said Ferguzon, recurring to his prudent counsel. "The river is broad; don't go too near the other shore, to be greeted with a volley of musket-balls that we can't return; keep on this side of the centre if possible."

He whom Ferguzon called now Roland, and again Cauvignac, and who answered to both names, doubtless because one was the name by which he was baptized, and the other his family name, or his *nom de guerre*, nodded assentingly.

"Never fear," he said, "I was just thinking of that; it's all very well for them who have nothing to take rash chances, but this business promises too well for me foolishly to run the risk of losing all the fruit of it; so if there is any imprudence committed on this occasion, it won't be by me. Off we go, boatman!"

The fisherman cast off his moorings, thrust his long pole into the watergrass, and the boat began to move away from the bank, at the same time that the Isson ferry-man's skiff put off from the opposite shore.

There was, near the centre of the stream, a little stockade, consisting of three stakes surmounted by a white flag, which served to point out to the long lighters going down the Dordogne the location of a dangerous cluster of rocks. When the water was running low, the black, slippery crest of the reef could be seen above the surface; but at this moment, when the Dordogne was full, the little flag, and a slight ripple in the water alone indicated its presence.

The two boatmen seemed by a common impulse to have fixed upon that spot as a convenient one for the interview between the two flags of truce, and both pulled in that direction; the ferry-man reached the flag first, and in accordance with his passenger's orders made his skiff fast to one of the rings in the stockade.

At that moment the fisherman turned to his passenger to take his orders, and was not a little surprised to find a masked man, closely wrapped in his cloak. Upon that discovery his feeling of dread, which had never left him, redoubled, and his voice trembled as he asked this strange personage what course he wished him to take.

"Make your boat fast to yonder piece of wood," said Cauvignac, pointing to one of the stakes, "and as near monsieur's boat as possible."

The boatman obeyed, and the two craft, brought close together by the current, permitted the plenipotentiaries to hold the following conference.

II

"What! you wear a mask, monsieur?" exclaimed the new-comer in a tone of surprise not unmixed with vexation. He was a stout man of some fifty-five to fifty-eight years, with the stern, glaring eye of a bird of prey, and a grizzly moustache and royale; although he wore no mask, he concealed his hair and his features as much as possible beneath a huge laced hat, and his figure and his clothes beneath a blue cloak of ample proportions.

Cauvignac, upon obtaining a view at close quarters of the individual who addressed him, could not restrain an involuntary movement of surprise.

"Well, well, monsieur, what's the matter?" demanded he of the blue cloak.

"Nothing, monsieur; I nearly lost my balance. I believe that you did me the honor of addressing me. What were you saying, pray?"

"I asked you why you are masked."

"That is a plain question," said the young man, "and I will reply with equal frankness; I am masked in order to conceal my face."

"Then it is a face that I know?"

"I think not; but having seen it once you might know it again later; and that, in my opinion, would be utterly useless."

"I should say that you were quite as outspoken as myself."

"Yes, when outspokenness can do me no harm."

"Does your frankness go so far as to lead you to disclose the secrets of others?"

"Why not, if such disclosure can be of advantage to me?"

"It's a singular profession that you practise."

"*Dame!* one does what one can do, monsieur; I have been, in succession, lawyer, doctor, soldier, and partisan; you see that I am not likely to go begging for a trade."

"What are you now?"

"Your humble servant," said the young man, bowing respectfully.

"Have you the letter in question?"

"Have you the blank signature?"

"Here it is."

"Shall we make the exchange?"

"One moment, monsieur," said the stranger in the blue cloak; "your conversation is delightful to me, and I should be sorry to lose my enjoyment of it so soon."

"Good lack! monsieur, it is quite at your service, as I myself am," rejoined Cauvignac. "Let us talk, by all means, if it is agreeable to you."

"Shall I step into your boat, or do you prefer to come aboard mine, so that our boatmen may be out of ear-shot in the other boat?"

"Useless, monsieur; you speak some foreign tongue, no doubt?"

"I can speak Spanish."

"And I; let us talk in Spanish, then, if you please."

"By all means! What motive," continued the gentleman, adopting from that moment the idiom agreed upon, "led you to inform the Duc d'Épernon of the infidelity of the lady in question?"

"I was desirous to be of service to that eminent nobleman, and to get into his good graces."

"Have you any ill-will to Mademoiselle de Lartigues?"

"Ill-will? By no manner of means! On the contrary, I must admit that I am under some obligation to her, and I should be extremely sorry were any mishap to befall her."

"Then Monsieur le Baron de Canolles is your enemy?"

"I never saw him; I know him only by reputation, and I must say that he is said to be a gallant knight and worthy gentleman."

"I am to understand that your action is not induced by hatred of any person?"

"Go to! if I had a grievance against Baron de Canolles I should challenge him to exchange shots or sword-thrusts with me, and he is too much of a man ever to decline an invitation of that kind."

"In that case I must recur to the reason you have given me."

"I think you can do no better."

"Very good! I understand that you have the letter which proves Mademoiselle de Lartigues to be unfaithful."

"Here it is. No offence, but this is the second time I have shown it to you."

The older gentleman glanced sadly from afar at the dainty paper, through which he could see the written characters.

The young man slowly unfolded the letter.

"You recognize the writing, do you not?"

"Yes."

"Then give me the blank signature, and you shall have the letter."

"In a moment. Will you allow me to ask you a question?"

"Ask it, monsieur."

The young man tranquilly folded the paper again, and replaced it in his pocket.

"How did you procure the letter?"

"I am quite willing to tell you."

"I am listening."

"You know that the somewhat extravagant government of the Duc d'Épernon has aroused a strong feeling against him in Guyenne?"

"Very well; go on."

"You know that the frightfully stingy government of Monsieur de Mazarin has aroused a tremendously strong feeling against him in the capital?"

"What have Monsieur de Mazarin and Monsieur d'Épernon to do with the matter?"

"One moment; these two strongly contrasted governments have produced a state of things much resembling a general war, in which every one has a share. At this moment Monsieur de Mazarin is fighting for the queen; you are fighting for the king; the coadjutor is fighting for Monsieur de Beaufort; Monsieur de Beaufort is fighting for Madame de Montbazon; Monsieur de La Rochefoucauld is fighting for Madame de Longueville; Monsieur le Duc d'Orléans is fighting for Mademoiselle Soyon; the Parliament is fighting for the people; lastly, Monsieur de Condé, who was fighting for France, has been imprisoned. Now I, who have no great stake to gain by fighting for the queen, for the king, for the coadjutor, for Monsieur de Beaufort, for Madame de Montbazon, for Madame de Longueville, for Mademoiselle Soyon, for the people, or for France, conceived the scheme of espousing no party whatever, but of following the one which I feel inclined to follow at the moment. Thus with me it is a question of expediency pure and simple. What say you to the idea?"

"It is ingenious, certainly."

"Consequently I have levied an army. You can see it drawn up yonder on the bank of the Dordogne."

"Five men? Nonsense!"

"That's one more than you have yourself; it doesn't look well, therefore, for you to treat it with contempt."

"Very ill clad," continued the older man, who was in ill-humor, and for that reason inclined to be censorious.

"True," rejoined his interlocutor, "they somewhat resemble the companions of Falstaff. Falstaff, by the way, is an English gentleman of my acquaintance. But to-night they will be newly equipped, and if you fall in with them to-morrow, you will admit that they are pretty fellows."

"Let us return to yourself. I am not concerned with your men."

"Very well; as I was saying, in the course of my warfare on my own account, we fell in with the tax-collector of this district, who was going from village to village, rounding out his Majesty's purse. So long as there was a single stiver uncollected we did escort duty for him faithfully, and I confess that, as I watched his money-bags filling, I was strongly tempted to join the king's faction. But the infernal confusion that reigned everywhere, together with a fit of spleen against Monsieur de Mazarin, and the complaints that we heard on all sides against Monsieur d'Épernon, brought us to our senses. We concluded that there was much to be said in favor of the justice of the princes' cause, and we embraced it with ardor; the collector completed his round of visits at the little house which stands by itself yonder among the poplars and sycamores."

"Nanon's house!" muttered the other; "yes, I see it."

"We watched until he came out, we followed him as we had been doing for five days, we crossed the Dordogne with him just below Saint-Michel, and when we were in midstream I told him of our conversion politically, and requested him, with all the courtesy of which I am capable, to turn over to us the cash in his possession. Would you believe, monsieur, that he refused? Thereupon, my comrades searched him, and as he was shrieking in a way to cause scandal, my lieutenant, a resourceful rascal,—you see him yonder, in a red cloak, holding my horse,—reflected that the water, by intercepting the air-currents, interfered with the continuity of sound; that is an axiom in physics which I, as a physician, understood and applauded. The author of the suggestion thereupon bent the recalcitrant tax-collector's head over toward the river, and held it a foot—no more—under water. As a matter of fact he ceased to shout, or, to put it more accurately, we ceased to hear him. We were able, therefore, to seize in the name of the princes all the money in his possession, and the correspondence which had been intrusted to him. I gave the money to my soldiers, who, as you justly observed, need to be newly equipped, and I kept the papers, this one among others: it seems that the worthy collector acted as Mercury for Mademoiselle de Lartigues."

"Indeed," muttered the old gentleman, "he was a creature of Nanon's if I mistake not. What became of the wretch?"

"Ah! you will see whether we did well to dip the wretch, as you call him, in the river. Why, except for that precaution he would have aroused the whole country. Fancy, when we took him out of the water, although he had been there hardly quarter of an hour, he was dead with rage!"

"You plunged him in again, no doubt?"

"As you say."

"But if the messenger was drowned—"

"I didn't say that he was drowned."

"Let us not haggle over words; if the messenger is dead—"

"Oh! as to that, he's dead enough."

"Monsieur de Canolles will not have received the letter, of course, and consequently will not keep the appointment."

"Oh! one moment; I make war on powers, not on private individuals. Monsieur de Canolles received a duplicate of the letter making the appointment; but as I considered that the autograph manuscript was of some value, I retained it."

"What will he think when he fails to recognize the writing?"

"That the person who hungers for a sight of him has employed another hand, as a measure of precaution."

The stranger eyed Cauvignac in evident admiration of such unbounded impudence combined with such perfect self-possession. He was determined, if possible, to find some means of frightening the reckless swashbuckler.

"What about the government," he said, "and the investigations that may be set on foot? Do you never think of that?"

"Investigations?" rejoined the younger man, with a laugh. "Oh! Monsieur d'Épernon has many other things to do besides investigate; and then, did I not tell you that I did what I did for the purpose of obtaining his favor? He would be ungrateful indeed if he didn't bestow it on me."

"I don't altogether understand," said the other, satirically, "how it ever occurred to you, who have, by your own admission, taken up the cause of the princes, to do Monsieur d'Épernon a service."

"And yet it's the simplest thing in the world: an inspection of the papers found upon the collector convinced me of the purity of the king's intentions; his Majesty is entirely justified in my eyes, and Monsieur le Duc d'Épernon is in the right a thousand times over as against his subordinates. That, therefore, is the just cause, and thereupon I embraced the just cause."

"Here's a scoundrel whom I will have hanged if he ever falls into my hands!" growled the old gentleman, pulling savagely at the ends of his bristly moustache.

"I beg your pardon?" said Cauvignac, winking under his mask.

"I said nothing. Let me ask you a question; what do you propose to do with the signature in blank which you demand?"

"Deuce take me if I've made up my mind! I asked for a signature in blank, because it is the most convenient thing, the easiest to carry, and the most elastic. It is probable that I shall keep it for some great emergency; but it is possible that I may throw it away on the first whim that comes to my mind; perhaps I may present it to you in person before the end of the week, perhaps it will not come back to you for three or four months, and then with a dozen or more endorsers, like a piece of commercial paper; but never fear, I shall not use it for any purpose for which you and I need blush. Noble blood counts for something, after all."

"You are of noble blood?"

"Yes, monsieur, the very noblest."

"In that case I will have him broken on the wheel," muttered the unknown; "that's the service his blank signature will do him!"

"Have you decided to give me the signature in blank?" asked Cauvignac.

"I must," was the reply.

"I don't force you to do it; let us understand each other. What I propose is an exchange; keep your paper if you choose, and I will keep mine."

"The letter?"

"The signature?"

And he held out the letter with one hand, while he cocked a pistol with the other.

"Don't disturb the repose of your pistol," said the stranger, throwing open his cloak; "for I have pistols, too, and they are all loaded. Fair play on both sides; here's your signature."

The exchange of documents was effected without further parley, and each of the parties examined that which was handed to him, carefully and in silence.

"Now, monsieur," said Cauvignac, "in which direction do you go?"

"I must cross to the right bank."

"And I to the left."

"How shall we arrange it? My men are where you propose to go, and yours where I propose to go."

"Why, nothing could be simpler; send my men over to me in your boat, and I will send yours over in mine."

"You have an inventive mind, and one that works very quickly."

"I was born to command an army."

"And so you do."

"Ah! true, I had forgotten," said the young man.

The stranger motioned to the ferry-man to cast off his boat, and pull to the opposite shore in the direction of the clump of woods which reached to the road.

The young man, who was perhaps expecting some treachery, stood half erect to look after him, with his hand still resting on the butt of his pistol, ready to fire at the least suspicious movement on the stranger's part. But the latter did not even deign to notice the distrust of which he was the object, and, turning his back on the young man with real or affected indifference, began to read the letter, and was soon entirely engrossed in its contents.

"Remember the hour," Cauvignac called after him; "eight o'clock this evening."

The stranger made no reply, and did not seem to have heard.

"Ah!" said Cauvignac to himself, caressing the butt of his pistol: "to think that, if I chose, I might throw open the succession to the government of Guyenne, and stop the civil war! But, with the Duc d'Épernon dead, what good would his signature in blank do me? and with the civil war at an end, what should I live on? Upon my word, there are times when I believe I am going mad. Vive le Duc d'Épernon and the civil war!—Come, boatman, to your oars, and pull to the other shore; we must not keep the worthy man waiting for his escort."

In a few moments Cauvignac approached the left bank of the Dordogne, just as the old gentleman was sending Ferguzon and his five bandits over to him in the ferry-man's boat. As he did not choose to be less prompt than he, he ordered his boatman to take the stranger's four men in his boat, and put them ashore on the other bank. In midstream the two boats met, and the occupants saluted one another courteously, as they passed on toward the point where their respective leaders were awaiting them. The old gentleman thereupon, with his escort, disappeared among the trees which stretched from the river-bank to the high-road; and Cauvignac, at the head of his army, took the path leading to Isson.

III

Half an hour after the scene we have described, the same window in Master Biscarros' hostelry which had been closed so suddenly was cautiously re-opened, and a young man of some sixteen or eighteen years, dressed in black, with sleeves puffed at the wrists, in the fashion of that day, rested his elbows on the window-sill, after carefully scrutinizing the road to right and left. A shirt of the finest linen protruded proudly from his doublet, and fell in wavy folds over his beribboned small-clothes. His small, slender hand, a true thoroughbred hand, toyed impatiently with his buckskin gloves, embroidered along the seams; a pearl-gray felt hat, surmounted by a magnificent blue feather, shaded his long, golden-chestnut locks, which formed a marvellously fitting frame for an oval face, with fair complexion, rosy lips, and black eyebrows. But truth compels us to state that this attractive ensemble, which was well adapted to make the youth one of the most charming of cavaliers, was for the moment ever so little clouded by an expression of ill-humor, caused no doubt by a season of profitless waiting; for he gazed with dilated eye along the road, which was already swimming in the evening mist.

In his impatience he struck his left hand with his gloves. At the sound, the landlord, who was plucking his last partridge, raised his head, and said, removing his cap, —

"At what hour will you sup, my young sir? We are only awaiting your orders to serve you."

"You know that I do not sup alone, but am awaiting a friend; when you see him coming, you may serve the supper."

"Ah, monsieur," rejoined Master Biscarros, "I wouldn't presume to censure your friend, for he is certainly free to come or not; but it's a very bad habit to keep people waiting."

"He has no such habit, and I am much surprised at his tardiness."

"I am something more than surprised, monsieur; I am deeply grieved, for the joint will be burned."

"Take it off the spit."

"Then it will be cold."

"Put another to the fire."

"It won't be cooked."

"In that case, my friend, do as you please," said the youth, unable, notwithstanding his ill-humor, to refrain from smiling at the inn-keeper's despair: "I intrust the matter to your supreme wisdom."

"There is no wisdom, not even King Solomon's own, that would make a warmed-over dinner eatable."

Having propounded that axiom, which Boileau was to express in verse twenty years later, Master Biscarros, shaking his head sadly, entered the inn.

Thereupon the youth, as if to cheat his impatience, drew back into the chamber, and was heard for a moment or two stamping noisily back and forth across the floor; but almost immediately, thinking that he heard horses' footsteps in the distance, he rushed to the window again.

"At last!" he cried; "there he is! God be praised!"

As he spoke, the head of a mounted man appeared beyond the thicket where the nightingale was singing, to whose melodious notes the young man seemed to pay no attention, doubtless because of his intense preoccupation. To his great astonishment, he waited in vain for the horseman to come out upon the road, for he turned to the right and rode in among the bushes, where his hat soon disappeared,—an unmistakable indication that he had alighted. A moment later the watcher saw through the branches, as they were cautiously put aside, a gray helmet, and the last rays of the setting sun were reflected on a musket-barrel.

The young man remained at his window lost in thought; evidently the man hiding in the thicket was not the friend he expected, and the impatient expression which darkened his mobile features gave place to an expression of curiosity.

Soon a second hat appeared beside the first, and the young man drew back out of sight.

The same gray helmet, the same glistening musket-barrel, the same manœuvring in the thicket. The new arrival addressed some words to the other, which the watcher could not hear because of the distance; and, in consequence doubtless of the information he received, he plunged into the hedge which ran parallel to the thicket, crouched behind a rock, and waited.

From his elevated position the young man could see his hat above the rock. Beside the hat gleamed a luminous point,—it was the end of the musket-barrel.

A feeling of terror took possession of the young gentleman's mind, and he drew back farther and farther as he watched.

"Oho!" he thought, "I wonder if they have designs on me and the thousand louis I have with me. But no; for, even if Richon comes, so that I can go on this evening, I am going to Libourne, and not to Saint-André-de-Cubzac, and so shall not pass the spot where those villains are in ambush. If my old Pompée were here, I would consult him. But what's this? If I'm not mistaken—yes, on my word, there are two more men! Gad! this has every appearance of an ambuscade in form."

He stepped still farther back, for it was true that at that moment two other horsemen appeared at the same point; but only one of these two wore the gray helmet. The other, astride a powerful black horse, and wrapped in the folds of an ample cloak, wore a hat trimmed with gold lace and adorned with a white feather; and beneath the cloak, as the evening breeze blew it aside, could be seen an abundance of rich embroidery upon a reddish doublet.

One would have said that the day was prolonging itself in order to light this scene, for the sun's last rays, as the luminary came forth from behind a bank of those dark clouds which sometimes stretch so picturesquely along the horizon at sundown, suddenly set ablaze a thousand rubies in the windows of a pretty little house, situated a hundred yards or less from the river, and which the young man would not otherwise have noticed, as it was in a great measure concealed by trees. This additional supply of light enabled him to see in the first place that the spies were watching the end of the village street and the little house with the shining windows, looking from one to the other; secondly, that the gray helmets seemed to have the greatest respect for the white feather; and lastly, that one of the windows in question was thrown open, and a woman appeared upon the balcony, looked about for a moment, as if she too were expecting some one, then re-entered the house as if she wished to avoid being seen.

As she disappeared, the sun sank behind the hill, and as it sank, the ground-floor of the house was immersed in darkness, and the light, gradually abandoning the windows, ascended to the slate roof, to disappear at last, after playing for a moment with a weather-vane consisting of a sheaf of golden arrows.

In the facts we have detailed there was ample material for any intelligent mind to build up a structure of probabilities, if not of certainties.

It was probable that the men were watching the isolated house, upon the balcony of which a woman had shown herself for an instant; it was probable that the woman and the men were expecting the arrival of one and the same person, but with very different intentions; it was probable that this person was to come from the village, and consequently to pass the inn, which was about half-way between the village and the thicket, as the thicket was about half-way between the inn and the house; it was probable that the horseman with the white feather was the leader of the horsemen with gray helmets, and, from the eagerness with which he stood up in his stirrups, in order to see farther, it was probable that he was jealous, and was watching in his own interest.

Just as the young man was concluding this chain of reasoning, the links of which fell naturally together in his mind, the door of his apartment opened and Master Biscarros appeared.

"My dear host," said the young man, without giving him time to explain the purpose of his visit,—a purpose which he guessed, however, "come hither, and tell me, if my question is not impertinent, whose is the small house which I see yonder,—a white speck among the poplars and sycamores."

The landlord followed with his eyes the direction in which the speaker's index finger pointed, and scratched his head.

"'Faith!" he replied, with a smile which he tried to render cunning, "sometimes it belongs to one person, sometimes to another; it's yours, if you have any reason for seeking solitude, whether you wish to conceal yourself, or simply to conceal some one else."

The young man blushed.

"But who lives there to-day?" he asked.

"A young lady who passes herself off for a widow, and whom the ghost of her first, and sometimes of her second husband, comes to visit from time to time. But there's one remarkable thing about it, and that is that the two ghosts seem to have an understanding with each other, and never return at the same time."

"Since when," asked the young man, with a smile, "has the fair widow occupied this house, which is so convenient for ghosts?"

"About two months. She keeps very much to herself, and no one, I think, can boast of having seen her during that time, for she goes out very rarely, and always heavily veiled. A little maid—a fascinating creature, on my word!—comes here every morning to order the meals for the day, and I send them to the house; she receives the dishes in the vestibule, pays handsomely for them, and shuts the door in the waiter's face. This evening, for example, there is a banquet on hand, and the partridge and quail you saw me plucking are for her."

"Whom does she entertain to-night?"

"One of the two ghosts I told you of, no doubt."

"Have you ever seen these ghosts?"

"Yes; but only passing along the road, after sunset, or before daylight."

"Nevertheless, I am sure that you have noticed them, dear Monsieur Biscarros; for, from the first word you spoke, I could see that you are a close observer. Come, what have you noticed in their appearance?"

"One is the ghost of a man of some sixty to sixty-five years; and that one I take to be the first husband, for it goes and comes like a ghost sure of the priority of its rights. The other is the ghost of a young man of twenty-six or twenty-eight, and this one is more timid, and has the appearance of a soul in torment; so I would swear that it's the ghost of the second husband."

"At what hour is the supper to be served to-night?"

"Eight o'clock."

"It is half after seven," said the young man, drawing from his fob a dainty little watch which he had already consulted several times; "you have no time to lose."

"Oh! it will be ready, never fear; but I came up to speak about your own, and to tell you that I have begun it all anew. So try, now, as your friend has delayed so long, to keep him away for another hour."

"Look you, my dear host," said the young gentleman, with the air of a man to whom the important question of a meal served at the proper moment was a secondary matter, "don't be disturbed about our supper, whenever the person whom I expect arrives, for we have much to talk about. If the supper isn't ready we will talk first; if it is ready, we will talk afterward."

"In good sooth, monsieur, you are a very accommodating gentleman, and since you are content to leave the matter in my hands, you shall not be disappointed; make your mind easy on that score."

Whereupon Master Biscarros made a low bow, to which the young man replied with a nod, and left the room.

"Now," said the young man to himself, resuming his station at the window with renewed interest, "I understand the whole affair. The lady is expecting somebody who is to come from Libourne, and the men in the bushes propose to accost him before he has time to knock at her door."

At that instant, as if to confirm the supposition of our sagacious observer, he heard the hoof-beats of a horse at his left. His eye instantly sought the thicket to observe the attitude of the men in ambush there. Although the darkness was beginning to obscure the different objects, it seemed to him that some of the men put aside the branches, while the others stood up to look over the rock, all alike preparing for a movement, which had every appearance of being an aggressive one. At the same time a sharp click, like the cocking of a musket, reached his ear thrice, and made him shudder. He at once turned in the opposite direction, to try and discern the person whose safety was menaced by that murderous sound, and spied a young man trotting briskly along upon a graceful, well-shaped horse. A handsome fellow he was, head erect, nose in air, and hand on hip, wearing a short cloak, lined with white satin, thrown gracefully over his right shoulder. Seen from a distance, he seemed to have a refined, poetic, joyous face. At closer quarters, it was seen to be a face with pure outlines, bright, clear complexion, keen eyes, lips slightly parted by the habit of smiling, a soft, black moustache, and fine, white teeth. A lordly way of twirling his switch, accompanied by a soft whistle, like that affected by the dandies of the epoch, following the fashion set by Monsieur Gaston d'Orléans, was not lacking, to make of the new-comer a perfect cavalier, according to the laws of good form then in vogue at the court of France, which was beginning to set the fashion for all the courts of Europe.

Fifty paces behind him, mounted upon a horse whose gait he regulated by that of his master's, rode an extremely consequential, high and mighty valet, who seemed to occupy a no less distinguished station among servants than his master among gentlemen.

The comely youth watching from the window of the inn, too young, doubtless, to look on in cold blood at such a scene as seemed imminent, could not restrain a shudder as he reflected that the two paragons who were approaching, with such absolute indifference and sense of security, would, in all probability, be shot down when they reached the spot where their foes were lying in ambush. A decisive conflict seemed to take place between the timidity natural at his age and his love for his neighbor. At last the generous sentiment carried the day, and as the gallant cavalier was riding by in front of the inn, without even looking toward it, the young man obeyed a sudden, irresistible impulse, leaned from the window, and cried,—

"Holé! monsieur, stop a moment, please, for I have something of importance to say to you."

At the sound of the voice, and the words which it uttered, the horseman raised his head, and seeing the young man at the window, stopped his horse with a movement of his hand which would have done honor to the best of squires.

"Don't stop your horse, monsieur, but ride toward me unconcernedly, as if you knew me."

The traveller hesitated a second; but realizing that he had to do with a gentleman of engaging countenance and pleasant manners, he removed his hat, and rode forward, smiling.

"Here I am, at your service, monsieur," he said; "what can I do for you?"

"Come still nearer, monsieur," continued he at the window; "or what I have to tell you cannot be told aloud. Put on your hat, for we must make them think that we are old acquaintances, and that you were coming to this inn to see me."

"But I don't understand, monsieur," said the traveller.

"You will understand directly; meanwhile put on your hat—good! Now come near, nearer! Give me your hand! That's it! Delighted to see you! Now listen; do not ride on beyond this inn, or you are lost!"

"What's the matter? Really, you terrify me," said the traveller, with a smile.

"The matter is that you are on your way to yonder little house where we see the light, are you not?"

The horseman started.

"Well, on the road to that house, at the bend in the road, in yonder dark thicket, four men are lying in wait for you."

"Oho!" exclaimed the traveller, gazing with all his eyes at the young man, who was quite pale. "Indeed! you are sure?"

"I saw them ride up, one after another, get down from their horses, and hide,—some behind the trees, others behind rocks. Lastly, when you rode out of the village just now, I heard them cock their muskets."

"The devil!" exclaimed the traveller, beginning to take alarm.

"Yes, monsieur, it's just as I tell you," continued the young man at the window; "if it were only not quite so dark you could see them, and perhaps recognize them."

"Oh! I have no need to see them; I know perfectly well who they are. But who told you that I was going to that house, monsieur, and that it is I they are watching for?"

"I guessed it."

"You are a very charming Œdipus; thanks! Ah! they propose to shoot me; how many of them are assembled for that praiseworthy purpose?"

"Four; one of whom seemed the leader."

"He is older than the others, is n't he?"

"Yes, as well as I could judge from here."

"Does he stoop?"

"He is round-shouldered, wears an embroidered doublet, white plume, brown cloak; his gestures are infrequent but imperative."

"As I thought; it's the Duc d'Épernon."

"The Duc d'Épernon!"

"Well, well, here I am telling you my business," said the traveller with a laugh. "I never do so with others; but no matter, you have done me so great a service that I don't care so much what I say to you. How are the men dressed who are with him?"

"Gray helmets."

"Just so; they are his staff-bearers."

"Become musket-bearers for to-day."

"In my honor; thanks! Now, do you know what you ought to do, my young gentleman?"

"No; but tell me your opinion, and if what I ought to do can be of any service to you, I am ready in advance to undertake it."

"You have weapons?"

"Why—yes; I have a sword."

"You have your servant?"

"Of course; but he is not here; I sent him to meet some one whom I expect."

"Very well; you ought to lend me a hand."

"To do what?"

"To charge the villains, and make them and their leader beg for mercy."

"Are you mad, monsieur?" cried the young man, in a tone which showed that he was not in the least inclined for such an expedition.

"Indeed, I ask your pardon," said the traveller; "I forgot that the affair had no interest for you."

Turning to his servant, who had halted when his master halted, he said, —

"Come here, Castorin!"

At the same time he put his hand to his holsters, as if to make sure that his pistols were in good condition.

"Ah, monsieur!" cried the young man at the window, putting out his arms as if to stop him, "monsieur, in Heaven's name do not risk your life in such an adventure! Rather come into the inn, and thereby avoid arousing the suspicion of the men who are waiting for you; consider that the honor of a woman is at stake."

"You are right," rejoined the horseman; "although, in this case, it's not her honor, precisely, but her material welfare. Castorin, my good fellow," he added, addressing his servant, who had joined him; "we will go no farther just now."

"What!" cried Castorin, almost as disappointed as his master, "what does monsieur say?"

"I say that Mademoiselle Francinette will have to do without the pleasure of seeing you this evening, as we shall pass the night at the Golden Calf; go in, therefore, order supper for me, and a bed to be got ready."

As he doubtless saw that Monsieur Castorin proposed to make some rejoinder, he accompanied his last words with a movement of the head which effectually precluded any more extended discussion. Castorin at once passed through the gate, crestfallen, and without venturing to say another word.

The traveller looked after him for an instant; then, after reflecting for another instant, seemed to have made up his mind what course to adopt. He alighted from his horse, passed through the gate on the heels of his lackey, over whose arm he threw his rein, entered the inn, and in two bounds was at the door of the room occupied by the young gentleman, who, when his door was suddenly thrown open, made an involuntary movement of surprise mingled with alarm, which the new-comer could not detect because of the darkness.

"And so," said the latter, approaching the young man with a jovial air, and cordially pressing a hand which was not offered him, "it's a settled fact that I owe you my life."

"Oh, monsieur, you exaggerate the service I have done you," said the young man, stepping back.

"No, no! no modesty; it's as I say. I know the duke, and he's an infernally brutal fellow. As for you, you are a model of perspicacity, a perfect phœnix of Christian charity. But tell me, my obliging and sympathetic friend, if you carried your thoughtfulness so far as to send word to the house."

"To what house?"

"*Pardieu!* to the house where I was going, — the house where I am expected."

"No," said the young man, "I did not think of it, I confess; and had I thought of it I had no way to do it. I have been here barely two hours myself, and I know no one in the house."

"The devil!" exclaimed the traveller with an anxious expression. "Poor Nanon! if only nothing happens to her."

"Nanon! Nanon de Lartigues!" exclaimed the young man in amazement.

"Upon my word! are you a sorcerer?" said the traveller. "You see men lying in wait by the roadside, and you divine whom they are waiting for; I mention a Christian name, and you divine the family name. Explain yourself at once, or I denounce you, and have you condemned to death at the stake by the parliament of Bordeaux!"

"Ah! but you surely will agree that one need not be very cunning to have solved that problem; once you had named the Duc d'Épernon as your rival, it was plain enough that if you named any Nanon whatsoever, it must be the beautiful, wealthy, and clever Nanon de Lartigues, by whom the duke is bewitched, so they say, and who really governs in his province; the result being that throughout Guyenne she is almost as bitterly detested as he is himself. And you were on your way to visit that woman?" the young man added, reproachfully.

"'Faith, yes, I confess it; and as I have called her name, I won't deny her. Besides, Nanon is misunderstood and slandered. She is a charming girl, faithful to her promises so long as she finds it agreeable to keep them, and devoted to the man she loves, so long as she loves him. I was to sup with her this evening, but the duke has upset the saucepan. Would you like me to present you to her to-morrow? Deuce take it! the duke must return to Agen sooner or later."

"Thanks," returned the young gentleman, dryly. "I know Mademoiselle de Lartigues by name only, and I have no desire for any further acquaintance with her."

"Well, you are wrong, *morbleu!* Nanon is a good person to know in every way."

The young man's brows contracted.

"Oho! I beg your pardon," said the astonished traveller; "but I thought that at your age—"

"I know that I am of an age at which such suggestions are ordinarily accepted," replied the other, noticing the bad effect his prudery seemed to have produced, "and I would gladly accept, were it not that I am simply a bird of passage here, and am compelled to continue my journey to-night."

"*Pardieu!* surely you will not go until I know the name of the gentle knight who so courteously saved my life?"

The young man hesitated for a moment before he replied,—

"I am the Vicomte de Cambes."

"Aha!" said his companion; "I have heard of a lovely Vicomtesse de Cambes, who has large estates near Bordeaux, and is a close friend of Madame la Princesse."

"She is a kinswoman of mine," said the young man, hastily.

"'Faith, viscount, I congratulate you, for they say that she is charming beyond compare. I hope you will present me to her, if the opportunity ever occurs. I am Baron de Canolles, captain in the Navailles regiment, and at present enjoying a leave of absence which Monsieur le Duc d'Épernon was pleased to grant me, at the recommendation of Mademoiselle de Lartigues."

"Baron de Canolles!" cried the viscount, gazing at his companion with the curiosity naturally aroused by that name, renowned in the love intrigues of the time.

"You know me?" said Canolles.

"By reputation only," the viscount replied.

"And by bad reputation, eh? What would you have? Every one follows his natural inclinations, and I love a life of excitement."

"You are perfectly free, monsieur, to live as you choose," rejoined the viscount. "Permit me, however, to express one thought that comes to my mind."

"What is it?"

"That there is a woman yonder, deeply compromised for your sake, upon whom the duke will wreak vengeance for his disappointment in your regard."

"The devil! do you think it?"

"Of course; although she is a somewhat frail person, Mademoiselle de Lartigues is a woman none the less, and compromised by you; it is for you to look to her safety."

"Gad! you are right, my young Nestor; and in the pleasure of conversing with you, I was near forgetting my obligations as a gentleman. We have been betrayed, and in all probability the duke knows all. It is very, true that Nanon is so clever that if she were warned in time, I would wager my life that she would make the duke apologize. Now let us see; are you acquainted with the art of war, young man?"

"Not yet," replied the viscount, with a laugh; "but I fancy I am likely to learn it where I am going."

"Well, here's your first lesson. In war, you know, when force is out of the question, we must resort to stratagem. Help me to carry out a stratagem."

"I ask nothing better. But in what way? Tell me."

"The inn has two doors."

"I know nothing about that."

"I know it; one that opens on the high-road, and another that opens into the fields. I propose to go out by the one that leads into the fields, describe a semi-circle, and knock at the back door of Nanon's house."

"Yes, so that you may be caught in the house!" cried the viscount. "You would make a fine tactician, upon my word!"

"Caught in the house?" repeated Canolles.

"Why, to be sure. The duke, tired of waiting, and failing to see you leave the inn, will go to the house himself."

"Yes; but I will simply go in and out again."

"Once inside, you won't come out."

"There's no doubt about it, young man," said Canolles, "you are a magician."

"You will be surprised, perhaps killed before her eyes; that's all there is about it."

"Pshaw!" said Canolles, "there are closets there."

"Oh!" exclaimed the viscount.

This *oh!* was uttered with such an eloquent intonation, it contained such a world of veiled reproach, of offended modesty, of charming delicacy, that Canolles stopped short, and darted a piercing glance at the young man, who was leaning on the window-sill.

Despite the darkness, he felt the full force of the glance, and continued in a playful tone, —

"Of course, you're quite right, baron; go by all means, but conceal yourself carefully, so that you may not be surprised."

"No, I was wrong," said Canolles, "and you are right. But how can I warn her?"

"It seems to me that a letter—"

"Who will carry it?"

"I thought that I saw a servant following you. A servant, under such circumstances, runs the risk of nothing worse than a few blows, while a gentleman risks his life."

"Verily I am losing my wits," said Canolles; "Castorin will do the errand to perfection, especially as I suspect that the rascal has allies in the house."

"You see that the matter can all be arranged here," said the viscount.

"Yes. Have you writing materials?"

"No; but they have them downstairs."

"Pardon me, I beg you," said Canolles; "upon my word, I can't imagine what has happened to me this evening, for I say one idiotic thing after another. No matter. Thanks for your good advice, viscount, and I shall act upon it immediately."

Without taking his eyes from the young man, whom he had been examining for some moments with strange persistency, Canolles backed to the door and descended the stairs, while the viscount muttered anxiously, —

"How he stares at me! can he have recognized me?"

Canolles meanwhile had gone down to the ground-floor, and having gazed for a moment with profound sorrow at the quail, partridge, and sweetmeats, which Master Biscarros was himself packing in the hamper upon the head of his assistant cook, and which another than he was to eat perhaps, although they were certainly intended for him, he asked to be shown to his room, called for writing materials, and wrote to Nanon the following letter: —

Dear Madame—About a hundred yards from your door, if nature had endowed your lovely eyes with the power to see in the dark, you could descry in a clump of trees Monsieur le Duc d'Épernon, who is awaiting my coming to have me shot, and compromise you wofully as a consequence. But I am by no means anxious to lose my life or to cause you to lose your peace of mind. Have no fear, therefore, in that direction. For my own part I propose to make use of the leave of absence which you procured for me the other day that I might take advantage of my freedom to come and see you. Where I am going, I have no idea; indeed, I am not sure that I shall go anywhere. However that may be, recall your fugitive adorer when the storm has passed. They will tell you at the Golden Calf in which direction I have gone. You will give me due credit, I trust, for my self-sacrifice. But your interests are dearer to me than my own enjoyment. I say my own enjoyment because I should have enjoyed pommelling Monsieur d'Épernon and his minions under their disguise. Believe me, dear lady, your most devoted and most faithful servant.

Canolles signed this effusion, overflowing with Gascon magniloquence, knowing the effect it would have upon the Gascon Nanon. Then he summoned his servant.

"Come hither, Master Castorin," said he, "and tell me frankly on what terms you are with Mademoiselle Francinette."

"But, monsieur," replied Castorin, wondering much at the question, "I don't know if I ought—"

"Have no fear, master idiot; I have no designs upon her, and you haven't the honor of being my rival. I ask the question simply for information."

"Ah! that's a different matter, monsieur, and I may say that Mademoiselle Francinette has deigned to appreciate my good qualities."

"Then you are on the best of terms with her, aren't you, monsieur puppy? Very good. Take this letter and go around by the fields."

"I know the road, monsieur," said Castorin, with a self-satisfied expression.

"'T is well. Knock at the back door. No doubt you know that door, too?"

"Perfectly well."

"Better and better. Take that road, knock at that door, and hand this letter to Mademoiselle Francinette."

"Then, monsieur," said Castorin, joyfully, "I may—"

"You may start instantly; you have ten minutes to go and come. This letter must be delivered to Mademoiselle Nanon de Lartigues at the earliest possible moment."

"But suppose they don't open the door, monsieur?" queried Castorin, suspecting that something had gone wrong.

"Why, you must be a fool in that case, for you should have some particular way of knocking, which makes it certain that a brave fellow like you won't be left outside; if that's not the case, I am much to be pitied for having such a dolt in my service."

"I have a private knock, monsieur," said Castorin, with his most conquering air; "first I knock twice softly, then a third—"

"I don't ask you how you knock, nor do I care, if the door is opened. Begone! and if you are taken by surprise, eat the paper, or I'll cut off your ears when you return, if it's not already done."

Castorin was off like a flash. But when he reached the foot of the staircase he stopped, and, in defiance of all rules, thrust the letter into the top of his boot; then he left the inn by the barn-yard door, and made a long circuit, sneaking through the bushes like a fox, jumping ditches like a greyhound, until at last he reached the rear door of the little house, and knocked in the peculiar fashion he had tried to explain to his master.

It proved to be so effective that the door opened instantly.

Ten minutes later, Castorin returned to the inn without accident, and informed his master that the letter was in the fair hands of Mademoiselle Nanon.

Canolles had employed these ten minutes in opening his portmanteau, laying out his *robe de chambre*, and ordering his supper to be served. He listened with visible satisfaction to Monsieur Castorin's report, and made a trip to the kitchen, giving his orders for the night in a loud tone, and yawning immoderately, like a man who is impatient for bed-time to arrive. These manœuvres were intended to convince the Duc d'Épernon, if he had put spies upon him, that the baron had never intended to go farther than the inn, where he had stopped for supper and lodging, like the unpretentious, inoffensive traveller he was. And the scheme really produced the result that the baron hoped. A man in the guise of a peasant, who was drinking in the darkest corner of the public room, called the waiter, paid his reckoning, rose, and went out unconcernedly, humming a tune. Canolles followed him to the door, and saw that he went toward the clump of trees; in a few moments he heard the receding steps of several horses,—the ambuscade was raised.

Thereupon the baron, with his mind at rest concerning Nanon, thought only of passing the evening as agreeably as possible; he therefore bade Castorin bring cards and dice, and, having done so, to go and ask the Vicomte de Cambes if he would do him the honor to receive him.

Castorin obeyed, and found at the vicomte's door an old, white-haired squire, who held the door half open, and replied surlily to his complimentary message,—

"Impossible at present; Monsieur le Vicomte is very much engaged."

"Very well," said Canolles, when the answer was reported to him, "I will wait."

As he heard considerable noise in the direction of the kitchen, to pass the time away he went to see what was going on in that important part of the establishment.

The uproar was caused by the return of the poor scullion, more dead than alive. At the bend in the road he was stopped by four men, who questioned him as to the objective point of his nocturnal expedition; and upon learning that he was carrying supper to the lady at the little house among the trees, stripped him of his cap, his white waistcoat and his apron. The youngest of the four then donned the distinctive garb of the victim's profession, balanced the hamper on his head, and kept on toward the little house in the place and stead of the scullion. Not long after, he returned, and talked in a low tone with the man who seemed the leader of the party. Then they restored his vest and cap and apron, replaced the hamper on his head, and gave him a kick in the stern to start him in the direction he was to follow. The poor devil asked for no more definite instructions; he started off at full speed, and fell half-dead with terror at the door of the inn, where he had just been picked up.

This episode was quite unintelligible to everybody except Canolles; and as he had no motive for explaining it, he left host, waiters, chambermaids, cook, and scullion to cudgel their brains over it; while they were outdoing one another in wild conjectures, he went up to the vicomte's door, and, assuming that the first message he had sent him by the mouth of Monsieur Castorin permitted him to dispense with a second formality of the same nature, he opened the door unceremoniously and went in.

A table, lighted and set with two covers, stood in the middle of the room, awaiting, to be complete, only the dishes with which it was to be embellished.

Canolles noticed the two covers, and drew a joyful inference therefrom.

However, the viscount when he saw him standing in the doorway, jumped to his feet so suddenly that it was easy to see that he was greatly surprised by the visit, and that the second cover was not intended for the baron, as he flattered himself for an instant that it was. His doubts were set at rest by the first words the viscount uttered.

"May I be permitted to know, Monsieur le Baron," he asked, walking to meet him ceremoniously, "to what new circumstance I am indebted for the honor of this visit?"

"Why," rejoined Canolles, somewhat taken aback by this ungracious reception, "to a very natural circumstance. I am hungry. I thought that you must be in the same plight. You are alone, I am alone; and I wished to have the honor of suggesting to you that we sup together."

The viscount looked at Canolles with evident distrust, and seemed to feel some embarrassment in answering him.

"Upon my honor!" said Canolles, laughing, "one would say that I frighten you; are you a knight of Malta, pray? Are you destined for the Church, or has your respectable family brought you up in holy horror of the Canolles? *Pardieu!* I shall not ruin you if we pass an hour together on opposite sides of a table."

"Impossible for me to go to your room, baron."

"Very well, don't do it. But as I am already here—"

"Even more impossible, monsieur; I am expecting some one."

This time Canolles was disarmed.

"You are expecting some one?" he said.

"Yes."

"'Faith," said Canolles, after a moment of silence, "I should almost prefer that you had let me go on at any risk, rather than spoil, by your manifest repugnance for my society, the service you rendered me, for which I fear that I have not as yet thanked you sufficiently."

The young man blushed and walked to Canolles' side.

"Forgive me, monsieur," he said in a trembling voice; "I realize how rude I am; and if it were not serious business, family matters, which I have to discuss with the person I expect, it would be both an honor and a pleasure to admit you as a third, although—"

"Oh, finish!" said Canolles; "whatever you say, I am determined not to be angry with you."

"Although," continued the viscount, "our acquaintance is one of the unforeseen results of mere chance, one of those fortuitous meetings, one of those momentary relations—"

"Why so?" queried Canolles. "On the contrary, the most sincere and enduring friendships are formed in this way: we simply have to give credit to Providence for what you attribute to chance."

"Providence, monsieur," the viscount rejoined with a laugh, "decrees that I depart two hours hence, and that, in all probability, I take the opposite direction to that you will take; receive, therefore, my sincere regrets at my inability to accept, gladly as I would do so if I could, the friendship you offer me so cordially, and of which I fully appreciate the worth."

"You are a strange fellow, upon my word," said Canolles, "and the generous impulse upon which you acted in the first place gave me quite a different idea of your character. But of course it shall be as you desire; I certainly have no right to persist, for I am your debtor, and you have done much more for me than I had any right to expect from a stranger. I will return, therefore, to my own room, and sup alone; but I assure you, viscount, it goes against my grain. I am not addicted to monologue."

Indeed, notwithstanding what he said, and his declared purpose to withdraw, Canolles did not withdraw; some power that he could not understand seemed to nail him to his place; he felt irresistibly drawn to the viscount, who, however, took up a candle and approached him with a charming smile.

"Monsieur," said he, extending his hand, "however that may be, and short as our acquaintance has been, I beg you to believe that I am overjoyed to have been of service to you."

Canolles heard nothing but the compliment; he seized the hand the viscount offered him, which was warm and soft, and, instead of answering his friendly, masculine pressure, was withdrawn at once. Realizing that his dismissal was none the less a dismissal, although couched in courteous phrase, he left the room, disappointed and thoughtful.

At the door he encountered the toothless smile of the old valet, who took the candle from the viscount's hands, ceremoniously escorted Canolles to his door, and hastened back to his master, who was waiting at the top of the stairs.

"What is he doing?" the viscount asked in an undertone.

"I think he has made up his mind to take supper alone," replied Pompée.

"Then he won't come up again?"

"I hope not, at least."

"Order the horses, Pompée; it will be so much time gained. But what is that noise?"

"I should say it was Monsieur Richon's voice."

"And Monsieur de Canolles?"

"They seem to be quarrelling."

"On the contrary, they are greeting each other. Listen!"

"If only Richon does n't say anything."

"Oh! there's no fear of that; he's very circumspect."

"Hush!"

As they ceased to speak, they heard Canolles' voice.

"Two covers, Master Biscarros," he cried. "Two covers! Monsieur Richon sups with me."

"By your leave, no," replied Richon; "it's impossible."

"The deuce! so you too propose to sup alone, like the young gentleman upstairs?"

"What gentleman?"

"The one upstairs, I say."

"What's his name?"

"Vicomte de Cambes."

"Oho! you know the viscount, do you?"

"*Pardieu!* he saved my life."

"He?"

"Yes, he."

"How was that?"

"Sup with me, and I'll tell you the whole story during supper."

"I cannot; I am to sup with him."

"Ah! yes; he is awaiting some one."

"Myself; and as I am late, you will allow me to leave you, will you not, baron?"

"*Sacrebleu!* no, I will not allow it!" cried Canolles. "I have taken it into my head that I will sup in company, and you will sup with me or I with you. Master Biscarros, two covers!"

But while Canolles turned his back to see if the order was executed, Richon darted rapidly up the staircase. When he reached the top stair a little hand met his and drew him into the viscount's room, the door of which immediately closed behind him, and was locked and bolted for greater security.

"In very truth," muttered Canolles, looking about in vain for Richon, and seating himself at his solitary table, "in very truth, I don't know what the people of this cursed country have against me; some of them run after me to kill me, and others avoid me as if I had the plague. *Corbleu!* my appetite is vanishing; I feel that I am growing melancholy, and I am capable of getting as drunk as a lansquenet to-night. Holé! Castorin, come here and be thrashed. Why, they are locking themselves in up there as if they were conspiring. Double calf that I am! of course they are conspiring; that's just it, and it explains everything. The next question is, in whose interest are they conspiring?—the coadjutor's? the princes'? the parliament's? the king's? the queen's? Monsieur de Mazarin's? 'Faith, they may conspire against any one they choose, it's all the same to me; and my appetite has returned. Castorin, order up my supper, and give me some wine; I forgive you."

Thereupon Canolles philosophically attacked the first supper that was prepared for the Vicomte de Cambes, which Master Biscarros was compelled to serve up to him, warmed over, for lack of supplies.

IV

Let us now see what was taking place under Nanon's roof while Baron de Canolles was vainly seeking some one to sup with him, until, growing weary of the profitless quest, he decided at last to sup by himself.

Nanon, whatever her enemies may have said or written—and among her enemies must be accounted the great majority of the historians who have devoted any space to her—was, at this period, a charming creature of some twenty-five or twenty-six years; small of stature, dark-skinned, but with a supple, graceful figure, bright, fresh coloring, eyes of deepest black, in whose limpid depths all the passions and emotions found expression: gay on the surface, in appearance a laughing siren. But Nanon was very far from giving her mind to the whims and follies which embroider with fantastic designs the silky and golden woof of which the life of a *petite-maîtresse* ordinarily consists. On the contrary, the most weighty conclusions, long and laboriously reasoned out in her shapely head, assumed an aspect no less seductive than clear when enounced by her vibrating voice, in which the Gascon accent was very marked. No one would have divined the untiring perseverance, the invincible tenacity, and the statesmanlike depth of insight which lay beneath that rosy, smiling mask, behind that look overflowing with voluptuous promise, and glowing with passion. And yet such were Nanon's qualities, good or bad according as we look at the face or the reverse of the medal. Such was the scheming mind, such the ambitious heart, to which her seductive body served as envelope.

Nanon was of Agen. Monsieur le Duc d'Épernon, son of that inseparable friend of Henri IV. who was in his carriage when Ravaillac's knife struck him, and was the object of suspicions which did not stop short of Marie de Médicis—Monsieur le Duc d'Épernon, appointed governor of Guyenne, where his arrogance, his insolence, and his exactions caused him to be generally execrated, was captivated by the little creature, who was the daughter of a simple attorney. He paid court to her, and conquered her scruples with great difficulty, and after a long defence maintained with the skill of a consummate tactician determined that the victor shall pay the full price of his victory.

But, as the ransom of her thenceforth ruined reputation, Nanon had despoiled the duke of his power and his freedom. At the end of the first six months of her liaison with the governor of Guyenne, she was the *de facto* ruler of that fair province, returning with interest the injuries and insults she had received from all those who had slighted or humiliated her. A queen by chance, she became a tyrant by design, shrewdly realizing the advisability of supplementing the probable brevity of her reign by abusing her power.

As a consequence, she seized upon everything she could reach,— treasure, influence, honors. She was enormously wealthy, distributed appointments, received visits from Mazarin and the leading noblemen at court. With admirable skill she made of the various elements that she had at her disposal a combination useful to her credit, and profitable to her fortune. Every service that Nanon rendered had its stated price. There was a regularly established tariff for appointments in the army and in the magistracy: Nanon would procure this position or that for some fortunate individual, but it must be paid for in hard cash or by a royal gift; so that when she relaxed her hold upon a fragment of power for the benefit of one person or another, she recouped the fragment in another form, giving up the authority, but retaining the money, which is its active principle.

This explains the duration of her reign; for men, in their hatred, hesitate to overthrow an enemy who will have any consolation remaining in his downfall. Vengeance thirsts for total ruin, for complete prostration. Nations are reluctant to expel a tyrant who would carry away their money, and depart with smiling face. Nanon de Lartigues had two millions.

And so she lived in a species of security over the volcano which was unceasingly shaking everything about her to its foundations. She had felt the popular hatred rise like the tide, increase in force, and assail with its waves the power of Monsieur d'Épernon, who, when hunted from Bordeaux in a day of wrath, had carried Nanon in his wake, as the ship carries the skiff. Nanon bent before the storm, ready to stand erect again when it should have passed; she had taken Monsieur de Mazarin for her model, and, an humble pupil, she practised at a distance the political tactics of the clever and pliable Italian. The cardinal's notice was attracted by this woman, who waxed great and wealthy by the same method which had made him a prime minister, possessed of fifty millions. He admired the little Gasconne; he did more than that,—he let her do as she chose. Perhaps we shall eventually know why.

Notwithstanding all this, and although some who claimed to be better informed averred that she corresponded directly with Monsieur de Mazarin, but little was said of the fair Nanon's political intrigues. Canolles himself, who, however, being young and rich and handsome, could not understand the need of intriguing, did not know what to think upon that point. As to love-affairs, whether it was that Nanon, in her preoccupation by more serious matters, had postponed them to a more convenient season, or that the gossip caused by Monsieur d'Épernon's passion drowned whatever noise any secondary amours might have made, even her enemies were not lavish of scandalous reports in her regard, and Canolles was justified in believing, as a matter of personal and national self-esteem, that Nanon was invincible before his appearance upon the scene. It may be that Canolles was, in truth, the beneficiary of the first real passion of that heart, hitherto accessible to ambition only; it may be that prudence had enjoined upon his predecessors absolute silence. At all events, Nanon, as mistress, was a fascinating woman; Nanon, insulted, was like to be a redoubtable foe.

The acquaintance between Nanon and Canolles had come about in the most natural way. Canolles, a lieutenant in the Navailles regiment, aspired to the rank of captain; in order to obtain the promotion, he was obliged to write to Monsieur d'Épernon, colonel-general of infantry. Nanon read the letter, and replied in the ordinary way, making a business appointment with Canolles. He selected from among his family jewels a magnificent ring, worth some five hundred pistoles (it was less expensive than to purchase a company), and betook himself to the place appointed for the meeting. But on this occasion Canolles, preceded by the renown of his previous triumphs, upset all Mademoiselle de Lartigues' calculations. It was the first time that he had seen Nanon; it was the first time that Nanon had seen him; they were both young, handsome, and clever. Their conversation consisted chiefly of reciprocal compliments; not a word was said concerning the business which brought them together, and yet the business was done. The next day Canolles received his captain's commission, and when the ring passed from his finger to Nanon's it was not as the price of gratified ambition, but as a pledge of mutual love.

V

A few words will suffice to explain Nanon's residence near the village of Matifou. As we have said, the Duc d'Épernon was intensely hated in Guyenne. Nanon, who had been honored by being transformed into his evil genius, was execrated. The popular outcry drove them from Bordeaux to Agen. But at Agen it began anew. One day the gilded carriage in which Nanon was driving to join the duke was overturned upon a bridge. By some unexplained means, Nanon found herself in the river, and Canolles pulled her out. One night Nanon's residence in the city took fire, and Canolles it was who made his way to her bedroom and saved her from the flames. Nanon concluded that the Agenois might probably succeed at the third trial. Although Canolles left her side as little as possible, it would be a miracle if he should always happen to be on hand at a given point to rescue her. She availed herself of the duke's absence on a tour through the province, and of an escort of twelve hundred men, of whom the Navailles regiment furnished its quota, to leave the city at the same time with Canolles, hurling defiance from her carriage windows at the populace, who would have liked nothing so much as to wreck the carriage, but dared not.

Thereafter the duke and Nanon selected, or rather Canolles had secretly selected for them, the little country-house where it was decided that Nanon should remain while an establishment was being prepared for her at Libourne. Canolles procured a leave of absence, ostensibly in order to attend to some private business at his home, really so that he might be at liberty to leave his regiment, which had returned to Agen, and to remain within a reasonable distance of Matifou, where his protecting presence was more necessary than ever.

In fact, events were becoming alarmingly serious. The princes of Condé, Conti, and Longueville, who had been arrested and imprisoned at Vincennes on the 17th January preceding, afforded an excellent pretext for civil war to the four or five factions which divided France at that epoch. The unpopularity of the Duc d'Épernon, who was known to be entirely devoted to the court, continued to increase, although it was reasonable to hope that it had reached its limit. A catastrophe, earnestly desired by all the factions, who, under the extraordinary conditions prevailing in France at the time, did not themselves know where they stood, was imminent. Nanon, like the birds which see the storm approaching, disappeared from the sky and betook herself to her leafy nest, there to await the result unknown and in obscurity.

She gave herself out as a widow, desirous of living in seclusion. So Master Biscarros described her, the reader will remember.

Monsieur d'Épernon paid her a visit, and announced his intention of being absent for a week. As soon as he took his leave of her, Nanon sent by the tax-collector, her *protégé*, a little note to Canolles, who was making use of his leave of absence to remain in the neighborhood. But, as we have seen, the original note had disappeared in the messenger's hands, and had become a copy under Cauvignac's pen. The reckless young nobleman was making all haste to obey the summons contained therein, when the Vicomte de Cambes stopped him four hundred yards from his destination. We know the rest.

Nanon therefore was awaiting Canolles, as a woman who loves is wont to await the loved one, consulting her watch ten times a minute, walking to the window again and again, listening to every sound, gazing questioningly at the sun as it sank in ruddy splendor behind the mountain, to give place to the first shades of night. The first knocking was at the front door, and she despatched Francinette thither; but it was only the pseudo-waiter from the inn, bringing the supper for which the guest was lacking. Nanon looked out into the hall and saw Master Biscarros' false servant, who, for his part, stole a glance into the bedroom, where a tiny table was set with two covers. Nanon bade Francinette keep the dishes hot, then sadly closed the door and returned to the window, which showed her the road still deserted as far as she could see it in the gathering darkness.

A second knock, a peculiar knock, was heard, this time at the back door, and Nanon cried,—

"Here he is!"

But still she feared that it was not he, and stopped in the middle of the room. The next moment the door opened, and Mademoiselle Francinette appeared on the threshold in evident consternation, holding the letter in her hand. Nanon spied the paper, rushed up to her, tore it from her hand, hastily opened it, and read it in an agony of fear.

The perusal of the letter was like a thunder-clap to Nanon. She dearly loved Canolles, but with her, ambition was almost equal to love, and in losing the Duc d'Épernon she would lose not only all her hopes of fortune to come, but perhaps her accumulated wealth as well. However, as she was a quick-witted siren, she began by putting out the candle, which would have caused her shadow to betray her movements, and ran to the window. It was time; four men were approaching the house, and were not more than fifty feet away. The man in the cloak walked first, and in the man in the cloak Nanon recognized the duke beyond a peradventure. At that moment Mademoiselle Francinette entered, candle in hand. Nanon glanced despairingly at the table and the two covers, at the two arm-chairs, at the two embroidered pillows, which displayed their insolent whiteness against the background of crimson damask bed-curtains, and at her fascinating *négligé*, which harmonized so well with all the rest.

"I am lost!" she thought.

But almost immediately her wits returned to her, and a smile stole over her face; like a flash she seized the plain glass tumbler intended for Canolles, and threw it out into the garden, took from its box a golden goblet adorned with the duke's arms, and placed beside his plate his silver cover; then, shivering with fear, but with a forced smile upon her face, she rushed down the stairs, and reached the door just as a grave, solemn blow was struck upon it.

Francinette was about to open the door, but Nanon caught her by the arm, thrust her aside, and said, with that swift glance which, with women taken by surprise, serves so well to complete their thought, —

"I am waiting for Monsieur le Duc, not for Monsieur de Canolles. Serve the supper!"

With that she drew the bolts herself, and threw herself upon the neck of the man with the white plume, who was preparing to greet her with a most savage expression.

"Ah!" she cried, "my dream did not play me false! Come, my dear duke, everything is ready, and we will go to supper at once."

D'Épernon was dumfounded; however, as a caress from a pretty woman is always acceptable, he allowed himself to be kissed.

But the next moment he remembered what overwhelming proof he possessed.

"One moment, mademoiselle," he said; "let us have an understanding, if you please."

With a wave of his hand to his followers, who drew back respectfully but did not go away altogether, the duke entered the house alone, with slow and measured step.

"Pray, what's the matter, my dear duke?" said Nanon, with such well-feigned gayety that any one might have thought it natural; "did you forget something the last time you were here, that you look around so carefully on all sides?"

"Yes," said the duke; "I forgot to tell you that I am not a consummate ass, a Géronte, such as Monsieur Cyrano de Bergerac introduces in his comedies, and having forgotten to tell it you, I have returned in person to prove it to you."

"I do not understand you, monseigneur," said Nanon, with the most tranquil and sincere expression imaginable. "Explain yourself, I beg."

The duke's eyes rested on the two arm-chairs, and passed thence to the two covers and the two pillows. There they paused for a longer time, while an angry flush overspread his face.

Nanon had foreseen all this, and she awaited the result of his scrutiny with a smile which disclosed her pearly teeth. But the smile strongly resembled a contraction of the nerves, and her teeth would have chattered if anguish had not kept them pressed tightly together.

The duke at last fixed his wrathful gaze upon her.

"I am still awaiting your Lordship's pleasure," said Nanon, with a graceful courtesy.

"My Lordship's pleasure is that you explain this supper."

"I have already told you that I dreamed that you would return to-day although you left me only yesterday. My dreams never fail to come true, so I ordered this supper purposely for you."

The duke made a grimace which he intended to pass off for an ironical smile.

"And the two pillows?" he said.

"Pray, is it monseigneur's intention to return to Libourne? In that case, my dream lied to me, for it told me that monseigneur would remain."

The duke made a second grimace even more significant than the first.

"And this charming *négligé*, madame? And these exquisite perfumes?"

"It is one of those I am accustomed to wear when I expect monseigneur. The perfume comes from sachets of *peau d'Espagne*, which I put in my wardrobes, and which monseigneur has often told me he preferred to all others, because it is the queen's favorite perfume."

"And so you were expecting me?" rejoined the duke, with a sneering laugh.

"Good lack, monseigneur," said Nanon, frowning; "I believe, God forgive me, that you would like to look in the closets. Are you jealous by any chance?"

Nanon laughed aloud, whereat the duke assumed his most majestic air.

"I, jealous? No, no! Thank God, I'm no such idiot as that. Being old and rich, I know naturally that I was made to be deceived, but I propose to prove to those who deceive me that I am not their dupe."

"How will you prove it, pray? I am curious to know."

"Oh! it will be an easy matter. I shall simply have to show them this paper."

He took a letter from his pocket.

"I don't dream, myself," he said; "at my age one doesn't dream, even when awake; but I receive letters. Read this one; it's very interesting."

Nanon shuddered as she took the letter the duke handed her, and started when she saw the writing; but the movement was imperceptible, and she read, —

"'Monseigneur le Duc d'Épernon is informed that a man who, for six months past, has been on familiar terms with Mademoiselle Nanon de Lartigues, will visit her this evening, and will remain to supper and to sleep.

"'As I do not desire to leave Monseigneur le Duc d'Épernon in uncertainty, he is informed that his fortunate rival is Monsieur le Baron de Canolles.'"

Nanon turned pale; the blow struck home.

"Ah! Roland! Roland!" she murmured, "I believed myself to be well rid of you."

"Am I well informed?" queried the duke, triumphantly.

"Not by any means," retorted Nanon; "and if your political police is no better organized than your amorous police, I pity you."

"You pity me?"

"Yes; for this Monsieur de Canolles, whom you gratuitously honor by believing him to be your rival, is not here, and you are at liberty to wait and see if he comes."

"He has come."

"He?" cried Nanon. "That is not true!"

There was an unmistakable accent of truth in this exclamation of the accused.

"I mean that he came within four hundred yards, and stopped at the Golden Calf, luckily for him."

Nanon saw that the duke was not nearly so well informed as she had supposed at first; she shrugged her shoulders as another idea, prompted doubtless by the letter, which she was folding and unfolding in her hands, began to take root in her mind.

"Is it possible," said she, "that a man of intellect, one of the cleverest politicians in the kingdom, allows himself to be gulled by anonymous letters?"

"That's all very well; but how do you explain this letter, anonymous or not?"

"Why, the explanation's very simple; it's simply a continuation of the generous proceedings of our friends at Agen. Monsieur de Canolles applied to you for leave of absence on account of urgent private business, and you granted it; they found out that he had come in this direction, and this absurd accusation has no other foundation than his journey."

Nanon noticed that the duke's features did not relax, but that his scowl became more pronounced.

"The explanation would answer, if the letter you attribute to your friends had not a certain postscript, which, in your confusion, you omitted to read."

The young woman shivered with terror; she realized that, if chance did not come to her assistance, she could not long continue the struggle.

"A postscript?" she repeated.

"Yes; read it," said the duke; "you have the letter in your hands."

Nanon tried to smile; but she felt that her distorted features would not lend their aid to any such demonstration; she contented herself, therefore, with reading aloud, in the firmest tones she could command, —

> "'I have in my possession Mademoiselle de Lartigues' letter to Monsieur de Canolles, making the appointment I mention for this evening. I will give up the letter in exchange for a paper signed in blank by Monsieur d'Épernon, to be handed to me by a man, alone in a boat on the Dordogne, opposite the village of Saint-Michel-la-Rivière, at six o'clock in the evening.'"

"And you were so imprudent—" continued Nanon.

"Your handwriting is so precious to me, dear lady, that I thought I could not pay too high a price for a letter of yours."

"And you revealed such a secret to the possible indiscretion of one of your servants! Oh! Monsieur le Duc!"

"Such confidences, madame, a man should receive in person, and I so received this one. I, myself, was waiting in the boat on the Dordogne."

"Then you have my letter?"

"Here it is."

Nanon made a superhuman effort to remember the exact contents of the letter, but it was impossible; her brain was beginning to be confused. She had no alternative, therefore, but to take her own letter and read it. It contained barely three lines; Nanon ran her eye over them in eager haste, and saw, with unspeakable delight, that the letter did not compromise her beyond all hope.

"Read it aloud," said the duke; "like you, I have forgotten what the letter contains."

Nanon found the smile she had sought in vain a few seconds before, and complied with the duke's suggestion.

"'I shall take supper at eight o'clock. Are you free? I am. If so, be punctual, my dear Canolles, and have no fear for our secret.'"

"I should say that that is explicit enough," cried the duke, pale with rage.

"That is my salvation," thought Nanon.

"So you have a secret with Monsieur de Canolles, have you?" continued the duke.

VI

Nanon realized that to hesitate for a second would be her destruction. Moreover, she had had time enough to develop in her brain the scheme suggested by the anonymous letter.

"Yes," said she, gazing fixedly at the duke, "I have a secret with that gentleman."

"You confess it?" cried Monsieur d'Épernon.

"I must; for one can conceal nothing from you."

"Oh!" shouted the duke.

"Yes, I was expecting Monsieur de Canolles," continued Nanon, calmly.

"You were expecting him?"

"I was expecting him."

"You dare admit it?"

"Freely. Tell me, now, do you know who Monsieur de Canolles is?"

"He is a jackanapes, whom I will punish cruelly for his impudence."

"He is a noble and gallant gentleman, to whom you will continue your benefactions."

"Oh! I swear by the Almighty that I will not!"

"No oaths, Monsieur le Duc; at all events, not until I have said what I have to say," rejoined Nanon, smiling sweetly.

"Say on, then, but waste no time."

"Haven't you, who are so skilful in probing the human heart to its lowest depths," said Nanon, "haven't you remarked my partiality for Monsieur de Canolles, my repeated solicitations in his interest?—the captain's commission I procured for him, the grant of money for a trip to Bretagne with Monsieur de Meilleraie, his recent leave of absence,—in a word, my constant efforts to gratify him?"

"Madame, madame!" said the duke, "you exceed all bounds!"

"For God's sake, Monsieur le Duc, wait until you hear the end!"

"Why should I wait any longer? What more is there for you to tell me?"

"That I have a most affectionate interest in Monsieur de Canolles."

"*Pardieu!* I know it well."

"That I am devoted to him, body and soul."

"Madame, you abuse—"

"That I will do my utmost to oblige him while I live, and all because—"

"Because he's your lover; that's not difficult to guess."

"Because," continued Nanon, seizing the wrathful duke's arm with a dramatic gesture, "because he is my brother!"

Monsieur d'Épernon's arm fell to his side.

"Your brother?" he said.

Nanon nodded affirmatively with a triumphant smile.

"This calls for an explanation," the duke cried, after a moment's reflection.

"Which I will give you," said Nanon. "When did my father die?"

"Why, about eight months since," replied the duke, after a short mental calculation.

"When did you sign the captain's commission for Canolles?"

"Eh? at about the same time."

"A fortnight later," said Nanon.

"A fortnight later; it's very possible."

"It is a sad thing for me to disclose another woman's shame, to divulge a secret which belongs to us alone, you understand. But your extraordinary jealousy drives me to it, your cruelty leaves me no alternative. I am like you, Monsieur le Duc, I lack generosity."

"Go on, go on!" cried the duke, beginning to yield to the fair Gasconne's imaginative flights.

"Very good; my father was an attorney of some note. Twenty-eight years ago he was still young, and he was always fine-looking. Before his marriage he was in love with Monsieur de Canolles' mother, whose hand was denied him because she was of noble blood, and he a plebeian. Love undertook the task of remedying the mistakes of nature, as it often does; and during Monsieur de Canolles, the elder's, absence from home—Now do you understand?"

"Yes; but how does it happen that this affection for Monsieur de Canolles took possession of you so recently?"

"Because I never knew of the bond between us until my father's death; because the secret was made known to me in a letter handed me by the baron himself, who then addressed me as his sister."

"Where is that letter?" queried the duke.

"Have you forgotten the fire which consumed everything I owned,—all my most valuable jewels and papers?"

"True," said the duke.

"Twenty times I have been on the point of telling you the story, feeling sure that you would do everything for him whom I call my brother under my breath; but he has always prevented me, always begged me to spare his mother's reputation, for she is still living. I have respected his scruples because I appreciated them."

"Ah! indeed!" said the duke, almost melted; "poor Canolles!"

"And yet," continued Nanon, "when he refused to let me speak, he threw away his own fortune."

"He's a high-minded youth," said the duke, "and his scruples do him honor."

"I did more than respect his scruples,—I swore that the mystery should never be revealed to any one on earth; but your suspicions caused the cup to overflow. Woe is me! I have forgotten my oath! Woe is me! I have betrayed my brother's secret!"

And Nanon burst into tears.

The duke fell upon his knees and kissed her pretty hands, which hung dejectedly at her side, while her eyes were raised toward heaven, as if imploring God's forgiveness for her perjury.

"You say, 'Woe is me!'" cried the duke; "say rather, 'Good luck for all!' I propose that poor Canolles shall make up for lost time. I don't know him, but I desire to know him. You shall present him to me, and I will love him like a son!"

"Say like a brother," rejoined Nanon, with a smile.

"Villanous informers!" she suddenly cried, passing to another train of thought, and crumpling the letter in her hand as if she proposed to throw it in the fire, but carefully placing it in her pocket, with a view of confronting its author with it later.

"Now that I think of it," said the duke, "why shouldn't the rascal come here? Why should I wait any longer before seeing him? I'll send at once to the Golden Calf to bid him come."

"Oh, of course," said Nanon, "so that he may know that I can conceal nothing from you, and that I have told you everything in utter disregard of my oath."

"I will be careful."

"Ah! Monsieur le Duc, do you wish me to quarrel with you?" retorted Nanon, with one of those smiles which demons borrow from angels.

"How so, my dear love?"

"Because you used to be more anxious for a *tête-à-tête* than now. Let us sup together, and to-morrow it will be time enough to send for Canolles. Between now and to-morrow," said Nanon to herself, "I shall have time to warn him."

"So be it," said the duke; "let us sup."

Haunted by a vestige of suspicion, he added, under his breath, —

"Between now and to-morrow I will not leave her side, and if she succeeds in inventing any method of warning him, she's a sorceress."

"And so," said Nanon, laying her hand upon the duke's shoulder, "I may venture to solicit my friend in my brother's interest?"

"Most assuredly!" rejoined d'Épernon; "as much as you choose. Is it money?"

"Money, indeed!" said Nanon. "He's in no need of money; indeed it was he who gave me the magnificent ring you have noticed, which was his mother's."

"Promotion, then?" said the duke.

"Ah! yes, promotion. We'll make him a colonel, won't we?"

"*Peste!/* how fast you go, my love! Colonel! To obtain that rank, he must have rendered his Majesty's cause some service."

"He is ready to render that cause whatever service may be pointed out to him."

"Indeed!" said the duke, looking at Nanon out of the corner of his eye, "I shall have occasion to send some one on a confidential mission to the court."

"To the court!" exclaimed Nanon.

"Yes," replied the old courtier; "but that would separate you."

Nanon saw that she must take some means to destroy this remnant of suspicion.

"Oh! don't be alarmed about that, my dear duke. What matters the separation, so long as there is profit in it? If he's near at hand, I can be of but little use to him—you are jealous; but, at a distance, you will extend your powerful patronage to him. Exile him, ex-patriate him if it's for his good, and don't be concerned about me. So long as I retain my dear duke's affection, have I not more than enough to make me happy?"

"Very well, it's agreed," said the duke; "to-morrow morning I will send for him, and give him his instructions. And now, as you suggest," he continued, casting a much more amiable glance upon the two chairs, the two covers, and the two pillows; "and now, my love, let us sup."

They took their places at the table, smiling amicably at each other; so that Francinette herself, although, in her capacity of confidential maid, she was well used to the duke's peculiarities and her mistress's character, believed that her mistress was perfectly tranquil in her mind, and the duke completely reassured.

VII

The gentleman whom Canolles greeted by the name of Richon, went up to the first floor of the Golden Calf, and was taking supper there with the viscount.

He was the person whose coming the viscount was impatiently awaiting when chance made him a witness of Monsieur d'Épernon's hostile preparations, and made it possible for him to render Baron de Canolles the important service we have described.

He had left Paris a week before, and Bordeaux the same day, and was therefore the bearer of recent news concerning the somewhat disturbed state of affairs, and the disquieting plots which were brewing all the way from Paris to Bordeaux. As he spoke, now of the imprisonment of the princes, which was the sensation of the day, again of the Parliament of Bordeaux, which was the ruling power of the neighborhood, and still again of Monsieur de Mazarin, who was the king of the moment, the young man silently watched his strong, bronzed face, his piercing, confident eye, his sharp, white teeth, which showed beneath his long, black moustache,— details which made Richon the perfect type of the true soldier of fortune.

"And so," said the viscount, after his companion had told what he had to tell, "Madame la Princesse is now at Chantilly?"

As is well known, both Duchesses de Condé were so called, but the additional title of Dowager was bestowed upon the elder of the two.

"Yes, and they look for you there at the earliest possible moment," said Richon.

"What is her situation?"

"She is practically in exile; her movements as well as her mother-in-law's are watched with the utmost care, for there is a shrewd suspicion at court that they do not mean to confine themselves to petitions to parliament, and that they are concocting something for the benefit of the princes more likely to prove efficacious. Unfortunately, as always, money—Speaking of money, have you received what was due you? That is a question I was strongly urged to ask you."

"I have succeeded with great difficulty in collecting about twenty thousand livres, and I have it with me in gold; that's all."

"All! *Peste!* viscount, it's easy to see that you are a millionnaire. To talk so contemptuously of such a sum at such a time! Twenty thousand francs! We shall be poorer than Monsieur de Mazarin, but richer than the king."

"Then you think that Madame la Princesse will accept my humble offering, Richon?"

"Most gratefully; it is enough to pay an army."

"Do you think that we shall need it?"

"Need what? an army? Most assuredly; and we are busily at work levying one. Monsieur de La Rochefoucauld has enlisted four hundred gentlemen on the pretext that he wishes them to be present at the obsequies of his father. Monsieur le Duc de Bouillon is about starting for Guyenne with an equal number. Monsieur de Turenne promises to make a descent upon Paris in the hope of surprising Vincennes, and carrying off the princes by a *coup de main*; he will have thirty thousand men,—his whole army of the North, whom he has seduced from the king's service. Oh! everything is going along well," Richon continued, "never fear; I don't know if we shall perform any great deeds, but at all events we shall make a great noise."

"Did you not fall in with the Duc d'Épernon?" interposed the young man, whose eyes sparkled with joy at this enumeration of forces, which augured well for the triumph of the party to which he was attached.

"The Duc d'Épernon?" repeated Richon, opening his eyes; "where do you suppose I fell in with him, I pray to know? I come from Agen, not from Bordeaux."

"You might have fallen in with him within a few steps of this place," replied the viscount, smiling.

"Ah! yes, of course, the lovely Nanon de Lartigues lives in the neighborhood, does she not?"

"Within two musket-shots of the inn."

"The deuce! that explains the Baron de Canolles' presence at the Golden Calf."

"Do you know him?"

"Whom? the baron? Yes. I might almost say that I am his friend, if Monsieur de Canolles were not of the oldest nobility, while I am only a poor *roturier*."

"*Roturiers* like yourself, Richon, are quite as valuable as princes in our present plight. Do you know, by the way, that I saved your friend, Baron de Canolles, from a thrashing, if not from something much worse."

"Yes; he said something of that to me, but I hardly listened to him, I was in such haste to join you. Are you sure that he didn't recognize you?"

"He could hardly recognize a person he had never seen."

"I should have asked if he did not guess who you are."

"Indeed," replied the viscount, "he looked at me very hard."

Richon smiled.

"I can well believe it," he said; "one doesn't meet young gentlemen of your type every day."

"He seemed to me a jovial sort of fellow," said the viscount, after a brief pause.

"A jovial fellow and a good fellow, too; he has a charming wit and a great heart. The Gascon, you know, is never mediocre in anything; he is in the front rank or is good for nothing. This one is made of good stuff. In love, as in war, he is at once a dandy and a gallant officer; I am sorry that he is against us. Indeed, as chance brought you in contact with him, you should have seized the opportunity to win him over to our side."

A fugitive blush passed like a flash over the viscount's pale cheeks.

"*Mon Dieu!*" continued Richon, with that melancholy philosophy which is sometimes found in men of the most vigorous temper, "are we so sober-minded and reasonable, pray, that we manage the torch of civil war in our adventurous hands as if it were an altar light? Is Monsieur le Coadjuteur, who, with a word, tranquillizes or arouses Paris, a very serious-minded man? Is Monsieur de Beaufort, whose influence in the capital is so great that he is called '*le roi des halles*' (King of the Markets), a very serious-minded man? Is Madame de Chevreuse, who makes and unmakes ministers at pleasure, a very serious-minded woman? or Madame de Longueville, who nevertheless sat on the throne at the Hôtel de Ville for three months? or Madame la Princesse de Condé, who, no longer ago than yesterday, was engrossed with dresses and jewels and diamonds? Lastly, is Monsieur le Duc d'Enghien, who is still playing with his jumping-jacks, in charge of women, and who will don his first breeches, perhaps, to turn all France topsy-turvy—is he a very serious-minded leader of a party? And myself, if you will allow me to mention my own name after so many illustrious ones, am I a very serious personage,—I, the son of a miller of Angoulême, and once a retainer of Monsieur de La Rochefoucauld,—I, to whom my master one day, instead of a cloak to brush, gave a sword, which I gallantly buckled on at my side, an embryo warrior? And yet the son of the miller of Angoulème, Monsieur de La Rochefoucauld's former *valet-de-chambre*, has risen to be a captain; he is levying a company, bringing together four or five hundred men, with whose lives he is about to play, as if God himself had given him the right; he is marching along on the road to greatness, some day to be colonel, or governor of a fortress—who knows? it may perhaps be his lot to hold for ten minutes, an hour, or a day, the destiny of a kingdom in his hands. This much resembles a dream, as you see, and yet I shall consider it a reality until the day when some great disaster awakens me—"

"And on that day," the viscount broke in, "woe to those who awaken you, Richon; for you will be a hero."

"A hero or a traitor, according as we are the strongest or the weakest. Under the other cardinal I should have looked twice, for I should have risked my head."

"Go to, Richon; do not try to make me believe that such considerations can influence a man like you, who are pointed to as one of the bravest soldiers in the whole army!"

"Oh! of course," said Richon, with an indescribable motion of his shoulders, "I was brave when King Louis XIII., with his pale face, his blue ribbon, and his eye gleaming like a carbuncle, cried in his strident voice, biting the ends of his moustache, 'The king is looking at you; forward, messieurs!' But when I am obliged to look at the same blue ribbon on the son's breast, which I can still see on the father's, and no longer behind me, but before my face; when I am obliged to shout to my soldiers, 'Fire on the King of France!'—on that day," continued Richon, shaking his head, "on that day, viscount, I fear that I shall be afraid, and aim badly—"

"What snake have you trodden on to-day, that you persist in putting things in the worst light, my dear Richon?" the young man asked. "Civil war is a deplorable thing, I know, but sometimes necessary."

"Yes, like the plague, the yellow fever, the black fever, fever of all colors. Do you think, for instance, Monsieur le Vicomte, that it is absolutely necessary that I, who have been so glad to grasp my good friend Canolles' hand this evening, should run my sword through his body to-morrow, because I serve Madame la Princesse de Condé, who laughs at me, and he Monsieur de Mazarin, at whom he laughs? Yet it may fall out so."

The viscount made a horrified gesture.

"Unless," pursued Richon, "I am out in my reckoning, and he makes a hole in me in one way or another. Ah! you people have no appreciation of what war is; you see nothing but a sea of intrigue, and plunge into it as if it were your natural element; as I said the other day to her Highness, and she agreed with me, 'You live in a sphere wherein the artillery fire which mows you down seems to you simple fireworks.'"

"In sooth, Richon, you frighten me," said the viscount, "and if I were not sure of having you at hand to protect me, I should not dare to start; but under your escort," he continued, holding out his little hand to the partisan, "I have no fear."

"My escort?" said Richon. "Oh, yes, you remind me of something I had forgotten; you will have to do without my escort, Monsieur le Vicomte; that arrangement has fallen through."

"Why, are you not to return to Chantilly with me?"

"I was to do so, in the event that my presence was not necessary here; but, as I was saying, my importance has increased to such a point that I received a positive command from Madame la Princesse not to leave the vicinity of the fort, upon which there are designs, it seems."

The viscount uttered an exclamation of dismay.

"What! I am to go without you?" he cried; "to go with no one but honest Pompée, who is a hundred times more a coward than I am myself? to travel half-way across France alone, or nearly so? Oh, no! I will not go, I swear it! I should die of fear before I arrived."

"Oh, Monsieur le Vicomte," rejoined Richon, laughing aloud, "do you forget the sword hanging by your side, pray?"

"Laugh if you please, but I will not budge. Madame la Princesse promised me that you should go with me, and I agreed to make the journey only on that condition."

"That's as you please, viscount," said Richon, with assumed gravity. "However, they count upon you at Chantilly; and have a care, for princes soon lose patience, especially when they expect money."

"To cap the climax," said the viscount, "I must start during the night—"

"So much the better," laughed Richon; "no one will see that you are afraid, and you will encounter greater cowards than yourself, who will run away from you."

"You think so?" said the viscount, by no means at ease, despite this reassuring suggestion.

"But there's another way of arranging the matter," said Richon; "your fear is for the money, is it not? Very well, leave the money with me, and I will send it by three or four trustworthy men. But, believe me, the best way to make sure that it arrives safely is to carry it yourself."

"You are right, and I will go, Richon; as my bravery must go all lengths, I will keep the money. I fancy that her Highness, judging by what you tell me, is even more in need of the money than of myself; so perhaps I should not be welcome if I arrived empty-handed."

"I told you, when I first came, that you have a very martial air; moreover, the king's soldiers are everywhere, and there is no war as yet; however, don't trust to them too much, but bid Pompée load his pistols."

"Do you say that simply to encourage me?"

"Of course; he who realizes his danger doesn't allow himself to be taken by surprise. You had best go now," continued Richon, rising; "the night will be fine, and you can be at Monlieu before morning."

"Will our friend, the baron, play the spy when we go?"

"Oh! at this moment he is doing what we have just done,—eating his supper, that is to say; and although his supper may not have been as good as ours, he is too much of a *bon-vivant* to leave the table without a weighty reason. But I will go down and keep his attention diverted."

"Apologize to him for me for my rudeness. I don't choose that he shall pick a quarrel with me, if we meet some day when he is less generously disposed than to-day; for your baron must be a very punctilious sort of fellow."

"You have hit the right word; he would be just the man to follow you to the ends of the world simply to cross swords with you; but I will make your excuses, never fear."

"Do so by all means; but wait till I am gone."

"You may be very sure that I will."

"Have you no message for her Highness?"

"Indeed I have; you remind me of the most important thing of all."

"Have you written to her?"

"No; there are but two words to say to her."

"What are they?"

"*Bordeaux. — Yes.*"

"She will know what they mean?"

"Perfectly; and on the faith of those two words she may set out in full confidence; you may say to her that I will answer for everything."

"Come, Pompée," said the viscount to the old squire, who just then partly opened the door, and showed his head in the opening; "come, my friend, we must be off."

"Oh!" exclaimed Pompée; "can it be that Monsieur le Vicomte thinks of starting now. There is going to be a frightful storm."

"What's that you say, Pompée?" rejoined Richon. "There's not a cloud in the sky."

"But we may lose our way in the dark."

"That would be a difficult thing to do; you have simply to follow the high-road. Besides, it's a superb moonlight night."

"Moonlight! moonlight!" muttered Pompée; "you understand, of course, that what I say is not on my own account, Monsieur Richon."

"Of course not," said Richon; "an old soldier!"

"When one has fought against the Spaniards, and been wounded at the battle of Corbie—"pursued Pompée, swelling up.

"One doesn't know what fear is, eh? Oh, well, that is most fortunate, for Monsieur le Vicomte is by no means at ease, I warn you."

"Oh!" exclaimed Pompée, turning pale, "are you afraid?"

"Not with you, my good Pompée," said the viscount. "I know you, and I know that you would sacrifice your own life before anything should happen to me."

"To be sure, to be sure," rejoined Pompée; "but if you are too much afraid, we might wait until to-morrow."

"Impossible, my good Pompée. So take the gold and put it in your saddle-bags; I will join you in a moment."

"It's a large sum to expose to the risks of a journey at night," said Pompée, lifting the bag.

"There's no risk; at all events, Richon says so. Are the pistols in the holsters, the sword in the scabbard, and the musket slung on its hook?"

"You forget," replied the old squire, drawing himself up, "that when a man has been a soldier all his life, he doesn't allow himself to be caught napping. Yes, Monsieur le Vicomte, everything is in its place."

"The idea," observed Richon, "that any one could be afraid with such a companion! A pleasant journey to you, viscount!"

"Thanks for the wish; but it's a long way," replied the viscount, with a residuum of distress which Pompée's martial bearing could not dissipate.

"Nonsense!" said Richon; "every road has a beginning and an end. My respectful homage to Madame la Princesse; tell her that I am at her service and Monsieur de La Rochefoucauld's while I live, and do not forget the two words,—*Bordeaux, Yes.* I will go and join Monsieur de Canolles."

"Look you, Richon," said the viscount, laying his hand upon his companion's arm as he put his foot on the first stair, "if this Canolles is such a gallant officer and honorable gentleman as you say, why should not you make some attempt to win him over to our side? He might overtake us at Chantilly, or even on the way thither; as I have some slight acquaintance with him, I would present him."

Richon looked at the viscount with such a strange smile that he, reading upon the partisan's face what was passing through his mind, made haste to add,—

"Consider that I said nothing, Richon, and act as you think you ought to act in the premises. Adieu!"

He gave him his hand and hastily returned to his room, whether in dread that Richon would see the sudden blush that overspread his face, or that Canolles, whose noisy laughter they could plainly hear, would hear their voices.

He therefore left the partisan to descend the stairs, followed by Pompée, who carried the valise with an air of studied indifference, so that no one might suspect the nature of its contents; having waited a few moments, he cast his eye around the room to make sure that he had forgotten nothing, extinguished the candles, stole cautiously down to the ground-floor, venturing a timid glance through the half-open door of a brilliantly lighted room on that floor, and, wrapping himself closely in a heavy cloak, which Pompée handed him, placed his foot in the squire's hand, leaped lightly into the saddle, scolded the old soldier good-naturedly for his moderation, and disappeared in the darkness.

As Richon entered the room occupied by Canolles, whom he had undertaken to entertain while the little viscount was making his preparations for departure, a joyful shout issuing from the baron's mouth, as he sat uncertainly upon his chair, proved that he bore no ill-will.

Upon the table, between two transparent bodies which had once been full bottles, stood a thick-set wicker-covered vessel, proud of its rotundity, through the interstices of which the bright light of four candles caused a sparkling as of rubies and topazes. It was a flask of the old Collioure vintage, whose honeyed flavor is so delicious to the overheated palate. Appetizing dried figs, biscuit, almonds, and high-flavored cheeses bore witness to the shrewdness of the inn-keeper's reckoning, as the two empty bottles and a third but half filled demonstrated its exactitude. Indeed, it was certain that whoever should partake of that tempting dessert would necessarily, however sober he might ordinarily be, consume a great quantity of liquid food.

Now Canolles did not plume himself upon being an anchorite. Perhaps, indeed, being a Huguenot (Canolles was of a Protestant family, and mildly professed the religion of his fathers),—perhaps, we say, being a Huguenot, Canolles did not believe in canonizing the pious hermits who had won a dwelling in heaven by drinking water and eating dried roots. And so, melancholy as he was, or in love if you please, Canolles was never insensible to the fumes of a good dinner, or to the sight of those bottles of peculiar shape, with red, yellow, or green seals, which confine, with the assistance of a trusty cork, the purest blood of Gascony, Champagne, or Burgundy. Under the present circumstances, therefore, Canolles had, as usual, yielded to the fascinations of that sight; from the sight he had passed to the smell, from the smell to the taste, and, three out of the five senses with which our kindly common mother, whom we call Dame Nature, has endowed her children, being fully satisfied, the two others awaited their turn patiently, and with beatific resignation.

It was at this juncture that Richon entered and found Canolles rocking on his chair.

"Ah I my dear Richon, you come in good time," he cried. "I was in great need of somebody to whom to sing Master Biscarros' praises, and I was almost reduced to the point of doing it to this idiot of a Castorin, who only knows how to drink, and whom I have never been able to teach to eat. Just look at that sideboard, my friend, and cast your eye over this table, at which I invite you to take a seat. Is not mine host of the Golden Calf a veritable artist, a man whom I can safely recommend to my friend the Duc d'Épernon? Listen to the details of this menu, and judge for yourself, Richon, for you know how to appreciate such things: *Potage de bisques; hors-d'œuvres*, pickled oysters, anchovies, small fowl; *capon aux olives*, with a bottle of Médoc, of which you see the corpse here; a partridge stuffed with truffles, peas *au caramel*, wild-cherry ice, irrigated by a bottle of Chambertin, here lying dead; furthermore, this dessert and this bottle of Collioure, which is trying hard to defend itself, but will soon go to join the others, especially if we join forces against it. *Sarpejeu!* I am in the best of humor, and Biscarros is a past master. Sit you down, Richon; you have supped, but what's the odds? I have supped, too, but that makes no difference, we will begin again."

"Thanks, baron," said Richon, with a laugh, "but I am not hungry."

"I grant you that; one may have ceased to be hungry, and still be athirst; taste this Collioure."

Richon held out his glass. "And so you have supped," continued Canolles,—"supped with your little rascal of a viscount? Oh! I beg your pardon, Richon, I am wrong; a charming boy, I mean, to whom I owe my present pleasure of looking at life on its beautiful side, instead of giving up the ghost through three or four holes, which the gallant Duc d'Épernon had it in contemplation to make in my skin. I am very grateful therefore to the charming viscount, the fascinating Ganymede. Ah! Richon, you have every appearance of being just what you are said to be,—a devoted servant of Monsieur de Condé."

"A truce to your pleasantry, baron," cried Richon, laughing uproariously; "don't say such things as that, or you will kill me with laughter."

"Kill you with laughter! Go to, my dear fellow! not you.

'Igne tantum perituri
Quia estes—
Landeriri.'

You know the lament, do you not? It's a Christmas carol, written by your patron upon the German river *Rhenus*, one morning when he was consoling one of his followers, who dreaded death by drowning. Oh! you devil of a Richon! No matter; I am shocked at your little gentleman,—to take so deep an interest in the first well-favored cavalier who passes!"

As he finished, Canolles fairly rolled off his chair, shrieking with laughter, and pulling at his moustache in a paroxysm of merriment, in which Richon could not help joining.

"Seriously, my dear Richon," Canolles resumed, "you are conspiring, aren't you?"

Richon continued to laugh, but somewhat less frankly.

"Do you know that I had a great mind to have you and your little gentleman arrested? *Corbleu!* that would have been amusing, and very easy too. I had the staff-bearers of my good gossip d'Épernon at hand. Ah! Richon to the guard-house and the little gentleman too! *landeriri!*"

At that moment they heard two horses galloping away from the inn.

"Oho!" said Canolles; "what might that be, Richon? Do you know?"

"I have a shrewd suspicion."

"Tell me, then."

"It's the little gentleman going away."

"Without bidding me adieu!" cried Canolles. "He is a consummate boor."

"Oh no, my dear baron; he's a man in a hurry, that's all."

Canolles frowned.

"What extraordinary manners!" said he. "Where was the fellow brought up? Richon, my friend, I tell you frankly that he does you no credit. That's not the way gentlemen should treat one another. *Corbleu!* if I had him here, I believe I would box his ears. The devil fly away with his father, who, from stinginess, I doubt not, gave him no governor."

"Don't lose your temper, baron," said Richon, with a laugh; "the viscount isn't so ill-bred as you think; for, as he went away, he bade me express to you his deep regret, and to say a thousand complimentary things to you."

"Nonsense! nonsense!" said Canolles; "court holy water, which transforms a piece of arrant impudence into a trifling rudeness; that's all of that. *Corbleu!* I'm in a ferocious humor! Pick a quarrel with me, Richon! You refuse? Wait a moment. *Sarpejeu!* Richon, my friend, I consider you an ill-favored villain!"

Richon began to laugh.

"In this mood, baron," said he, "you would be quite capable of winning a hundred pistoles from me this evening, if we should play. Luck, you know, always favors the disappointed."

Richon knew Canolles, and designedly opened this vent for his ill-humor.

"Ah! *pardieu!*" he cried; "let us play. You are right, my friend, and the suggestion reconciles me to your company. Richon, you are a very agreeable fellow; you are as handsome as Adonis, Richon, and I forgive Monsieur de Cambes.—Cards, Castorin!"

Castorin hurried in, accompanied by Biscarros; together they prepared a table, and the two guests began to play. Castorin, who had been dreaming for ten years of a martingale at *trente-et-quarante,* and Biscarros, whose eye gleamed covetously at the sight of money, stood on either side of the table looking on. In less than an hour, notwithstanding his prediction, Richon had won forty pistoles from his opponent, whereupon Canolles, who had no more money about him, bade Castorin bring him a further supply from his valise.

"It's not worth while," said Richon, who overheard the order; "I haven't time to give you your revenge."

"What's that? you haven't time?" exclaimed Canolles.

"No; it is eleven o'clock," said Richon, "and at midnight I must be at my post."

"Nonsense! you are joking!" rejoined Canolles.

"Monsieur le Baron," observed Richon, gravely, "you are a soldier, and consequently you know the rigorous rules of the service."

"Then why didn't you go before you won my money?" retorted Canolles, half-smiling, half-angry.

"Do you mean to reproach me for calling upon you?"

"God forbid! But consider; I haven't the slightest inclination to sleep, and I shall be frightfully bored here. Suppose I should propose to bear you company, Richon?"

"I should decline the honor, baron. Affairs of the nature of that upon which I am engaged are transacted without witnesses."

"Very good! You are going—in what direction?"

"I was about to beg you not to ask me that question."

"In what direction has the viscount gone?"

"I am obliged to tell you that I have no idea."

Canolles looked at Richon to make sure that there was no raillery in his disobliging answers; but the kindly eye and frank smile of the governor of Vayres disarmed his curiosity, if not his impatience.

"Well, well, you are a perfect treasure-house of mysteries, my dear Richon; but no compulsion. I should have been disgusted enough if any one had followed me three hours ago, although, after all, the man who followed me would have been as disappointed as I was myself. So one last glass of Callioure and good luck to you!"

With that, Canolles refilled the glasses, and Richon, having emptied his to the baron's health, took his leave; nor did it once occur to the baron to watch to see in which direction he went. Left to his own resources, amid the half-burned candles, empty bottles, and scattered cards, he fell a prey to one of those fits of depression which no one can understand without experiencing them, for his jovial humor throughout the evening had its origin in a disappointment which he had labored to forget, with but partial success.

He dragged his feet along toward his bedroom, casting a sidelong glance, half regretful, half-angry, through the window in the hall toward the isolated house, where a single window, through which a reddish light shone, intercepted from time to time by more than one shadow, proved with sufficient certainty that Mademoiselle de Lartigues was passing a less lonely evening than himself.

On the first stair, the toe of Canolles' boot came in contact with some object; he stooped and picked up one of the viscount's diminutive pearl-gray gloves, which he had dropped in his haste to leave Master Biscarros' hostelry, and which he probably did not consider of sufficient value to waste his time in searching for it.

Whatever may have been Canolles' reflections in a moment of misanthropy not to be wondered at in an offended lover, there was not at the isolated house a whit more real satisfaction than at the Golden Calf.

Nanon was restless and anxious throughout the night, revolving in her mind a thousand schemes to warn Canolles, and she resorted to every device that a well-developed female brain could suggest in the way of cunning and trickery to extricate herself from her precarious situation. Her only object was to steal one minute from the duke to speak to Francinette, or two minutes to write a line to Canolles upon a scrap of paper.

But you would have said that the duke, suspecting all that was passing through her mind, and reading her anxiety through the mask of cheerfulness which her face wore, had sworn to himself that he would not vouchsafe to her one moment of that liberty which was so essential to her peace of mind.

Nanon had a sick-headache; Monsieur d'Épernon would not hear of her rising to get her bottle of salts, but went to look for it himself.

Nanon pricked herself with a pin, and a ruby drop appeared at the end of her taper finger; she essayed to go to her toilet-case for a piece of the famous rose-taffeta, which was just coming into favor, but Monsieur d'Épernon, with indefatigable devotion to her comfort, rose, prepared the rose-taffeta with disheartening dexterity, and locked the toilet-case.

Nanon thereupon pretended to be sleeping soundly; almost immediately the duke began to snore. At that, Nanon opened her eyes, and by the glimmer of the night-light in its alabaster vessel on a table by the bed, she tried to take the duke's own tablets from his doublet, which was within her reach; but just as she had the pencil in her hand, and was about tearing off a leaf of paper, the duke opened one eye.

"What are you doing, my love?" he asked.

"I was looking to see if there isn't a calendar in your tablets."

"For what purpose?"

"To see when your birthday comes."

"My name is Louis, and my birthday falls on August 25th, as you know; so you have abundant time to prepare for it, dear heart."

And he took the tablets from her hands and replaced them in his doublet.

By this last manœuvre, Nanon had at all events secured pencil and paper. She stowed them away under her bolster, and very adroitly overturned the night-light, hoping to be able to write in the dark; but the duke immediately rang for Francinette, and loudly demanded a light, declaring that he could not sleep unless he could see. Francinette came running in before Nanon had had time to write half of her sentence, and the duke, to avoid another similar mishap, bade the maid place two candles on the chimney-piece. Thereupon Nanon declared that she could not sleep with so much light, and resolutely turned her face to the wall, awaiting the dawn in feverish impatience and anxiety easy to understand.

The dreaded day broke at last, and bedimmed the light of the two candles. Monsieur le Duc d'Épernon, who prided himself upon his strict adherence to a military mode of life, rose as the first ray of dawn stole in through the jalousies, dressed without assistance, in order not to leave his little Nanon for an instant, donned his *robe de chambre*, and rang to ask if there were any news.

Francinette replied by handing him a bundle of despatches which Courtauvaux, his favorite outrider, had brought during the night.

The duke began to unseal them and to read with one eye; the other eye, to which he sought to impart the most affectionate expression he could command, he did not once remove from Nanon.

Nanon would have torn him in pieces if she could.

"Do you know what you ought to do, my dear?" said he, after he had read a portion of the despatches.

"No, monseigneur; but if you will give your orders, they shall be obeyed."

"You should send for your brother," said the duke. "I have here a letter from Bordeaux containing the information I desired, and he might start instantly, so that when he returned, I should have an excuse for giving him the promotion you suggest."

The duke's face was a picture of open-hearted benevolence.

"Courage!" said Nanon to herself; "there is a possibility that Canolles will read in my eyes what I want to say, or will understand a hint. Send yourself, my dear duke," she said aloud, for she suspected that if she undertook to do the errand herself, he would not allow her.

D'Épernon called Francinette, and despatched her to the inn with no other instructions than these, —

"Say to Monsieur le Baron de Canolles that Mademoiselle de Lartigues expects him to breakfast."

Nanon darted a meaning glance at Francinette, but, eloquent as it was, Francinette could not read in it, "Tell Monsieur le Baron de Canolles that I am his sister."

Francinette departed on her errand, satisfied that there was a needle under the rock, and that the needle might prove to be a good, healthy serpent.

Meanwhile Nanon rose, and took up a position behind the duke, so that she might be able, at the first glance she exchanged with Canolles, to warn him to be on his guard; and she busied herself in constructing a sentence by means of which she might at the outset convey to the baron all that he ought to know, in order that he might not sing false in the family trio about to be performed.

Out of the corner of her eye she could see the whole of the road as far as the turn where Monsieur d'Épernon and his men had lain in ambush the night before.

"Ah!" exclaimed the duke, "Francinette is returning." And he fixed his eyes upon Nanon's, who was compelled to look away from the road to meet his gaze.

Nanon's heart was beating as if it would burst through her breast; she had seen no one but Francinette, and it was Canolles whom she hoped to see, and to read in his face some comforting assurance.

Steps were heard upon the stairs; the duke prepared a smile which was at once condescending and affable; Nanon forced back the flush which mounted to her cheeks, and summoned all her strength for the conflict.

Francinette tapped gently at the door.

"Come in!" said the duke.

Nanon conned the famous sentence with which she proposed to greet Canolles.

The door opened; Francinette was alone. Nanon gazed eagerly into the reception-room; there was no one there.

"Madame," said Francinette, with the imperturbable self-possession of a comedy soubrette, "Monsieur le Baron de Canolles has left the Golden Calf."

The duke stared, and his face grew dark.

Nanon threw back her head and drew a long breath.

"What!" exclaimed the duke; "Monsieur de Canolles is not at the Golden Calf."

"You are surely mistaken, Francinette," chimed in Nanon.

"Madame," said Francinette, "I tell you what Monsieur Biscarros himself told me."

"He must have guessed the whole truth," murmured Nanon. "Dear Canolles! as quick-witted and clever as he is gallant and handsome!"

"Go at once to Master Biscarros," said the duke, with a face like a thundercloud, "and—"

"Oh! I fancy," said Nanon, hastily, "that he knew you were here, and disliked to disturb you. Poor Canolles is so timid!"

"Timid!" echoed the duke; "that isn't the reputation he bears, unless I am much mistaken."

"No, madame," said Francinette; "Monsieur le Baron has really gone."

"How does it happen, madame, I pray to know, that the baron is afraid of me, when Francinette was instructed to invite him in your name? Did you tell him I was here, Francinette? Answer!"

"I could not tell him, Monsieur le Duc, as he was not there."

Notwithstanding this rejoinder, which was uttered with an absence of hesitation that betokened sincerity, the duke seemed to have become as suspicious as ever. Nanon, in her joy at the turn the affair had taken, could not find strength to say a word.

"Must I return and summon Master Biscarros?" queried Francinette.

"Most assuredly," said the duke, in his harshest voice; "but no; wait a moment. Remain here; your mistress may need you, and I will send Courtauvaux."

Francinette vanished. Five minutes later, Courtauvaux knocked at the door.

"Go and bid the landlord of the Golden Calf come hither, and bring with him a breakfast menu! Give him these ten louis, so that the breakfast may be a good one!" said the duke.

Courtauvaux received the money on the skirt of his coat, and took himself off at once to execute his master's orders.

He was a servant of good family, and knowing enough at his trade to give lessons to all the Crispins and Mascarillos of the day. He found Biscarros, and said to him, —

"I have induced monsieur to order a good breakfast; and he gave me eight louis. I keep two, of course, for my commission, and here are six for you. Come at once."

Biscarros, tremulous with joy, tied a white apron around his loins, pocketed the six louis, and pressing Courtauvaux's hand, followed close upon his heels as he trotted away toward the little house.

VIII

This time Nanon was without apprehension; Francinette's intelligence had reassured her completely, and she was even very anxious to talk with Biscarros. He was ushered in, therefore, immediately upon his arrival.

Biscarros entered the room with his apron politely tucked in his belt, and cap in hand.

"You had at your house yesterday a young gentleman, Monsieur le Baron de Canolles, did you not?" said Nanon.

"What has become of him?" added the duke.

Biscarros, somewhat ill at ease, for the outrider and the six louis made him more than suspect the great personage under the *robe de chambre*, replied evasively:

"He has gone, monsieur."

"Gone?" said the duke; "really gone?"

"Really."

"Where has he gone?" Nanon asked.

"That I cannot tell you; for, in very truth, I do not know, madame."

"You know at least in which direction he went?"

"He took the Paris road."

"At what hour did he take that road?" asked the duke.

"About midnight."

"And without saying anything?" queried Nanon, timidly.

"Without saying anything; he simply left a letter, and bade me hand it to Mademoiselle Francinette."

"Well, why haven't you handed it to her, knave?" said the duke; "is that all the respect you have for a nobleman's command?"

"I did hand it to her, monsieur; I did indeed!"

"Francinette!" roared the duke.

Francinette, who was listening at the door, made but one bound from the reception-room into the bedroom.

"Why didn't you give your mistress the letter Monsieur de Canolles left for her?"

"Why, monseigneur—" murmured the maid, in deadly terror.

"Monseigneur!" thought the amazed Biscarros, shrinking into the most remote corner of the room; "Monseigneur! it must be some prince in disguise."

"I had not asked her for it," Nanon, pale as a ghost, hastened to say.

"Give it me," said the duke, extending his hand.

Poor Francinette slowly held out the letter, turning to her mistress with a look which seemed to say,—

"You see that it's no fault of mine; that imbecile of a Biscarros has ruined everything."

Two fierce gleams shot from Nanon's eyes, and pierced Biscarros in his corner. The sweat stood in great drops on the poor wretch's brow, and he would have given the six louis he had in his pocket to be standing in front of his oven with the handle of a saucepan in his hand.

Meanwhile the duke had taken the letter and opened it, and was reading. As he read, Nanon stood beside him, paler and colder than a statue, feeling as if no part of her were alive save her heart.

"What does all this mean?" queried the duke.

Nanon knew by that question that the letter did not compromise her.

"Read it aloud, and I can explain it perhaps," said she.

"'Dear Nanon,'" the duke began.

He turned to his companion, who became more composed with every second, and bore his gaze with admirable self-possession.

"'Dear Nanon,'" the duke resumed:—

> "'I am availing myself of the leave of absence I owe to your good offices, and to divert my mind, I am going for a short gallop on the Paris road. Au revoir; I commend my fortune to your attention.'

"*Ah ça!* why, this Canolles is mad!"

"Mad? Why so?" rejoined Nanon.

"Does a sane man start off in this way at midnight, without a reason for so doing?"

"I should say as much," said Nanon to herself.

"Come, explain his departure to me."

"Eh! *mon Dieu!* monseigneur," said Nanon, with a charming smile, "nothing can be easier than that."

"She, too, calls him monseigneur," muttered Biscarros. "He is a prince, beyond question."

"Well, tell me."

"What! can you not guess which way the wind blows?"

"Not in the least."

"Canolles is twenty-seven years old; he is young, handsome, thoughtless. What particular form of madness do you suppose he prefers? Love. He must have seen some fair traveller pass Master Biscarros' door, and have followed her."

"He's in love, you think?" cried the duke, smiling at the very natural reflection that, if Canolles was in love with any traveller whatsoever, he was not in love with Nanon.

"Why, yes, of course he's in love. Isn't that it, Master Biscarros?" said Nanon, enchanted to see that the duke accepted her suggestion. "Come, answer freely; have I not guessed aright?"

Biscarros thought that the moment had come to reestablish himself in the young woman's good graces by assenting freely to whatever she might say, and with a smile about four inches wide blooming upon his lips, he said,—

"In very truth, madame may be right."

Nanon stepped toward him, shuddering in spite of herself.

"It is so; is it not?" she said.

"I think so, madame," replied Biscarros, with a knowing air.

"You think so?"

"Yes; wait a moment; indeed, you open my eyes."

"Ah! tell us about it, Master Biscarros," rejoined Nanon, beginning to feel the first pricks of jealousy; "come, tell us what fair travellers tarried at your hostelry last night."

"Yes, tell us," said Monsieur d'Épernon, stretching out his legs, and making himself comfortable in an easy chair.

"There were no lady travellers," said Biscarros.

Nanon breathed again.

"But," continued the inn-keeper, not suspecting that every word he uttered made Nanon's heart leap, "there was a little fair-haired gentleman, very plump and dainty, who didn't eat or drink, and who was afraid to resume his journey after dark. A young gentleman who was afraid," repeated Biscarros, with an extremely-cunning nod; "you understand, do you not?"

"Ha! ha! ha!" laughed the duke, condescendingly, biting freely at the hook.

Nanon answered his laughter with something very like gnashing of the teeth.

"Go on!" said she; "it's a charming story! Of course the little gentleman was awaiting Monsieur de Canolles."

"No, no; he was waiting for a tall, moustachioed gentleman to sup with him, and was even somewhat uncivil to Monsieur de Canolles when he proposed that they should sup together. But that worthy gentleman was not discouraged by so small a matter. He's an enterprising young man, apparently, and 'faith, after the departure of the tall man, who turned to the right, he rode after the short one, who turned to the left."

With this Rabelaisian conclusion, Biscarros, observing the duke's expansive features, thought that he might indulge in an ascending scale of roars of laughter, of so stentorian quality that the windows rattled.

The duke, whose mind was entirely relieved from a great weight, would have embraced Biscarros if the least drop of noble blood had flowed in his veins. As for Nanon, with pallid cheeks, and a convulsive smile frozen upon her lips, she listened to every word that fell from the inn-keeper's lips, with that devouring faith which leads the jealous to drink freely to the dregs the poison which destroys their lives.

"What leads you to think," said she, "that your little gentleman is a woman, and that Monsieur de Canolles is in love with her, rather than that he is riding about the country because he is bored, or to gratify a whim?"

"What makes me think so?" replied Biscarros, determined to bring conviction home to the minds of his hearers. "Wait, and I will tell you."

"Yes, tell us, my good friend," said the duke. "Egad! you are an amusing fellow."

"Monseigneur is too kind," said Biscarros. "It was like this."

The duke became all ears, and Nanon listened with clenched fists.

"I suspected nothing, and had taken the little fair-haired cavalier for a man readily enough, when I met Monsieur de Canolles half-way upstairs, with a candle in his left hand, and in his right a small glove, which he was examining, and passionately smelling—"

"Ho! ho! ho!" roared the duke, whose spleen vanished with amazing rapidity, as soon as he ceased to have any apprehension on his own account.

"A glove!" exclaimed Nanon, trying to remember if she had not left such a pledge in the possession of her knight; "a glove like this?"

As she spoke, she handed the inn-keeper one of her own gloves.

"No," said Biscarros, "a man's glove."

"A man's glove? Monsieur de Canolles staring at a man's glove, and passionately smelling it? You are mad!"

"No; for it belonged to the little gentleman, the pretty little blond cavalier, who neither ate nor drank, and was afraid of the dark,—a tiny glove, in which madame could hardly put her hand, although madame certainly has a pretty hand—"

Nanon gave a sharp little cry, as if she had been struck by an invisible arrow.

"I trust," said she, with a mighty effort, "that you have all the information you desire, monseigneur; that you know all you wished to know."

With trembling lips, clenched teeth, and gleaming eyes, she pointed with outstretched finger to the door, while Biscarros, noticing these indications of wrath upon the young woman's face, was altogether non-plussed, and stood with mouth and eyes wide open.

"If the young gentleman's absence is such a calamity," he thought, "his return would be a blessed thing. I will flatter this worthy nobleman with a hopeful suggestion, that he may have a hearty appetite."

In pursuance of this determination, Biscarros assumed his most gracious expression, gracefully put his right leg forward, and remarked,—

"After all, though the gentleman has gone, he may return at any moment."

The duke smiled at this beginning.

"True," he said; "why should he not return? Perhaps, indeed, he has returned already. Go and ascertain, Monsieur Biscarros, and let me know."

"But the breakfast?" said Nanon, hastily; "I am dying of hunger."

"To be sure," said the duke; "Courtauvaux will go. Come here, Courtauvaux; go to Master Biscarros' inn, and see if Monsieur le Baron de

Canolles has returned. If he is not there, ask questions, find out what you can, look for him in the neighborhood. I am anxious to breakfast with him. Go!"

Courtauvaux left the room, and Biscarros, noticing the embarrassed silence of the others, prepared to put forth a new expedient.

"Don't you see that madame is motioning you to retire?" said Francinette.

"One moment! one moment!" cried the duke; "deuce take me! but you're losing your head now, my dear Nanon. What about the menu, pray? I am like you; I am half famished. Here, Master Biscarros, put these six louis with the others: they are to pay for the diverting tale you have been telling us."

Thereupon he bade the historian give place to the cook, and we hasten to say that Master Biscarros shone no less brilliantly in the second rôle than the first.

Meanwhile Nanon had reflected and realized at a glance the situation in which she was placed if Master Biscarros' supposition were well-founded. In the first place, was it well-founded? and, after all, even if it were, was not Canolles excusable? For what a cruel thing for a gallant fellow like him was this broken appointment! How insulting the espionage of the Duc d'Épernon, and the necessity imposed upon him, Canolles, of looking on, so to speak, at his rival's triumph! Nanon was so deeply in love herself that, attributing this prank to a paroxysm of jealousy, she not only forgave Canolles, but pitied him, and congratulated herself, perhaps, on being loved so well as to have incited him to take this petty revenge upon her. But the evil must be cut off at its root, and the progress of this incipient passion must be checked at all hazards.

At that point, a terrifying thought passed through Nanon's mind, and well-nigh struck her dumb.

Suppose that this meeting between Canolles and the little gentleman was by appointment.

But no; she was mad to think of it, for the little fellow awaited the arrival of a man with moustaches, and was rude to Canolles; perhaps Canolles did not himself detect the stranger's sex until he happened upon the little glove.

No matter! Canolles must be thwarted.

Summoning all her energy, she returned to the duke, who had just dismissed Biscarros, laden with compliments and instructions.

"What a misfortune, monsieur," said she, "that that madcap's folly deprives him of an honor like that you were about to bestow upon him! If he had been here, his future was assured; his absence may ruin everything."

"But," said the duke, "if we find him—"

"No danger of that," rejoined Nanon; "if there's a woman in the case, he will not have returned."

"What would you have me do, my love? Youth is the age of pleasure; he is young, and is amusing himself."

"But," said Nanon, "I am more sensible than he, and it's my opinion that we should interfere a little with his unseasonable amusement."

"Ah! scolding sister!" cried the duke.

"He will take it ill of me at the moment, perhaps; but he will unquestionably thank me for it later."

"Very well; have you a plan? I ask nothing better than to adopt it if you have."

"I have one."

"Tell it me."

"Do you not wish to send him to the queen with urgent intelligence?"

"To be sure; but if he has not returned—"

"Send a messenger after him; and as he is on the road to Paris, it will be so much time gained."

"*Pardieu!* you are right."

"Leave it to me, and Canolles shall have the order to-night or to-morrow morning. I will answer for it."

"Whom will you send?"

"Do you need Courtauvaux?"

"Not in the least."

"Give him to me, then, and I will send him with my instructions."

"Oh! what a head for a diplomatist! you have a future before you, Nanon."

"May I remain forever under so good a master! that is the height of my ambition," said Nanon, throwing her arm around the old duke's neck, whereat he trembled with delight.

"What a delightful joke to play upon our Celadon!" said she.

"It will be a charming story to tell, my love."

"Upon my word! I should like to go in chase of him myself, to see how he'll receive the messenger."

"Unhappily, or rather happily, that is out of the question, and you must needs remain with me."

"True; but let us lose no time. Write your order, duke, and place Courtauvaux at my disposal."

The duke took a pen and wrote upon a bit of paper these two words:—

"Bordeaux.—No,"

and signed his name.

He then enclosed this laconic despatch in an envelope, on which he wrote the following address:—

"To her Majesty, Queen Anne of Austria, Regent of France."

Nanon meanwhile wrote a few lines, which she placed with the other, after showing them to the duke:—

My Dear Baron,—The accompanying despatch is for her Majesty the queen, as you see. On your life, carry it to her instantly; the welfare of the kingdom is at stake!

Your loving sister,

Nanon.

Nanon had hardly finished the letter, when they heard hurried footsteps at the foot of the stairs, and Courtauvaux ran up quickly and opened the door, with the expansive expression of a bearer of news which he knows to be awaited with impatience.

"Here is Monsieur de Canolles, whom I met within a hundred yards of the house," he said.

The duke uttered an exclamation of good-humored surprise. Nanon turned pale, and darted to the door, muttering,—

"It is written that I shall not escape the meeting."

At that moment a new personage appeared in the doorway, arrayed in a magnificent costume, holding his hat in his hand, and with a most gracious smile upon his lips.

IX

A thunder-bolt falling at Nanon's feet would certainly have caused her no greater surprise than this unexpected apparition, and would not, in all probability, have extorted from her a more sorrowful exclamation than that which escaped from her mouth involuntarily.

"He?" she cried.

"To be sure, my dear little sister," replied a most affable voice. "But I beg your pardon," added the owner of the voice, as he espied the Duc d'Épernon; "perhaps I intrude."

He bowed to the ground to the governor of Guyenne, who replied with a gracious gesture.

"Cauvignac!" muttered Nanon, but so low that the name was pronounced by her heart rather than by her lips.

"Welcome, Monsieur de Canolles," said the duke, with a most benevolent expression; "your sister and I have done naught but talk of you since last evening, and since last evening we have been most desirous of seeing you."

"Ah! you wished to see me? indeed!" said Cauvignac, turning to Nanon, with a look in which there was an indescribable expression of irony and suspicion.

"Yes," said Nanon; "Monsieur le Duc has been kind enough to express a wish that you should be presented to him."

"Naught save the fear of intruding upon you, monseigneur," said Cauvignac, bowing to the duke, "has prevented me from seeking that honor before this."

"On my word, baron," said the duke, "I admire your delicacy, but I feel bound to reproach you for it."

"Reproach me for my delicacy, monseigneur? Oho!"

"Yes; for if your good sister had not looked out for your interests—"

"Ah!" exclaimed Cauvignac, with an eloquent, reproachful glance at Nanon; "ah! my good sister has looked out for the interests of Monsieur—"

"Her brother," interposed Nanon, hastily; "what could be more natural?"

"And then to-day; to what do I owe the pleasure of seeing you?"

"True," said Cauvignac; "to what do you owe the pleasure of seeing me, monseigneur?"

"Why, to chance, to mere chance, which led you to return."

"Aha!" said Cauvignac to himself; "it seems that I had gone away."

"Yes, you went away, you bad brother; and without letting me know, except by a word or two, which had no other effect than to increase my anxiety."

"What would you have, dear Nanon? we must make allowances for a man in love," said the duke, with a smile.

"Oho! this is becoming complicated," said Cauvignac; "it seems now that I am in love."

"Come, come," said Nanon, "confess that you are."

"I won't deny it," rejoined Cauvignac, with a meaning smile, seeking to glean from some eye some hint of the truth, to guide him in constructing a lusty lie.

"Very good," said the duke; "but let us breakfast, if you've no objection. You can tell us of your love-affairs as we sit at the table, baron.—Francinette, a cover for Monsieur de Canolles. You haven't breakfasted, captain, I trust?"

"No, monseigneur; and I confess that the fresh morning air has sharpened my appetite prodigiously."

"Say the night air, you rascal," said the duke; "for you have been on the road all night."

"'Faith!" muttered Cauvignac, "the brother-in-law guessed aright there. Very good! I admit it; the night air—"

"In that case," the duke continued, giving his arm to Nanon, and leading the way to the dining-room, followed by Cauvignac, "I trust that you will find here the wherewithal to defeat your appetite, however strongly constituted it may be."

It was the fact that Master Biscarros had outdone himself; the dishes were not numerous, but delicious and exquisitely served. The yellow wine of Guyenne, and the red Burgundy fell from the bottles like golden pearls and cascades of rubies.

Cauvignac ate very heartily.

"The boy handles his knife and fork very cleverly," said the duke. "But you do not eat, Nanon."

"I am no longer hungry, monseigneur."

"Dear sister!" cried Cauvignac; "to think that the pleasure of seeing me has taken away her appetite! Indeed, I can but be grateful to her for loving me so dearly."

"This chicken-wing, Nanon?" said the duke.

"Give it to my brother, monseigneur; give it to my brother," replied Nanon, who saw Cauvignac emptying his plate with terrifying rapidity, and dreaded his raillery after the food had disappeared.

Cauvignac held out his plate with a grateful smile. The duke placed the wing upon the plate, and Cauvignac replaced the plate on the table before him.

"Well, what have you been doing that's worth the telling, Canolles?" said the duke, with a familiarity which seemed to Cauvignac of most hopeful augury. "It is understood that I am not speaking of love-affairs."

"Nay; do speak of them, monseigneur; speak of them," rejoined the younger man, whose tongue was beginning to be unloosed by successive doses of Médoc and Chambertin, and who, moreover, was in a very different situation from those people who borrow a name themselves, in that he had no fear of being interfered with by his double.

"Oh, monseigneur, he's very skilful at raillery," said Nanon.

"In that case, we can place him in the same category with the little gentleman," the duke suggested.

"Yes," said Nanon, "the little gentleman you met last evening."

"Ah! yes, in the road," said Cauvignac.

"And afterwards at Master Biscarros' hôtel," the duke added.

"And afterwards at Master Biscarros' hôtel," assented Cauvignac; "it's true, by my faith."

"Do you mean that you really did meet him?" queried Nanon.

"The little gentleman?"

"Yes."

"What sort of person was he? Tell us frankly," said the duke.

"Egad!" replied Cauvignac; "he was a charming little fellow,—fair and slender and refined, and travelling with a caricature of a squire."

"It's the same man," said Nanon, biting her lips.

"And you are in love with him?"

"With whom?"

"With this same little, fair, slender, refined gentleman."

"Oh, monseigneur!" exclaimed Cauvignac, "what do you mean?"

"Have you still the pearl-gray glove on your heart?"

"The pearl-gray glove?"

"Yes; the one you were smelling and kissing so passionately last evening."

This last phrase removed Cauvignac's perplexity.

"Ah!" he cried, "your little gentleman was a woman, was she? On my word of honor, I suspected as much."

"There can be no doubt now," murmured Nanon.

"Give me some wine, sister mine," said Cauvignac. "I can't imagine who emptied the bottle that stands beside me, but there's nothing in it."

"Go to!" exclaimed the duke; "his complaint can be cured, as his love doesn't interfere with his eating or drinking; and the king's business will not suffer."

"The king's business suffer!" cried Cauvignac. "Never! The king's business first of all! the king's business, is sacred. To his Majesty's health, monseigneur."

"I may rely upon your loyalty, baron?"

"Upon my loyalty to the king?"

"Yes."

"I should say you may rely upon it. I would gladly be drawn and quartered for him—at times."

"Your loyalty is easily understood," said Nanon, fearing that, in his enthusiasm for the Médoc and Chambertin, Cauvignac might forget the part he was playing, and clothe himself in his own individuality.

"Aren't you a captain in his Majesty's service, by virtue of Monsieur le Duc's favor?"

"I shall never forget it!" said Cauvignac, laying his hand, upon his heart, with tearful emotion.

"We will do better, baron; we will do better hereafter," said the duke.

"Thanks, monseigneur, thanks!"

"And we have already begun."

"Indeed!"

"Yes. You are too bashful, my young friend," continued d'Épernon. "When you are in need of anything, you must come to me. Now that there is no need to beat around the bush; now that you are no longer called upon to conceal your identity; now that I know that you are Nanon's brother—"

"Monseigneur," cried Cauvignac, "henceforth I will apply to you in person."

"You promise?"

"I give you my word."

"You will do well. Meanwhile, your sister will explain to you what is to be done now; she has a letter to intrust to you in my behalf. Perhaps your fortune is in the missive which I place in your hands on her recommendation. Follow your sister's advice, young man, follow her advice; she has an active brain, a keen intellect, and a noble heart. Love your sister, baron, and you will be established in my good graces."

"Monseigneur," exclaimed Cauvignac, effusively, "my sister knows how dearly I love her, and that I long for nothing so much as to see her happy, powerful, and—rich."

"Your fervor gratifies me," said the duke; "pray remain with Nanon, while I go hence to have a reckoning with a certain consummate villain. By the way, baron, perhaps you may be able to give me some information concerning the scoundrel."

"Gladly," said Cauvignac. "Only it will be necessary for me to know to what scoundrel you refer, monseigneur; there are many of them, and of every variety in these days."

"You are right; but this one is one of the most brazen-faced it has ever been my lot to fall in with."

"Indeed!"

"Imagine, if you please, that the gallows-bird extorted my signature in blank, in exchange for the letter your sister wrote you yesterday, which he procured by an infamous deed of violence."

"A signature in blank! upon my word! But what interest had you, pray, in possessing the letter of a sister to her brother?"

"Do you forget that I knew nothing of the relationship?"

"Ah! true."

"And I was idiotic enough—you will forgive me, won't you, Nanon?" continued the duke, holding out his hand to the young woman—"I was idiotic enough to be jealous of you!"

"Indeed! jealous of me! Oh! monseigneur, you were very, very wrong!"

"I was about to ask you if you had any suspicion as to the identity of the rascal who played informer?"

"No, not the slightest. But you understand, monseigneur, that such acts do not go unpunished, and some day you will know who did it."

"Oh! yes, certainly I shall know it some day, and I have taken precautions in abundance to that end; but I would have preferred to know it immediately."

"Ah!" rejoined Cauvignac, pricking up his ears; "ah! you say you have taken precautions to that end, monseigneur?"

"Yes, yes! And the villain," continued the duke, "will be very fortunate if my signature in blank doesn't lead to his being hanged."

"Why, how can you distinguish that particular signature from all the other orders you give out, monseigneur?"

"Because I made a private mark upon it."

"A mark?"

"Yes; an invisible mark, which I can render visible with the aid of a chemical process."

"Well, well!" said Cauvignac, "that is certainly a most ingenious device, monseigneur; but you must be careful that he doesn't suspect the trap."

"Oh! there's no danger of that; who do you think is likely to tell him of it?"

"True! true!" replied Cauvignac; "not Nanon, surely, nor I—"

"Nor I," said the duke.

"Nor you. So you are right, monseigneur; you cannot fail to know some day who the man is, and then—"

"Then, as I shall have kept my agreement with him, for he will have obtained whatever he chose to use the signature for, I will have him hanged."

"*Amen!*" said Cauvignac.

"And now," continued the duke, "as you can give me no information concerning the miscreant—"

"No, monseigneur; in very truth, I cannot."

"As I was saying, I will leave you with your sister.—Nanon, give the boy precise instructions, and above all things, see that he loses no time."

"Never fear, monseigneur."

"Adieu to you both."

He waved his hand gracefully to Nanon, bestowed a friendly nod upon her brother, and descended the stairs, saying that he should probably return during the day.

Nanon went with the duke to the head of the stairs.

"*Peste!*" said Cauvignac to himself, "my gallant friend did well to warn me. Ah! he's no such fool as he seems. But what shall I do with his signature? *Dame!* I'll do what I would do with a note; discount it."

"Now, monsieur," said Nanon, returning, and closing the door behind her, "now let us understand each other."

"My dear little sister," Cauvignac replied, "I came hither for the purpose of having a talk with you; but in order to talk at our ease, we must be seated. Sit you down, therefore, I beg."

As he spoke, he drew a chair near to his own and motioned to Nanon that it was intended for her.

Nanon seated herself with a frown, which augured ill for the harmony of the interview.

"First of all," said she, "why are you not where you should be?"

"Ah! my dear little sister, that is hardly courteous. If I were where I should be, I should not be here, and consequently you would not have the pleasure of seeing me."

"Did you not wish to take orders?"

"No, not I; say rather, that certain persons who are interested in me, notably yourself, wished to force me to take orders; but personally, I have never had a particularly earnest vocation for the Church."

"But you were educated for a religious life?"

"Yes, sister; and I believe I have piously profited by that fact."

"No sacrilege, monsieur; do not joke on sacred subjects."

"I am not joking, dear sister; I am simply stating facts. Look you; you sent me to the Minim brethren at Angoulème to prepare for the priesthood."

"Well?"

"I studied diligently there. I know Greek like Homer, Latin like Cicero, and theology like John Huss. Having nothing more to learn among those worthy monks, I left their establishment, still following out your wishes, and went to the Carmelites at Rouen, to make profession of faith."

"You forget to say that I had promised you a yearly allowance of a hundred pistoles, and that I kept my promise. A hundred pistoles for a Carmelite was more than enough, I should say."

"I don't deny it, my dear sister; but the convent always claimed my allowance on the pretext that I was not yet a Carmelite."

"Even so, did you not, when you consecrated your life to the Church, take a vow of poverty?"

"If I did make such a vow, dear sister, I give you my word that I have faithfully lived up to it; no one was ever poorer than I."

"But how did you leave the convent?"

"Ah! there you are! In the same way that Adam left the earthly paradise; it was knowledge that undid me, sister; I knew too much."

"What's that? you knew too much?"

"Yes. Imagine, if you can, that among the Carmelites, who have not the reputation of being Erasmuses or Descartes, I was looked upon as a prodigy, — of learning, be it understood. The result was that when Monsieur le Duc de Longueville came to Rouen to urge that city to declare in favor of the parliament, I was sent to harangue Monsieur de Longueville; the which I did in such elegant and well-chosen language, that Monsieur de Longueville not only expressed himself as well pleased with my eloquence, but asked me if I would be his secretary. This happened just as I was about to take the vows."

"Yes, I remember; and on the pretext that you were saying farewell to the world, you asked me for a hundred pistoles, which were given into your own hands."

"And they are the only ones I received, on the word of a gentleman!"

"But you were to renounce the world."

"Yes, such was my intention; but such was not the intention of Providence, which probably had other plans for me. It made a different disposition of me through the medium of Monsieur de Longueville; it was not its will that I should remain a monk. I therefore conformed to the will of a merciful Providence, and I am free to say that I do not repent having done so."

"Then you are no longer in the Church?"

"No, not for the moment, at least, my dear sister. I do not dare say that I may not return to it some day; for what man can say to-day what he will do to-morrow? Has not Monsieur de Rancé recently founded the Trappist order? Perhaps I shall follow in his footsteps, and found some new order. But for the moment I have dallied with war, you see, and that has made me profane and impure for some time to come; at the first opportunity I shall purify myself."

"You a fighting man!" exclaimed Nanon, with a shrug.

"Why not? *Dame!* I won't pretend to say that I am a Dunois, a Duguesclin, a Bayard, a knight without fear and without reproach. No, I am not so vainglorious as to claim that I have not some trifling peccadilloes to be ashamed of, nor will I ask, like the famous condottiere Sforza, what fear is. I am a man, and, as Plautus says: '*Homo sum et nihil humani me alienum puto;*' which means: 'I am a man, and nothing pertaining to mankind is strange to me.' I do know what fear is, therefore, but that does not prevent my being courageous on occasion. I handle a sword or a pistol prettily enough when I am driven to it. But my real bent, my decided vocation, is diplomacy. Unless I am sadly mistaken, my dear Nanon, I am on the way to become a great politician. A fine career is politics; Monsieur de Mazarin will rise very high if he's not hanged. And I am like Monsieur de Mazarin; so that one of my apprehensions, the greatest of them all, in fact, is, that I may be hanged. Fortunately, I have you, dear Nanon, and that gives me great confidence."

"So you are a warrior?"

"And a courtier, too, at need. Ah! my sojourn with Monsieur de Longueville was of the greatest benefit to me."

"What did you learn when you were with him?"

"What one always learns in the service of princes, — to fight, to intrigue, to betray."

"And those accomplishments —"

"Raised me to the very highest position."

"Which you have lost?"

"*Dame!* Hasn't Monsieur de Condé lost his? A man can't rule events. Dear sister, I, poor creature that I am, have governed Paris."

"You?"

"Yes, I."

"For how long a time?"

"For an hour and three quarters, watch in hand."

"You governed Paris?"

"With despotic power."

"How did that come about?"

"In the simplest way imaginable. You must know that Monsieur le Coadjuteur, Monsieur de Gondy, the Abbé de Gondy—-"

"Well?"

"Was absolute master of the city. Well, at that precise moment, I was in the service of Monsieur le Duc d'Elbœuf; he is a Lorraine prince, and one need not be ashamed to belong to him. For the time being, Monsieur d'Elbœuf was at enmity with the coadjutor. So I led an uprising in favor of Monsieur d'Elbœuf, in the course of which I captured—"

"Whom? the coadjutor?"

"No; I shouldn't have known what to do with him, and should have been much embarrassed. I captured his mistress, Mademoiselle de Chevreuse."

"Why, that was a terrible thing to do!" cried Nanon.

"Isn't it a terrible thing that a priest should have a mistress? At all events, that's what I said to myself. My purpose was, therefore, to carry her away, and carry her so far that he would never see her again. I sent word to him of my purpose; but the devil of a man uses arguments one can't resist; he offered me a thousand pistoles."

"Poor woman! to be thus bargained for!"

"Nonsense! on the contrary, she should have been overjoyed, for that proved how dearly Monsieur de Gondy loved her. None but men of the Church are so devoted as all that to their mistresses. I fancy that it's because they are forbidden to have them."

"You are rich, then?"

"Rich?"

"Of course, after all these acts of brigandage."

"Don't speak of it; look you, Nanon, I was most unlucky. Mademoiselle de Chevreuse's maid, whom no one thought of ransoming, and who consequently remained with me, took the money from me."

"I hope that you retained at least the good-will of those in whose interest you acted in putting this affront upon the coadjutor."

"Ah! Nanon, that proves how little you know of princes. Monsieur d'Elbœuf was reconciled with the coadjutor. In the treaty they entered into I was sacrificed. I was forced therefore to enter the service of Monsieur de Mazarin, who is a contemptible creature; and as the pay was by no means commensurate with the work to be done, I accepted an offer that was made me to incite another *émeute* in honor of Councillor Broussel, the object being to secure the election of the Chancellor Seguier. But my men, the bunglers! only half killed him. In that affray I was in greater danger than ever before threatened me. Monsieur de la Meilleraie fired a pistol at me almost point-blank. Luckily, I stooped in time; the bullet whistled over my head, and the illustrious marshal killed no one but an old woman."

"What a tissue of horrors!" exclaimed Nanon.

"Why no, dear sister; simply the necessities of civil war."

"I can understand that a man capable of such things might have dared to do what you did yesterday."

"What did I do, pray?" queried Cauvignac with the most innocent expression; "what did I dare?"

"You dared to throw dust in the eyes of so eminent a man as Monsieur d'Épernon. But what I cannot understand, and would never have believed, is that a brother, fairly laden with favors at his sister's hands, could in cold blood form a plan to ruin that sister."

"Ruin my sister?—I?" said Cauvignac.

"Yes, you!" retorted Nanon. "I had no need to wait for the tale you have just told me, which proves that you are capable of anything, to recognize the handwriting of this letter. Tell me! do you deny that this unsigned letter was written by you?"

And Nanon indignantly held before her brother's eyes the denunciatory letter the duke had handed her the night before.

Cauvignac read it composedly.

"Well," said he, "what have you to say against this letter? Is it not couched in well-turned phrase? If you thought so, I should be very sorry for you, for it would prove that your literary taste is vitiated."

"This is not a question of the composition, monsieur, but of the fact itself. Did you, or did you not write this letter?"

"Unquestionably I did. If I had proposed to deny the fact, I should have disguised my handwriting; but it was useless. I have never intended to hide it from you; indeed, I was anxious that you should recognize the letter, as coming from me."

"Oh!" exclaimed Nanon, with a horrified gesture, "you admit it!"

"It is a last relic of humility, dear sister; yes, I may as well tell you that I was actuated by a desire for revenge—"

"Revenge?"

"Yes, most naturally—"

"Revenge upon me, you wretch! Pray, consider what you are saying. What injury have I ever done you that the thought of seeking revenge should enter your mind?"

"What have you done to me? Ah! Nanon, put yourself in my place. I left Paris because I had too many enemies there; 't is the misfortune of all men who dabble in politics. I returned to you—I implored you. Do you remember? You received three letters,—you won't say that you did not recognize my hand; it was precisely the same as in this anonymous letter, and furthermore, those letters were signed,—I wrote you three letters, begging for a hundred beggarly pistoles—a hundred pistoles! to you, who had millions, it was the merest trifle. But a hundred pistoles, as you know, is my favorite figure. Very good; my sister ignored me! I presented myself at my sister's house; my sister's door was closed in my face! Naturally, I made inquiries. 'Perhaps she is in want,' I said to myself;'if so, this is the time to show her that her benefactions have not fallen on stony soil. Perhaps she is no longer free; in that case her treatment of me is pardonable.' You see my heart sought excuses for you, until I learned that my sister was free, happy, wealthy, and rich—rich, richer, richest!—and that one Baron de Canolles, a stranger, had usurped my privileges, and was enjoying her protection in my place. Thereupon jealousy turned my head."

"Say cupidity. You sold me to Monsieur d'Épernon as you sold Mademoiselle de Chevreuse to the coadjutor! What business was it of yours, I pray to know, that I was on friendly terms with Monsieur le Baron de Canolles?"

"What business was it of mine? None at all, and I should not even have thought of interfering if you had continued to be on friendly terms with me."

"Do you know that if I were to say a single word to Monsieur d'Épernon, if I should tell him the whole truth, you would be lost?"

"Certainly."

"You heard with your own ears from his mouth a moment since, what fate is in store for the man who extorted that signature in blank from him."

"Don't speak of it; I shuddered to the very marrow of my bones; and it needed all my self-control to prevent me from betraying myself."

"And you say that you do not tremble now, although you confess your acquaintance with fear?"

"No; for such an open confession on your part would show that Monsieur de Canolles is not your brother, and that note of yours, being addressed to a stranger, would take on very sinister meaning. It is much better, believe me, to have made the disingenuous confession you have made, ungrateful sister—I dare not say blindly, I know you too well for that; but consider, pray, how many advantages, all foreseen by me, result from this little episode, for which all the credit is due to my thoughtfulness. In the first place, you were greatly embarrassed, and dreaded the arrival of Monsieur de Canolles, who, not having been warned, would have floundered around terribly in the midst of your little family romance. My presence, on the other hand, has made everything smooth; your brother is no longer a mystery. Monsieur d'Épernon has adopted him, and in a very flattering way, I am bound to say. Now, therefore, the brother is under no further necessity of skulking in corners; he is one of the family; *ergo*, correspondence, appointments without, and why not within?—provided always that the brother with black eyes and hair is careful not to come face to face with Monsieur d'Épernon. One cloak bears an astonishing resemblance to another, deuce take it! and when Monsieur d'Épernon sees a cloak leave your house, who is to tell him whether it is or is not a brother's cloak? So there you are, free as the wind. But to do you this service, I have unbaptized myself; my name is Canolles, and that's a nuisance. You ought to be grateful to me for the sacrifice."

Nanon was struck dumb by this resistless flood of eloquence, the fruit of inconceivable impudence, and she could think of no arguments to oppose to it. Cauvignac made the most of his victory, and continued,—

"And now, dear sister, as we are united once more after so long a separation; as you have found a real brother, after so many disappointments, confess that henceforth you will sleep in peace,—thanks to the shield which love stretches over you; you will lead as tranquil a life as if all Guyenne adored you, which is not precisely the fact, you know; but Guyenne must bend to our will. In short, I have taken my station at your threshold; Monsieur d'Épernon procures a colonel's commission for me; instead of six men, I have two thousand. With those, two thousand men I will perform again the twelve tasks of Hercules; I shall be created duke and peer; Madame d'Épernon dies; Monsieur d'Épernon marries you—"

"Before all this happens you must do two things," said Nanon, shortly.

"What are they, dear sister? Tell me; I am listening."

"First of all, you must return the duke's signature in blank to him; otherwise, you will be hanged. You heard your sentence from his own lips. Secondly, you must leave this house instantly, or not only am I ruined forever, for which you care nothing, but you will be involved in my ruin,—a consideration which will cause you to think twice, I trust, before you decide."

"These are my answers, dear lady: the signature in blank is my property, and you can't prevent my getting myself hanged, if such is my good pleasure."

"God forbid!"

"Thanks! I shall do nothing of the kind; never fear. I declared my aversion to that kind of death a few moments since; I shall keep the document, therefore, unless you have a craving to purchase it from me, in which case we may come to terms."

"I have no use for it; I give them away."

"Lucky Nanon!"

"You will keep it, then?"

"Yes."

"At the risk of what may happen to you?"

"Don't be alarmed; I have a place for it. As to taking my leave, I shall make no such blunder, being here by the duke's invitation. Furthermore, in your desire to be rid of me, you forget one thing."

"What is that?"

"The important commission the duke mentioned, which is likely to make my fortune."

Nanon turned pale.

"Why, you know perfectly well that it was not intended for you," she said. "You know that to abuse your present position would be a crime, for which you would have to pay the penalty one day or another."

"For that reason I don't propose to abuse it. I am anxious to use it, nothing more."

"Besides, Monsieur de Canolles is named in the commission."

"Very good; am I not Baron de Canolles?"

"Yes; but his face, as well as his name, is known at court. Monsieur de Canolles has been there several times."

"*A la bonne heure!* that's a strong argument; it's the first you have put forward, and you see that I yield to it."

"Moreover, you might fall in with your political opponents there," said Nanon; "and perhaps your face, although under a different name, is as well known as Monsieur de Canolles'."

"Oh! that would amount to nothing, if, as the duke says, the mission is destined to result advantageously to France. The message will be the messenger's safeguard. A service of such importance implies pardon for him who renders it, and amnesty for the past is always the first condition of political conversions. And so, dear sister, it is not for you, but for me, to impose conditions."

"Well, what are yours?"

"In the first place, as I was saying, the first condition of every treaty,—general amnesty."

"Is that all?"

"Secondly, the adjustment of our accounts."

"It would seem that I owe you something, then?"

"You owe me the hundred pistoles, which you inhumanly refused me."

"Here are two hundred."

"Good! I recognize the real Nanon in that."

"But I give them to you on one condition."

"What is that?"

"That you repair the wrong you have done."

"That is no more than fair. What must I do?"

"You must take horse and ride along the Paris road until you overtake Monsieur de Canolles."

"In that case, I lose his name."

"You restore it to him."

"And what am I to say to him?"

"You will hand him this order, and make sure that he sets out instantly to execute it."

"Is that all?"

"Absolutely."

"Is it necessary that he should know who I am?"

"On the contrary, it is of the utmost importance that he should not know."

"Ah! Nanon, do you blush for your brother?"

Nanon did not reply; she was lost in thought.

"How can I be sure," she began, after a moment's silence, "that you will do my errand faithfully? If you held anything sacred, I would require your oath."

"You can do better than that."

"How?"

"Promise me a hundred more pistoles after the errand is done."

"It's a bargain," said Nanon, with a shrug.

"Mark the difference. I ask you for no oath, and your simple word is enough for me. We will say a hundred pistoles to the man who hands you from me Monsieur de Canolles' receipt."

"Yes; but you speak of a third person; do you not expect to return yourself?"

"Who knows? I have business myself which requires my presence in the neighborhood of Paris."

Nanon could not restrain an exclamation of delight

"Ah! that's not polite," said Cauvignac, with a laugh; "but never mind, dear sister, no malice."

"Agreed; but to horse!"

"Instantly; simply time to drink a stirrup cup."

Cauvignac emptied the bottle of Chambertin into his glass, saluted his sister deferentially, vaulted into the saddle, and disappeared in a cloud of dust.

X

The moon was just rising as the viscount, followed by the faithful Pompée, left Master Biscarros' hostelry behind him, and started off on the road to Paris.

After about quarter of an hour, which the viscount devoted to his reflections, and during which they made something like a league and a half, he turned to the squire, who was gravely bobbing up and down in his saddle, three paces behind his master.

"Pompée," the young man asked, "have you my right glove by any chance?"

"Not that I am aware of, monsieur," said Pompée.

"What are you doing to your portmanteau, pray?"

"I am looking to see if it is fastened on securely, and tightening the straps, for fear the gold may rattle. The rattle of gold is a fatal thing, monsieur, and leads to unpleasant meetings, especially at night."

"It's well done of you, Pompée, and I love to see that you are so prudent and careful."

"Those are very natural qualities in an old soldier, Monsieur le Vicomte, and are well adapted to go with courage; however, as rashness is not courage, I confess my regret that Monsieur Richon couldn't come with us; for twenty thousand livres is a risky burden, especially in such stormy times as these."

"What you say is full of common-sense, Pompée, and I agree with you in every point," the viscount replied.

"I will even venture to say," continued Pompée, emboldened in his fear by the viscount's approbation, "that it is imprudent to take the chances we are taking. Let us halt a moment, if you please, while I inspect my musket."

"Well, Pompée?"

"It seems to be in good condition, and the man who undertakes to stop us will have a bad quarter of an hour. Oho! what do I see yonder?"

"Where?"

"A hundred yards ahead of us, to the right; look, over there."

"I see something white!"

"Yes, yes!" said Pompée, "white; a cross-belt, perhaps. I am very anxious, on my honor, to get behind that hedge on the left. In military language that is called intrenching; let us intrench ourselves, Monsieur le Vicomte."

"If those are cross-belts, Pompée, they are worn by the king's soldiers; and the king's soldiers don't rob peaceful travellers."

"Don't you believe it, Monsieur le Vicomte, don't you believe it! On the contrary, we hear of nothing but road-agents, who use his Majesty's uniform as a cloak under which to commit innumerable villanies, each one more damnable than the last; and lately, at Bordeaux, two of the light-horse were broken on the wheel. I think I recognize the uniform of the light-horse, monsieur."

"Their uniform is blue, Pompée, and what we see is white."

"True; but they often put on a blouse over their uniform; that's what the villains did who were recently broken on the wheel at Bordeaux. It seems to me that they are gesticulating a great deal; they are threatening. That's their tactics, you see, Monsieur le Vicomte; they lie in ambush like this, by the road, and, carbine in hand, compel the traveller to throw his purse to them from a distance."

"But, my good Pompée," said the viscount, who, although considerably alarmed, kept his presence of mind, "if they threaten from a distance with their carbines, do the same with yours."

"Yes; but they don't see me," said Pompée; "so any demonstration on my part would be useless."

"Well, if they don't see you, they can hardly be threatening you, I should say."

"You understand absolutely nothing of war," retorted the squire, ill-humoredly; "the same thing is going to happen to me here that happened at Corbie."

"Let us hope not, Pompée; for, if I remember aright, Corbie is where you were wounded."

"Yes, and a terrible wound. I was with Monsieur de Cambes, and a rash gentleman he was! We were doing patrol duty one night to investigate the place where the battle was to be fought. We spied some cross-belts. I urged him not to do a foolhardy thing that would do no good; he persisted and marched straight up to the cross-belts. I turned my back angrily. At that moment, a cursed ball—viscount, let us be prudent!"

"Prudent we will be, Pompée: I ask nothing better. But it seems to me that they do not move."

"They are scenting their prey. Wait."

The travellers, luckily for them, had not to wait long. In a moment the moon shone out from behind a black cloud, and cast a bright light upon two or three shirts drying behind a hedge, with sleeves outstretched, some fifty paces away.

They were the cross-belts which reminded Pompée of his ill-fated patrol at Corbie.

The viscount laughed heartily, and spurred his horse; Pompée followed him, crying: —

"How fortunate that I did not follow my first impulse; I was going to send a ball in that direction, and it would have made me a second Don Quixote. You see, viscount, the value of prudence and experience in warfare!"

After a period of deep emotion, there is always a period of repose; having safely passed the shirts, the travellers rode on two or three leagues peacefully enough. It was a superb night; a clump of trees by the roadside made a broad shadow, black as ebony, across the road.

"I most assuredly do not like the moonlight," said Pompée. "When you can be seen from a distance you run the risk of being taken by surprise. I have always heard men versed in war say that of two men who are looking for each other the moon never helps but one at a time. We are in the bright light, Monsieur le Vicomte, and it isn't prudent."

"Very well, let us ride in the shadow, Pompée."

"Yes, but if men were lying hidden in the edge of the wood, we should literally run into their mouths. In war time you never approach a wood until it has been reconnoitred."

"Unfortunately," rejoined the viscount, "we lack scouts. Isn't that what they call the men who reconnoitre woods, brave Pompée?"

"Yes, yes," muttered the squire. "Deuce take Richon, why didn't he come? We could have sent him forward as advance-guard, while we formed the main body of the army."

"Well, Pompée, what shall we do? Shall we stay in the moonlight, or go over into the shadow?"

"Let us get into the shadow, Monsieur le Vicomte; it's the most prudent way, I think."

"Shadow it is."

"You are afraid, Monsieur le Vicomte, aren't you?"

"No, my dear Pompée, I swear I'm not."

"You would be foolish, for I am here and on the watch; if I were alone, you understand, this would trouble me very little. An old soldier fears neither God nor devil. But you are a companion as hard to watch as the gold I have on behind; and the double responsibility alarms me. Ah! what is that black form I see over there? This time it is moving."

"There's no doubt about that," said the viscount.

"See what it is to be in the shadow; we see the enemy, and he doesn't see us. Doesn't it seem to you as if the villain has a musket?"

"Yes; but he's alone, Pompée, and there are two of us."

"Monsieur le Vicomte, men who travel alone are most to be feared; for their being alone indicates a determined character. The famous Baron des Adrets always went by himself. Look! he's aiming at us, or I'm much mistaken! He 's going to fire; stoop!"

"Why, no, Pompée, he's simply changing his musket from one shoulder to the other."

"Never mind, we must stoop all the same; it's the custom; let us receive his fire with our noses on our saddles."

"But you see that he doesn't fire, Pompée."

"He doesn't fire?" said the squire, raising his head. "Good! he must be afraid; our determined bearing has intimidated him. Ah! he's afraid! Let me speak to him, and do you speak after me, and make your voice as gruff as possible."

The shadow was coming toward them.

"*Holé!* friend, who are you?" cried Pompée.

The shadow halted with a very perceptible start of terror.

"Do you shout now," said Pompée.

"It's useless," said the viscount; "the poor devil is frightened enough already."

"Ah! he's afraid!" said Pompée, raising his weapon.

"Mercy, monsieur!" exclaimed the man, falling on his knees, "mercy! I am only a poor pedler, and I haven't sold as much as a pocket-handkerchief for a week; I haven't a sou about me."

What Pompée had taken for a musket was the yard-stick with which the poor devil measured off his wares.

"Pray understand, my friend," said Pompée, majestically, "that we are no thieves, but fighting men, travelling at night because we are afraid of nothing; go your way in peace; you are free."

"Here, my friend," the milder voice of the viscount interposed, "here's a half-pistole for the fright we gave you, and may God be with you!"

As he spoke, the viscount, with his small white hand, gave the poor devil a half-pistole, and he walked away, thanking Heaven for the lucky meeting.

"You were wrong, Monsieur le Vicomte, you were very wrong," said Pompée, a few steps farther on.

"Wrong, wrong! wherein, pray?"

"In giving that man a half-pistole. At night you should never admit that you have money about you; look you, wasn't it that coward's first cry that he hadn't a sou?"

"True," said the viscount, smiling; "but he's a coward, as you say, while we, as you also said, are fighting men, who fear nothing."

"Between being afraid and being suspicious, Monsieur le Vicomte, there is as great a distance as between fear and prudence. Now, it isn't prudent, I say again, to let a stranger whom you meet on the high-road see that you have money."

"Not when the stranger is alone and unarmed?"

"He may belong to an armed band; he may be only a spy sent forward to see how the land lies. He may return with a crowd, and what can two men, however brave they may be, do against a crowd?"

This time the viscount realized the reasonableness of Pompée's reproof, or rather, to cut the lecture short, pretended to admit his guilt, and they rode on until they reached the bank of the little river Saye, near Saint-Genès.

There was no bridge, and they were obliged to ford the stream.

Pompée, thereupon, delivered a learned discourse upon the passage of rivers, but as a discourse is not a bridge, they were not the less obliged to ford the stream after the discourse was concluded.

Fortunately, the river was not deep, and this latest incident afforded the viscount further proof that things seen at a distance, especially at night, are much more alarming than when seen at close quarters.

He was really beginning, therefore, to feel safe, especially as the day would break in about another hour, when, as they were in the midst of the wood which lies about Marsas, the two travellers suddenly drew rein; they could hear, far in their rear, but distinctly, the hoof-beats of galloping horses.

At the same moment their own horses raised their heads, and one of them neighed.

"This time," said Pompée, in a stifled voice, seizing the bridle of his companion's horse, "this time, Monsieur le Vicomte, you will show a little docility, I trust, and be guided by the experience of an old soldier. I hear a troop of mounted men; they are pursuing us. Of course it's your pretended pedler's band; I told you so, imprudent youth that you are! Come, no useless bravado, but let us save our lives and our money! Flight is often a means of winning the battle; Horace pretended to fly."

"Very well, let us fly, Pompée," said the viscount, trembling from head to foot.

Pompée drove in his spurs; his horse, an excellent roan, leaped forward with a zeal that inflamed the ardor of the viscount's barb, and they dashed away at full speed, followed by a train of sparks, as their iron-shod hoofs flew along the hard road.

This race lasted about half an hour; but instead of gaining ground, it seemed to the fugitives that their enemies were coming nearer.

Suddenly a voice issued from the darkness,—a voice which, mingling with the hissing sound produced by the speed at which they were riding, seemed like the muttered menace of the spirits of the night.

It made the gray hair stand erect on Pompée's head.

"They cried 'Stop!'" he muttered; "they cried 'Stop!'"

"Well, shall we stop?" asked the viscount.

"By no means!" cried Pompée; "let us double our speed, if possible. Forward! forward!"

"Yes, yes! forward! forward!" cried the viscount, as thoroughly terrified now as his defender.

"They are gaining, they are gaining!" said Pompée; "do you hear them?"

"Alas! yes."

"They are not more than thirty—Listen, they are calling us again. We are lost!"

"Founder the horses, if we must," said the viscount, more dead than alive.

"Viscount! viscount!" shouted the voice. "Stop! stop! stop, old Pompée!"

"It is some one who knows us, some one who knows we are carrying money to Madame la Princesse, some one who knows we are conspirators; we shall be broken on the wheel alive!"

"Stop! stop!" the voice persisted.

"They are shouting to some one to stop us," said Pompée; "they have some one ahead of us; we are surrounded!"

"Suppose we turn into the field, and let them pass?"

"A good idea," said Pompée; "let us try it."

They guided their horses with rein and knee at the same time, and turned to the left; the viscount's mount, skilfully handled, leaped the ditch, but Pompée's heavier beast took off too late, the ground gave way under his feet, and he fell, carrying his rider down with him. The squire emitted a shriek of despair.

The viscount, who was already fifty paces away, heard his cry of distress, and although sadly frightened himself, turned and rode back to his companion.

"Mercy!" howled Pompée. "Ransom! I surrender; I belong to the house of Cambes!"

A loud shout of laughter was the only response to this pitiful appeal; and the viscount, riding up at that moment, saw Pompée embracing the stirrup of the conqueror, who, in a voice choking with laughter, was trying to reassure him.

"Monsieur le Baron de Canolles!" exclaimed the viscount.

"*Sarpejeu!* yes. Go to, viscount, it isn't fair to lead people who are looking for you such a race as this."

"Monsieur le Baron de Canolles!" echoed Pompée, still doubting his good luck; "Monsieur le Baron de Canolles and Monsieur Castorin!"

"Why, yes, Monsieur Pompée," said Castorin, rising in his stirrups to look over his master's shoulder, as he bent forward, laughing, over his saddle-bow; "what are you doing in that ditch?"

"You see!" said Pompée. "My horse fell just as I was about to intrench myself, taking you for enemies, in order to make a vigorous defence! Monsieur le Vicomte," he continued, rising and shaking himself, "it's Monsieur de Canolles."

"You here, monsieur!" murmured the viscount, with something very like joy, which was reflected in his tone in spite of himself.

"'Faith, yes, it's myself," replied Canolles, gazing at the viscount with a degree of pertinacity which his finding of the glove sufficiently explained. "I was bored to death in that inn. Richon left me after winning my money. I learned that you had taken the Paris road. Luckily I had business in the same direction, so I set out to overtake you; I didn't suspect that I should have to run such a race to do it! *Peste!* my young gentleman, what a horseman you are!"

The viscount smiled, and stammered a few words.

"Castorin," continued Canolles, "assist Monsieur Pompée to mount. You see that he can't quite manage it, notwithstanding his skill."

Castorin dismounted and lent a hand to Pompée, who finally regained his seat.

"Now," said the viscount, "we will ride on, by your leave."

"One moment," said Pompée, much embarrassed; "one moment, Monsieur le Vicomte; it seems to me that I miss something."

"I should say as much," said the viscount; "you miss the valise."

"Oh! *mon Dieu!*" ejaculated Pompée, feigning profound astonishment.

"Wretch!" cried the viscount, "can you have lost it?"

"It can't be far away, monsieur," Pompée replied.

"Isn't this it?" inquired Castorin, picking up the object in question, which he found some difficulty in lifting.

"It is," said the viscount.

"It is," echoed Pompée.

"It isn't his fault," said Canolles, anxious to make a friend of the old squire; "in his fall the straps broke and the valise fell off."

"The straps are not broken, monsieur, but cut," said Castorin. "Look!"

"Oho! Monsieur Pompée," said Canolles, "what does that mean?"

"It means," said the viscount, sternly, "that, in his terror at being pursued by robbers, Monsieur Pompée cleverly cut the straps of the valise so that he might not have the responsibility of being the treasurer. In military parlance, what is that ruse called, Monsieur Pompée?"

Pompée tried to excuse himself by putting the blame on his hunting-knife which he had imprudently drawn; but, as he could give no satisfactory explanation, he remained under the suspicion, in the viscount's eyes, of having chosen to sacrifice the valise to his own safety.

Canolles was more lenient.

"Nonsense! nonsense!" said he; "that may or may not be; but strap the valise on again. Come, Castorin, help Monsieur Pompée. You were right, Master Pompée, to be afraid of robbers; the valise is heavy, and would be a valuable prize."

"Don't joke, monsieur," said Pompée, with a shudder; "all joking is equivocal at night."

"You are right, Pompée, always right; and so I propose to act as escort to you and the viscount. A re-enforcement of two men may be of some use to you."

"Yes, indeed!" cried Pompée, "there is safety in numbers."

"What say you to my offer, viscount?" said Canolles, who observed that the viscount welcomed his obliging suggestion with less enthusiasm than the squire.

"I, monsieur," was the reply, "recognize therein your usual desire to oblige, and I thank you very sincerely; but our roads are not the same, and I should dislike to put you to inconvenience."

"What!" said Canolles, greatly disappointed to find that the struggle at the inn was to begin again in the high-road; "what! our roads are not the same? Aren't you going to—"

"Chantilly," said Pompée, hastily, trembling at the thought of pursuing his journey with no other companion than the viscount.

That gentleman made an impatient gesture, and if it had been daylight, an angry flush might have been seen to mount to his cheeks.

"Why," cried Canolles, without seeming to notice the furious glance with which the viscount blasted poor Pompée,—"why, Chantilly lies directly in my way. I am going to Paris, or rather," he added with a laugh, "I have no business, my dear viscount, and I don't know where I am going. Are you going to Paris? so am I. Are you going to Lyons? I am going to Lyons. Are you going to Marseilles? I have long had a passionate desire to see Provence, and I am going to Marseilles. Are you going to Stenay, where his Majesty's troops are? let us go to Stenay together. Though born in the South, I have always had a predilection for the North."

"Monsieur," rejoined the viscount, in a determined tone, due doubtless to his irritation against Pompée, "you force me to remind you that I am travelling alone on private business of the utmost importance; and forgive me, but if you insist, you will compel me, to my great regret, to tell you that you annoy me."

Nothing less than the thought of the little glove, which lay hidden upon his breast between his shirt and doublet, would have restrained the baron, who was as quick-tempered and impulsive as any Gascon, from an outburst of wrath. However, he did succeed in controlling himself.

"Monsieur," he replied in a more serious tone, "I have never heard it said that the high-road belonged to one person more than to another. Indeed, if I mistake not, it is called the king's road, as an indication that all his Majesty's subjects have an equal right to use it. I am, therefore, upon the king's road with no purpose of annoying you; indeed I am here to make myself useful to you, for you are young, weak, and practically undefended. I did not suppose that I looked like a highway-man. But since you so imply, I must needs admit my unprepossessing appearance. Forgive my intrusion, monsieur. I have the honor of presenting my respects to you. *Bon voyage!*"

With that, Canolles, having saluted the viscount, rode to the other side of the road, followed by Castorin in the flesh and by Pompée in spirit.

Canolles acted throughout this scene with such perfect courtesy his gestures were so graceful, the brow which his broad felt hat shaded was so unruffled, and surrounded by such silky black hair, that the viscount was even less impressed by his words than by his lofty bearing. He had moved away, as we have said, followed by Castorin, sitting stiff and straight in his saddle. Pompée, who remained with the viscount, sighed in a heartrending way, fit to break the hearts of the stones in the road. Thereupon the viscount, having duly reflected, urged his horse forward, joined Canolles, who pretended not to see or hear him, and whispered in an almost inaudible voice,—

"Monsieur de Canolles!"

Canolles started and turned his head; a thrill of pleasure ran through his veins; it seemed to him as if all the music of the heavenly spheres were taking part in a divine concert for his benefit alone.

"Viscount!" said he.

"Listen, monsieur," continued the viscount, in a soft, sweet voice; "really I am distressed at the thought of being guilty of any discourtesy to one so courteous and obliging as yourself. Forgive my timidity, I pray you; I was brought up by relatives whose affection for me made them reluctant to let me out of their sight; I ask you once more, therefore, to forgive me; I have not intended to offend you, and I trust you will permit me to ride beside you, as a proof of our sincere reconciliation."

"Marry! that I will!" cried Canolles, "a hundred and a thousand times, yes! I bear no malice, viscount, and to prove it—"

He put out his hand, into which fell or slipped a little hand as soft and shrinking as a sparrow's claw.

During the rest of the night the baron talked incessantly. The viscount listened, and laughed now and then.

The two servants rode behind,—Pompée explaining to Castorin how the battle of Corbie was lost, when it might perfectly well have been won, if they had not neglected to summon him to the council of war held in the morning.

"But how did you get out of your affair with Monsieur d'Épernon?" said the viscount, as the first rays of daylight appeared.

"It was no difficult matter," Canolles replied; "according to what you told me, viscount, it was he who had business with me, not I with him; either he got tired of waiting for me and went his way, or he was obstinate about it and is waiting still."

"But what of Mademoiselle de Lartigues?" queried the viscount, with some hesitation.

"Mademoiselle de Lartigues cannot be at home with Monsieur d'Épernon, and at the Golden Calf with me, at one and the same time. We mustn't ask a woman to do the impossible."

"That is no answer, baron. I ask you how it is that you could bear to leave Mademoiselle de Lartigues, being so fond of her as you are."

Canolles gazed at the viscount with eyes which already saw too clearly, for it was quite light by this time, and there was no other shadow on the young man's face than that cast by his hat.

The baron felt a mad impulse to reply by speaking his thoughts; but the presence of Pompée and Castorin, and the viscount's serious expression held him back; moreover, he was not yet absolutely free from doubt.

"Suppose that I am mistaken, and that it should prove to be a man, despite the little glove and little hand; upon my soul, I never should dare look him in the face again!"

He took patience therefore and answered the viscount's question with one of those smiles which serve to answer any question.

They stopped at Barbézieux for breakfast and to breathe their horses. Canolles breakfasted with the viscount, and as they sat at table gazed admiringly at the hand whose perfumed envelope had caused him such lively emotion. Furthermore, the viscount was bound in common courtesy to remove his hat before taking his seat, and as he did so he disclosed such a wealth of lovely, soft hair that any other than a man in love, and consequently blind, would have been relieved of all uncertainty; but Canolles dreaded the awakening too keenly not to prolong the dream as much as possible. There was something fascinating to him in the viscount's disguise, which permitted him to indulge in a multitude of little familiarities which a more thorough acquaintance or a complete confession would have forbidden. He therefore said not a word to lead the viscount to think that his incognito was detected.

After breakfast they resumed their journey, and rode until dinner. Gradually, a feeling of weariness, which he found more and more difficulty in concealing, caused a haggard look to appear on the viscount's face, and a slight shivering of his whole body, of which Canolles in a friendly way asked him the cause. Thereupon Monsieur de Cambes would smile and pretend that the feeling had passed away, and even suggest quickening their pace; which Canolles refused to do, saying that they had a long distance still to travel, and that they must therefore spare their horses.

After dinner the viscount found some difficulty in rising. Canolles darted to his assistance.

"You need rest, my young friend," said he; "a continuous journey like this would kill you before you finish the third stage. We will not ride to-night, but go to bed. I propose that you shall have a good night's sleep, and may I die if the best room in the inn is not given you!"

The viscount looked at Pompée with such an expression of terror that Canolles could not conquer his desire to laugh.

"When we undertake so long a journey," said Pompée, "we ought each to have a tent."

"Or one tent for two," observed Canolles, with the most natural air; "that would be quite enough."

The viscount shivered from head to foot.

The blow struck home, and Canolles saw that it did; out of the corner of his eye he noticed that the viscount made a sign to Pompée. Pompée went to his master's side, who said a few words to him in an undertone, and a moment later the old squire, muttering some excuse, rode on ahead and disappeared.

An hour and a half after this incident, which Canolles did not seek to have explained, as they rode into a considerable village the two travellers spied the squire standing in the doorway of a hostelry of decent appearance.

"Aha!" said Canolles, "it would seem that we are to pass the night here, eh, viscount?"

"Why, yes, baron, if you choose."

"Nonsense! it is for you to choose. As I told you I am travelling for pleasure, while you tell me that you are travelling on business. I'm afraid that you won't fare very well in this hovel."

"Oh! a night is soon passed."

They halted, and Pompée, more alert than Canolles, darted forward and took his master's stirrup; moreover, it occurred to Canolles that such an attention would be absurd from one man to another.

"Show me to my room at once," said the viscount. "In truth, you are right, Monsieur de Canolles," he continued, turning to his companion, "I am really extremely fatigued."

"Here it is, monsieur," said the hostess, throwing open the door of a good-sized room on the ground-floor, looking on the court-yard, but with bars at the windows, and nothing but the garret above.

"Where is mine, pray?" cried Canolles, casting his eyes cautiously at the door next the viscount's, and at the thin partition, which would have been very slender protection against a curiosity so thoroughly sharpened as his.

"Yours?" said the hostess. "Come this way, monsieur, and I'll take you to it."

Without apparently noticing Canolles' ill-humor, she led him to the farther end of an exterior corridor, lavishly supplied with doors, and separated from the viscount's room by the width of the court-yard.

The viscount stood at his door looking after them.

"Now," said Canolles, "I am sure of my fact; but I have acted like a fool. To put a bad face on the matter would ruin me irretrievably; I must assume my most gracious air."

He went out again upon the sort of gallery formed by the exterior corridor, and cried, —

"Good-night, my dear viscount; sleep well! you sadly need it. Shall I wake you in the morning? No? Very well, then, do you wake me when you choose. Good-night!"

"Good-night, baron!"

"By the way," continued Canolles, "is there nothing you lack? shall I lend you Castorin to wait upon you?"

"Thanks! I have Pompée; he sleeps in the next room."

"A wise precaution; I will see that Castorin does the same. A prudent measure, eh, Pompée? One can't take too many precautions at an inn. Good-night, viscount!"

The viscount replied by echoing the compliment, and closed his door.

"Very good, very good, viscount," murmured Canolles; "to-morrow it will be my turn to engage quarters for the night, and I'll have my revenge. Aha! he pulls both curtains close at his window; he hangs up a cloth to intercept his shadow! *Peste!* a very modest youth is this little gentleman; but it's all the same. To-morrow."

Canolles entered his room grumbling, undressed in high dudgeon, went to sleep swearing, and dreamed that Nanon found the viscount's pearl-gray glove in his pocket.

XI

The next morning Canolles was in even more jovial humor than on the preceding day; the Vicomte de Cambes too gave freer rein to his natural animation. Even the dignified Pompée became almost playful in describing his campaigns to Castorin. The whole morning passed in pleasant conversation.

At breakfast Canolles apologized for leaving the viscount; but he had, he said, a long letter to write to one of his friends who lived in the neighborhood, and he told him also that he intended to call upon another friend of his, whose house was situated three or four leagues beyond Poitiers, almost on the high-road. Canolles inquired about this last-named friend, whose name he mentioned to the inn-keeper, and was told that he would find his house just before reaching the village of Jaulnay, and could easily identify it by its two towers.

Thereupon, as Castorin was to leave the party to deliver the letter, and as Canolles too was to make a détour, the viscount was asked to decide where they should pass the night. He glanced at a little map which Pompée carried in a case, and suggested the village of Jaulnay. Canolles made no objection, and even carried his perfidy so far as to say aloud: —

"Pompée, if you are sent on before as quarter-master, as you were yesterday, secure a room for me, if possible, near your master's, so that we may talk together a little."

The crafty squire exchanged a glance with the viscount and smiled, fully determined to do nothing of the sort. Castorin, meanwhile, who had received his instructions beforehand, took the letter and was told to join the rest of the party at Jaulnay.

There was no danger of mistaking the inn, as Jaulnay could boast but one, —the Grand Charles-Martel.

The horses were saddled, and they set out. About five hundred yards beyond Poitiers, where they dined, Castorin took a cross-road to the right. They rode on for about two hours. At last they came to a house, which Canolles, from the description given him, recognized as his friend's. He pointed it out to the viscount, repeated his request to Pompée as to the location of his room, and took a cross-road to the left.

The viscount was entirely reassured. His manœuvre of the previous evening had been successful without a contest, and the whole day had passed without the slightest allusion to it. He no longer feared that Canolles would place any obstacle in the way of his wishes, and as soon as he saw in the baron nothing more than a kindly, jovial, witty travelling companion, he desired nothing better than to finish the journey in his company. And so, whether because the viscount deemed it a useless precaution, or because he did not wish to part company with his squire, and remain alone in the high-road, Pompée was not even sent on ahead.

They reached the village at nightfall; the rain was falling in torrents. As good luck would have it, there was a vacant room with a good fire. The viscount, who was in haste to change his clothes, took it, and sent Pompée to engage a room for Canolles.

"It is already done," said Pompée, the selfish, who was beyond measure anxious to go to bed himself; "the hostess has agreed to look out for him."

"'T is well. My toilet-case?"

"Here it is."

"And my bottles?"

"Here they are."

"Thanks. Where do you sleep, Pompée?"

"At the end of the corridor."

"Suppose I need you?"

"Here is a bell; the hostess will come—"

"That will do. The door has a good lock, has it not?"

"Monsieur can see for himself."

"There are no bolts!"

"No, but there's a stout lock."

"Good; I will lock myself in. There's no other entrance?"

"None that I know of."

Pompée took the candle and made the circuit of the room.

"See if the shutters are secure."

"They are all hooked."

"Very well. You may go, Pompée."

Pompée went out, and the viscount turned the key in the lock.

An hour later, Castorin, who had arrived first at the inn, and was quartered near Pompée, without his knowledge, left his room on tiptoe, and opened the door to admit Canolles.

Canolles, with beating heart, glided into the inn, and leaving Castorin to secure the door, inquired the location of the viscount's room and went upstairs.

The viscount was just about to retire when he heard footsteps in the corridor.

The viscount, as we have seen, was very timid; the footsteps startled him, and he listened with all his ears?

The footsteps stopped at his door. An instant later some one knocked.

"Who's there?" inquired a voice, with such a terrified accent, that Canolles could not have recognized it, had he not already had occasion to study all its variations.

"I!" said Canolles.

"What! you?" rejoined the voice, passing from terror to dismay.

"Yes. Fancy, viscount, that there's not a single unoccupied room in the inn. Your idiot of a Pompée didn't think of me. Not another inn in the whole village—and as your room has two beds—"

The viscount glanced in dismay at the two twin beds standing side by side in an alcove, and separated only by a table.

"Well, do you understand?" continued Canolles. "I claim one of them. Open the door quickly, I beg, for I am dead with cold—"

At that there was a great commotion inside the room, the rustling of clothes and hurried steps.

"Yes, yes, baron," said the viscount's voice, more dismayed than ever, "yes, I am coming, I—"

"I am waiting. But in pity's name make haste, dear friend, if you don't wish to find me frozen stiff."

"Forgive me; but I was asleep, you see—"

"What! I thought I saw a light."

"No, you were mistaken."

And the light was at once extinguished. Canolles made no complaint.

"I am here—I can't find the door," the viscount continued.

"I should think not," said Canolles. "I hear your voice at the other end of the room. This way, this way—"

"Oh! I am looking for the bell to call Pompée."

"Pompée is at the other end of the corridor, and will not hear you. I tried to wake him to find out something, but 't was impossible. He is sleeping like the deaf idiot he is."

"Then I will call the hostess."

"Nonsense! the hostess has given up her bed to one of her guests, and has gone to the attic to sleep. So no one will come, my dear friend. After all, why call anybody? I need no assistance."

"But I—"

"Do you open the door, and I will thank you. I will feel my way to the bed, turn in, and that's the whole of it. Open the door, I beg."

"But there must be other rooms," said the viscount, in despair, "even if they are without beds. It's impossible that there are no other rooms. Let us call and inquire."

"But it's after half-past ten, my dear viscount. You will rouse the whole establishment. They will think the house is on fire. The result would be to keep everybody awake all night, and I am dying for want of sleep."

These last words seemed to reassure the viscount to some extent. Light steps approached the door, and it was softly opened.

Canolles entered and locked the door behind him. The viscount had fled precipitately.

The baron found himself in almost total darkness, for the last embers of the fire, which was dying out, gave out but a feeble flickering light. The atmosphere was warm and heavy with the perfumes which denote the most assiduous attention to the toilet.

"Ah! thanks, viscount," said Canolles; "in truth, one is much more comfortable here than in the corridor."

"You are anxious to go to sleep, baron?"

"Yes, most assuredly. Tell me which is my bed, or let me light the candle."

"No, no, it's useless!" said the viscount, hastily. "Your bed is here at the left."

As the viscount's left was the baron's right, the baron turned to the left, fell in with a window, near the window a small table, and upon the table the bell which the agitated viscount had sought in vain. To make assurance doubly sure, he put the bell in his pocket.

"What did you say?" he cried. "Are we playing at blind-man's buff? You ought at least to cry *casse-cou*. What the devil are you fumbling for there in the dark?"

"I am looking for the bell, to call Pompée."

"But what the devil do you want of Pompée?"

"I want—I want him to make up a bed beside mine."

"For whom?"

"For himself."

"For himself! What are you talking about, viscount? Servants in our room! Go to! you act like a frightened girl. Fie, fie! we are old enough to defend ourselves. No; just give me your hand and guide me to my bed, which I cannot find—or else let us light the candle."

"No, no, no!" cried the viscount.

"If you won't give me your hand, you ought at least to pass me the end of a thread; for I am in a veritable labyrinth."

He walked, with arms outstretched, in the direction from which the voice came; but he saw something like a shadow flit by him, accompanied by a wave of sweetest perfume; he closed his arms, but, like Virgil's Orpheus, embraced nothing but air.

"There! there!" said the viscount at the other end of the room; "you are close beside your bed, baron."

"Which of the two is mine?"

"It matters little! I shall not go to bed."

"What's that! you won't go to bed?" exclaimed Canolles, turning about at this imprudent speech; "what will you do, pray?"

"I shall pass the night on a chair."

"Nonsense!" said Canolles. "I certainly shall not allow any such child's play; come, viscount, come!"

As the fire on the hearth blazed up for an instant before dying altogether, Canolles caught sight of the viscount crouching in a corner between the window and the commode, wrapped in his cloak.

The blaze was no more than a flash; but it was sufficient to guide the baron and to make the viscount understand that he was lost. Canolles walked straight toward him with arms outstretched, and although the room was dark once more, the poor fellow realized that he could not again elude his pursuer.

"Baron! baron!" he faltered; "come no nearer, I implore you; not a step nearer, if you are a gentleman!"

Canolles stopped; the viscount was so near him that he could hear his heart beat, and could feel his warm breath coming in gasps; at the same time a delicious, intoxicating perfume, a blending of all the perfumes which emanate from youth and beauty, a perfume ten thousand times sweeter than that of the sweetest flowers, seemed to envelop him and make it impossible for him to obey the viscount, even had he desired to do so.

However, he stood for an instant where he was, his hands stretched out toward those other hands, which were ready to repulse him, and with the feeling that he had but to take one step more to touch that charming body, whose suppleness and grace he had so much admired during the last two days.

"Mercy! mercy!" murmured the viscount; "mercy!"

His voice died away upon his lips and Canolles felt his body glide by the curtains of the window and fall at his feet.

His breast dilated; there was a something in the imploring voice that told him that his adversary was half vanquished.

He stepped forward, put out his hands and met the young man's clasped in supplication; he had not the strength to cry out, but heaved a pitiful sigh.

Suddenly the galloping of a horse was heard beneath the window; there was a hurried knocking at the door, followed by a great outcry.

"M. le Baron de Canolles!" a voice shouted.

"Ah! God, I thank thee! I am saved!" murmured the viscount.

"The devil take the beast!" exclaimed Canolles; "couldn't he have waited until to-morrow morning?"

"M. le Baron de Canolles!" cried the voice. "M. le Baron de Canolles! I must speak with him on the instant."

"Well, what's the matter?" said the baron, stepping toward the window.

"Monsieur! Monsieur!" called Castorin at the door; "they are asking for you,—you are wanted."

"But who is it, varlet?"

"A courier."

"From whom?"

"M. le Duc d'Épernon."

"What does he want with me?"

"The king's service."

At that magic phrase, which it was impossible not to heed, Canolles, still grumbling, opened the door and went downstairs.

Pompée's snoring could be distinctly heard.

The courier had entered the inn, and was waiting below: Canolles joined him, and turned pale as he read Nanon's letter; for, as the reader will have guessed, the courier was Cauvignac himself, who, having started nearly ten hours after Canolles, was unable to overtake him before the second night, ride as hard as he might.

Cauvignac's answers to his questions left Canolles in no doubt as to the necessity of losing no time. He read the letter a second time, and the phrase, *Your loving sister, Nanon*, told him what had happened; that is to say, that Mademoiselle had cleared her skirts by passing him off as her brother.

Canolles had frequently heard Nanon herself speak in most unflattering terms of this brother whose place he had taken. This fact added not a little to the ill grace with which he prepared to obey the duke's behest.

"'T is well," said he to Cauvignac, without opening a credit for him at the inn, or emptying his purse into his hands, which he would have been certain to do under other circumstances; "'t is well; tell your master that you overtook me, and that I obeyed him instantly."

"Shall I say nothing to Mademoiselle de Lartigues?"

"Yes; tell her that her brother appreciates the feeling which dictates her action, and is deeply indebted to her. —Castorin, saddle the horses."

Without another word to the messenger, who was thunderstruck by this ungracious reception, Canolles went up once more to the viscount's room, and found him pale and trembling, and completely dressed.

"You may set your mind at rest, viscount," said Canolles; "you are rid of me for the rest of your journey. I am about to take my leave in the king's service."

"When?" the viscount asked with a vestige of apprehension.

"Instantly; I am going to Mantes, where the court now is."

"Adieu, monsieur."

The young man could hardly utter the words, and sank upon a chair, not daring to meet his companion's eye.

Canolles stepped up to him.

"I shall never see you again in all probability," he said, with deep emotion.

"Who knows?" said the viscount, trying to smile.

"Promise one thing to a man who will never forget you," said Canolles, laying his hand upon his heart; and his tone and his gesture alike indicated absolute sincerity.

"What is it?"

"That you will sometimes think of him."

"I promise."

"Without anger?"

"Yes."

"Will you give me any token in support of your promise?"

The viscount put out his hand.

Canolles took the trembling hand in his own, with no purpose to do aught but press it, but in obedience to an impulse stronger than his will, he put it to his lips and imprinted an ardent kiss upon it, then rushed from the room, murmuring:—

"Ah! Nanon! Nanon! can you ever make up to me what you have caused me to lose?"

XII

If we now turn aside for a moment and cast a glance at the princesses of the house of Condé in their exile at Chantilly, of which Richon drew such a distressing picture to the viscount, this is what we shall see.

Beneath the spreading chestnuts, powdered with snowy blossoms, on the smooth, velvety lawns sloping down to the peaceful blue ponds, a swarm of laughing, chatting, singing promenaders wandered to and fro. Here and there amid the tall grass could be seen the figure of a solitary reader, lost in waves of verdure, where naught could be distinctly seen save the white page of the book in her hand, which belonged perhaps to M. de la Calprenède's *Cléopâtre*, to M. d'Urfé's *Astrée*, or to Mademoiselle de Scudéry's *Grand Cyrus*. Beneath the arbors of honeysuckle and clematis could be heard the sweet strains of lutes, and invisible voices singing. At intervals a horseman, bearing a despatch, passed like a flash along the main avenue leading to the château.

Meanwhile, upon the terrace, three women, dressed in satin, and followed at a distance by mute and respectful equerries, were walking gravely to and fro with ceremonious, majestic gestures: in the middle, a lady of noble and stately figure, despite her fifty-seven years, was holding forth magisterially upon affairs of state; at her right, a young lady clad in garments of sombre hue, and holding herself stiffly erect, listened with contracted brows to her neighbor's learned views; at her left another older lady, the stiffest and primmest of the three, because she was of less illustrious rank, was talking, listening, and meditating all at once.

The lady in the middle was the dowager princess, mother of the victor of Rocroy, Norlingen and Lens, who was just beginning, since he had become an object of persecution, and the persecution had landed him at Vincennes, to be called the Great Condé, a name which posterity has continued to bestow upon him. This lady, upon whose features could still be detected traces of that beauty which made her the object of the last and maddest of all the passions of Henri IV., had been wounded in her mother love, and in her pride as princess of the blood, by a *facchino Italiano*, who was called Mazarini when he was Cardinal Bentivoglio's servant, but who was now called His Eminence Cardinal Mazarin, since he had become Anne of Austria's lover, and First Minister of the Kingdom of France.

He it was who dared to imprison Condé, and to send the noble prisoner's wife and mother into exile at Chantilly.

The lady at her right was Claire-Clémence de Maillé, Princesse de Condé, who, in accordance with an aristocratic custom of the time, was called Madame la Princesse simply, to signify that the wife of the head of the Condé family was the first princess of the blood, *the* princess *par excellence*: she was always proud, but her pride had gained in intensity since her persecution, and she had become haughty and supercilious.

It was the fact that her husband's imprisonment raised her to the rank of a heroine, after being compelled to play only a secondary part so long as he was free; her state was more deplorable than widowhood, and her son, the Duc d'Enghien, just completing his seventh year, was more interesting than an orphan. The eyes of the nation were upon her, and without fear of being laughed at, she dressed in mourning. Since the forced exile of these two weeping women by direction of Anne of Austria their piercing shrieks had changed to muttered threats: from being the victims of oppression they had become rebels. Madame la Princesse, Themistocles in a mobcap, had her Miltiades in petticoats, and the laurels of Madame de Longueville, for an instant Queen of Paris, disturbed her slumbers.

The duenna at the left was the Marquise de Tourville, who did not venture to write novels, but exercised her pen upon political subjects: she did not make war in person like the valorous Pompée, nor did she, like him, receive a bullet at the battle of Corbie; but her husband, who was a highly esteemed officer, was wounded at La Rochelle and killed at Fribourg,—the result being that she inherited his fortune, and fancied that she inherited at the same time his genius for war. Since she joined the Princesses de Condé at Chantilly she had sketched three plans of campaign, all of which had successively aroused the enthusiasm of the ladies of the suite, and had been, not abandoned, but postponed until the moment when the sword should be drawn and the scabbard thrown away. She did not dare put on her husband's uniform, although she sometimes longed to do so; but she had his sword hanging in her room over the head of her bed, and now and then, when she was alone, she would draw it from its sheath with an exceedingly martial air.

Chantilly, notwithstanding its holiday aspect, was in reality nothing but a vast barrack, and a diligent search would have discovered powder in the cellars, and bayonets in the hedgerows.

The three ladies, in their lugubrious promenade, bent their steps toward the main door of the château, and seemed to be expecting the arrival of some messenger with important news. Several times the princess dowager had said, shaking her head and sighing:—

"We shall fail, my daughter! we shall be humiliated."

"We must expect to pay something as the price of the great glory we are to win," said Madame de Tourville, without relaxing the stiffness of her demeanor in any respect; "there is no victory without a combat!"

"If we fail, if we are vanquished," said the young princess, "we will avenge ourselves!"

"Madame," said the princess dowager, "if we fail, it will be that God has vanquished Monsieur le Prince. Pray, would you dream of seeking to be revenged on God?"

The younger princess bowed her head before her mother-in-law's superb humility; indeed, these three personages, saluting one another thus and offering incense at one another's shrine, were not unlike a bishop and two deacons, who make God the pretext of their mutual homage.

"Neither Monsieur de Turenne, Monsieur de La Rochefoucauld, nor Monsieur de Bouillon," murmured the dowager; "they all fail us at once!"

"And no money!" added Madame de Tourville.

"On whom can we rely," said Madame la Princesse, "if Claire herself has forgotten us?"

"Who tells you, my daughter, that Madame de Cambes has forgotten us?"

"She does not return."

"Perhaps she has been prevented; the roads are watched by Monsieur de Saint-Aignan's army, you know."

"At all events she could write."

"How can you wish that she should put upon paper a reply of such moment,—the adhesion of a city like Bordeaux to the party of the princes? No, that is not the aspect of the affair which disturbs me most by any means."

"Moreover," suggested Madame de Tourville, "one of the three plans which I had the honor to lay before your Highness proposed an uprising in Guyenne as a certain means of accomplishing an object."

"Yes, yes, and we will recur to it, if necessary," replied Madame la Princesse: "but I agree with Madame my mother, and I begin to think that

Claire must have fallen under suspicion; otherwise she would be here before this. Perhaps her farmers have failed to keep their word; a peasant will always seize an opportunity to avoid paying his debts. And who can say what the Guyenne people may or may not have done despite their promises? Gascons!"

"Braggarts!" said Madame de Tourville; "brave individually, it may be, but bad soldiers *en masse*. They do very well to shout, 'Vive Monsieur le Prince!' when they're afraid of the Spaniard; that's all."

"They have a thorough detestation for Monsieur d'Épernon, however," said the princess dowager; "they hanged him in effigy at Agen, and promised to hang him in person at Bordeaux, if he ever returned there."

"He will return there, and hang the braggarts themselves," said Madame la Princesse, indignantly.

"And all this," rejoined Madame de Tourville, "is the fault of Monsieur Lenet—Monsieur Pierre Lenet," she repeated affectedly, "the stubborn adviser whom you persist in keeping by you, and who is good for nothing but to thwart all our plans. If he had not frowned upon my second plan, the purport of which was, you remember, to take by surprise the château de Vayres, Île Saint-Georges, and the fort of Blaye, we should be besieging Bordeaux ere now, and Bordeaux would be obliged to capitulate."

"I prefer, with deference to their Highnesses' opinion, that Bordeaux should open its gates of its own free will," said a voice behind Madame de Tourville, in a tone of respect, not unmixed with a tinge of irony. "A city that capitulates yields to force and incurs no obligation; whereas a city which opens its gates freely, thereby compromises itself, and must needs follow to the end the fortunes of those to whom it has offered itself."

The three ladies turned and saw Pierre Lenet, who, as they were taking one of their turns toward the main door of the château upon which their eyes were constantly fixed, had emerged from a smaller door on a level with the terrace, and approached them from behind.

What Madame de Tourville said was true in part. Pierre Lenet, one of Monsieur le Prince's advisers, a cold, grave, but very shrewd man, was commissioned by the prisoner to keep an eye on his friends and foes alike, and it must be said that he had much more difficulty in preventing the prince's friends from compromising his cause than in foiling the evil designs of his foes. But, being endowed with the cleverness and craft of a lawyer, and accustomed to the sharp practice and jugglery of the tribunals, he usually triumphed, either by some timely counterplot or by passive opposition. It was at Chantilly itself that the battles had to be fought which taxed his powers to the utmost. The self-esteem of Madame de Tourville, the impatience of Madame la Princesse, and the aristocratic inflexibility of the dowager were quite as hard to deal with as the astuteness of Mazarin, the pride of Anne of Austria, and the indecision of the parliament.

Lenet, to whom the princes addressed their correspondence, had established a rule that he would give the princesses no news except at what he himself deemed an opportune time; for, as feminine diplomacy is not always shrouded in mystery, which is the cardinal principle of the masculine variety, many of Lenet's plans had been in this way betrayed by his friends to his enemies.

The two princesses, who, notwithstanding the opposition they encountered at his hands, none the less appreciated Pierre Lenet's devotion, and especially his usefulness, welcomed him with a friendly gesture; there was even the shadow of a smile upon the dowager's lips.

"Well, my dear Lenet," she said, "you heard Madame de Tourville complaining, or rather commiserating us. Everything is going from bad to worse. Ah! my dear Lenet, our affairs! our affairs!"

"Madame," said Lenet, "I am very far from taking so gloomy a view of our affairs as your Highness. I hope much from time, and from a change in the tide of fortune. You know the proverb: 'Everything succeeds with him who knows how to wait.'"

"Time, and a change in the tide of fortune!" exclaimed Madame la Princesse; "that's philosophy, and not politics, Monsieur Lenet!"

Lenet smiled.

"Philosophy is useful in all things, madame, especially in politics; it teaches us not to be over-elated with success, and to be patient in adversity."

"I care not!" said Madame de Tourville. "I would give more to see a courier than for all your maxims; don't you say the same, Madame la Princesse?"

"Yes, I confess it," replied Madame de Condé.

"Your Highness will be satisfied in that case, for you will receive three to-day," rejoined Lenet, as coolly as before.

"What, three?"

"Yes, madame. The first has been seen on the Bordeaux road, the second is coming from Stenay, and the third from La Rochefoucauld."

The two princesses uttered an exclamation of joyful surprise. Madame de Tourville bit her lips.

"It seems to me, my dear Monsieur Pierre," she said in a wheedling tone, to conceal her vexation, and wrap in a coating of sugar the bitter remark she was about to make, "it seems to me that a skilful necromancer like yourself ought not to stop short after such a fine start, and that, having announced the arrival of the couriers, you should tell us the contents of their despatches."

"My knowledge, madame, doesn't extend as far as you think," said he, modestly, "it confines itself to being a faithful servitor. I announce, but I do not guess."

At the same moment, as if Lenet were in reality served by a familiar spirit, they spied two horsemen, who came riding through the great gate of the château, and galloped up the avenue. Immediately a swarm of idlers, deserting the lawns and flower-gardens, swooped down to the avenue railings to have their share of the news.

The horsemen dismounted, and one of them, tossing to the other, who seemed to be his servant, the bridle-rein of his foam-covered steed, ran rather than walked toward the princesses who came forward to meet him, and stepped upon the balcony at one end as he stepped upon it at the other.

"Claire!" cried Madame la Princesse.

"Yes, your Highness. Accept my most humble respects, madame."

Kneeling upon one knee, the young man tried to take the princess's hand to imprint a respectful kiss upon it.

"Come to my arms, dear viscountess, to my arms!" cried Madame de Condé, raising her.

Having submitted to Madame la Princesse's embrace with all possible respect, the cavalier turned to the princess dowager, to whom he made a low bow.

"Speak quickly, dear Claire!" said she.

"Yes, speak," added Madame de Condé. "Have you seen Richon?"

"Yes, madame, and he entrusted me with a message for you."

"Good news or bad?"

"I do not know myself; the message consists of two words."

"What are they? Quick! I am dying with impatience."

The keenest anxiety was depicted on the features of both princesses.

"'Bordeaux—Yes,'" said Claire, herself anxious as to the effect the two words would produce.

But she was soon reassured, for the princesses received them with a triumphant exclamation, which brought Lenet from the other end of the balcony.

"Lenet! Lenet! come! come!" cried Madame la Princesse, "you do not know the news our good Claire brings us."

"Yes, madame," said Lenet, smiling; "I do know it; that is why I did not hurry to meet her."

"What! you know it?"

"'Bordeaux—Yes,'—isn't that it?"

"In truth, my dear Pierre, you must be a sorcerer!" said the dowager.

"If you knew it, Lenet," said Madame la Princesse, reproachfully, "why, seeing our anxiety, did you not relieve it with those two words!"

"Because I wished to allow Madame de Cambes to receive the reward of her fatiguing journey," replied Lenet, with a motion of his head toward Claire, who was deeply moved, "and also because I feared an explosion of joy on the part of your Highnesses, out on the terrace in everybody's sight."

"You are right, Pierre, always right, my good Pierre!" said Madame la Princesse. "Let us say nothing."

"And we owe this to the gallant Richon," said the princess dowager. "Hasn't he done well, Compère Lenet, and aren't you content with him?"

Compère was the princess dowager's pet word; it was a reminiscence of Henri IV., who used it frequently.

"Richon is a man of brain and energy, madame, and I pray your Highness to believe that if I had not been as sure of him as of myself I would not have recommended him."

"What shall we do for him?" said Madame la Princesse.

"We must give him some important post," said the dowager.

"Some important post? Your Highness cannot think of doing so," interposed Madame de Tourville, sourly; "you forget that Monsieur Richon is not of gentle birth!"

"Nor am I, madame," retorted Lenet; "which fact does not prevent Monsieur le Prince from having some confidence in me, I believe. Most assuredly do I admire and respect the nobility of France; but there are circumstances in which a noble heart, I venture to say, is worth more than an ancient coat of arms."

"Why did not good Richon come himself to tell us this joyful tidings?" asked Madame la Princesse.

"He remained in Guyenne to raise troops. He told me that he could already count upon nearly three hundred men, but he says that, from want of time, they will be but ill equipped to take the field, and he would much prefer that we should obtain for him the command of a place like Vayres, or Île Saint-George. There, he says, he would be sure of making himself useful to your Highnesses."

"But how can we obtain it?" asked the princess. "We are in too bad odor at court at this moment to recommend any one, and if we should undertake it, whoever we might recommend would become on the instant an object of suspicion."

"Perhaps, madame," said the viscountess, "a method which Monsieur Richon himself suggested to me may be practicable."

"What is that?"

"Monsieur d'Épernon is, it appears," continued the viscountess, blushing, "very much in love with a certain young woman."

"Ah! yes, the fair Nanon," said Madame la Princesse, disdainfully; "we know about that."

"Well, it seems that the duc d'Épernon can refuse nothing to this young woman, and that she disposes of whatever any one chooses to purchase from her. Could not you purchase a commission for Monsieur Richon?"

"It would be money well placed," said Lenet.

"True, but the chest is empty, as you well know, Monsieur le conseiller," said Madame de Tourville.

Lenet turned with a smile to Madame de Cambes.

"This is the moment, madame," said he, "to prove to their Highnesses that you have forgotten nothing."

"What do you mean, Lenet?"

"He means, madame, that I am fortunate enough to be able to offer you a paltry sum, which I have collected with much difficulty from my farmers. The offering is a very modest one, but I could do no more,—twenty thousand livres!" she continued, hesitating and lowering her eyes, ashamed to offer so small a sum to the two first ladies in the realm next to the queen.

"Twenty thousand livres!" they cried with one accord.

"Why, it's a fortune in times like these," continued the dowager.

"Dear Claire!" exclaimed Madame la Princesse, "how can we ever repay our obligation to her?"

"Your Highness will think of that later."

"Where is this money?" inquired Madame de Tourville.

"In her Highness's apartment, whither I bade Pompée, my squire, to carry it."

"Lenet," said Madame la Princesse, "you will remember that we owe this sum to Madame de Cambes."

"It is already carried to her credit," said Lenet, producing his tablets, and pointing out the viscountess's twenty thousand livres set down, under that date, in a column, the total of which would have alarmed the princesses somewhat if they had taken the trouble to add it.

"Pray how did you succeed in reaching here, dear Claire?" said Madame la Princesse; "for we are told that Monsieur de Saint-Aignan is watching the road, and searching every traveller, for all the world like a customs officer."

"Thanks to Pompée's superior wisdom, madame, we avoided that danger, by making a tremendous détour, which delayed us a day and a half, but assured our safety. Except for that I should have arrived day before yesterday."

"Have no uneasiness on that score, madame," said Lenet, "there is no time lost as yet; but we must see to it that we make good use of to-day and to-morrow. To-day, as your Highnesses will remember, we expect three couriers; one has already arrived, the other two are still to come."

"May we know the names of these others, monsieur?" asked Madame de Tourville, still hoping to catch the counsellor at fault, for she was constantly at war with him; and though the war was not declared, it was none the less real.

"The first, if my expectations are fulfilled, will be Gourville; he comes from the Duc de La Rochefoucauld."

"From the Prince de Marsillac, you mean," rejoined Madame de Tourville.

"Monsieur le Prince de Marsillac is now Duc de La Rochefoucauld, madame."

"His father is dead, then?"

"A week since."

"Where did he die?"

"At Verteuil."

"And the second?" asked Madame la Princesse.

"The second is Blanchefort, captain of Monsieur le Prince's guards. He comes from Stenay, from Monsieur de Turenne."

"In that case," said Madame de Tourville, "I think that, to avoid any loss of time, we should recur to the first plan I suggested in the probable event of the adhesion of Bordeaux, and the alliance of Messieurs de Turenne and de Marsillac."

Lenet smiled as usual.

"Pardon me, madame," said he, in his most courteous tone; "but the plans formed by Monsieur le Prince himself are at this moment in process of execution, and bid fair to be entirely successful."

"The plans formed by Monsieur le Prince," retorted Madame de Tourville, sharply; "by Monsieur le Prince, who is in the donjon of Vincennes, and has no communication with anybody!"

"Here are his Highness's orders, written by his own hand, dated yesterday," said Lenet, taking from his pocket a letter from the Prince de Condé, "and received by me this morning; we are in correspondence."

The paper was almost snatched from his hands by the two princesses, who devoured, with tears of joy, all that it contained.

"Ah! do Lenet's pockets contain the whole kingdom of France?" said the princess dowager, laughingly.

"Not yet, madame, not yet; but with God's help I will so act as to make them large enough for that. Now," continued Lenet, with a significant glance at the viscountess, "Madame la Vicomtesse must stand in need of rest; for her long journey—"

The viscountess understood that Lenet wished to be left alone with the princesses, and at a smile from the dowager which confirmed that impression, she courtesied respectfully and took her leave.

Madame de Tourville remained and promised herself an ample harvest of mysterious information; but upon an almost imperceptible sign from the dowager to her daughter-in-law, the two princesses spontaneously, by a stately reverence, executed in accordance with all the rules of etiquette, signified to Madame de Tourville that the political conclave in which she was summoned to take part had reached its term. The lady of theories understood the hint perfectly, returned their salute by a reverence even more solemn and ceremonious than theirs, and withdrew, calling upon God to bear witness to the ingratitude of princes.

The ladies passed into their study, and Pierre Lenet followed them.

"Now," said he, after making sure that the door was securely locked, "if your Highnesses care to receive Gourville, he has arrived and changed his clothes, not daring to present himself in his travelling costume."

"What news does he bring?"

"That Monsieur de La Rochefoucauld will be here this evening or to-morrow with five hundred gentlemen."

"Five hundred gentlemen!" cried the princess; "why, 't is a veritable army!"

"Which will add to the difficulties of our journey. I should have preferred five or six faithful servitors only to all this display; we could more easily conceal our movements from Monsieur de Saint-Aignan. Now it will be almost impossible to reach the South without being molested."

"If we are molested, so much the better!" cried the princess; "for if we are molested we will fight, and we shall win; Monsieur de Condé's spirit will march with us."

Lenet glanced at the dowager as if to ask her opinion also; but Charlotte de Montmorency, who grew to womanhood during the civil wars of Louis XIII. and had seen so many noble heads bend to enter a prison, or roll upon the scaffold for having sought to hold themselves erect, sadly passed her hand across her brow, laden with painful memories.

"Yes," said she, "we are reduced to that alternative; to hide or to fight,—a frightful state of things! We were living in peace, with such glory as God had bestowed upon our house; we had no other desire, at least I hope that no one of us had any other, than to remain in the station to which we were born,—and lo! the exigencies of the time force us to contend against our master."

"Madame," interposed the younger princess, impetuously, "I look with less anguish than your Highness upon the necessity to which we are reduced. My husband and my brother are undergoing confinement unworthy of their rank; that husband and that brother are your sons; furthermore, your daughter is proscribed. These facts assuredly justify whatever enterprises we may undertake."

"True," said the dowager, with melancholy resignation; "true, I endure it all with more patience than yourself, madame; but it is because it seems as if it were our destiny to be proscribed or imprisoned. I had no sooner become the wife of your husband's father, than I was compelled to leave France, pursued by the love of King Henri IV. We had no sooner returned than we were consigned to Vincennes, pursued by the hatred of Cardinal de Richelieu. My son, who is in prison to-day, was born in prison, and after thirty-two years has renewed his acquaintance with the room in which he was born. Alas! your father-in-law, Monsieur le Prince, was right in his gloomy prophecies. When the result of the battle of Rocroy was made known to him, when he was taken into the great hall hung with flags captured from the Spaniards, he said, turning to me: 'God knows the joy that my son's exploit affords me; but remember, madame, that the more glory our family acquires, the greater will be the misfortunes that overtake it. If it were not that I bear the arms of France, too noble a blazonry to be cast aside, I would take for my crest a falcon betrayed and recaptured by the ringing of his bells, with this legend: *Fama nocet.*' We have made too much noise in the world, my daughter, and that is what injures us. Do not you agree with me, Lenet?"

"Madame," Lenet replied, deeply afflicted by the memories awakened by the princess, "your Highness is right; but we have gone too far to retreat now; more than that; in circumstances like our present ones, it is most essential to make up our minds promptly. We must not deceive ourselves as to our situation. We are free only in appearance; the queen has her eye upon us, and Monsieur de Saint-Aignan is blockading us. The question we have to solve is, how we are to leave Chantilly despite the queen's vigilance and Monsieur de Saint-Aignan's blockade."

"Leave Chantilly! why, we will leave it with heads erect!" cried Madame la Princesse.

"I am of the same opinion," said the princess dowager. "The Condés are not Spaniards, and they do not play false. They are not Italians, and they do not resort to trickery. What they do, they do in broad daylight, with heads erect."

"Madame," said Lenet, in a tone of conviction, "God is my witness that I will be the first to execute your Highness's commands, whatever they may be; but in order to leave Chantilly in the way you describe, we must fight our way. You do not intend, of course, to become women again in the day of battle, after taking a man's part in council. You will march at the head of your supporters, and you will be the ones to furnish your soldiers with their war-cry. But you forget that closely connected with your precious lives, another life, no less precious, is beginning to assume prominence; that of the Duc d'Enghien, your son and grandson. Will you incur the risk of burying in the same grave the present and the future of your family? Do you imagine that Mazarin will not make use of the father as a hostage, when such rash enterprises are undertaken in the name of the son? Have you forgotten the secrets of the donjon of Vincennes, which were investigated under such melancholy circumstances by the Grand Prior of Vendôme, by Marshal d'Ornano, and by Puylaurens? Have you forgotten the fatal chamber, which, as Madame de Rambouillet says, is worth its weight in arsenic? No, mesdames," continued Lenet, clasping his hands, "no; you will hearken to the advice of your faithful counsellor; you will take your departure from Chantilly as it is fitting that persecuted women should do. Remember that your surest weapon is weakness. A child bereft of its father, a woman bereft of her husband, a mother bereft of her son, escape as they may from the snare in which they are caught. Before you act or speak openly, wait until you no longer serve as guaranties to the stronger party. Prisoners, your supporters will remain mute; free, they will declare themselves, having no further reason to fear that any one will dictate to them the conditions of your ransom. Our plan is concerted with Gourville. We are sure of a strong escort, which will protect us from insult on the road; for to-day twenty different factions are in the field, and preying indiscriminately upon friend and foe. Give your consent. Everything is in readiness."

"Leave Chantilly in disguise! like malefactors!" cried the young princess. "Oh! what will my husband say when he learns that his mother, his wife, and his son have done such a shameful thing?"

"I know not what he will say, madame, but if you succeed he will owe his liberty to you! if you fail, you risk the loss of none of your advantages, especially not your position, as you would do by a battle."

The dowager reflected a moment before she said sadly:—

"Dear Monsieur Lenet, convince my daughter; for, so far as I personally am concerned, I am compelled to remain here. I have struggled on until now, but at last, I must succumb; the pain which is consuming me, and which I try in vain to hide, that I may not bring discouragement on those about me, will soon hold me fast upon a bed of suffering, which will perhaps be my death-bed. But, as you have said, we must, before everything, look to the fortune of the Condés. My daughter and my grandson will leave Chantilly, and will, I trust, be sufficiently well-advised to abide by your counsel,—I say more,—by your commands. Command, Lenet, and you will be obeyed!"

"You are pale, madame!" cried Lenet, supporting the dowager, as Madame la Princesse, alarmed at her sudden pallor, took her in her arms.

"Yes," said the dowager, growing manifestly weaker; "yes, the glad tidings of to-day have done me more harm than the anguish of the last few days. I feel that an internal fever is consuming me, but let us make no sign; at such a moment, it might work severe injury to our cause."

"Madame," said Lenet, in a low voice, "your Highness's indisposition would be a blessing from heaven, if it did not cause you to suffer. Keep your bed, and spread the report that you are ill. Do you, madame," he continued, addressing the young princess, "summon your physician Bourdelot, and as we shall soon need to make a requisition upon the stables, let it be known everywhere that it is your purpose to have a stag-hunt in the park. In that way no one will be surprised to see men, weapons, and horses in large numbers."

"Do it yourself, Lenet. But how can it be that so clear-sighted a man as you are does not feel that this hunting-party, given at the very moment that my mother falls ill, will cause remark?"

"That is all provided for, madame. Is not day after to-morrow Monsieur le Duc d'Enghien's seventh birthday, when he is to be taken from the charge of women?"

"Yes."

"Very well! we will say that this hunting-party is given to celebrate the young prince's first pair of breeches, and that her Highness was so determined that her illness should not interfere with this function that you could but yield to her wishes."

"An excellent idea!" cried the dowager, with a joyful smile, proud and delighted at the thought of this manner of proclaiming the virility of her grandson; "yes, it's an excellent suggestion, and you are indeed a worthy counsellor, Lenet."

"But should Monsieur le Duc d'Enghien follow the hunt in a carriage?" asked the princess.

"No, madame, on horseback. Oh! let not your mother's heart take alarm. I have devised the expedient of a small saddle, which Vialas, his equerry, will place immediately in front of his own; in that way, Monsieur le Duc d'Enghien will be seen, and in the evening we can take our departure in all security; for Monsieur d'Enghien will be able to go anywhere on foot or in the saddle; whereas, in a carriage he would be arrested at the first obstacle."

"You think, then, that we should go?"

"Day after to-morrow in the evening, if your Highness has no reason for postponing your departure."

"Oh, no! on the contrary, let us escape from our prison at the earliest possible moment, Lenet."

"Once away from Chantilly, what is your plan?" the dowager inquired.

"We shall pass through Monsieur de Saint-Aignan's forces, finding some means to tie a bandage over his eyes. We shall join Monsieur de La Rochefoucauld and his escort, and go on to Bordeaux, where we are expected. Once in the possession of the second city in the realm, the capital of the South, we can negotiate or make war, as seems best to your Highness. However, I have the honor to remind you, madame, that, even at Bordeaux, we shall have no chance of holding out for a considerable time, unless we have control of some posts in the vicinity to divert the attention of the royal troops. Two of these posts especially are of the greatest importance: Vayres, which commands the Dordogne, and would keep open a way to send supplies into the city; and Île Saint-Georges, which the Bordelais themselves consider the key of their city. But we will think of that later; for the moment let us confine ourselves to the method of leaving this place."

"Nothing can be simpler, I think," said Madame la Princesse. "We are alone and masters here, whatever you may say, Lenet."

"Rely upon nothing, madame, until you are at Bordeaux. Nothing is simple, in a contest with the diabolical mind of Monsieur de Mazarin, and if I waited until we were alone to describe my plan to your Highness, it was to satisfy my conscience, I assure you; for I tremble at this moment for the secrecy of my plan, which my single brain conceived, and which no ears but yours have heard. Monsieur de Mazarin doesn't learn things, he divines them."

"Oh! I defy him to divine this," said the princess. "But let us assist my mother to her apartment; I will immediately give out the fact of a hunting-party for day after to-morrow. Do you look to the matter of invitations, Lenet."

"Rely upon me, madame."

The dowager went to her apartment, and at once took to her bed. Boudelot, family physician to the Condés, and preceptor to Monsieur le Duc d'Enghien, was summoned; the report of her sudden indisposition was quickly circulated, and within half an hour arbors, balconies, gardens were deserted, all the guests hastening to the princess dowager's antechamber.

Lenet passed the whole day in writing, and that same evening above fifty invitations were sent out in all directions in the hands of the numerous retainers of that royal establishment.

XIII

The next day but one following, which was the day appointed for putting Pierre Lenet's plans in execution, was one of the gloomiest of spring days, a season which is traditionally called the most beautiful of the year, but which is always, especially in France, the most disagreeable.

A fine, soaking rain was falling in the parterres of Chantilly, streaking the clumps of trees in the garden and the hedge-rows in the park with a grayish mist. In the great court-yards fifty horses, all ready saddled, were standing about the hitching posts, sad-eyed, with ears drooping, impatiently pawing the ground; packs of hounds in couples were waiting in groups of twelve, breathing noisily, gaping between whiles, and striving by their united efforts to run away with the groom, who was wiping the rain-soaked ears of his favorites.

The whippers-in, in chamois livery, with their hands behind their backs and their horns slung over their shoulders, wandered hither and thither. Some few officers, inured to storms by their experience at Rocroy or Lens, defied the rain, and whiled away the weary time of waiting by talking together in groups upon the terraces and outer staircases.

Every one was notified that it was a ceremonious occasion, and had assumed his most solemn expression to see Monsieur le Duc d'Enghien wearing his first pair of breeches, hunt his first stag. Every officer in the prince's service, every adherent of the illustrious family, invited by Lenet's circular letter, had fulfilled what he considered his bounden duty by hastening to Chantilly. The anxiety aroused in the first instance by the condition of the princess dowager was dissipated by a favorable bulletin from Bourdelot. She had been bled, and had that morning taken an emetic, the universal panacea at that period.

At ten o'clock all Madame de Condé's personal guests had arrived; each one was admitted upon presenting his letter of invitation, and those who, by any chance, had neglected to bring it, upon being recognized by Lenet were admitted by the Swiss at a nod from him. These guests, with the household staff, constituted a body of eighty or ninety men, most of whom were gathered about the superb white horse, upon whose back, just in front of the great French saddle, was a little velvet seat with a back, intended for

Monsieur le Duc d'Enghien, where he was to take his place when Vialas, his equerry, should have taken his seat upon the principal saddle.

However, there was as yet no suggestion of beginning the hunt, but they seemed to await the arrival of additional guests.

About half-past ten, three gentlemen, followed by six valets all armed to the teeth, and carrying valises so swollen that one would have said they were starting out to make the tour of Europe, rode in at the gate and noticing the posts in the court-yard, apparently put there for that purpose, attempted to hitch their horses to them.

Immediately a man dressed in blue, with a silver baldric, halberd in hand, accosted the new-comers, who, by their drenched clothing and their mud-stained boots, were easily recognized as travellers from a distance.

"Whence come you, messieurs?" said this functionary.

"From the North," one of them replied.

"Whither go you?"

"To the burial."

"The proof?"

"You see our crêpe."

It was a fact that the three masters had each a piece of crêpe on their swords.

"Excuse me, messieurs," said the halberdier; "the château is yours. There is a table spread, an apartment warmed, servants awaiting your orders; your people will be entertained in the servants' quarters."

The gentlemen, who were honest rustics, half-starved and inquisitive, bowed, dismounted, threw their reins to their servants, and having been shown the way to the dining-hall, betook themselves thither. A chamberlain awaited them at the door, and acted as their guide.

Meanwhile the horses were taken off the hands of the strange servants by the servants of the house, taken to the stables, rubbed down, brushed, watered, and confronted with a trough well supplied with oats and a rack filled with hay.

The three gentlemen had hardly taken their places at the table, when six other horsemen, followed by six lackeys armed and equipped like those we have described, rode in as they did, and like them, seeing the posts, essayed to hitch their horses to the rings. But the man with the halberd, who had received strict orders, approached them and repeated his questions.

"Whence come you?" said he.

"From Picardy. We are officers in Turenne."

"Whither go you?"

"To the burial."

"The proof."

"You see our crêpe."

And like their predecessors, they pointed to the crêpe attached to the hilt of their rapiers.

The same attention was shown to them, and they followed the others to the dining-hall; the same care was bestowed upon their horses, who followed the other horses to the stables.

Behind them came four others, and the same scene was renewed.

Between half-past ten and noon, two by two, four by four, five by five, alone or in parties, shabbily or sumptuously dressed, but all well mounted, well armed, and well equipped, a hundred cavaliers made their appearance, all of whom were questioned according to the same formula, and replied by stating whence they came and that they were going to the burial, and by exhibiting their crêpe.

When they had all dined, and become acquainted with one another, while their people were being entertained and their horses were resting, Lenet entered the room where they were all assembled, and said to them:—

"Messieurs, Madame la Princesse thanks you by my mouth for the honor you have done her by calling upon her on your way to join Monsieur le Duc de La Rochefoucauld, who awaits your coming to celebrate the obsequies of his late father. Look upon this house as your own, and deign to take part in the diversion of a stag hunt, ordered to take place this afternoon by Monsieur le Duc d'Enghien, who dons to-day his first pair of breeches."

A murmur of approbation and gratitude welcomed the first part of Lenet's harangue, who, like a practised orator, paused for that purpose.

"After the hunt," he continued, "you will sup with Madame la Princesse, who desires to thank you in person; thereafter you will be at liberty to continue your journey."

Some of the gentlemen paid particular attention to the announcement of this programme, which seemed to some extent to impose fetters on their free will; but in all likelihood they had been warned by Monsieur de La Rochefoucauld to expect something of the sort, for not one of them murmured. Some went to inspect their horses; others had recourse to their portmanteaux to put themselves in fit condition to appear before the princesses; while others remained at table, talking about the state of affairs in the country, which seemed to have some affinity with the events of the day.

Many walked about beneath the main balcony where Monsieur le Duc d'Enghien, his toilet completed, was expected to appear for the last time before his final farewell to female attendants.

The young prince in his nursery, surrounded by nurses and playthings, did not realize his own importance. But the pride of birth manifested itself in full measure, and he gazed impatiently at the rich, yet simple costume in which he was to be dressed for the first time. It was a black velvet suit trimmed with unpolished silver, which made it appear as if he were dressed in mourning: indeed his mother, who was determined at all hazards to pose as a widow, thought seriously of speaking of him in a certain harangue as the *"poor orphaned prince."*

But there was one who eyed these splendid garments even more longingly than the prince. A few feet from him, another child, a few months older than he, with red cheeks and light hair, overflowing with health and strength and childish petulance, was devouring with hungry eyes the luxurious surroundings of his more fortunate playfellow. Several times, unable to repress his curiosity, he had ventured to approach the chair upon which the fine clothes were spread out, and had slyly patted the velvet and caressed the trimming, while the little prince was looking in another direction. But at last it happened that he brought back his eyes in time, and Pierrot drew his hand away too late.

"Take care!" cried the prince, sharply: "take care, Pierrot, you'll spoil my new breeches; they're 'broidered velvet, Pierrot, and it fades when you touch it. I forbid you touching my breeches!"

Pierrot hid the guilty hand behind his back, twisting his shoulders this way and that, as children of all ranks do when they are crossed.

"Don't be angry, Louis," said Madame la Princesse to her son, whose features were disfigured by an ugly grimace. "If Pierrot touches your suit again, he shall be whipped."

Pierrot changed his sulky expression for a threatening one.

"Monseigneur's a prince," he said, "but I'm a gardener; and if monseigneur is to keep me from touching his clothes, I won't let him play with my Guinea hens. Ah! I'm stronger than monseigneur, and he knows it."

These imprudent words were no sooner out of Pierrot's mouth, than the prince's nurse, who was Pierrot's mother, seized the independent youngster by the wrist, and said: —

"Pierrot, you forget that monseigneur is your master, the master of everything in the château and around the château, and so your Guinea hens are his."

"Why, I thought he was my brother," said Pierrot.

"Your foster-brother, yes."

"If he's my brother, we ought to share; and if my Guinea hens are his, his clothes are mine."

The nurse was about to reply by a demonstration of the difference between a uterine brother and a foster-brother, but the young prince, who wished Pierrot to witness his triumph from beginning to end, because he was especially desirous to excite Pierrot's admiration and envy, did not give her time.

"Don't be afraid, Pierrot," said he; "I am not angry with you, and you shall see me in a little while on my fine white horse, and my nice little saddle! I am going to hunt, and I shall kill the stag!"

"Oh! yes," retorted the irreverent Pierrot, "you'll stay a long while on horseback! You wanted to ride my donkey the other day, and my donkey threw you off on to the ground!"

"Yes, but to-day," rejoined the prince, with all the majesty he could summon to his assistance and find in his memory, — "to-day I represent my papa, and I shall not fall. Besides, Vialas will hold me in his arms."

"Come, come," said Madame la Princesse, to cut short the discussion between the children, "come and dress the prince! One o'clock is striking, and all our friends are waiting impatiently. Lenet, bid them give the signal for departure."

XIV

At the same instant the blast of the horn rang out in the court-yard and reached the most distant corners of the château. Thereupon each guest ran to his horse, finding him fresh and well-rested, thanks to the care that had been bestowed upon him, and vaulted into the saddle. The huntsman with his stag-hounds, the whippers-in with their packs, were the first to set out. Then the gentlemen drew up in line, and the Duc d'Enghien, mounted on the white horse, and held in his seat by Vialas, made his appearance, surrounded by maids of honor, equerries, and gentlemen in waiting, and followed by his mother in a dazzling costume and riding a jet-black horse. By her side, upon a horse which she rode with charming grace, was the Vicomtesse de Cambes, adorable in her female garb, which she had at last resumed to her great joy.

All search for Madame de Tourville had been made in vain since the night before; she had disappeared: like Achilles, she was sulking in her tent.

This brilliant cavalcade was greeted with unanimous acclamations. The guests stood up in their stirrups, pointing out Madame la Princesse, and Monsieur le Duc d'Enghien, who were strangers to most of the gentlemen, they having never been to court, and being unfamiliar with all this royal pomp. The child bowed with a fascinating smile, Madame la Princesse with majestic affability; they were the wife and son of the man whom his bitterest enemies called the first general in Europe. The first general in Europe was persecuted, pursued, imprisoned by the self-same persons whom he had saved from a foreign foe at Lens, and defended against the rebels at Saint-Germain. This was more than was necessary to arouse enthusiasm, and the enthusiasm knew no bounds.

Madame la Princesse drank in with avidity all these proofs of her popularity; then, upon Lenet's whispering a few words in her ear, she gave the signal for departure, and they soon passed from the gardens into the park, all the gates of which were guarded by soldiers of the Condé regiment. Behind the hunters the wickets were locked; and as if that precaution were insufficient to make sure that no false brother should take part in the festivities, the soldiers remained on sentry duty behind the wicket, and a halberdier, dressed and armed like the one in the court-yard, stood beside each of them, with orders to open to none but those who could answer the three questions which composed the countersign.

A moment after the gates were locked, the notes of the horn, and the furious baying of the hounds, announced that the stag was away.

Meanwhile, on the other side of the park, opposite the wall built by the Constable Anne de Montmorency, six horsemen had halted in the road to listen to the horns and the dogs, and seemed to be taking counsel together as they patted the necks of their panting steeds.

In view of their entirely new costumes, the glistening accoutrements of their horses, the glossy cloaks which fell jauntily from their shoulders over their horses' tails, the magnificence of the weapons which could be seen through artistically devised openings, it was rather astonishing that such smart, well-favored cavaliers should hold aloof at a time when all the nobility of the neighborhood were assembled at the château of Chantilly.

These resplendent worthies were eclipsed, however, by their leader, or by him who appeared to be their leader; plumed hat, gilded baldric, elegant boots with golden spurs, a long sword with carved, open-work hilt,—such, with the accompaniment of a superb sky-blue cloak à l'Espagnole, was this gentleman's equipment.

"*Pardieu!*" he exclaimed, after a moment of deep reflection, during which his five comrades gazed at one another in astonishment, "how do we get into the park? By the gate or the wicket? Let us present ourselves at the first gate or the first wicket, and we shall get in all right. Cavaliers of our cut are not left outside when men dressed like those we met this morning are admitted."

"I tell you again, Cauvignac," replied one of the five, "that those same ill-clad men, who, notwithstanding their dress and their rustic bearing, are in the park at this moment, had a great advantage over us,—the countersign. We haven't it, and we can't get in."

"You think so, Ferguzon?" said the first speaker, with some deference for the opinion of his lieutenant; our readers will have recognized in him the adventurer whom they met in the early pages of this narrative.

"Do I think so? I am sure of it. Do you imagine that these people are hunting for the sake of hunting? *Tarare!* they are conspiring, that's certain."

"Ferguzon is right," said a third; "they are conspiring, and we sha'n't be able to get in."

"A stag-hunt isn't a bad thing, however, when one falls in with it on the road."

"Especially when one is tired of hunting men, eh, Barrabas?" said Cauvignac. "Well, it shall not be said that we allowed this one to pass under our noses. We are all that any one need be to cut a decent figure at this *fête*; we are as shiny as new crown-pieces. If Monsieur le Duc d'Enghien needs soldiers, where will he find smarter ones than we? If he needs conspirators, where will he find any more fashionably dressed? The least gorgeous of us has the bearing of a captain!"

"And you, Cauvignac," rejoined Barrabas "would pass at need for a duke and peer."

Ferguzon said nothing; he was reflecting.

"Unfortunately," continued Cauvignac, laughing, "Ferguzon is not inclined to hunt to-day."

"*Peste!*" said Ferguzon, "I've no special objection to hunting; it's a gentlemanly amusement which suits me to a T. So I don't despise it myself, nor try to dissuade others. I simply say that an entrance to the park where they are hunting is made impossible by locked gates."

"Hark!" cried Cauvignac, "there are the horns sounding the tally-ho."

"But," continued Ferguzon, "what I say doesn't necessarily mean that we may not hunt."

"How can we hunt, blockhead, if we can't get in?"

"I don't say that we can't get in," rejoined Ferguzon.

"How the devil can we get in, if the gates, which are open to others, are locked in our faces?"

"Why shouldn't we make a breach in this little wall, for our private use,—a breach through which we and our horses can pass, and behind which we certainly shall find no one to call us to account?"

"*Hourra!*" cried Cauvignac, waving his hat joyfully. "Full reparation! Ferguzon, you are the one brainy man among us! And when I have overturned the King of France, and placed Monsieur le Prince on his throne, I will demand Signor Mazarino Mazarini's place for you. To work, my boys, to work!"

With that, Cauvignac sprang to the ground, and, assisted by his companions, one of whom sufficed to hold all the horses, he began to tear down the wall, already in a somewhat shaky condition.

In a twinkling the five workers opened a breach three or four feet wide. Then they remounted and followed Cauvignac into the park.

"Now," said he, riding in the direction whence the sound of the horns seemed to come, "now, be refined and courteous, and I invite you to take supper with Monsieur le Duc d'Enghien."

XV

We have said that our six gentlemen of recent manufacture were well mounted; their horses also had the advantage over those of the cavaliers who arrived in the morning, that they were fresh. They therefore soon overtook the main body of the hunt, and took their places among the hunters without the least objection from any quarter. The great majority of the guests were from different provinces, and were not acquainted with one another; so that the intruders, once in the park, might easily pass for guests.

Everything would have passed off as well as they could have wished, if they had kept to their proper station, or even if they had been content with outstripping the others and riding among the huntsmen and whippers-in. But it was not so. In a very few moments Cauvignac seemed to reach the conclusion that the hunt was given in his honor; he snatched a horn from the hands of one of the whippers-in, who did not dare refuse to give it to him, took the lead of the huntsmen, rode in front of the captain of the hunt again and again, cut through woods and hedges, blowing the horn in any but the right way, confusing the *vue* with the *lancer*, the *debuché* with the *rembuché*, running down the dogs, overturning the whippers-in, saluting the ladies with a jaunty air when he rode by them, swearing, yelling, and losing his head when he lost sight of them, and at the last coming upon the stag, just as the animal, after swimming across the great pond, turned upon his pursuers and stood at bay.

"*Hallali! Hallali!* cried Cauvignac, "the stag is ours! *Corbleu!* we have him."

"Cauvignac," said Ferguzon, who was only a length behind him. "Cauvignac, you'll get us all turned out of the park. In God's name be more quiet!"

But Cauvignac heard not a word, and, seeing that the animal was getting the best of the dogs, dismounted and drew his sword, shouting with all the strength of his lungs:—

"*Hallali! Hallali!*"

His companions, excepting always the prudent Ferguzon, encouraged by his example, were preparing to swoop down upon their prey, when the captain of the hunt interposed.

"Gently, monsieur," he said, waving Cauvignac aside with his knife; "Madame la Princesse directs the hunt. It is for her, therefore, to cut the stag's throat, or to concede that honor to such person as she may please."

Cauvignac was recalled to himself by this sharp reprimand; and as he fell back with decidedly bad grace, he found himself suddenly surrounded by the crowd of hunters, the delay having given them time to come up. They formed a great circle about the beast, driven to bay at the foot of an oak, and surrounded by all the dogs.

At the same moment Madame la Princesse was seen galloping up, preceding Monsieur le Duc d'Enghien, the gentlemen in waiting and the ladies, who had made it a point of honor not to leave her. She was greatly excited, and it was easy to imagine that she looked upon this simulacrum of war as the prelude to a real war.

When she reached the centre of the circle she stopped, cast a haughty glance about her, and noticed Cauvignac and his comrades, whom the officers of the hunt were eying uneasily and suspiciously.

The captain drew near to her, knife in hand. It was the knife ordinarily used by Monsieur le Prince; the blade was of the finest steel and the handle of silver-gilt.

"Does your Highness know yonder gentleman?" he said in a low tone, glancing at Cauvignac out of the corner of his eye.

"No," said she, "but he was admitted, so he is undoubtedly known to some one."

"He is known to no one, your Highness; every one whom I have questioned sees him to-day for the first time."

"But he could not pass the gates without the countersign."

"No, of course not," replied the captain; "and yet I venture to advise your Highness to be on your guard."

"First of all, we must know who he is," said the princess.

"We shall soon know, madame," Lenet, who had ridden up with the princess, observed with his habitual smile. "I have sent a Norman, a Picard, and a Breton to talk with him, and he will be closely questioned; but for the moment, do not seem to be talking about him, or he will escape us."

"Cauvignac, said Ferguzon, "I think that we are being discussed in high places. We shall do well to suffer an eclipse."

"Do you think so?" said Cauvignac. "'Faith, what's the odds? I propose to be in at the death, come what come may."

"It's a stirring spectacle, I know," said Ferguzon, "but we may have to pay more for our places than at the Hôtel de Bourgogne."

"Madame," said the captain, presenting the knife to the princess, "to whom is your Highness pleased to grant the honor of putting the stag to death?"

"I reserve it for myself, monsieur," said the princess; "a woman of my station should accustom herself to the touch of steel and the sight of blood."

"Namur," said the captain to the arquebusier, "be ready."

The arquebusier stepped forward, arquebuse in hand, and took up his position within twenty feet of the animal. This manœuvre was intended to ensure the princess's safety if the stag, driven to despair, as sometimes happens, should attack her instead of waiting meekly to be killed.

Madame la Princesse dismounted, and with sparkling eyes, glowing cheeks, and lips slightly parted, walked toward the animal, who was almost entirely buried under the dogs, and seemed to be covered with a carpet of a thousand colors. Doubtless the animal did not believe that death was to come to him from the hand of the lovely princess, from which he had eaten many and many a time; he had fallen upon his knees, and he tried to rise, letting fall from his eyes the great tear-drop which accompanies the death agony of the stag and the deer. But he had not time; the blade of the knife, glistening in the sun's rays, disappeared to the hilt in his throat; the blood spurted out into the princess's face; the stag raised his head, and, casting a last reproachful glance at his beautiful mistress, fell forward and died.

At the same instant all the horns blew the death-blast, and a mighty shout arose: "*Vive* Madame la Princesse!" while the young prince stood up in his saddle and clapped his little hands in high glee.

Madame la Princesse withdrew the knife from the animal's throat, glanced around with the look of an Amazon in her eyes, handed the dripping knife to the captain of the hunt, and remounted. Lenet thereupon drew nigh.

"Does Madame la Princesse wish me to tell her," said he, with a smile, "of whom she was thinking when she cut the poor beast's throat a moment since?"

"Yes, Lenet, I should be glad to have you tell me."

"She was thinking of Monsieur de Mazarin, and would have been glad to have him in the stag's place."

"Yes," cried the princess, "that is quite true, and I would have cut his throat without pity, I swear to you: but really, Lenet, you are a sorcerer!"

She turned to the rest of the company.

"Now that the hunt is at an end, messieurs," said she, "please follow me. It is too late now to start another stag, and besides, supper awaits us."

Cauvignac acknowledged this invitation by a most graceful bow.

"Pray, what are you doing, captain?" queried Ferguzon.

"*Pardieu* I am accepting! Didn't you hear Madame la Princesse invite us to supper, as I promised you that she would?"

"Cauvignac, you may take my advice or not, but if I were in your place I would make for the breach in the wall."

"Ferguzon, my friend, your natural perspicacity plays you false. Didn't you notice the orders given by yonder gentleman in black, who has the expression of a fox when he laughs, and of a badger when he doesn't laugh? Ferguzon, the breach is guarded, and to make for the breach is to indicate a purpose to go out as we came in."

"But if that's the case, what is to become of us?"

"Never fear! I will answer for everything."

With that assurance the six adventurers took their places in the midst of the gentlemen, and rode with them toward the château.

Cauvignac was not mistaken; they were closely watched.

Lenet rode on the outskirts of the cavalcade. On his right was the captain of the hunt, and on his left the intendant of the Condé estates.

"You are sure," said he, "that no one knows those men?"

"No one; we have questioned more than fifty gentlemen, and the reply is always the same; perfect strangers to everybody."

The Norman, the Picard, and the Breton had no further information to impart. But the Norman had discovered a breach in the park wall, and like an intelligent man had stationed guards there.

"We must have recourse, then, to a more efficacious method," said Lenet. "We must not allow a handful of spies to compel us to send away a hundred gallant fellows without accomplishing anything. Look to it, Monsieur l'Intendant, that no one is allowed to leave the court-yard, or the gallery where the horsemen are to be entertained. Do you, Monsieur le

Capitaine, as soon as the door of the gallery is closed, station a picket guard of twelve men with loaded muskets, in case of accident. Go! I will not lose sight of them."

Lenet had no great difficulty in performing the duties he had imposed upon himself. Cauvignac and his companions evinced no desire to fly. Cauvignac rode among the foremost, twisting his moustache with a killing air; Ferguzon followed him, relying upon his promise, for he knew his leader too well not to be sure that he would not be caught in that trap, even if it had no second issue. Barrabas and the other three followed their captain and lieutenant, thinking of nothing but the excellent supper that awaited them; they were in fact rather dull fellows, who with absolute indifference abandoned the intellectual portion of their social relations to their two leaders, in whom they had full and entire confidence.

Everything took place in accordance with Lenet's intention, and his orders were carried out to the letter. Madame la Princesse took her place in the great reception-room under a canopy, which served her for a throne. Her son was beside her, dressed as we have described.

The guests exchanged glances; they had been promised a supper, but it was evident that they were to listen to a speech.

The princess at last rose and began to speak. Her harangue[1] was well calculated to arouse enthusiasm and make converts to her cause. On this occasion Clémence de Maillé-Brézé gave free rein to her feelings, and openly attacked Mazarin. Her hearers, electrified by the reminder of the insult offered to the whole nobility of France in the persons of the princes, and even more, it may be, by the hope of making an advantageous bargain with the court in case of success, interrupted the discourse again and again, calling God to witness, at the tops of their voices, that they would do faithful service in the cause of the illustrious house of Condé, and would help to rescue it from the state of degradation to which Mazarin wished to reduce it.

[1]Lovers of speeches will find this one entire in the memoirs of Pierre Lenet. For our own part, we agree with Henri IV., who claimed that he owed his gray hairs to the long speeches he had been compelled to listen to.

"And so, messieurs," cried the princess, bringing her harangue to an end, "the support of your valor, the free offering of your devotion is what the orphan before you asks of your noble hearts. You are our friends—at all events you present yourselves here as such. What can you do for us?"

After a moment of solemn silence began one of the grandest and most affecting scenes that can be imagined.

One of the gentlemen bowed with deep respect to the princess.

"My name," said he, "is Gérard de Montalent; I bring with me four gentlemen, my friends. We have among us five good swords and two thousand pistoles, which we place at Monsieur le Prince's service. Here are our credentials, signed by Monsieur le Duc de La Rochefoucauld."

The princess bowed, took the letter from the hands of the speaker, passed it to Lenet, and motioned to the gentlemen to take their places at her right.

As soon as they had obeyed her command another gentleman rose.

"My name is Claude-Raoul de Lessac, Comte de Clermont. I come with six gentlemen, my friends. We have each a thousand pistoles, which we ask to be allowed to pour into your Highness's treasure-chest. We are well armed and equipped, and a small daily wage will suffice for our needs. Here are our credentials, signed by Monsieur le Duc de Bouillon."

"Step to my right, gentlemen," said the princess, taking Monsieur de Bouillon's letter, which she read, as she read the other, and passed to Lenet, "and accept my grateful thanks."

The gentlemen obeyed.

"My name is Louis-Ferdinand de Lorges, Comte de Duras," said a third. "I come without friends and without money, my sword my only wealth and my only strength; with it I cut my way through the enemy, when I was besieged in Bellegarde. Here are my credentials from Monsieur le Vicomte de Turenne."

"Come hither, monsieur," said the princess, taking the letter with one hand, and giving him the other to kiss. "Come and stand by my side: I make you one of my brigadiers."

The same course was followed by all the gentlemen; all were provided with credentials, from Monsieur de La Rochefoucauld, Monsieur de Bouillon, or Monsieur de Turenne; all delivered their letters and passed to the right of the princess; when there was no more room on that side they took their places at her left.

The centre of the great hall became gradually empty. Soon there remained only Cauvignac and his fellows, a solitary group, and upon them many suspicious and threatening glances were cast, accompanied by angry murmurs.

Lenet glanced toward the door. It was securely locked. He knew that the captain and twelve armed men were on the other side. Bringing his piercing gaze to bear upon the strangers, he said:—

"And you, messieurs; who are you? Will you do us the honor to tell us your names, and show us your credentials?"

The beginning of this scene, the probable ending of which disturbed him beyond measure, had cast a shadow over the face of Ferguzon, and his uneasiness gradually infected his companions, who, like Lenet, glanced in the direction of the door; but their leader, majestically enveloped in his cloak, had maintained throughout an impassive demeanor. At Lenet's invitation he stepped forward, and said, saluting the princess with ostentatious gallantry: —

"Madame, my name is Roland de Cauvignac, and I bring with me for your Highness's service these five gentlemen, who belong to the first families of Guyenne, but desire to retain their incognito."

"But you did not, of course, come to Chantilly, without being recommended to us by some one," said the princess, thinking with dismay of the terrible tumult which would result from the arrest of these six men. "Where are your credentials?"

Cauvignac bowed as if he recognized the justness of the question, felt in the pocket of his doublet, and took from it a folded paper which he handed to Lenet with a low bow.

Lenet opened and read it and a joyful expression overspread his features, contracted a moment before by very natural apprehension.

While Lenet was reading, Cauvignac cast a triumphant glance upon the assemblage.

"Madame," said Lenet, stooping to whisper in the princess's ear, "see what unexpected good fortune; a paper signed in blank by Monsieur d'Épernon!"

"Monsieur," said the princess, with her most gracious smile; "thrice I thank you, — for my husband, for myself, for my son."

Surprise deprived all the spectators of the power of speech.

"Monsieur," said Lenet, "this paper is so valuable that it cannot be your intention to give it into our hands unconditionally. This evening, after supper, we will talk together, if you please, and you can then tell me in what way we can be of service to you."

With that, Lenet put the precious paper in his pocket and Cauvignac had the requisite delicacy to abstain from asking him for it.

"Well," said he to his companions, "did I not invite you to take supper with Monsieur le Duc d'Enghien?"

"Now, to supper!" said the princess.

At the word the folding doors were thrown open and disclosed a table spread with a sumptuous repast in the great gallery of the château.

The feast was very animated and noisy; the health of Monsieur le Prince, proposed again and again, was drunk each time by all the guests on their knees, sword in hand, and uttering imprecations against Mazarin fierce enough to bring the walls down on their heads.

Every one did honor to the good cheer of Chantilly. Even Ferguzon, the prudent Ferguzon, yielded to the charms of the vintage of Burgundy, with which he became acquainted for the first time. Ferguzon was a Gascon, and had previously been in a position to appreciate no other wines than those of his own province, which he considered excellent, but which had achieved no great renown at that period, if the Duc de Saint-Simon is to be believed.

But it was not so with Cauvignac. Cauvignac, while appreciating at their full worth the vintages of Moulin-à-Vent, Nuits, and Chambertin, was very moderate in his libations. He had not forgotten Lenet's cunning smile, and he thought that he needed all his faculties in order to make a bargain with the crafty counsellor which he would not have occasion to repent having made. He aroused the admiration of Ferguzon, Barrabas, and the other three, who, failing to appreciate the reason of his temperance, were simple enough to think that he was beginning to reform.

Toward the close of the banquet, as the toasts were becoming more frequent, the princess vanished, taking the Duc d'Enghien with her, and leaving her guests free to prolong the revelry as far into the night as they chose. Everything had taken place according to her wishes, and she gives a circumstantial narrative of the scene in the salon, and the banquet in the gallery, omitting nothing save the words Lenet whispered in her ear as she rose from the table:—

"Do not forget, your Highness, that we start at ten o'clock."

It was then close upon nine, and the princess began her preparations.

Meanwhile Lenet and Cauvignac exchanged glances. Lenet rose, Cauvignac did the same. Lenet left the gallery by a small door in a corner; Cauvignac understood the manœuvre and followed him.

Lenet led Cauvignac to his cabinet. The adventurer strode along behind with a careless, confident air. But his hand toyed negligently with the hilt of a long dagger thrust in his belt, and his keen, quick eye peered through half-opened doors, and scanned every fluttering curtain.

He did not fear treachery precisely, but it was a matter of principle with him always to be prepared for it.

Once in the cabinet, which was dimly lighted by a lamp, but was quite untenanted, as a swift glance showed him, Cauvignac took the seat to which Lenet waved him on one side of the table whereon the lamp was burning. Lenet took his seat on the other side.

"Monsieur," said Lenet, to win the adventurer's confidence at the outset, "in the first place, here is your signature in blank, which I return to you. It is yours, is it not?"

"It belongs, monsieur," replied Cauvignac, "to him in whose possession it happens to be, for, as you see, it bears no other name than that of Monsieur le Duc d'Épernon."

"When I ask if it is yours, I mean to ask if it is in your possession with Monsieur le Duc d'Épernon's consent."

"I have it from his own hand, monsieur."

"It was neither stolen, then, nor extorted from him by violence?—I do not say by you, but by some other person from whom you received it. Perhaps you have it only at second hand?"

"It was given me by the duke himself, I tell you,—voluntarily, in exchange for a paper which I handed him."

"Did you agree with Monsieur d'Épernon to use this signature of his for any particular purpose, and for no other?"

"I made no agreement whatsoever with Monsieur d'Épernon."

"The person in whose hands it is may use it, then, with perfect safety?"

"He may."

"If that is so, why do you not make use of it yourself?"

"Because if I keep it I can use it for but one purpose, while by giving it to you, I can purchase two things with it."

"What are these two things?"

"Money, first of all."

"We have almost none."

"I will be reasonable."

"And the second thing?"

"A commission in the army of the princes."

"The princes have no army."

"They soon will have one."

"Would you not prefer a commission to raise a company?"

"I was about to make that very suggestion to you."

"The question of the money is left for decision, then."

"Yes, the question of the money."

"What amount do you expect?"

"Ten thousand livres. I told you that I would be reasonable."

"Ten thousand livres?"

"Yes. You must surely advance me something toward arming and equipping my men."

"Indeed, it's not an exorbitant request."

"You agree, then?"

"It's a bargain."

Lenet produced a commission all signed, inserted the names given him by the young man, affixed Madame la Princesse's seal, and handed it to Cauvignac; he then opened a strong-box which contained the treasure of the rebels, and took out ten thousand livres in gold pieces, which he arranged in piles of twenty each.

Cauvignac counted them scrupulously one after another; when that task was completed he nodded to Lenet, to signify that the paper with Monsieur d'Épernon's signature was his. Lenet took it and placed it in the strong-box, thinking, doubtless, that so precious a treasure could not be too carefully guarded.

Just as he was placing the key of the chest in his pocket, a valet came running in, all aghast, to tell him that his presence was required on business of importance.

Consequently Lenet and Cauvignac left the cabinet,—Lenet to follow the servant, Cauvignac to return to the banqueting-hall.

Meanwhile Madame la Princesse was making her preparations for departure, which consisted in changing her party dress for an Amazonian costume, equally suitable for the carriage or the saddle; in assorting her papers so that she might burn those that were worthless, and set aside the valuable ones to be taken with her; lastly, in collecting her diamonds, which she had had removed from their settings, that they might occupy less space, and be more easily available in case of an emergency.

Monsieur le Duc d'Enghien was to travel in the suit he had worn at the hunt, as there had been no time to order another one made. His equerry, Vialas, was to remain constantly at the carriage door, riding a white horse of the purest racing blood, so that he might take him upon the little saddle and gallop away with him, if need were. They were afraid at first that he would fall asleep, and sent for Pierrot to come and play with him; but it was an unnecessary precaution; the proud satisfaction of being dressed as a man was quite enough to keep him awake.

The carriages, which were ordered to be made ready as if to drive Madame la Vicomtesse de Cambes to Paris, were driven to a dark avenue of chestnuts, where it was impossible to see them, and were waiting there, doors open and coachmen in their places, within twenty paces of the main gate. They were all ready for the signal, which was to be given by a blast from the hunting-horns. Madame la Princesse, with her eyes fixed upon the clock, which marked five minutes less than ten o'clock, had already left her seat and was walking toward her son to take him by the hand, when the door was hastily thrown open, and Lenet burst into, rather than entered the room.

Madame la Princesse, seeing his pale face, and his anxious expression, lost color herself.

"Oh, *mon Dieu!*" said she, running to meet him, "what has happened? What is the matter?"

"The matter is," Lenet replied in a voice choked with excitement, "that a gentleman has arrived, and requests speech of you on behalf of the king."

"Great God!" ejaculated the princess, "we are lost! Dear Lenet, what are we to do?"

"There is but one thing to be done."

"What is it?"

"Undress Monsieur le Duc d'Enghien immediately and dress Pierrot in his clothes."

"But I won't have you take off my clothes and give them to Pierrot!" cried the young prince, ready to burst into tears at the mere thought, while Pierrot, in an ecstasy of joy, feared that he could not have heard aright.

"We must do it, monseigneur," said Lenet, in the impressive tone which comes to one in emergencies, and which has the power of inspiring awe even in a child, "or else they will take you and your mamma this very moment to the same prison where your father is."

The prince said no more, while Pierrot, on the other hand, was quite unable to control his feelings, and indulged in an indescribable explosion of joy and pride; they were-both taken to a room on the ground-floor near the chapel, where the metamorphosis was to take place.

"Luckily," said Lenet, "the princess dowager is here; otherwise we were surely outwitted by Mazarin."

"How so?"

"Because the messenger was in duty bound to begin by calling upon her, and he is in her antechamber at this moment."

"This messenger is a mere spy, of course, sent here from the court to watch us?"

"Your Highness has said it."

"His orders, then, are not to lose sight of us."

"Yes; but what care you, if you are not the person he keeps in sight?"

"I fail to understand you, Lenet."

Lenet smiled.

"I understand myself, madame, and I will answer for everything. Dress Pierrot as a prince, and the prince as a gardener, and I will undertake to teach Pierrot his lesson."

"Oh, *mon Dieu!* let my son go away alone!"

"Your son will go with his mother, madame."

"Impossible!"

"Why so? If they find a false Duc d'Enghien here, they may well find a false Princesse de Condé!"

"Oh! splendid! Now I understand, good Lenet! dear Lenet! But who will represent me?" added the princess, anxiously.

"Have no fear on that score, madame," replied the imperturbable counsellor. "The Princesse de Condé whom I propose to make use of, and who I intend shall be kept in sight by Monsieur de Mazarin's spy, has just undressed in hot haste, and is getting into your bed at this moment."

Let us go back for a moment, and see what had taken place prior to Lenet's conversation with the princess.

While the guests were still sitting about the festive board, toasting the princes and cursing Mazarin, while Lenet was bargaining with Cauvignac in his cabinet for the possession of Monsieur d'Épernon's signature, and while Madame la Princesse was making her preparations for departure, a horseman made his appearance at the main gate of the château, followed by his servant, and rang the bell.

The concierge opened the gate, but behind the concierge the new-comer found the halberdier whom we already know.

"Whence come you?" he demanded.

"From Mantes," was the reply.

So far all was well.

"Whither go you?" the halberdier continued.

"To wait upon the princess dowager of Condé, then upon Madame la Princesse, and lastly upon Monsieur le Duc d'Enghien."

"You cannot enter!" said the halberdier, barring the way with his halberd.

"By order of the king!" rejoined the new-comer, taking a paper from his pocket.

At these awe-inspiring words the halberd was lowered, the sentinel called an usher, that official hurried to the spot, and his Majesty's messenger, having delivered his credentials, was immediately ushered into the château.

Fortunately, it was a very extensive structure, and the apartments of the dowager were far removed from the gallery, where the last scene of the noisy festival we have described was still in progress.

If the messenger had requested an interview with Madame la Princesse in the first place, the whole plan of escape would in truth have been thwarted. But etiquette demanded that he should first pay his respects to the elder princess; so the first *valet de chambre* ushered him into a large cabinet, adjoining her Highness's bedroom.

"Pray accept her Highness's apologies, monsieur," said he, "but her Highness was taken suddenly ill day before yesterday, and was bled for the third time less than two hours since. I will make known your arrival to her, and I shall have the honor of ushering you into her presence in a moment."

The gentleman bowed in token of acquiescence, and was left alone, entirely unaware that three curious pairs of eyes were observing his countenance through the key-hole and trying to recognize him.

These three pairs of eyes belonged to Lenet, to Vialas, the princess's equerry, and to La Roussière, captain of the hunt. In the event that either one of the three had recognized the gentleman, that one was to enter the room, and on the pretext of entertaining him while he waited, to divert his attention and thus gain time.

But no one of the three was able to recognize the man whom they were so deeply interested in winning over to their cause. He was a well-favored youth in the uniform of an officer of infantry; he gazed about, with an indifferent air which might easily have been attributed to distaste for his errand, at the family portraits and the furniture of the cabinet, paying particular attention to the portrait of the dowager, to whom he was soon to be introduced,—a portrait which was made when she was in the very flower of her youth and beauty.

It was but a very few minutes before the *valet de chambre* returned, as he had promised, and conducted the messenger to the princess dowager's bedroom.

Charlotte de Montmorency was sitting up in bed; her physician, Bourdelot, was just leaving her bedside. He met the officer at the door and saluted him ceremoniously; the officer returned his salutation in the same manner.

When the princess heard the visitor's footsteps and the few words he exchanged with the physician, she made a rapid sign with her hand in the direction of the passage beside the bed, whereupon the heavily fringed hangings which enveloped the bed except on the side where they were drawn apart for the reception of her visitor, moved slightly for two or three seconds.

In the passage were the younger princess and Lenet, who had entered by a secret door cut in the wainscoting, eager to ascertain the purport of the king's messenger's visit to Chantilly.

The officer walked into the room, and halting a few feet from the door, bowed with a greater show of respect than etiquette absolutely demanded.

The princess dowager's great black eyes were dilated with the superb expression of a queen about to give free rein to her wrath; her silence was heavy with impending storms. With her white hand, made even whiter than usual by the blood-letting, she motioned to the messenger to deliver to her the letter of which he was the bearer.

The officer extended his hand toward hers, and respectfully placed therein Anne of Austria's letter; then waited until the princess should have read the four lines it contained.

"Very good," muttered the dowager, folding the paper with affected coolness; "I understand the queen's meaning, shrouded as it is in polite phrases; I am your prisoner."

"Madame," the officer began, in dire embarrassment.

"A prisoner easy to guard, monsieur," continued Madame de Condé, "for I am in no condition to fly very far; and I have, as you must have seen as you came in, a stern keeper in the person of my physician, Monsieur Bourdelot."

As she spoke the dowager looked more attentively at the messenger, whose countenance was sufficiently pre-possessing to soften somewhat the harsh reception due the bearer of such a communication.

"I knew," she continued, "that Monsieur de Mazarin was capable of much unseemly violence; but I did not believe him to be so faint-hearted as to fear a sick old woman, a helpless widow, and an infant, for I presume that the order of which you are the bearer, applies to the princess my daughter, and the duke my grandson, as well as to myself?"

"Madame," returned the young man, "I should be in despair were your Highness to judge me by the functions which I am unhappily compelled to perform. I arrived at Mantes bearing a message for the queen. The postscript of the message recommended the messenger to her Majesty; the queen thereupon graciously bade me remain in attendance upon her, as she would in all probability have need of my services. Two days later the queen sent me hither; but while accepting, as in duty bound, the mission, whatever it might be, which her Majesty deigned to intrust to me, I will venture to say that I did not solicit it, and furthermore that I would have refused it if kings were accustomed to brook a refusal."

With that the officer bowed again, with no less respect than before.

"I augur well from your explanation, and, since you have given it, I have some hope that I may be permitted to be ill without being molested. But no false shame, monsieur; tell me the truth at once. Shall I be watched even in my own apartments, as my poor son is at Vincennes? Shall I be allowed to write, and will my letters be opened, or not? If, contrary to all appearance, I am ever able to leave my bed again, will my walks be restricted?"

"Madame," replied the officer, "these are the instructions which the queen did me the honor to give me with her own mouth: 'Go,' said her Majesty, 'and assure my cousin of Condé that I will do whatever the welfare of the realm will permit me to do for the princes. In this letter I beg her to receive one of my officers, who will serve as intermediary between her and myself for such communications as she may wish to make to me. You will be that officer.' Such, madame," added the young man, with renewed demonstrations of respect, "were her Majesty's own words."

The princess listened to this recital with the careful attention of one seeking to detect in a diplomatic note the hidden meaning often depending upon the use of a certain word, or upon the placing of a comma in a particular spot.

After a moment's reflection, having discovered, doubtless, in the message the meaning that she had feared from the first to find therein, that is to say, espionage pure and simple, she said, pressing her lips together:

"You will take up your abode at Chantilly, monsieur, as the queen desires; furthermore, if you will say what apartment will be most agreeable to you, and most convenient for executing your commission, that apartment shall be yours."

"Madame," rejoined the officer, with a slight frown, "I have had the honor of explaining to your Highness many things not included in my instructions. Between your Highness's wrath and the queen's command I am in a dangerous position, being naught but a poor officer, and above all a wretched courtier. However, it seems to me that your Highness would be more generous to abstain from humiliating a man who is merely a passive instrument. It is distasteful to me, madame, to have to do what I am doing. But the queen has so ordered, and it is for me to obey the queen's commands to the letter. I did not seek the position,—I should have been glad had it been given to another; it seems to me that that is much to say."

And the officer raised his head with a blush which caused a similar blush to overspread the princess's haughty countenance.

"Monsieur," she replied, "whatever our social station, we owe obedience to her Majesty, as you have said. I will therefore follow the example set by you, and will obey as you obey. You must understand, however, how hard it is to be unable to receive a worthy gentleman like yourself without being at liberty to do the honors of one's house as one would like. From this moment you are master here. Order, and you shall be obeyed."

The officer bowed low as he replied:—

"God forbid, madame, that I should forget the distance which separates me from your Highness, and the respect I owe to your illustrious family! Your Highness will continue to be mistress in your own house, and I will be the first of your servants."

Thereupon the young gentleman withdrew, without embarrassment, without servility or arrogance, leaving the dowager a prey to anger, which was the more intense in that she found it impossible to vent it upon one so discreet and respectful as the messenger.

The result was that Mazarin was the theme that evening of a conversation which would have struck the minister down if curses had the power to kill from a distance, like projectiles.

The gentleman found in the antechamber the servant who announced him.

"Now, monsieur," said the latter, "Madame la Princesse de Condé, with whom you have requested an audience on the queen's behalf, consents to receive you; be pleased to follow me."

The officer understood that this form of speech served to spare the pride of the princess, and seemed as grateful for the honor bestowed upon him as if it were not made compulsory by the terms of his commission. He followed the valet through divers apartments until they reached the door of the princess's bedroom.

There the valet turned about.

"Madame la Princesse," he said, "retired upon returning from the hunt, and as she is greatly fatigued she will receive you in bed. Whom shall I announce to her Highness?"

"Announce Monsieur le Baron de Canolles on behalf of her Majesty the queen regent," was the reply.

At this name, which the pseudo-princess heard from her bed, she uttered a smothered exclamation, which, had it been overheard, would sadly have compromised her identity, and hastily pulled her hair over her eyes with the right hand, while with the left she pulled the rich coverlid of her bed well over her face.

"Admit the gentleman," she said, in a disguised voice.

The officer stepped inside the door.

MADAME DE CONDÉ

I

The room into which Canolles was ushered was a vast apartment, with hangings of sombre hue, and lighted by a single night-lamp upon a bracket between two windows; the feeble light which it cast was, however, sufficient to enable one to make out a large picture immediately above the lamp, representing a woman holding a child by the hand. At the four corners of the frame shone the three golden *fleurs-de-lys*, from which it was necessary only to take away the heart-shaped bend to make of them the three *fleurs-de-lys* of France. In the depths of a large alcove, which the light hardly reached at all, could be seen, beneath the heavy coverlid of a magnificent bed, the woman upon whom the name of the Baron de Canolles had produced so striking an effect.

The gentleman began once more to go through with the customary formalities; that is to say, he took the requisite three steps toward the bed, bowed, and took three steps more. Thereupon, two maids, who had doubtless been assisting to disrobe Madame de Condé, having withdrawn, the valet closed the door and Canolles was left alone with the princess.

It was not for Canolles to begin the conversation, and he waited until he should be spoken to; but as the princess seemed determined to maintain silence, the young officer concluded that it would be better for him to disregard the proprieties than to remain in such an embarrassing position. He was fully alive, however, to the fact that the storm portended by this disdainful silence would probably burst forth at the first words which should break it, and that he was about to be submerged by a second flood of princely wrath, even more to be feared than the first, in that this princess was younger and more interesting.

But the extreme nature of the insult put upon him of itself emboldened the young gentleman, and bowing a third time, in accordance with his feelings, that is to say, with stiff formality, indicative of the ill-humor which was brewing in his Gascon brain, he began: —

"Madame, I have had the honor to request, on behalf of her Majesty the queen regent, an audience of your Highness; your Highness has deigned to grant my request. Now, may I not beg that your Highness will crown your gracious reception by letting me know by a word, by a sign, that you are aware of my presence and are ready to listen to me?"

A movement behind the curtains and beneath the bed-clothes warned Canolles that he might expect a reply; and a moment later he heard a voice so choked with emotion as to be almost inaudible.

"Speak, monsieur," said the voice; "I am listening."

Canolles assumed an oratorical tone, and began:—

"Her Majesty the queen sends me to you, madame, to assure your Highness of her desire to continue upon friendly terms with you."

There was a very perceptible stir in the passage beside the bed, and the princess, interrupting the orator, said in a broken voice:—

"Monsieur, say no more of her Majesty the queen's friendly feeling for the family of Condé; there is direct proof of the contrary feeling in the vaults of the donjon of Vincennes."

"Well, well," thought Canolles, "it seems that they have talked the matter over, for they all say the same thing."

Meanwhile there was more stir in the passage, which the messenger did not notice, on account of the embarrassment caused by his peculiar situation.

"After all, monsieur," the princess continued, "what do you desire?"

"I desire nothing, madame," said Canolles, drawing himself up. "It is her Majesty the queen who desires that I should come to this château, that I should be admitted to the honor of your Highness's society, unworthy as I am, and that I should contribute to the utmost of my ability to restore harmony between two princes of the blood royal, at enmity for no cause at such a sad time as this."

"For no cause?" cried the princess; "do you say that there was no cause for our rupture?"

"I beg pardon, madame," rejoined Canolles. "I say nothing; I am not a judge, but an interpreter simply."

"And until the harmony of which you speak is restored the queen sets spies upon me, on the pretext—"

"And so I am a spy!" exclaimed Canolles, exasperated beyond measure. "The word is out at last! I thank your Highness for your frankness."

As a feeling of desperation began to take possession of him he fell into one of those superb attitudes which painters seek so earnestly to impart to the figures in their inanimate tableaux, and which actors endeavor to assume in their *tableaux vivants.*

"So it is definitely decided that I am a spy!" he continued. "In that case, madame, I pray you treat me as such wretches are commonly treated; forget that I am the envoy of a queen, that that queen is responsible for every act of mine, that I am simply an atom obeying her breath. Order me turned out of doors by your servants, order your gentlemen to put me to death, place me face to face with people whom I can answer with club or sword; but do not, I pray you, madame, who are placed so high by birth, by merit, and by misfortune, do not insult an officer who but fulfils his bounden duty as soldier and as subject!"

These words straight from the heart, sad as a moan, and harsh as a reproach, were calculated to produce and did produce a profound impression. While listening to them the princess raised herself upon her elbow, with glistening eyes and trembling hand.

"God forbid," said she, extending her hand almost imploringly toward the messenger when he had ceased to speak. "God forbid that I should intentionally insult so gallant a gentleman as yourself! No, Monsieur de Canolles, I do not suspect your loyalty; consider my words unsaid; they were unkind, I admit, and I have no wish to wound you. No, no, you are a noble-hearted gentleman, Monsieur le Baron, and I do you full and entire justice."

As the princess, in the act of uttering these words, impelled, doubtless, by the same generous impulse which drew them from her heart, had involuntarily thrust her head forward out of the shadow of the heavy curtains, thereby exposing to view her white forehead, her luxuriant blond hair, her bright red lips, and her lovely eyes, wet with tears, Canolles started back, for it was as if a vision had passed before his eyes, and it seemed to him as if he were once more inhaling a perfume the memory of which alone sufficed to intoxicate him. It seemed to him that one of the golden doors through which pass lovely dreams, opened to bring back to him the vanished swarm of gladsome thoughts and joys of love. He gazed with more assurance and with new light at the bed, and in a second, by the passing glare of a flash which lighted up the whole past, he recognized in the princess lying before him the Vicomte de Cambes.

For some moments his agitation had been so great that the princess could attribute it to the stern reproach which had stung him so deeply, and as her impulsive movement lasted but an instant, as she drew back almost immediately into the shadow, covered her eyes once more, and hid her slender white hand, she essayed, not without emotion, but without anxiety, to take up the conversation where she had left it.

"You were saying, monsieur?" said she.

But Canolles was dazzled, fascinated; visions were passing and repassing before his eyes, and his brain was in a whirl; his senses forsook him; he was on the point of throwing respect to the wind, and of asking questions. But an instinctive feeling, perhaps that which God implants in the hearts of those who love, which women call bashfulness, but which is nothing more nor less than avarice, counselled Canolles to dissemble still and wait; not to put an end to his dream, not to compromise by an imprudent, hasty word the happiness of his whole life.

He did not add a gesture or a word to what he was called upon to do or say. Great God! what would become of him if this great princess should suddenly recognize him; if he should inspire her now with horror as he had inspired her with suspicion at Master Biscarros' inn; if she should recur to the accusation she had abandoned; and if she should conclude that it was his purpose to avail himself of his official position, of a royal command, to continue a pursuit, which was pardonable so long as the Vicomte or Vicomtesse de Cambes was its object, but became rank insolence, almost a crime, when directed, against a princess of the blood?

"But," he suddenly reflected, "is it possible that a princess of her name and station could have been travelling about alone with a single attendant?"

Thereupon, as always happens under such circumstances, when a wavering, despairing hope seeks something to revive it, Canolles in desperation let his eyes wander about the room until they fell upon the portrait of the woman holding her son by the hand.

At the sight a ray of light flashed through his mind, and he instinctively stepped nearer to the portrait. The pseudo-princess could not restrain a slight exclamation, and when Canolles, hearing her voice, turned his head, he saw that her face was altogether hidden from him.

"Oho!" said Canolles to himself, "what does that mean? Either it was the princess whom I met in the Bordeaux road, or I am the victim of a trick, and the person in that bed is not the princess. At all events, we will soon see."

"Madame," he said, abruptly, "I know not what to think of your present silence, and I recognize—"

"Whom do you recognize?" hastily exclaimed the lady in the bed.

"I recognize the fact," continued Canolles, "that I have been so unfortunate as to inspire in you the same feeling I inspired in the princess dowager."

"Ah!" the voice involuntarily gave utterance to this sigh of relief.

Canolles' remark was not strictly logical, perhaps, and had little relevancy to their conversation, but his purpose was accomplished. He noticed the sensation of terror which prompted the interruption, and the joyful sensation with which his last words were received.

"But," he continued, "I am none the less compelled to say to your Highness, distasteful as it is to me, that I am to remain at the château and accompany your Highness wherever it may be your pleasure to go."

"So that I cannot be alone even in my own apartments?" cried the princess. "Ah! monsieur, that is worse than an indignity!"

"I have informed your Highness that such are my instructions; but I beg you to have no fears on that score," added Canolles, with a piercing glance at the occupant of the bed, and emphasizing every word; "you should know better than any one that I am not slow to yield to a woman's entreaties."

"I?" cried the princess, whose tone denoted more embarrassment than surprise. "In truth, monsieur, I cannot fathom your meaning; I have no idea to what circumstance you allude."

"Madame," rejoined Canolles, bowing, "I thought that the servant who announced me to your Highness mentioned my name. I am Baron de Canolles."

"Indeed," said the princess in a more confident voice; "what matters it to me, monsieur?"

"I thought that having already had the honor of obliging your Highness—"

"Of obliging me! how, I pray to know?" retorted the voice, in a changed tone, which reminded Canolles of a certain very wrathful, but at the same time very timorous voice, which he remembered too well.

"By carrying out my instructions to the letter," he replied with the utmost respect.

The princess's apprehension seemed to be allayed once more.

"Monsieur," said she, "I have no wish to make you remiss in your duty; carry out your instructions, whatever they may be."

"Madame, I am as yet, I am happy to say, entirely unskilled in the persecution of women, and know even less of the method to be employed in insulting a princess. I have the honor therefore to repeat to your Highness what I have already said to the princess dowager, that I am your very humble servant. Deign to give me your word that you will not leave the château unaccompanied by me, and I will relieve you of my presence, which, as I can well understand, is hateful to your Highness."

"But in that case, monsieur," said the princess, quickly, "you will not carry out your orders."

"I shall do what my conscience tells me that I ought to do."

"Monsieur de Canolles, I swear that I will not leave Chantilly without giving you due notice."

"Then, madame," said Canolles, bowing to the ground, "forgive me for having been the involuntary cause of arousing your wrath for an instant. Your Highness will not see me again until you are pleased to summon me."

"I thank you, baron," said the voice, with a joyful inflection, which seemed to find an echo in the passage. "Go, go! I thank you; to-morrow I shall have the pleasure of seeing you again."

This time the baron recognized, beyond possibility of mistake, the voice, the eyes, and the unspeakably delicious smile of the fascinating being who slipped between his fingers, so to speak, the night that the courier brought him the order from the Duc d'Épernon. A last glance at the portrait, dimly lighted as it was, showed the baron, whose eyes were beginning to be accustomed to the half-darkness, the aquiline nose of the Maillé family, the black hair and deep-set eyes of the princess; while the woman before him, who had just played through the first act of the difficult part she had undertaken, had the eye level with the face, the straight nose with dilated nostrils, the mouth dimpled at the corners by frequent smiling, and the plump cheeks which denote anything rather than the habit of serious meditation.

Canolles knew all that he wished to know; he bowed once more as respectfully as if he still believed that he was in the princess's presence, and withdrew to the apartment set apart for him.

II

Canolles had formed no definite plan of action. Once in his own quarters he began to stride rapidly back and forth, as undecided folk are wont to do, without noticing that Castorin, who was awaiting his return, rose when he saw him, and was following him, holding in his hands a *robe de chambre*, behind which he was hardly visible.

Castorin stumbled over a chair and Canolles turned about.

"Well," said he, "what are you doing with that *robe de chambre?*"

"I am waiting for monsieur to take off his coat."

"I don't know when I shall take off my coat. Put the *robe de chambre* on a chair and wait."

"What! monsieur does not propose to take off his coat?" queried Castorin, who was by nature a capricious rascal, but seemed on this occasion more intractable than ever. "Monsieur does not intend to retire at once?"

"No."

"When does monsieur intend to retire, pray?"

"What's that to you?"

"It's a great deal to me, as I am very tired."

"Ah! indeed!" exclaimed Canolles, pausing in his walk, and looking Castorin in the face, "you are very tired, are you?"

It was easy to read upon the lackey's face the impertinent expression common to all servants who are dying with the longing to be turned out of doors.

Canolles shrugged his shoulders.

"Go and wait in the antechamber," said he; "when I have need of you I will ring."

"I forewarn monsieur that if he delays long, he will not find me in the antechamber."

"Where shall you be, I pray to know?"

"In my bed. It seems to me that after travelling two hundred leagues it is high time to go to bed."

"Monsieur Castorin," said Canolles, "you are a clown."

"If monsieur considers a clown unworthy to be his servant, monsieur has but to say the word, and I will relieve him of my services," rejoined Castorin, with his most majestic air.

Canolles was not in a patient mood, and if Castorin had possessed the power to catch a glimpse even of the shadow of the storm that was brewing in his master's mind, it is certain that, however anxious he might have been to be free, he would have chosen another time to hazard the suggestion. Canolles walked up to him, and took one of the buttons of his doublet between his thumb and forefinger,—the familiar trick, long afterwards, of a much greater man than poor Canolles ever was.

"Say that again," said he.

"I say," rejoined Castorin with unabated impudence, "that if monsieur is not content with me I will relieve monsieur of my services."

Canolles let go the button, and went gravely to get his cane. Castorin was not slow to grasp the meaning of that manœuvre.

"Monsieur," he cried, "beware what you do! I am no longer a common valet; I am in the service of Madame la Princesse!"

"Oho!" said Canolles, lowering the cane which was already in the air; "oho! you are in the service of Madame la Princesse?"

"Yes, monsieur, since half an hour ago."

"Who engaged you to take service with her?"

"Monsieur Pompée, her intendant."

"Monsieur Pompée?"

"Yes."

"Well! why didn't you tell me so at once?" cried Canolles. "Yes, yes, my dear Castorin, you are quite right to leave my service, and here are two pistoles to indemnify you for the blows I was on the point of giving you."

"Oh!" ejaculated Castorin, not daring to take the money; "what does that mean? Is monsieur making sport of me?"

"Not so. On the contrary I bid you by all means be Madame la Princesse's servant. When is your service to begin, by the way?"

"From the moment that monsieur gives me my liberty."

"Very well; I give you your liberty from to-morrow morning."

"And until then?"

"Until to-morrow morning you are my servant and must obey me."

"Willingly! What are monsieur's orders?" said Castorin, deciding to take the two pistoles.

"I order you, as you are so desirous to sleep, to undress and get into my bed."

"What? what is monsieur's meaning? I do not understand,"

"You don't need to understand, but simply to obey. Undress at once; I will assist you."

"Monsieur will assist me?"

"To be sure; as you are to play the part of the Baron de Canolles, I must needs play the part of Castorin."

Thereupon, without awaiting his servant's leave, the baron removed his doublet and hat and put them on himself, and locking the door upon him before he had recovered from his surprise, ran rapidly downstairs.

He was at last beginning to see through the mystery, although certain parts of it were still enveloped in mist. For two hours past it had seemed to him as if nothing of all that he had seen or heard was perfectly natural. The attitude of every one at Chantilly was constrained and stiff; everybody that he met seemed to be playing a part, and yet the various details all seemed to harmonize in a way which indicated to the queen's envoy that he must redouble his watchfulness if he did not choose to be himself the victim of some grand mystification.

The presence of Pompée in conjunction with that of the Vicomte de Cambes cleared away many doubts, and the few which still remained in Canolles' mind were completely dissipated when, as he left the court-yard, he saw, notwithstanding the profound darkness of the night, four men coming toward him and about to enter the door through which he had just passed. They were led by the same valet who ushered him into the presence of the princess. Another man wrapped in a great cloak followed behind.

The little party halted in the doorway awaiting the orders of the man in the cloak.

"You know where he lodges," said the latter, in an imperious tone, addressing the valet, "and you know him, for you introduced him. Do you watch him, therefore, and see that he doesn't leave his apartment; station your men on the stairway, in the corridor, anywhere, so that, without suspecting it, he may be watched himself, instead of watching their Highnesses."

Canolles made himself more invisible than a ghost in the darkest corner he could find; from there, unseen himself, he saw his five keepers pass through the door, while the man in the cloak, having made sure that they were carrying out his orders, returned the same way that he came.

"This gives me no very definite information," said Canolles to himself as he looked after him, "for it may be simply their indignation that leads them to return like for like. If that devil of a Castorin won't cry out or do some idiotic thing! I did wrong not to gag him; unluckily it's too late now. Well, I must commence my round."

With that, Canolles cast a keen glance around, then crossed the court-yard to that wing of the building behind which the stables were located.

All the life of the château seemed to have taken refuge in that locality. He could hear horses pawing the ground, and hurried footsteps. In the harness-room there was a great clashing of bits and spurs. Carriages were being rolled out of the sheds, and voices, stifled by apprehension, but which could be distinguished by listening attentively, were calling and answering one another. Canolles stood still for a moment listening. There was no room for doubt that preparations for departure were in progress.

He swiftly traversed the distance between the wings, passed through an arched gateway, and reached the front of the château.

There he stopped.

The windows of the ground-floor apartments were too brilliantly illuminated for him not to divine that a large number of torches were lighted inside, and as they went and came, causing great patches of light to sweep across the level turf, Canolles understood that that was the centre of activity, and the true seat of the enterprise.

He hesitated at first to pry into the secret which they were trying to hide from him. But he reflected that his position as an agent of the queen, and the responsibility thereby imposed upon him, would excuse many things to the satisfaction of the most scrupulous conscience. So he crept cautiously along the wall, the base of which was made all the darker by the brilliantly lighted windows, which were some six or seven feet from the ground. He stepped upon a stepping-stone, thence to a projection in the wall, clung with one hand to a ring, with the other to the window-sill, and darted through a corner of the window the keenest and most searching glance that ever made its way into the sanctuary of a conspiracy.

This is what he saw.

A woman standing before a toilet-table and putting in place the last pin necessary to hold her travelling-hat upon her head, and near by, several maids dressing a child in hunting costume. The child's back was turned to Canolles, and he could see nothing but his long, blond curls. But the light of two six-branched candelabra, held upon either side of the toilet-table by footmen in the attitude of caryatides, shone full upon the lady's face, in which Canolles at once recognized the original of the portrait he had recently examined in the half-light of the princess's apartment. There were the long face, the stern mouth, the imperiously curved nose of the woman whose living image stood before Canolles. Everything about her betokened the habit of domination,—her imperious gesture, her sparkling eye, the abrupt movement of her head.

In like manner everything in the bearing of those about her betokened the habit of unquestioning obedience,—their frequent bowing, the haste with which they ran to bring whatever she might ask for, their promptness in responding to the voice of their sovereign, or anticipating her commands.

Several officials of the household, among whom Canolles recognized the *valet de chambre*, were pouring into portmanteaux, trunks, and chests, some jewels, others money, and others the various portions of that woman's arsenal known as the toilet. The little prince, meanwhile, was playing about among the assiduous servitors, but by a strange fatality Canolles was unable to catch a glimpse of his face.

"I suspected it," he muttered; "they are putting a trick upon me, and these people are making preparations to go away. Very good: but I can with a wave of my hand change this scene of mystification into a scene of lamentation; I have only to run out upon the terrace and blow this silver whistle three times, and in five minutes two hundred men will have burst into the château in answer to its shrill blast, will have arrested the princesses and bound all these fellows hand and foot who are laughing together so slyly. Yes," he continued, but now it was his heart that spoke rather than his lips; "yes, but I should bring irretrievable ruin upon that other, who is sleeping, or pretending to sleep, over yonder; she will hate me, and it will be no more than I deserve. "Worse than all, she will despise me, saying that I have acted the spy to the end—and yet, if she obeys the princess, why should not I obey the queen?"

At that moment, as if chance were determined to combat these symptoms of returning resolution, a door of the apartment where the princess was dressing opened, and gave admittance to two persons, a man of fifty years and a woman of twenty, who hurried in with joyful faces. At that sight Canolles' whole heart passed into his eyes, for he recognized the lovely hair, the fresh lips, the speaking eye of the Vicomte de Cambes, as that individual, with smiling face, respectfully kissed the hand of Clémence de Maillé, Princesse de Condé. But on this occasion the viscount wore the garments of her own sex, and made the loveliest viscountess on the face of the earth.

Canolles would have given ten years of his life to hear their conversation; but to no purpose did he glue his ear to the glass; an unintelligible buzzing was all that he could hear. He saw the princess bid the younger woman adieu, and kiss her on the brow, saying as she did so something which made all the others laugh; he then saw the viscountess return to the state apartments with some inferior officials clothed in the uniforms of their superiors. He even saw the worthy Pompée, swollen with pride, in orange coat trimmed with silver-lace, strutting about with noble mien, and like Don Jophet of Armenia, leaning upon the hilt of an enormous rapier, in attendance upon his mistress, as she gracefully raised the train of her long satin robe.

Then, through another door at the left, the princess's escort began to file out noiselessly, led by Madame de Condé herself, whose bearing was that of a queen, not of a fugitive. Next to her came Vialas, carrying in his arms the little Duc d'Enghien, wrapped in a cloak; then Lenet, carrying a carved casket and divers bundles of papers, and last of all the intendant of the château, closing the procession, which was preceded by two officers with drawn swords.

They all left the room by a secret passageway. Canolles immediately leaped down from his post of observation and ran to the gateway, where the lights had meanwhile been extinguished; and he saw the whole cortège pass silently through on the way to the stables; the hour of departure was at hand.

At that moment Canolles thought only of the duties imposed upon him by the mission with which the queen had intrusted him. In the person of this woman who was about to leave the château, he was allowing armed civil war to go abroad and gnaw once more at the entrails of France. Certes, it was a shameful thing for him, a man, to become a spy upon a woman, and her keeper; but the Duchesse de Longueville, who set fire to the four corners of France, she was a woman too.

Canolles rushed toward the terrace, which overlooked the park, and put the silver whistle to his lips.

It would have been all up with the preparations for departure! Madame de Condé would not have left Chantilly, or, if she had done so, would not have taken a hundred steps before she and her escort were surrounded by a force thrice her own; and thus Canolles would have fulfilled his mission without the least danger to himself; thus, at a single blow, he would have destroyed the fortune and the future of the house of Condé, and would by the same blow have built up his own fortune upon the ruins of theirs, and have laid the foundations of future grandeur, as the Vitrys and Luynes did in the old days, and more recently the Guitauts and Miossens, under circumstances which were perhaps of less moment to the welfare of the realm.

But Canolles raised his eyes to the apartment where the soft, sad light of the night-lamp shone behind curtains of red velvet, and he fancied that he could see the shadow of his beloved outlined upon the great white window-blinds.

Thereupon all his resolutions, all his selfish arguments faded away before the gentle beams of that light, as the dreams and phantoms of the night fade away before the first beams of the rising sun.

"Monsieur de Mazarin," he said to himself in a passionate outburst, "is so rich that he can afford to lose all these princes and princesses who seek to escape him; but I am not rich enough to lose the treasure which belongs henceforth to me, and which I will guard as jealously as a dragon. At this moment she is alone, in my power, dependent upon me; at any hour of the day or night I can enter her apartment; she will not fly without telling me, for I have her sacred word. What care I though the queen be deceived and Monsieur de Mazarin lose his temper? I was told to watch Madame la Princesse, and I am watching her. They should have given me her description or have set a more practised spy than myself upon her."

With that, Canolles put the whistle in his pocket, listened to the grinding of the bolts, heard the distant rumbling of the carriages over the bridge in the park, and the clattering of many horses' hoofs, growing gradually fainter, until it died away altogether. When everything had disappeared, when there was nothing more to see or hear, heedless of the fact that he was staking his life against a woman's love,—that is to say, against a mere shadow of happiness,—he glided into the second deserted court-yard, and cautiously ascended the staircase leading to his apartment, the darkness being unrelieved by the faintest gleam of light.

But, cautious as his movements were, when he reached the corridor he unavoidably stumbled against a person who was apparently listening at his door, and who uttered a muffled cry of alarm.

"Who are you? Who are you?" demanded the person in question, in a frightened voice.

"Pardieu!" said Canolles, "who are you yourself, who prowl about this staircase like a spy?"

"I am Pompée."

"Madame la Princesse's intendant?"

"Yes, yes,-Madame la Princesse's intendant."

"Ah! that's a lucky chance; I am Castorin."

"Castorin, Monsieur de Canolles' valet?"

"Himself."

"Ah! my dear Castorin," said Pompée, "I'll wager that I gave you a good fright."

"Fright?"

"Yes! *Dame!* when one has never been a soldier—Can I do anything for you, my dear friend?" continued Pompée, resuming his air of importance.

"Yes."

"Tell me what it is."

"You can inform Madame la Princesse immediately that my master desires to speak with her."

"At this hour?"

"Even so."

"Impossible!"

"You think so?"

"I am sure of it."

"Then she will not receive my master?"

"No."

"By order of the king, Monsieur Pompée! Go and tell her that."

"By order of the king!" cried Pompée. "I will go."

He ran precipitately downstairs, impelled at once by respect and fear, two greyhounds which are quite capable of making a tortoise run at their pace.

Canolles kept on and entered his room, where he found Castorin snoring lustily, stretched out magisterially in a large easy-chair. He resumed his uniform and awaited the result of his latest step.

"'Faith!" he said to himself, "if I don't do Monsieur de Mazarin's business very successfully, it seems to me that I don't do badly with my own."

He waited in vain, however, for Pompée's return; and after ten minutes, finding that he did not come, nor any other in his stead, he resolved to present himself unannounced. He therefore aroused Monsieur Castorin, whose bile was soothed by an hour's sleep, bade him, in a tone which admitted no reply, to be ready for any thing that might happen, and bent his steps toward the princess's apartments.

At the door he found a footman in very ill humor, because the bell rang just as his service was at an end, and he was looking forward, like Monsieur Castorin, to a refreshing slumber after the fatiguing day.

"What do you wish, monsieur?" he asked when he saw Canolles.

"I request the honor of paying my respects to Madame la Princesse."

"At this hour, monsieur?"

"What's that? 'at this hour'?"

"Yes, it seems to me very late."

"How dare you say that, villain?"

"But, monsieur—" stammered the footman.

"I no longer request, I demand," said Canolles, in a supremely haughty tone.

"You demand? Only Madame la Princesse gives orders here."

"The king gives orders everywhere. By the king's order!"

The lackey shuddered and hung his head.

"Pardon, monsieur," he said, trembling from head to foot, "but I am only a poor servant, and cannot take it upon myself to open Madame la Princesse's door; permit me to go and awaken a chamberlain."

"Are the chamberlains accustomed to retire at eleven o'clock at the château of Chantilly?"

"They hunted all day," faltered the footman.

"In truth," muttered Canolles, "I must give them time to dress some one as a chamberlain. Very well," he added aloud; "go; I will wait."

The footman started off on the run to carry the alarm through the château, where Pompée, terrified beyond measure by his unfortunate encounter, had already sown unspeakable dismay.

Canolles, left to his own devices, pricked up his ears and opened his eyes.

He heard much running to and fro in the salons and corridors; he saw by the light of expiring torches men armed with muskets taking their places at the angles of the stairways; on all sides he felt that the silence of stupefaction which reigned throughout the château a moment before was succeeded by a threatening murmur.

Canolles put his hand to his whistle and drew near a window, whence he could see the dark mass of the trees, at the foot of which he had stationed the two hundred men he brought with him.

"No," said he, "that would simply lead to a pitched battle, and that is not what I want. It's much better to wait; the worst that can happen to me by waiting is to be murdered, while if I act hastily I may ruin her."

Canolles had no sooner come to the end of this reflection than the door opened and a new personage appeared upon the scene.

"Madame la Princesse is not visible," said this personage, so hurriedly that he had not time to salute the gentleman; "she is in bed, and has given positive orders that no one be admitted."

"Who are you?" said Canolles, eying the new-comer from head to foot. "And who taught you to speak to a gentleman with your hat on your head?"

As he asked the question Canolles coolly removed the man's hat with the end of his cane.

"Monsieur!" cried the latter, stepping back with dignity.

"I asked you who you are."

"I am—I am, as you can see by my uniform, captain of her Highness's guards."

Canolles smiled. He had had time to scrutinize his interlocutor, and saw that he was dealing with some butler with a paunch as round as his bottles, some prosperous Vatel imprisoned in an official doublet, which, from lack of time, or superabundance of belly, was not properly secured.

"Very good, master captain of the guards," said Canolles, "pick up your hat and answer."

The captain executed the first branch of Canolles' injunction like one who had studied that excellent maxim of military discipline: "To know how to command, one must know how to obey."

"Captain of the guards!" continued Canolles. "*Peste!* that's a fine post to hold!"

"Why, yes, monsieur, well enough; but what then?" observed that official, drawing himself up.

"Don't swell out so much, Monsieur le Capitaine," said Canolles, "or you will burst off the last button, and your breeches will fall down about your heels, which would be most disgraceful."

"But who are you, monsieur?" demanded the pretended captain, taking his turn at asking questions.

"Monsieur, I will follow the example of urbanity set by you, and will answer your question as you answered mine. I am captain in the regiment of Navailles, and I come hither in the king's name as his ambassador, clothed with powers—which will be exerted in a peaceful or violent manner, according as his Majesty's commands are or are not obeyed."

"Violent!" cried the pretended captain. "In a violent manner?"

"Very violent, I give you warning."

"Even where her Highness is personally concerned?"

"Why not? Her Highness is his Majesty's first subject, nothing more."

"Monsieur, do not resort to force; I have fifty men-at-arms ready to avenge her Highness's honor."

Canolles did not choose to tell him that his fifty men-at-arms were simply footmen and scullions, fit troops to serve under such a leader, and that, so far as the princess's honor was concerned, it was at that moment riding along the Bordeaux road with the princess.

He replied simply, with that indifferent air which is more terrifying than an open threat, and is familiar to brave men and those who are accustomed to danger:—

"If you have fifty men-at-arms, Monsieur le Capitaine, I have two hundred soldiers, who form the advance-guard of the royal army. Do you propose to put yourself in open rebellion against his Majesty?"

"No, monsieur, no!" the stout man hastened to reply, sadly crestfallen; "God forbid! but I beg you to bear me witness that I yield to force alone."

"That is the least I can do for you as your brother-in-arms."

"Very well; then I will take you to Madame the Princess Dowager, who is not yet asleep."

Canolles had no need to reflect to appreciate the terrible danger that lay hidden in this snare; but he turned it aside without ceremony, thanks to his omnipotence.

"My orders are, not to see Madame the Princess Dowager, but the younger princess."

The captain of the guards once more bent his head, imparted a retrograde movement to his great legs, trailed his long sword across the floor, and stalked majestically through the door between two sentries, who stood trembling there throughout the scene we have described, and were very near quitting their post when they heard of the presence of two hundred men, — so little disposed were they to become martyrs to fidelity in the sacking of the château of Chantilly.

Ten minutes later the captain returned, followed by two guards, and with wearisome formality undertook to escort Canolles to the apartment of the princess, to which he was at last introduced without further delay.

He recognized the room itself, the furniture, the bed, and even the perfume, but he looked in vain for two things: the portrait of the true princess which he had noticed at the time of his first visit, and to which he owed his first suspicion of the trick they proposed to play him; and the figure of the false princess, for whom he had made so great a sacrifice.

The portrait had been removed; and as a precautionary measure, somewhat tardily adopted, the face of the person on the bed was turned toward the wall with true princely impertinence. Two women were standing in the passage between the bed and the wall.

The gentleman would willingly have passed over this lack of courtesy; but as the thought came to his mind that possibly some new substitution had enabled Madame de Cambes to take flight as the princess had done, his hair stood on end with dismay, and he determined to make sure at once of the identity of the person who occupied the bed, by exerting the supreme power with which he was clothed by his mission.

"Madame," said he with a low bow, "I ask your Highness's pardon for presenting myself at this hour, especially after I had given you my word that I would await your commands; but I have noticed a great stir in the château—"

The person in the bed started, but did not reply. Canolles looked in vain for some indication that the woman before him was really the one he sought, but amid the billows of lace and the soft mass of quilts and coverlets it was impossible for him to do anything more than distinguish a recumbent form.

"And," he continued, "I owe it to myself to satisfy myself that this bed still contains the same person with whom I had the honor of half an hour's conversation."

These words were followed, not by a simple start, but by a downright contortion of terror. The movement did not escape the notice of Canolles, who was alarmed by it.

"If she has deceived me," he thought, "if, despite her solemn promise, she has fled, I will leave the château. I will take horse, I will place myself at the head of my two hundred men, and I will capture my runaways, though I have to set fire to thirty villages to light my road."

He waited a moment longer; but the person in the bed did not speak or turn toward him; it was evident that she wished to gain time.

"Madame," said Canolles, at last giving vent to a feeling of impatience, which he had not the courage to conceal, "I beg your Highness to remember that I am sent hither by the king, and in the king's name I demand the honor of seeing your face."

"Oh! this inquisition is unendurable," exclaimed a trembling voice, which sent a thrill of joy through the young officer's veins; for he recognized therein a quality which no other voice could counterfeit. "If it is, as you say, the king who compels you to act thus, the king is still a mere child, and does not yet know the duties of a gentleman; to force a woman to show her face is no less insulting than to snatch away her mask."

"There is a phrase, madame, before which women bend the knee when it is uttered by a king, and kings when it is uttered by destiny. That phrase is: 'It must be.'"

"Very well, since it must be, since I am alone and helpless against the king's order and his messenger's persistence, I obey, monsieur; look at me."

Thereupon the rampart of pillows, bed-clothes, and laces which protected the fair besieged was suddenly put aside, and through the improvised breach appeared the blond head and lovely face which the voice led him to expect to see,—the cheeks flushed with shame, rather than with indignation. With the swift glance of a man accustomed to equivalent, if not strictly similar situations, Canolles satisfied himself that it was not anger which kept those eyes, veiled by velvety eyelashes, bent upon the ground, or made that white hand tremble, as it confined the rebellious waves of hair upon an alabaster neck.

The pseudo-princess remained for an instant in that attitude, which she would have liked to make threatening, but which expressed nothing more than vexation, while Canolles gazed at her, breathing ecstatically, and repressing with both hands the tumultuous, joyful beating of his heart.

"Well, monsieur," said the ill-used fair one after a few seconds of silence, "has my humiliation gone far enough? Have you scrutinized me at your leisure? Your triumph is complete, is it not? Show yourself a generous victor, then, and retire."

"I would be glad to do so, madame; but I must carry out my instructions to the end. Thus far I have performed only that part of my mission which concerns your Highness; but it is not enough to have seen you; I must now see Monsieur le Duc d'Enghien."

A terrible silence followed these words, uttered in the tone of a man who knows that he has the right to command, and who proposes to be obeyed. The false princess raised herself in bed, leaning upon her hand, and fixed upon Canolles one of those strange glances which seemed to belong to none but her, they expressed so many things at once. It seemed to say: "Have you recognized me? Do you know who I really am? If you know, forgive me and spare me; you are the stronger, so take pity on me."

Canolles understood all that her glance said to him; but he hardened himself against its seductive eloquence, and answered it in spoken words:—

"Impossible, madame; my orders are explicit."

"Let everything be done as you choose, then, monsieur, as you have no consideration for rank or position. Go; these ladies will take you to my son's bedside."

"Might not these ladies, instead of taking me to your son, bring your son to you, madame? It seems to me that that would be infinitely preferable."

"Why so, monsieur?" inquired the false princess, evidently more disturbed by this latest request than by any previous one.,

"Because, in the meantime, I could communicate to your Highness a part of my mission which must be communicated to you alone."

"To me alone?"

"To you alone," Canolles replied, with a lower reverence than any he had achieved as yet.

The princess's expression, which had changed from dignity to supplication, and from supplication to anxiety, now changed once more to abject terror, as she fixed her eyes upon Canolles' face.

"What is there to alarm you so in the idea of a *tête-à-tête* with me, madame?" said he. "Are you not a princess, and am not I a gentleman?"

"Yes, you are right, monsieur, and I am wrong to be alarmed. Yes, although I now have the pleasure of seeing you for the first time, your reputation as a courteous, loyal gentleman has come to my ears. Go, mesdames, and bring Monsieur le Duc d'Enghien to me."

The two women came forth from the passage beside the bed, and walked toward the door; they turned once to be sure that the order was intended to be obeyed, and at a gesture confirming the words of their mistress, or of her *locum tenens*, left the room.

Canolles looked after them until they had closed the door. Then his eyes, sparkling with joy, returned to the princess.

"Tell me, Monsieur de Canolles," said she, sitting up and folding her hands, "tell me why you persecute me thus."

As she spoke she looked at the young officer, not with the haughty gaze of a princess, which she had tried with but poor success, but with a look so touching and so full of meaning that all the details of their first meeting, all the intoxicating episodes of the journey, all the memories of his nascent love came rushing over him, and enveloped his heart as with perfumed vapor.

"Madame," said he, stepping toward the bed, "it is Madame de Condé whom I am here to watch in the king's name, — not you, who are not Madame de Condé."

The young woman to whom these words were addressed gave a little shriek, became pale as death, and pressed one of her hands against her heart.

"What do you mean, monsieur?" she cried; "who do you think I am?"

"Oh! as for that," retorted Canolles, "I should be much embarrassed to explain; for I would be almost willing to swear that you are the most charming of viscounts were you not the most adorable of viscountesses."

"Monsieur," said the pretended princess, hoping to awe Canolles by reasserting her dignity, "of all you say to me I understand but one thing, and that is that you insult me!"

"Madame," said Canolles, "we do not fail in respect to God because we adore him. We do not insult angels because we kneel before them."

And Canolles bent forward as if to fall on his knees.

"Monsieur," said the countess, hastily, checking him with a gesture, — "monsieur, the Princesse de Condé cannot suffer—"

"The Princesse de Condé, madame, is at this moment riding along the Bordeaux road on a good horse, accompanied by Monsieur Vialas her equerry, Monsieur Lenet her adviser, her gentlemen in waiting, her officers, her whole household, in short; and she has no concern in what is taking place between the Baron de Canolles and the Vicomte, or Vicomtesse, de Cambes."

"What are you saying, monsieur? Are you mad?"

"No, madame; I am simply telling you what I have myself seen and heard."

"In that case, if you have seen and heard all that you say, your mission should be at an end."

"You think so, madame? Must I then return to Paris, and confess to the queen that, rather than grieve the woman whom I love (I name no one, madame, so do not look so angrily at me), I have violated her orders, allowed her enemy to escape, and closed my eyes to what I saw,—that I have, in a word, betrayed, yes, betrayed the cause of my king?"

The viscountess seemed to be touched, and gazed at the baron with almost tender compassion.

"Have you not the best of all excuses," said she, "the impossibility of doing otherwise? Could you, alone, stop Madame la Princesse's imposing escort? Do your orders bid you to fight fifty gentlemen single-handed?"

"I was not alone, madame," said Canolles, shaking his head. "I had, and still have, in the woods yonder, not five hundred yards away, two hundred soldiers, whom I can summon in a moment by blowing my whistle. It would have been a simple matter, therefore, for me to stop Madame la Princesse, who would have found resistance of no avail. But even if the force under my command had been weaker than her escort, instead of four times stronger, I could still have fought, and sold my life dearly. That would have been as easy to me," the young man continued, bending forward more and more, "as it would be sweet to me to touch that hand if I dared."

The hand upon which the baron's glowing eyes were fixed, the soft, plump, white hand, had fallen outside the bed, and moved nervously at every word the baron spoke. The viscountess herself, blinded by the electric current of love, the effects of which she had felt in the little inn at Jaulnay, could not remember that she ought to withdraw the hand which had furnished Canolles with so happy a simile; she forgot her duty in the premises, and the young man, falling upon his knees, put his lips timidly to the hand, which was sharply withdrawn at the contact, as if a red-hot iron had burned it.

"Thanks, Monsieur de Canolles," said she. "I thank you from the bottom of my heart for what you have done for me; believe that I shall never forget it. But I pray you to double the value of the service by realizing my position and leaving me. Must we not part, now that your task is ended?"

This *we*, uttered in a tone so soft that it seemed to contain a shade of regret, made the most secret fibres of Canolles' heart vibrate painfully. Indeed, excessive joy is almost always accompanied by something very like pain.

"I will obey, madame," said he; "but I will venture to observe, not as a pretext for disobedience, but to spare you possible remorse hereafter, that if I obey I am lost. The moment that I admit my error, and cease to pretend to be deceived by your stratagem, I become the victim of my good-nature. I am declared a traitor, imprisoned—shot, it may be; and it will be no more than just, for I am a traitor."

Claire cried out in dismay, and herself seized Canolles' hand, which she immediately let fall again with charming confusion.

"Then what are *we* to do?"

The young man's heart swelled. That blessed *we* seemed in a fair way to become Madame de Cambes' favorite pronoun.

"What! ruin you!—you, who are so kind and generous!" she exclaimed. "I ruin you? Oh! never! At what sacrifice can I save you? Tell me! tell me!"

"You must permit me, madame, to play my part to the end. It is essential, as I told you but now, that I seem to be your dupe, and that I report to Monsieur de Mazarin what I *see*, not what I know."

"Yes, but if it is discovered that you have done all this for me, that we have met before, that you have seen my face, then I shall be the one to be ruined: do not forget that!"

"Madame," said Canolles, with admirably simulated melancholy, "I do not think, judging from your coldness, and the dignity which it costs you so little to maintain in my presence, that you are likely to divulge a secret which, after all, has no existence in your heart, at all events."

Claire made no reply; but a fleeting glance, an almost imperceptible smile, replied in a way to make Canolles the happiest of men.

"I may remain, then?" he said, with an indescribable smile.

"Since it must be so!" was the reply.

"In that case, I must write to Monsieur de Mazarin."

"Yes, go."

"What's that?"

"I told you to go and write to him."

"Not so. I must write to him here, from your room; I must date my letter at the foot of your bed."

"But it's not proper."

"Here are my instructions, madame; read them for yourself."

And Canolles handed a paper to the viscountess, who read:—

"'Monsieur le Baron de Canolles will keep Madame la Princesse and her son, Monsieur le Duc d'Enghien, in sight—'"

"In sight," said Canolles.

"In sight; yes, so it says."

Claire realized all the advantage that a man as deeply in love as Canolles was might take upon the strength of such instructions, but she also realized how great a service she would render the princess by prolonging the deception of the court.

"Write, then," she said, resignedly.

Canolles questioned her with his eyes, and in the same way she indicated a secretary, which contained all the essentials for writing. Canolles opened it, took therefrom pen, ink, and paper, placed them upon a table, moved the table as near as possible to the bed, asked permission to be seated, as if Claire were still in his eyes Madame la Princesse, and wrote the following despatch to Monsieur de Mazarin:—

"MONSEIGNEUR,—I arrived at the château of Chantilly at nine o'clock in the evening; you will see that I travelled with all diligence, as I had the honor to take leave of your Eminence at half-past six.

"I found the two princesses in bed,—the princess dowager quite seriously ill, Madame la Princesse tired out after hunting all day.

"According to your Eminence's instructions I waited upon their Highnesses, who immediately dismissed all their guests, and I am at this moment keeping watch upon Madame la Princesse and her son."

"And her son," Canolles repeated, turning to the viscountess. "The devil! that sounds like a lie, and yet I would prefer not to lie."

"Have no fear," rejoined Claire, laughing; "if you haven't seen my son yet, you shall see him very soon."

"And her son," resumed Canolles, echoing her laugh.

"I have the honor of writing this letter to your Eminence in Madame la Princesse's bedroom, sitting by her bedside."

He signed his name, and, having respectfully asked Claire's permission, pulled a bell-cord. A *valet de chambre* answered the bell.

"Call my servant," said Canolles; "and when he is in the antechamber inform me."

Within five minutes the baron was informed that Monsieur Castorin was waiting.

"Take this letter," said Canolles, "and carry it to the officer in command of my two hundred men; bid him send an express to Paris with it."

"But, Monsieur le Baron," rejoined Castorin, who looked upon such an errand in the middle of the night as one of the most disagreeable things imaginable, "I thought that I told you that Monsieur Pompée had engaged me to take service with Madame la Princesse."

"Very good; I transmit this order to you on behalf of Madame la Princesse.—Will not your Highness deign to confirm what I say?" he added, turning toward the bed. "You are aware how important it is that this letter be delivered at once."

"Go," said the spurious princess, with a majestic accent and gesture.

Castorin bowed to the ground and left the room.

"Now," said Claire, holding out both her little hands imploringly to Canolles, "you will leave me, will you not?"

"Pardon me; but your son, madame?"

"True," replied Claire, with a smile; "you shall see him."

The words were hardly out of her mouth when some one scratched at the door, as the custom was at that time. It was Cardinal de Richelieu, influenced, doubtless, by his love for cats, who introduced this style of knocking. During his long reign people scratched at Monsieur de Richelieu's door; afterwards at Monsieur de Chavigny's, who was entitled to succeed him in this regard, were it only as his natural heir; and, lastly, at Monsieur de Mazarin's. Therefore they might well scratch at Madame la Princesse's door.

"They are coming," said Madame de Cambes.

"'T is well. I resume my official character."

He moved the table away and the chair, put on his hat, and stood in a respectful attitude, four steps from the princess's bed.

"Come in," said Claire.

Thereupon the stateliest procession imaginable filed into the room. There were ladies' in waiting, chamberlains, functionaries of all grades,—the whole ordinary retinue of the princess.

"Madame," said the first *valet de chambre*, "Monseigneur le Duc d'Enghien has been awakened. He can now receive his Majesty's messenger."

Canolles' eyes, as he looked at Madame de Cambes, said as plainly as his voice could have done:—

"Is this in accordance with our agreement?"

This look, eloquent with the entreaty of a heart in distress, was perfectly understood, and in gratitude, doubtless, for all that Canolles had done,—perhaps in some measure to gratify the love for mischief which is invariably hidden in the depths of the best woman's heart,—

"Bring Monsieur le Duc d'Enghien hither," said Claire; "monsieur will see my son in my presence."

They hastened to obey, and a moment later the young prince was led into the room.

We have seen that, while he was watching every detail of the last preparations for Madame la Princesse's departure, Canolles saw the young prince playing and running about, but did not see his face. He did, however, notice his costume, which was a simple hunting-suit. He thought, therefore, that it could not be in his honor that he was arrayed in the magnificent costume in which he now saw him. His former idea, that the prince had gone with his mother, became almost a certainty; but he gazed at the heir of the illustrious Prince de Condé for some time in silence, and an imperceptible smile played about his lips, although his demeanor was no less respectful than before.

"I am too happy," he said, with a low bow, "to be vouchsafed the honor of presenting my respects to Monseigneur le Duc d'Enghien."

Madame de Cambes, upon whose face the child's great wondering eyes were fixed, motioned to him to bow; and as it seemed to her that the air with which Canolles was following the scene was too scornful by half, she said, with a malicious deliberation which made the baron shudder, "My son, this gentleman is Monsieur de Canolles, sent hither by his Majesty. Give Monsieur de Canolles your hand to kiss."

At that command Pierrot, who had been taken in charge and drilled by Lenet, as he had agreed, put out a hand which he had had neither the time nor the means to transform into a gentleman's hand, and Canolles had no choice but to bestow, amid the stifled laughter of the spectators, a kiss upon that hand, which one less skilled in such matters than he would have had no difficulty in identifying as anything but an aristocratic member.

"Ah! Madame de Cambes!" muttered Canolles, "you shall pay me for that kiss!" And he bowed respectfully to Pierrot in acknowledgment of the honor done him. Realizing that after this trial, which was the last upon the programme, it was impossible for him to remain longer in a woman's bedroom, he turned toward the bed and said: —

"My duties for this evening are fulfilled, and it remains for me to ask your permission to retire."

"Go, monsieur," said Claire; "you see that we are very quiet here, so that nothing need disturb the tranquillity of your slumbers."

"Before I retire I venture to solicit a very great boon, madame."

"What might it be?" asked Madame de Cambes, uneasily, for the baron's tone indicated that he was planning to take revenge upon her.

"To grant me the same favor that I have received from the prince your son."

The viscountess was fairly caught. It was impossible to refuse an officer in the king's service the formal favor he thus solicited in public, and Madame de Cambes extended her trembling hand to Canolles.

He walked toward the bed as he might have walked toward the throne of a queen, took by the ends of the fingers the hand that was held out to him, knelt upon one knee, and imprinted upon the soft, white, trembling flesh a long kiss, which all the bystanders attributed to profound respect, and which the viscountess alone recognized as the equivalent of an ardent loving embrace.

"You promised me, you swore, indeed," said Canolles in an undertone, as he rose, "not to leave the château without informing me. I rely upon your promise and your oath."

"You may rely upon them, monsieur," said Claire, falling back upon her pillow, almost in a swoon.

Canolles, through whose whole being her tone sent a thrill of joy, tried to read in his fair prisoner's eyes confirmation of the hope her tone gave him. But those eyes were hermetically closed.

Canolles reflected that locked caskets are the ones which contain the most precious treasures, and he left the room with paradise in his heart.

To tell how our gentleman passed that night; to tell how his sleep and his waking were one long dream, during which he lived over and over again in his mind all the details of the chimerical adventure which had placed in his keeping the most precious treasure that a miser could ever hide away beneath the wings of his heart; to tell of the plans he devised for making the future subservient to the needs of his love and the whims of his imagination; to set forth the arguments that he used to convince himself that he was doing what he ought, —would be an utter impossibility; for folly is a wearisome thing to any other mind than a fool's.

Canolles fell asleep very late, if the feverish delirium which alternated with his waking moments can be called sleep; and yet the dawn had scarcely whitened the tops of the poplar-trees, and had not descended to the tranquil surface of the lovely ponds, where sleep the water-lilies, whose flowers open only in the sunlight, when he leaped out of bed, and, dressing himself in haste, went down into the garden. His first visit was to the wing occupied by the princess; his first glance at the window of her apartment. Either the princess was not yet asleep, or she was already awake, for a light, too bright to be produced by a mere night-lamp, shone through the closely drawn damask curtains. Canolles stopped short at the sight, which undoubtedly caused a number of insane conjectures to pass through his mind at the same instant, and, abandoning his tour of inspection, he stepped behind the pedestal of a statue which hid him from view; there, alone with his chimera, he began that everlasting dialogue of true lovers, who see the beloved object in all the poetic emanations of nature.

The baron had been at his observatory for half an hour, or thereabout, and was gazing with unspeakable bliss at the curtains which any other than he would have passed indifferently by, when a window upon the gallery opened, and the honest face of Master Pompée appeared in the opening. Everything connected with the viscountess possessed the deepest interest for Canolles; so he turned his gaze away from the seductive curtains, and thought he could detect a desire on Pompée's part to establish communication with him by signs. At first Canolles was not sure that the signs were addressed to him, and looked about to discover if any other person was near; but Pompée, observing his uncertainty, accompanied his motions with a whistle, which would have been a decidedly unseemly method for a squire to adopt to attract the attention of the ambassador of his Majesty the King of France, had it not had an excuse in the shape of a small white object almost imperceptible to any other eyes than those of a lover, who immediately recognized in the white object a folded paper.

"A note!" thought Canolles? "she's writing to me. What does that mean?"

He drew near, trembling with apprehension, although his first sentiment was exceeding joy; but there always is a certain tincture of dread in the great joys of a lover, which is perhaps its chiefest charm: to be sure of one's happiness is to be happy no longer.

As Canolles approached, Pompée ventured to expose the paper more and more, and at last he put out his arm while Canolles held his hat. The two men understood each other to admiration, as we see; the former let the note fall, and the other caught it very skilfully, and then darted into a clump of trees to read it at his leisure, while Pompée, fearful of taking cold, no doubt, quickly closed the window.

But one does not read like that the first note he has ever received from the woman of his choice, especially when there can be no reason for its unforeseen arrival, unless it be to aim a blow at his happiness. For what could the viscountess have to say to him if there had been no change in the programme agreed upon between them the night before? The note therefore must of necessity contain some distressing news.

Canolles was so thoroughly convinced of this that he did not even put the paper to his lips as a lover would ordinarily do in the like circumstances. On the contrary, he turned it over and over with increasing dread. However, it must be opened at some time, so he summoned all his courage, broke the seal, and read as follows:—

"Monsieur,—I hope you will agree with me that to remain longer in our present position is altogether impossible. It must be excessively disagreeable to be looked upon as a detestable spy by the whole household; on the other hand I have reason to fear that, if I receive you more affably than Madame la Princesse would be likely to do in my place, we shall be suspected of playing a comedy, which would inevitably end in the loss of my reputation."

Canolles wiped his brow; his presentiments had not deceived him. With the daylight, the great banisher of visions, all his golden dreams disappeared. He shook his head, heaved a sigh, and read on:—

"Pretend to discover the stratagem to which we resorted; there is a very simple method of making that discovery, and I will myself furnish the materials if you will promise to do as I ask. You see that I do not seek to conceal how much I rely upon you. If you will do as I ask I will send you a portrait of myself, upon which are my crest and my name. You can say that you found it on one of your night rounds, and that you discovered in that way that I am not the princess.

"Need I say that you have my permission, if indeed you attach any value to the portrait, to keep it as a token of my heartfelt, undying gratitude to you, if you take your departure this morning?

"Leave us without seeing me again, if possible, and you will take with you all my gratitude, while I shall always remember you as one of the noblest and most loyal gentlemen I have ever known."

Canolles read the note through once more, and stood as if turned to stone. Whatever favor a letter of dismissal may contain, no matter how sweet the honey in which a farewell or a refusal is clothed, refusal, farewell, dismissal, are none the less cruel to the heart of a lover. The portrait was a lovely thing to have, no doubt about that; but the motive for offering it detracted greatly from its value. And then, of what use is a portrait when the original is at hand, when one holds her fast and need not let her go?

True; but Canolles, who did not hesitate to risk incurring the wrath of the queen and Mazarin, trembled at the thought of Madame de Cambes' frown.

And yet, how the woman had made sport of him, first of all on the road, then at Chantilly, by taking the place of Madame la Princesse, and again, only the night before, by giving him a hope which she snatched away again in the morning! But, of all her deceptions, this was the most heartless. On the road she did not know him, and simply got rid of an inconvenient companion, nothing more. In taking Madame de Condé's place, she obeyed orders, and played the part assigned her by her suzerain, —she could not do otherwise; but this time she did know him, and after she had expressed her appreciation of his self-sacrifice, and had twice uttered that *we* which had touched the deepest chords of his heart, to retrace her steps, disavow her kindly feeling, deny her gratitude, in a word, write such a letter as that, was, in Canolles' sight, worse than cruelty, —it was almost mockery. So he lost his temper, and raged inwardly, heedless of the fact that behind those curtains—the lights having been all extinguished as the daylight rendered them useless—a fair spectator, well hidden by the heavy hangings, looked on at the pantomime of his despair, and shared it perchance.

"Yes, yes," he thought, and accompanied the thought with expressive gestures,—"yes, 't is a dismissal in due form, a commonplace ending to a great event, a poetic hope changed to brutal disappointment. But I will not submit to the ridicule she proposes to heap upon me. I prefer her hatred to this pretended gratitude she prates of. Ah! yes, I imagine myself relying upon her promise now! As well rely upon the constancy of the wind and the tranquillity of the ocean. Ah! madame, madame," he continued, turning toward the window, "you have escaped me twice; but I give you my word that if I ever have another such opportunity you shall not escape me the third time."

With that, Canolles returned to his apartment, intending to dress and gain access to the viscountess, though he were obliged to resort to force. But upon glancing at the clock, he discovered that it was barely seven. No one had yet risen in the château.

Canolles dropped into an arm-chair and closed his eyes, to collect his thoughts, and, if possible, drive away the phantoms that were dancing about him; he opened them again at short intervals to consult his watch.

Eight o'clock struck and the château began to show signs of life. Canolles waited another half-hour with infinite impatience; at last he could contain himself no longer, but went downstairs and accosted Pompée, who was proudly taking the air in the main court-yard, surrounded by lackeys to whom he was describing his campaigns in Picardy under the late king.

"You are her Highness's intendant?" said Canolles, as if he then saw poor Pompée for the first time.

"Yes, monsieur," replied the wondering squire.

"Be good enough to inform her Highness that I crave the honor of paying my respects to her."

"But, monsieur, her Highness—"

"Has arisen."

"But—"

"Go!"

"But I thought that monsieur's departure—"

"My departure will depend upon the interview I propose to have with her Highness."

"I say that because I have no orders from my mistress."

"And I say this," retorted Canolles, "because I have an order from the king."

As he spoke he majestically clapped his hand upon the pocket of his doublet,—a gesture which he adopted as the most satisfactory in its results of all those he had employed since his arrival.

But even as he executed this *coup d'état*, our ambassador felt that his courage was deserting him. In fact, since the preceding night, his importance had greatly diminished. Twelve hours, or very nearly that, had elapsed since Madame la Princesse left Chantilly; doubtless she had travelled all night; she must therefore be twenty or twenty-five leagues away. Let Canolles and his men make what speed they might, they could not hope to overtake her; and if they should overtake her, what assurance was there that the escort of a hundred gentlemen with which she set out was not ere this increased to three or four hundred devoted adherents? To be sure, Canolles might still, as he said the night before, die in the performance of his duty; but had he the right to lead to certain death the men who accompanied him, and thus force them to pay the bloody penalty of his amorous caprice? Madame de Cambes, if he had been in error as to her feeling for him, if her distress was mere comedy,—Madame de Cambes might then openly make sport of him; he would have to endure the jeering of the lackeys and of the soldiers hidden in the forest; the wrath of Mazarin and the queen; and worse than all, his new-born passion would be nipped in the bud, for never did woman love a man whom she designed, though but for an instant, to make ridiculous.

As he was turning these thoughts over and over in his mind, Pompée returned, with lowered crest, to say that his mistress was awaiting him.

On this occasion all ceremony was done away with; the viscountess received him in a small salon adjoining her apartment, fully dressed, and standing. Traces of a sleepless night, which she had tried in vain to efface, were plainly visible upon her charming features. A slight dark circle about her eyes was an especially eloquent indication that those eyes had hardly been closed during the night.

"You see, monsieur," she began, without giving him time to speak, "that I comply with your wish, but in the hope, I confess, that this interview will be the last, and that you will reciprocate by complying with mine."

"Forgive me, madame," said Canolles; "but after what took place between us last evening, I made bold to hope that your demands would be less severe, and I was confident that, after what I had done for you,—for you alone, for I do not know Madame de Condé,—you would deign to endure my further presence at Chantilly."

"Yes, monsieur, I confess that on the impulse of the moment—in the perplexity necessarily consequent upon my present position—the thought of the great sacrifice you were making for me, and the interests of Madame la Princesse, which demanded that I should gain time for her, drew from my lips certain words which accorded but ill with my thought. But during this long night I have reflected; it is out of the question that both of us should remain longer at the château."

"Out of the question, madame!" said Canolles. "Do you forget that everything is possible for him who speaks in the king's name?"

"Monsieur de Canolles, I hope that before all else you are a gentleman, and that you will not take unfair advantage of the position in which my devotion to her Highness has placed me."

"Madame," rejoined Canolles, "before all else I am a madman. *Mon Dieu!* you must have seen it, for no one but a madman could do what I have done. So take pity on my madness, madame; do not send me away, I implore you!"

"Then I will leave the place, monsieur; yes, I will bring you back to your duty, in spite of yourself. We will see if you will resort to force to stop me, if you will expose us both to public scandal. No, no, monsieur," the viscountess continued, in a tone which Canolles had not heard before. "No, you will see upon reflection that you cannot remain forever at Chantilly; you will remember that you are expected elsewhere."

This last phrase cast a bright light upon Canolles' perplexity. It recalled to his mind the scene at Biscarros' inn, and Madame de Cambes' discovery of his liaison with Nanon, and everything was made clear.

This insomnia was caused by memories of the past, not by present anxiety. This determination of the morning, which led her to avoid Canolles, was not the result of reflection, but was a manifestation of jealousy.

For a moment there was silence between them, as they stood there face to face; but during that silence both were listening to the thoughts which whispered with the beating of their hearts.

"Jealous!" Canolles was saying; "jealous! Ah! now I understand it all. Yes, yes, she would make sure that I love her enough to sacrifice all other love! This is a test!"

Meanwhile Madame de Cambes communed thus with herself:—

"I am simply a passing fancy for Monsieur de Canolles. He met me on the road just when he was obliged to leave Guyenne, and followed me as the traveller follows a jack-o'-lantern; but his heart is in that little house among the trees, whither he was going the evening that I met him. It is impossible for me to keep by my side a man who loves another, and whom I might perchance be weak enough to love myself, if I were to be longer in his company. Oh! not only should I betray my honor, but the interests of Madame la Princesse, were I to sink so low as to love the agent of her persecutors."

As if replying to her own thoughts she cried abruptly:—

"No, no, you must go, monsieur: go, or I go!"

"You forget, madame, that I have your promise not to leave the château without informing me of your purpose."

"Very well, monsieur, I now inform you that I propose to leave Chantilly instantly."

"And do you imagine that I will allow it?"

"What!" cried the viscountess; "you will detain me by force?"

"Madame, I know not what I may do, but I do know that it is impossible for me to part from you."

"Then I am your prisoner?"

"You are a woman whom I have already lost twice, and whom I do not propose to lose a third time."

"Aha! violence?"

"Yes, madame, violence," replied Canolles, "if there is no other way to keep you."

"Oh! what extreme felicity," cried Madame de Cambes, "to detain by force a woman who shrieks, who demands her freedom, who does not love you, who detests you!"

Canolles started back, and made a rapid mental effort to distinguish between the words and the thought that prompted them. He realized that the moment had come to stake his all upon a single cast.

"Madame," said he, "the words that you have just uttered, with such evident sincerity that there is no mistaking their meaning, have removed all uncertainty from my mind. You shrieking, you a slave! I detain a woman who does not love me, who detests me! Nay, nay, madame, have no fear; that shall never be. I did think, judging from my own happiness in being with you, that you would perhaps endure my presence; I hoped that, after I had thrown away my reputation, my peace of mind, my future, mayhap my honor, you would reward me for this sacrifice by the gift of a few brief hours, which I am fated never to enjoy. All this might have been had you loved me,—yes, even had I been indifferent to you; for you are kind of heart, and would have done for compassion's sake what another would have done for love. But I find that I have not mere indifference to reckon with, but hatred; that puts a different face upon the matter, as you say. I crave your pardon, madame, for failing to realize that one who loves so madly could be hated in return. It is for you to remain here, queen, mistress, and free in this château as everywhere; it is for me to withdraw, and I withdraw accordingly. In ten minutes you will be fully at liberty once more. Adieu, madame, adieu, forever!"

And Canolles, whose despair, assumed at first, had become quite genuine and distressful toward the close of his address, saluted Madame de Cambes and turned upon his heel, groping blindly for the door, which he could not find, and repeating the word, "Adieu! adieu!" with an accent of such profound melancholy that, coming from the heart, it went straight to the heart. Unfeigned affliction has a voice of its own as truly as the tempest.

Madame de Cambes did not anticipate this unquestioning obedience on the part of Canolles; she had marshalled her forces for a struggle, not for a victory, and her calculations were all set at naught by this combination of humility and love. As the baron was walking toward the door, putting out his arms at random, and giving utterance to something very like a sob, he suddenly felt that a hand was laid upon his shoulder with a most significant pressure; it did not touch him, simply, it stopped him.

He turned his head. She was still standing in front of him. Her arm still rested gracefully upon his shoulder, and the dignified expression which her face wore an instant before had melted away in a lovely smile.

"Well, well, monsieur!" said she, "is this the way you obey the queen? You would go hence when your orders bid you stay, traitor that you are!"

Canolles with a sharp cry fell upon his knees, and pressed his burning brow against the hands she held out to him.

"Oh! I shall die with joy!" he exclaimed.

"Alas! do not be overjoyful yet," said the viscountess; "for my object in stopping you is simply that we might not part thus, that you might not go hence with the idea that I am an ingrate, that you might voluntarily give back the promise I gave you, that you might come to look upon me as a friend, at least, since the fact that we belong to opposite parties will prevent our ever being anything more to each other."

"Oh! *mon Dieu!*" cried Canolles, "am I deceived again? You do not love me?"

"Let us not talk about our sentiments, baron; rather let us talk of the risk we both run by remaining here. Go yourself, or allow me to go; it must be."

"What do you say, madame?"

"The truth. Leave me here; return to Paris; tell Mazarin, tell the queen what has happened. I will assist you to the best of my ability; but go, go!"

"Must I tell you again," cried Canolles, "that to leave you would be death to me?"

"No, no, you will not die, for you will retain the hope that in happier days we shall meet again."

"Chance has thrown me in your way, madame, or, rather, has placed you in my way twice already; but chance will have grown weary in well-doing, and if I leave you now I shall never see you again."

"Then I will seek you out."

"Oh! madame, ask me to die for you; death is an instant's suffering, and all is over. But do not ask me to leave you again. At the bare thought my heart is breaking. Why, consider, pray, that I have hardly seen you, hardly spoken with you."

"Well, then, if I allow you to remain to-day, if you are at liberty to see me and talk to me throughout the day, will you be content? Tell me."

"I make no promises."

"Nor I, if that is so. But, as I did some time since promise to give you due notice of my departure, know that I leave this place an hour hence."

"Must I do whatever you wish? Must I obey you in every point? Must I set aside my own volition and follow yours blindly? If I must do all that, be content. You have before you a slave, ready to obey. Command me, madame, command me."

Claire gave the baron her hand, and said, in her softest and most winning voice:—

"I ask a new promise in exchange for mine; if I do not leave your side from now until nine o'clock this evening, will you go at nine o'clock?"

"I swear it."

"Come, then; the sky is blue and gives promise of a beautiful day; there is dew upon the grass, sweet perfume in the air, and balm among the trees. *Holé! Pompée.*"

The worthy intendant, who had doubtless been instructed to remain outside the door, made his appearance at once.

"My saddle-horses," said Madame de Cambes, assuming her princely expression; "I will ride this morning to the ponds, and return by the farm, where I will breakfast. You will accompany me, Monsieur le Baron," she continued; "it is a part of your duties, as you have received her Majesty's commands never to lose sight of me."

A suffocating cloud of joy blinded the baron, and enveloped him, like the masses of vapor in which the immortal gods of old were carried up to heaven; he went where he was led, unresistingly, almost without volition; he was intoxicated, he was mad. Soon, amid a charming wood, through shadowy avenues, where hanging branches softly swept across his brow, he opened once again his eyes to things of earth. He was on foot, his heart oppressed by pleasure so intense that it was well-nigh pain, his hand in hers, and she as pale, as silent, and as happy, too, as he.

Behind them Pompée stalked along, so near that he could see, so far away that he could not hear.

III

This blissful day came to an end at last, as every dream must do; the hours had passed like seconds to the thrice happy gentleman, and yet it seemed to him as if enough memorable incidents were crowded into that one day to fill three ordinary lives. Every avenue in the park was enriched with the memory of a word or a smile from the viscountess; a look, a gesture, a finger laid upon the lip, everything had its meaning. As they stepped aboard the boat she pressed his hand; when they stepped ashore again she leaned upon his arm; as they walked along by the park wall, she was tired and sat down; and again and again, as a thrill of pleasure swept like a lightning flash before the young man's eyes, the landscape, lighted up by a fantastic gleam, was indelibly imprinted on his mind in its least details.

Canolles was not to leave the viscountess during the day; at breakfast she invited him to dinner, at dinner she invited him to supper.

Amid all the pomp which the pretended princess displayed in her reception of the king's messenger, Canolles could discern the winning attentions of the woman who loves. He forgot the valets, etiquette, the world; he even forgot the promise he had given to take his departure, and fancied himself installed for a blissful eternity in this terrestrial paradise, of which he would be the Adam, and Madame de Cambes the Eve.

But when night fell, when the supper came to an end, after passing off, like all the other incidents of that day, in ineffable bliss, when a maid of honor had duly introduced Monsieur Pierrot, still disguised as the Duc d'Enghien, who seized the opportunity to eat as much as four princes of the blood together would have done, when the clock began to strike, and Madame de Cambes, glancing up at it, made sure that it was about to strike ten times, she said, with a sigh:—

"Now it is time."

"Time for what?" rejoined Canolles, trying to smile, and to ward off a great disaster by a jest.

"Time to keep the promise you gave me."

"Ah! madame," said Canolles, sadly, "you forget nothing, do you?"

"Perhaps I might have forgotten, like yourself; but here is something that refreshes my memory;" and she took from her pocket a letter that was handed her just as they took their seats at the table.

"From whom is that letter?" queried Canolles.

"From Madame la Princesse, who bids me join her."

"I understand that this is a mere pretext! I am grateful to you for showing me such consideration."

"Make no mistake, Monsieur de Canolles," rejoined the viscountess, taking no pains to conceal her sadness. "Had I not received this letter, I should have reminded you of your promise at the proper time, just as I have done now. Do you think that the people about us can much longer avoid detecting the understanding between us? Our relations, you will agree, are not those of a persecuted princess with her persecutor. But if this separation is so painful to you as you pretend, let me tell you, Monsieur le Baron, that it rests with you to make it unnecessary that we should separate."

"Say what you mean! oh, say!" cried Canolles.

"Do you not guess?"

"Yes, madame, I do, indeed; I cannot be mistaken. You mean to suggest that I should espouse the cause of Madame la Princesse."

"She speaks of it herself in this letter," said Madame de Cambes, eagerly.

"I am glad that the idea did not originate with you, and I thank you for the embarrassment with which you broached the subject. Not that my conscience revolts at the thought of following this or that party; no, I have no convictions; indeed, who, save those personally interested, have convictions in this war? When the sword has once left the scabbard, what care I whether the blow comes from one side or another? I do not know the court, nor do I know the princes; with an independent fortune and without ambition, I have no expectations from either party. I am an officer, and that's the end of it."

"In that case you will consent to go with me?"

"No."

"But why not, pray, if things are as you say?"

"Because you would esteem me less."

"Is that the only obstacle?"

"My word for it."

"Then you need have no fear."

"You don't yourself believe what you are saying now," rejoined Canolles, shaking his finger at her with a smile. "A turncoat is the same thing as a traitor; the first word is a little softer, but they are synonymous."

"Ah, well! perhaps you are right," said Madame de Cambes, "and I will urge you no further. If you had been in any ordinary position I would have tried to win you over to the cause of the princes; but as an envoy of the king, intrusted with a confidential mission by her Majesty the queen regent and the first minister of the crown, honored with the good-will of Monsieur le Duc d'Épernon, who, notwithstanding the suspicions I entertained at first, is your very zealous patron, so I am told—"

Canolles blushed.

"I will say no more on that subject, but listen to me, baron; we do not part forever, be sure; I have a presentiment that we shall meet again."

"Where?" asked Canolles.

"I have no idea; but meet again we certainly shall."

Canolles sadly shook his head.

"I dare not count upon it, madame," said he; "there is war between us, and that is too great an obstacle when, at the same time, there is no love."

"Pray, do you count this day as nothing?" asked the viscountess, in a soul-thrilling tone.

"It is the only day that I am sure that I have lived since I came into the world."

"Then you see that you are ungrateful."

"Grant me a second day like this one—"

"I cannot; I must leave Chantilly to-night."

"I don't ask it for to-morrow, nor for the day after to-morrow; I simply ask you for some day in the future. Select whatever time you choose, whatever place you choose, but give me a certainty to live upon; I should suffer too much if I had naught but a hope."

"Where shall you go upon leaving me?"

"To Paris, to report upon the success of my mission."

"And then?"

"To the Bastille, perhaps."

"But assuming that you do not go there?"

"I shall return to Libourne, where my regiment should be."

"And I to Bordeaux, where I expect to find Madame la Princesse. Do you know any out-of-the-way village on the road from Bordeaux to Libourne?"

"I know one, the memory of which is almost as dear to me as that of Chantilly."

"Jaulnay?" queried the viscountess, with a smile.

"Jaulnay," echoed Canolles.

"Very well; I shall need four days to go to Jaulnay; it is now Tuesday. I will stop there all day on Sunday."

"Oh! thanks, thanks!" cried Canolles, pressing against his lips a hand which Madame de Cambes had not the courage to withdraw.

"Now," said she, after a moment's pause, "we must play out our little comedy to the end."

"Ah, yes, madame; the comedy which is to cover me with ridicule in the eyes of all Prance. But I have nothing to say; it was I who would have it so, it was I who—I cannot say selected the part that I play therein—but arranged the catastrophe which brings it to a close."

Madame de Cambes lowered her eyes.

"Now tell me what I have still to do," said Canolles, coolly; "I await your orders, and am ready for anything."

Claire was so deeply moved that Canolles could see the velvet folds of her dress rise and fall with the uneven, hurried beating of her heart.

"You are making a very great sacrifice for me, I know; but pray believe me when I say that my gratitude will live forever. Yes, you are about to incur disgrace at court for my sake, and to be severely censured. Monsieur, care nothing for that, I beg you, if it affords you any pleasure to know that you have made me happy."

"I will try, madame."

"Believe me, baron," continued Madame de Cambes, "the bitter grief which I read upon your face causes me no less bitter remorse. It may be that others would recompense you more fully than I; but, monsieur, a recompense accorded so readily would not worthily pay for your self-sacrifice."

As she spoke, Claire hung her head with a sigh.

"Is that all you have to say to me?"

"Stay," said the viscountess, taking from her breast a portrait which she handed to Canolles; "take this portrait, and at every pang that this unhappy affair causes you, look at it, and say to yourself that you suffer for her whose image is before you, and that every such pang is paid for in regret."

"Is that all?"

"In esteem."

"Is that all?"

"In sympathy."

"Ah! madame, one word more!" cried Canolles. "Why should it cost you so dear to make me altogether happy?"

Claire stepped quickly toward him, put out her hand, and opened her mouth to add:—

"In love."

But simultaneously with her mouth, the door was thrown open and the pseudo-captain of the guards appeared upon the threshold, accompanied by Pompée.

"I will finish at Jaulnay," said the viscountess.

"Your sentence, or your thought?"

"Both; one always expresses the other."

"Madame," said the captain of the guards, "your Highness's carriage is waiting."

"Feign astonishment," said Claire, in an undertone.

"Where does your Highness propose to go?" he asked, with a smile of pity for his own plight.

"I am going away."

"But does your Highness forget that I am instructed by her Majesty not to leave you for an instant?"

"Monsieur, your mission is at an end."

"What does this mean?"

"That I am not her Highness, Madame la Princesse de Condé, but Madame la Vicomtesse de Cambes, her first maid of honor. Madame la Princesse left Chantilly last evening, and I go to join her."

Canolles did not stir. It was plainly most distasteful to him to continue to play this comedy before an audience of lackeys.

Madame de Cambes, to encourage him, bestowed one of her sweetest glances upon him; that glance restored his courage in some measure.

"So the king has been deceived," he said. "And where is Monsieur le Duc d'Enghien?"

"I have given orders that Pierrot return to his flower-beds," said a grave voice at the door.

It was the voice of the princess dowager, who was standing near the door, supported by two of her tire-women.

"Return to Paris, to Mantes, to the court, in a word, wherever it may be; your mission here is at an end. You will say to the king that the persecuted have resorted to stratagem, which renders fruitless the use of force. You are at liberty, however, to remain at Chantilly, to stand guard over me, who have not left, and shall not leave the château, because such is not my design. With this, Monsieur le Baron, I take my leave of you."

Canolles, red with shame, could hardly summon strength to bend his head, as he glanced at the viscountess, and murmured reproachfully:—

"O, madame! madame!"

She understood the glance and heard the words.

"I crave your Highness's permission," she said, "to play the part of Madame la Princesse one moment more. I desire to thank Monsieur le Baron de Canolles, in the name of his illustrious hosts who have left this château, for the respect he has shown, and the great delicacy he has exhibited in the performance of so difficult a mission. I venture to believe, madame, that your Highness has the same opinion, and to hope, therefore, that you will add your acknowledgments to mine."

The dowager was touched by these earnest words, and it may be that her profound sagacity suggested to her some part of this new secret grafted upon the old; so it was that her voice was not entirely free from emotion as she uttered the following words:—

"For all that you have done against us, monsieur, oblivion; for all that you have done for my family, gratitude."

Canolles knelt upon one knee at the feet of the princess, who gave him that hand to kiss whereon Henri IV. had imprinted so many kisses.

It was the last act of the play, it was an irrevocable dismissal. There was nothing left for Canolles to do but to take his leave. And so he withdrew to his apartment, and lost no time in writing to Mazarin the most despairing report imaginable; he preferred not to be present to suffer the consequences of the first outburst of anger. That done he passed out through the servants of the château, with some apprehension that he might be insulted by them, to the court-yard, where his horse awaited him.

As he was about to put his foot in the stirrup, these words were uttered by an imperious voice:—

"Do honor to the envoy of his Majesty, the king, our master!"

Thereupon every head was bent before Canolles, who, with a low bow toward the window at which the princess was standing, drove his spurs into his horse, and disappeared, with head erect.

Castorin, awakened from the seductive dream which he owed to Pompée, the false intendant, followed his master with lowered crest.

IV

It is full time to return to one of the most important personages of this narrative, whom we shall find riding an excellent horse along the road from Paris to Bordeaux, with five companions, whose eyes sparkled at every sound that came from a bag filled with gold crowns, hanging at Ferguzon's saddle-bow. The melody rejoiced and refreshed the little troop, as the music of the drum and fife imparts renewed life to the soldier on the march.

"Never mind, never mind," one of the men was saying; "ten thousand livres is a pretty little sum."

"You might say," rejoined Ferguzon, "that it is a magnificent sum, if it owed nothing to anybody; but it owes a company to Madame la Princesse. *Nimium satis est*, as the ancients used to say; which may be translated thus: 'Nothing less than too much is enough. Now, my dear Barrabas, we haven't that desirable *enough* which is equivalent to *too much*."

"How much it costs to appear to be an honest man!" said Cauvignac; "all that we took from the royal tax-gatherer has gone into equipments, doublets, and trimming. We cut as fine a figure as any nobleman, and we carry luxury so far as to have purses; to be sure, there's nothing in them. Oh, appearances!"

"Speak for us, captain, and not for yourself," said Barrabas. "You have the purse and ten thousand livres to boot."

"My good fellow," said Cauvignac, "did you not hear, or did you misunderstand what Ferguzon just said touching our obligation to Madame la Princesse? I am not of those who promise one thing and do another. Monsieur Lenet paid over ten thousand livres to me to raise a company, and if I don't raise it may the devil fly away with me! On the day when it is raised he will owe me forty thousand more. When that time comes, if he doesn't pay the forty thousand livres we will see."

"With ten thousand livres!" cried four satirical voices in chorus; for Ferguzon, whose confidence in his leader's resources was unbounded, seemed to be the only one of the troop convinced that Cauvignac would attain the promised result; "with ten thousand livres you will raise a company?"

"Yes," said Cauvignac, "when some one thinks fit to add something to it."

"Who is there, pray, to add anything to it?" asked a voice.

"Not I," said Ferguzon.

"Who, then?" Barrabas asked.

"*Pardieu!* the first comer. Stay, I see a man yonder on the road. You will see—"

"I understand," said Ferguzon.

"Is that all?" queried Cauvignac.

"And admire."

"Yes," said one of the horsemen, drawing nigh Cauvignac, "yes, I understand that you can always be depended on to keep your promises, captain; but we may lose by being too honest. To-day we are necessary; but if the company is raised to-morrow, officers in the confidence of the princes will be assigned to it, and we, who have had all the trouble of raising it, shall be dismissed."

"You are an idiot, in five letters, my dear Carrotel, and this isn't the first time I have told you so," said Cauvignac. "The pitiful logic you have just perpetrated deprives you of the rank I proposed to give you in the company; for it is evident that we shall be the six officers of this nucleus of an army. I should have appointed you sub-lieutenant at the outset, Carrotel; now you will be only a sergeant. Thanks to the nonsense you just heard, Barrabas, you, who have held your tongue, will hold that position until, Ferguzon having been hanged, you are promoted to the lieutenancy by right of seniority. But let us not lose sight of my first recruit, whom I see yonder."

"Have you any idea who the man is, captain?" Ferguzon asked.

"Not the slightest."

"He should be a tradesman; he wears a black cloak."

"Are you sure?"

"Look when the wind raises it; do you see?"

"If he wears a black cloak, he's a wealthy citizen; so much the better. We are recruiting for the service of the princes, and it is important that the company should be made up of good men. If it were for that wretch of a Mazarin, anything would be good enough; but for the princes, deuce take me!—Ferguzon, I have an idea that my company will do me honor, as Falstaff says."

The whole troop spurred forward to overtake the citizen, who was riding peaceably along in the middle of the road.

When the worthy man, who was mounted upon a sleek mule, observed the magnificently arrayed horsemen galloping up behind him, he rode off to the side of the road with due respect, and saluted Cauvignac.

"He is well-mannered," said that worthy; "that's a great point. "He doesn't know the military salute, but we will teach him that."

He returned the salute, then rode up beside the traveller.

"Monsieur," he began, "be good enough to tell us if you love the king."

"*Parbleu!* yes," was the reply.

"Admirable!" said Cauvignac, rolling his eyes in delight. "And the queen?"

"The queen! I have the greatest veneration for her."

"Excellent! and Monsieur de Mazarin?"

"Monsieur de Mazarin is a great man, monsieur, and I admire him."

"Perfect! In that case, we have had the good fortune to fall in with a faithful servitor of his Majesty?"

"I pride myself upon it, monsieur."

"And are prepared to prove your zeal for him?"

"On every occasion."

"How luckily this comes about! such meetings as this never happen except on the high-road."

"What do you mean?" queried the tradesman, beginning to eye Cauvignac with some uneasiness.

"I mean, monsieur, that you must come with us."

The tradesman almost leaped out of his saddle in surprise and terror.

"Go with you! Whither, monsieur, in God's name?"

"I am not altogether sure, myself; wherever we go."

"Monsieur, I travel only with people whom I know."

"That is quite right, and shows you to be a prudent man; so I will proceed to tell you who we are."

The tradesman made a gesture, as if to say that he had already guessed. Cauvignac continued, without seeming to notice the gesture:—

"I am Roland de Cauvignac, captain of a company, which is not present, it is true, but is worthily represented by Louis-Gabriel Ferguzon, my lieutenant, by Georges-Guillaume Barrabas, my sub-lieutenant, by Zéphérin Carrotel, my sergeant, and by these two gentlemen, one of whom is my quartermaster and the other my sergeant-major. You know us now, monsieur," continued Cauvignac, with his most benign smile, "and I venture to hope that you feel no antipathy for us."

"But, monsieur, I have already served his Majesty in the urban guard, and I pay my taxes, tithes, and so forth, regularly."

"Very good, monsieur," rejoined Cauvignac; "and I do not propose to enlist you in his Majesty's service, but in that of Messieurs les Princes, whose unworthy representative you see before you."

"In the service of the princes, the king's enemies!" cried the honest fellow, more and more amazed; "then why did you ask me if I loved his Majesty?"

"Because, monsieur, if you did not love the king, if you had accused the queen or blasphemed against Monsieur de Mazarin, I should not have dreamed of disturbing you; in that case you would have been sacred to me as a brother."

"But, monsieur, I am not a slave; I am not a serf."

"No, monsieur, you are a soldier; that is to say, you have it in your power to become a captain like myself, or a marshal of France like Monsieur de Turenne."

"Monsieur, I have had a large amount of experience of courts in my life."

"Ah! so much the worse, monsieur, so much the worse! it's a wretched habit to get into, this going to law. I never did any of it myself; it may have been because I studied for the bar."

"But by having so many lawsuits I have learned the laws of the kingdom."

"There are great numbers of them. You know, monsieur, that from the *Pandects* of Justinian down to the decree of Parliament, which provided, apropos of the death of Maréchal d'Ancre, that no foreigner should ever be first minister of France, there have been eighteen thousand seven hundred and seventy-two laws, to say nothing of ordinances; but there are privileged brains which have an astounding memory; Pico della Mirandole spoke twelve languages at eighteen. What good has your knowledge of these laws ever done you, monsieur?"

"The good of knowing that people are not to be kidnapped on the high-road without warrant."

"I have such warrant, monsieur, and here it is."

"From Madame la Princesse?"

"From her Highness in person."

And Cauvignac respectfully raised his hat.

"Then there are two kings in France?" cried the tradesman.

"Even so, monsieur; that is why I do myself the honor of asking you to accord your preference to mine, and why I deem it my duty to enlist you in my service."

"Monsieur, I will appeal to the Parliament."

"There's a third king, and you will probably have occasion to serve it as well. Our politics are built upon broad lines! Forward, monsieur!"

"But it's impossible, monsieur; I have an appointment upon important business."

"Where?"

"At Orléans."

"With whom?"

"My attorney."

"What is the business?"

"It concerns certain financial transactions."

"The service of the State should be every man's first business, monsieur."

"Can't the State do without me?"

"We relied upon you, and we should miss you, in good sooth! However, if, as you say, money matters occasion your visit to Orléans—"

"Yes, monsieur, money matters."

"How much money is concerned?"

"Four thousand livres."

"Which you are going to receive?"

"No, which I am going to pay."

"To your attorney?"

"Even so, monsieur."

"On account of a lawsuit?"

"On account of a lawsuit lost."

"'Pon my word, this deserves consideration. Four thousand livres!"

"Four thousand livres."

"That is just the sum you would pay out in case Messieurs les Princes would consent that your place should be filled by a mercenary."

"Nonsense! I could procure a substitute for a hundred crowns."

"A substitute of your commanding appearance, a substitute who rides muleback with his toes turned out like you, a substitute who knows eighteen thousand seven hundred and seventy-two laws! Go to, monsieur! for an ordinary man a hundred crowns would certainly be enough; but if we are to be content with ordinary men, it's not worth while to enter into competition with the king. We need men of your merit, of your rank, of your stature. What the devil! don't cry yourself down; it seems to me that you are worth fully four thousand livres!"

"I see what you are coming at," cried the tradesman; "this is downright robbery with force and arms."

"Monsieur, you insult us," said Cauvignac, "and we would flay you alive by way of reparation for the insult, if we were less anxious to maintain the reputation of the adherents of the princes. No, monsieur; give me your four thousand livres, but do not look upon it as extortion, I beg; it is a necessity."

"Who will pay my attorney?"

"We will."

"You?"

"We."

"But will you bring me a receipt?"

"In due form."

"Signed by him?"

"Signed by him."

"That puts a different face on the matter."

"As you see. So you accept?"

"I must, as I can't do otherwise."

"Give us your attorney's address, then, and such other information as we can't do without."

"I told you that it was a judgment resulting from the loss of a lawsuit."

"Against whom?"

"Against a certain Biscarros, claimant, as heir of his wife, who was a native of Orléans."

"Attention!" said Ferguzon.

Cauvignac winked at him as if to say "Never fear, I am on the watch."

"Biscarros," he repeated; "isn't he an inn-keeper in the outskirts of Libourne?"

"Just so,—between Libourne and Saint-Martin-de-Cubzac."

"At the sign of the Golden Calf?"

"The same. Do you know him?"

"A little."

"The villain! to get judgment against me for a sum—"

"Which you didn't owe him?"

"Oh! yes. I owed it—but I hoped never to pay it."

"I understand; it's very hard."

"For that reason, I give you my word that I would much rather see the money in your hands than in his."

"If that is so, I think you will be content."

"But my receipt?"

"Come with us, and you shall have it in due form."

"How will you go to work to get it?"

"That's my affair."

They pursued their journey toward Orléans, where they arrived two hours later. The tradesman conducted his captors to the inn nearest his attorney's office. It was a frightful den, with the appropriate name of the Dove of the Ark.

"Now," said he, "what are we to do? I would be very glad not to part from my four thousand livres except as against a receipt."

"Don't let that disturb you. Do you know your attorney's handwriting?"

"Perfectly."

"When we bring you his receipt, you will make no objection to handing the money over to us?"

"None! But my attorney will never give his receipt without the money; I know him too well."

"I will advance the sum," said Cauvignac. As he spoke he took from his wallet four thousand livres, half in louis, and the rest in half-pistoles, and arranged them in piles before the wondering eyes of the tradesman.

"Now," said he, "tell us your attorney's name."

"Master Rabodin."

"Very good; take a pen and write."

The tradesman obeyed.

> "MASTER RABODIN,—I send you the four thousand livres, damages and costs due upon the judgment in favor of Master Biscarros, whom I strongly suspect of a purpose to make an improper use of it. Be kind enough to hand the bearer your receipt—"

"What next?" queried the tradesman.

"Date and sign it."

The tradesman did as he was bid.

"Now," said Cauvignac to Ferguzon, "take this letter and money, disguise yourself as a miller, and call upon the attorney."

"What shall I do there?"

"Give him the money and take his receipt."

"Is that all?"

"That's all."

"I don't understand."

"So much the better! the errand will be done all the better for that."

Ferguzon's confidence in his captain was unbounded, so he walked toward the door without another word.

"Order up some wine, and of the best," said Cauvignac; "monsieur must be thirsty."

Ferguzon bowed and went out. Within the half-hour he returned, and found Cauvignac at table with the tradesman, both doing honor to that famous Orléans wine which rejoiced the Gascon palate of Henri IV.

"Well?" said Cauvignac, inquiringly.

"Here is the receipt."

"Is that what you desire?"

And Cauvignac passed the piece of stamped paper to the tradesman.

"Precisely."

"Is the receipt in proper form?"

"It is."

"Then you have no objection to giving me your money in exchange for it?"

"None at all."

"Give it me, then."

The tradesman counted out the four thousand livres. Cauvignac placed them in his bag, where they replaced the four thousand recently taken therefrom.

"And now my release is paid for, is it?"

"*Mon Dieu*, yes, unless you absolutely insist upon serving."

"No, not personally; but—"

"But what? Let us hear," said Cauvignac. "I have a presentiment that we sha'n't part until we have done some more business together."

"It is very possible," said the tradesman, whose serenity was completely restored the instant the receipt was in his hands. "I have a nephew—"

"Aha!"

"A stubborn, troublesome fellow."

"Of whom you would gladly be rid?"

"No, not just that; but who would make an excellent soldier, I am sure."

"Send him to me, and I'll make a hero of him."

"You will take charge of him?"

"With pleasure."

"I have also a godson, a deserving lad, who is anxious to take orders, and for whom I am obliged to pay heavily for board."

"So that you would prefer that he should take the musket, eh? Send me the godson and the nephew; it will cost you only five hundred livres for the two."

"Five hundred livres! I don't understand."

"Why, of course, they have to pay on entering the company."

"Then why did you make me pay for the privilege of not entering it?"

"There were special reasons for that. Your nephew and your godson will pay two hundred and fifty livres each, and you will never hear of them again."

"The devil! that's an alluring prospect, do you know? They will be well cared for?"

"I give you my word that when they have once tasted service under my orders, they wouldn't change places with the Emperor of China. Ask these good fellows how I keep them. Tell him, Barrabas; tell him, Carrotel."

"In truth," said Barrabas, "we live like lords."

"And how are they clothed? Look for yourself."

Carrotel executed a pirouette in order to exhibit his resplendent costume from every point of view.

"Certainly there is nothing to be said in the matter of equipment," said the tradesman.

"So you will send me your two youths?"

"I am very anxious to do so. Do you make a long stay here?"

"No, we shall leave to-morrow morning; but we will go slowly so that they may overtake us. Give us the five hundred livres and the bargain's made."

"I have only two hundred and fifty."

"Give them the other two hundred and fifty; indeed that will furnish you with an excuse for sending them to me; if you had no pretext for sending them they might suspect something."

"But they may say that one of them alone can do the errand."

"You must tell them that the roads are not safe, and give them each twenty-five livres; that will be by way of advance on their pay."

The tradesman stared at him in wondering admiration.

"Upon my word," said he, "it takes a soldier to find a way out of every difficulty!"

Having counted out the two hundred and fifty livres to Cauvignac, he withdrew, overjoyed to have found an opportunity to be rid, for five hundred livres, of a nephew and godson who cost him more than two hundred pistoles a year.

V

"Now, Master Barrabas," said Cauvignac, "have you in your valise a coat something less elegant than the one you are wearing,—one in which you might pass for an employee of the custom-house?"

"I have the tax-collector's coat, you know, that we—"

"Very good! and you have his commission, too, no doubt?"

"Lieutenant Ferguzon bade me not lose it, and I have taken great care of it."

"Lieutenant Ferguzon is the most farseeing man of my acquaintance. Array yourself as a tax-collector and take the commission with you."

Barrabas went out, and returned ten minutes later, completely transformed.

He found Cauvignac dressed wholly in black, and looking enough like a court officer to deceive anybody.

They went together to the attorney's quarters. Master Rabodin lived in a third-floor apartment, consisting of a reception-room, an office, and a closet. There were other rooms, no doubt, but as they were not open to clients we will say nothing about them.

Cauvignac passed through the reception-room, left Barrabas in the study, cast a sympathetic glance in passing at the two clerks who were pretending to write busily while playing at *marelle*, and entered the *sanctum sanctorum*.

Master Rabodin was sitting in front of a desk so laden with papers that the respectable attorney seemed to be literally buried up in writs and records and judgments. He was a tall, gaunt, sallow man, clad in a black coat which fitted as closely to his body as an eel's skin. When he heard Cauvignac's footsteps, he straightened up his long, bent backbone, and raised his head, which then appeared above the breastwork by which he was surrounded.

For an instant Cauvignac thought that he had discovered the basilisk, an animal regarded as fabulous by modern scientists, so brightly did the attorney's little eyes shine with the ominous glitter of avarice and cupidity.

"Monsieur," said Cauvignac, "I ask your pardon for calling upon you without previous appointment; but," he added with his most charming smile, "it is a privilege of my office."

"A privilege of your office!" exclaimed Master Rabodin. "What is your office, pray?"

"I am an exempt in his Majesty's service, monsieur."

"An exempt in his Majesty's service?"

"I have that honor."

"I do not understand, monsieur."

"You will understand in a moment. You know Monsieur Biscarros, do you not?"

"Certainly I know him; he is my client."

"What do you think of him?"

"What do I think of him?"

"Yes."

"Why, I think—I think—I think that he's a very worthy man."

"Well, monsieur, you are mistaken."

"What's that?—mistaken?"

"Your worthy man is a rebel."

"A rebel?"

"Yes, monsieur, a rebel, who takes advantage of the isolated situation of his inn to make it a hotbed of conspiracy."

"God bless my soul!"

"Who has bound himself to poison the king, the queen, and Monsieur de Mazarin, if they happen to put up at his inn."

"You don't mean it!"

"And whom I have arrested and taken to the prison at Libourne, on a charge of *lèse-majesté.*"

"Monsieur, you horrify me," said Master Rabodin, falling back in his chair.

"That is not all, monsieur," continued the false exempt; "you, also, are involved in the affair."

"I, monsieur!" cried the attorney, turning from orange-yellow to apple-green; "I involved in it! how, in God's name?"

"You have in your possession a sum of money which the villain Biscarros destined for the payment of an army of rebels."

"It is true, monsieur, that I have received for him—"

"Four thousand livres! he was subjected to the torture of the *brodequins*, and at the eighth wedge he admitted that you had that sum."

"I have it, monsieur, but I have had it only an instant."

"So much the worse, monsieur, so much the worse!"

"Why so much the worse?"

"Because I shall be obliged to make sure of your person."

"Of my person?"

"Certainly; the complaint names you as accomplice."

The attorney turned from apple-green to bottle-green.

"Ah! if you hadn't received that sum," continued Cauvignac, "it would be a different matter; but you admit having received it, and that is against you, you see."

"Monsieur, suppose I agree to give it up; suppose I hand it to you instantly; suppose I make oath that I have no connection with this villain Biscarros?"

"You would lie under grave suspicion none the less. However, I think I may say that immediate surrender of the money—"

"Monsieur, I will give it to you this very moment!" cried Master Rabodin. "It is still there, in the bag in which it was handed to me. I have verified the amount, and that's all."

"Is it exact?"

"Count it yourself, monsieur, count it yourself."

"Nay, monsieur, by your leave, nay; for I am not empowered to touch his Majesty's money; but I have with me the tax-collector of Libourne, who was assigned to accompany me in order to take charge of the different sums which Biscarros scattered broadcast to be collected again at need."

"It is a fact that he was very urgent that I should send the four thousand livres to him the moment that I received them."

"You see! Doubtless he is already informed that Madame la Princesse has left Chantilly, and is on her way to Bordeaux, and is getting together all his resources in order to make himself prominent among her adherents."

"The wretch!"

"And you suspected nothing?"

"Nothing, monsieur, nothing."

"Had nobody warned you?"

"Nobody."

"What's that you say?" said Cauvignac, pointing to the tradesman's letter which lay open on Master Rabodin's desk, with a number of other papers. "How dare you say that when you yourself furnish me with proof to the contrary?"

"Proof?"

"Damnation! read."

Rabodin read, in a trembling voice: —

> "I Master Rabodin, — I send you the four thousand livres damages and costs due upon the judgment in favor of Master Biscarros, whom I strongly suspect of a purpose to make an improper use of it.'"

"An improper use!" Cauvignac repeated. "You see that your client's unsavory reputation has reached as far as this."

"Monsieur, I am overwhelmed," said the attorney.

"I cannot conceal from you, monsieur," said Cauvignac, "that my orders are strict."

"Monsieur, I swear that I am innocent."

"*Pardieu!* Biscarros said the same until he was put to the question; but at the fifth wedge he changed his tone."

"I tell you, monsieur, that I am ready to hand you the money. Here it is; take it, for it burns my hands."

"Let us do things regularly," said Cauvignac. "I have already told you that it's no part of my business to handle the king's money."

He walked to the door leading to the office.

"Come in, Monsieur le Receveur," said he; "each to his own duty."

Barrabas came forward.

"Monsieur admits everything," said Cauvignac.

"What's that? — I admit everything?" cried the attorney.

"Yes, you admit that you were in correspondence with Biscarros."

"Monsieur, I have never received more than two letters from him, and I have written him only one."

"Monsieur admits that he was in possession of funds belonging to the accused."

"Here they are, monsieur. I have never received any money for him except these four thousand livres, and I am ready to hand them to you."

"Monsieur le Receveur," said Cauvignac, "as your commission authorizes you to do, take this money and give a receipt in his Majesty's name."

Barrabas handed his commission to the attorney, who pushed it away with his hand, not choosing to insult him by reading it.

"Now," said Cauvignac, while Barrabas, for fear of an error, was counting the money, "now you must come with me."

"I must go with you?"

"Certainly; didn't I tell you that you are under suspicion?"

"But, monsieur, I swear to you that his Majesty has no more faithful servitor than myself."

"It's not enough to swear to it, you must furnish proofs."

"Very well, monsieur, I will furnish proofs."

"Let's see them."

"My whole past life."

"That's not enough; we require a guaranty for the future."

"Point out to me what I can do, and I will do it."

"There is one infallible way of proving your devotion."

"What is that?"

"There is one of my friends, a captain, in Orléans at this moment, raising a company for the king."

"Well?"

"It would be well done of you to enlist in his company."

"I, monsieur!—an attorney?"

"The king is sorely in need of attorneys, monsieur, for his affairs are terribly involved."

"I would do it willingly, monsieur; but what about my office?"

"You can leave it to be run by your clerks."

"Impossible! How could they arrange to procure my signature?"

"Pardon, messieurs, if I venture to say a word," said Barrabas.

"Most assuredly!" said the attorney; "say on, monsieur, say on."

"It seems to me that if monsieur, who would make but a sorry soldier—"

"Yes, monsieur, you are right; sorry, indeed," interposed the attorney.

"If monsieur would offer your friend, or the king, in his stead—"

"What, monsieur? what can I offer the king?"

"His two clerks."

"Why, certainly!" cried the attorney; "certainly, and with great pleasure. Let your friend take them both. I give them to him; they are two delightful fellows."

"One of them seemed a mere child."

"Fifteen, monsieur; he's fifteen; and a first-class performer on the drum.—Fricotin, step this way," he shouted.

Cauvignac made a gesture with his hand, indicating that he desired Monsieur Fricotin to be left where he was.

"What of the other?" he asked.

"Eighteen, monsieur; five feet six inches tall, aspiring to become a porter at Saint-Sauveur, and, consequently, already familiar with the mode of handling a halberd.—This way, Chalumeau."

"But he squints horribly, unless I am much mistaken," said Cauvignac, making a second gesture similar to the first.

"So much the better, monsieur; so much the better! You can make him do sentry duty; and as he squints out, he can see both to right and left, while an ordinary man can only see straight ahead."

"That's an advantage, I agree; but you understand that the king is in sore straits financially; pleading with cannon-balls is much more costly than pleading with words. The king cannot burden himself with the equipment of these two youngsters; it's quite all he can do to undertake to train and pay them."

"Monsieur," said Rabodin, "if that is all that is necessary to prove my devotion to the king—why, I will make the sacrifice."

Cauvignac and Barrabas looked at each other.

"What do you think, Monsieur le Receveur?" said Cauvignac.

"I think that monsieur seems to be acting in good faith," Barrabas replied.

"And that we must be considerate with him, eh? Give monsieur a receipt for five hundred livres."

"Five hundred livres!"

"A receipt for that sum to pay for the equipment of two young soldiers, whom Master Rabodin in his zeal offers his Majesty."

"May I expect to be left at peace in consideration of this sacrifice, monsieur?"

"I think so."

"Shall I not be molested?"

"I hope not."

"And suppose that I am prosecuted, without regard to justice?"

"You are at liberty to make use of my testimony. But will your two clerks consent?"

"They will be overjoyed."

"You are sure of it?"

"Yes. But it would be best not to tell them—"

"Of the honor in store for them, eh?"

"It would be more prudent."

"What are we to do, then?"

"Oh! it's a simple matter enough. I will send them to your friend. What is his name?"

"Captain Cauvignac."

"I will send them to your friend Captain Cauvignac, upon some pretext or other; it had better be somewhere outside of Orléans, to avoid a possible scandal."

"Yes, and so that the Orléanais may not be seized with the desire to scourge you with rods, as Camillus did the schoolmaster in ancient times."

"I will send them to him, then, outside the city."

"On the high-road from Orléans to Tours, for example."

"At the first public-house."

"Yes; they will find Captain Cauvignac at table. He will offer them a glass of wine and they will accept. He will propose the king's health, which they will drink with enthusiasm, and there they are soldiers! Now you may call them."

The attorney called the young men. Fricotin was a little fellow, hardly four feet tall, thick-set, quick and active; Chalumeau was a great booby of five feet six, thin as an asparagus-stalk, and red as a carrot.

"Messieurs," said Cauvignac, "Master Rabodin here proposes to show his confidence in you by sending you upon an errand of importance. To-morrow morning you will go to the first inn outside the city on the Tours road, to fetch a package of papers relating to the suit of Captain Cauvignac against Monsieur de La Rochefoucauld. Master Rabodin will give you twenty-five livres each for the service."

Fricotin, who was a credulous youth, leaped three feet into the air. But Chalumeau, who was by nature suspicious, looked at Cauvignac and the attorney at the same moment, with an expression of doubt which made him squint three times as badly as usual.

"Stay, stay!" exclaimed Master Rabodin; "one moment. I didn't agree to pay the fifty livres."

"Which sum," continued the false exempt, "Master Rabodin will recoup in his fees in the suit between Captain Cauvignac and Monsieur le Duc de La Rochefoucauld."

Master Rabodin hung his head; he was fairly caught. He must go through the door that was pointed out to him, or else through the door of a prison.

"Very good," said he. "I consent; but I hope you will give me a receipt for all this."

"Look at this," said Barrabas, "and see if I haven't anticipated your desire;" and he handed him a paper on which these words were written:—

"Received from Master Rabodin, his Majesty's faithful subject, the sum of five hundred livres, as a voluntary offering, to assist him in his war against the princes."

"If you insist," said Barrabas, "I will put the two clerks in the receipt."

"No, no," said the attorney, hastily; "it's quite right as it is."

"By the way," said Cauvignac, "tell Fricotin to bring his drum, and Chalumeau his halberd; it will be so much less to buy."

"But on what pretext shall I tell them to do that?"

"*Pardieu!* as a means of amusing themselves on the road."

With that the pretended exempt and pretended collector took their departure, leaving Master Rabodin bewildered at the thought of the danger he had escaped, and only too happy to have come so well out of it.

VI

The next morning everything passed off as Cauvignac had planned. The nephew and godson were the first to arrive, both mounted on the same horse; then came Fricotin and Chalumeau, one with his drum, the other with his halberd. There was some little opposition to be overcome when it was explained to them that they had the honor of being enrolled in the service of the princes; but all opposition vanished before the threats of Cauvignac, the promises of Ferguzon, and the logic of Barrabas.

The horse of the nephew and godson was assigned to the duty of carrying the baggage, and as Cauvignac's commission authorized him to raise a company of infantry, the two raw recruits could say nothing.

They set out at once. Cauvignac's march resembled a triumph. The ingenious freebooter had found a way to bring into the war the most persistent advocates of peace. Some he induced to embrace the cause of the king, others the cause of the princes. Some believed they were enlisting in the service of the Parliament, others in that of the King of England, who was talking of a descent upon Scotland to attempt the conquest of his dominions. There was naturally, at first, some little lack of uniformity in the colors, some discord in the sentiments of the troops, whom Lieutenant Ferguzon, despite his persuasive powers, found it difficult to reduce to the level of passive obedience. However, by resorting constantly to secrecy and mystery, which were necessary, so Cauvignac said, to the success of the operation, they were induced to go forward, soldiers and officers alike, without knowing where they were going, or what they were to do.

Four days after leaving Chantilly Cauvignac had collected twenty-five men; a very pretty little nucleus of an army. Many rivers which make a great noise when they flow into the sea, have a less imposing origin.

Cauvignac was in search of a convenient centre of operations. He reached a little village between Châtellerault and Poitiers, which seemed to suit his purposes. It was the village of Jaulnay. Cauvignac recognized it as the place where he had delivered an order to Canolles on a certain evening, and he established his headquarters there at the inn, where he remembered that he had supped very comfortably on the evening in question. As to that, he had no choice, for, as we have said before, it was the only inn in the place.

Thus established, on the principal highway from Paris to Bordeaux, Cauvignac had behind him the troops of Monsieur de La Rochefoucauld, who was besieging Saumur, and before him those of the king, who were concentrated in Guyenne. Holding out a hand to either, and abstaining from hoisting any colors whatsoever until the proper time, he set about collecting a hundred men, with whom at his back he might make the most of his opportunities. Recruiting went merrily forward, and in a very short time his task was well-nigh half done.

One day, having passed the whole morning in hunting men, he was standing, as usual, on the watch, at the door of the inn, talking with his lieutenant and sub-lieutenant, when he spied a young lady on horseback at the end of the village street, followed by a squire, also on horseback, and two mules laden with trunks.

The ease with which the fair Amazon handled her steed, and the stiff, haughty bearing of the squire, awakened a slumbering memory in Cauvignac's mind. He laid his hand upon Ferguzon's arm,—his lieutenant was indisposed that day, and his manner was somewhat dejected,—and said, pointing to the traveller:—

"There's the fiftieth soldier of the Cauvignac regiment, or I'm damned!"

"Who? that young lady?"

"Precisely."

"Nonsense! we already have a nephew who was to be an advocate, a godson who was to be a priest, two attorney's clerks, two druggists, a doctor, three bakers, two country bumpkins; that's enough of that kind of soldiers, God knows! without adding a woman to them; for some day or other we shall have to fight."

"Very true; but our cash only amounts to twenty-five thousand livres" (it appears that the cash as well as the troop had taken pattern by the snowball), "and if we could reach a good round figure, thirty thousand livres, say, it seems to me that it wouldn't be a bad scheme."

"Ah! if you look at it from that point of view, I am with you, and haven't a word to say."

"Hush! you will see."

Cauvignac approached the young woman, who, having drawn rein in front of one of the windows of the inn, was questioning the hostess, who assured her that she could be accommodated with a room.

"Your servant, young gentleman," he said, with a cunning expression, putting his hand to his hat in a free and easy way.

"Young gentleman, did you say?" said the lady, with a smile.

"Yes, viscount."

The lady blushed.

"I am at a loss to know what you mean, monsieur," she said.

"Oh! yes, you do, and the half-inch of blush on your cheeks proves it."

"You certainly are mistaken, monsieur."

"Nay, nay! on the contrary, I am perfectly sure of what I say."

"A truce to your jesting, monsieur."

"I am not jesting, monsieur, and if you wish for proofs, you shall have them. I had the honor to meet you, it will soon be three weeks ago, dressed according to your sex, on the banks of the Dordogne, on which occasion you were attended by your faithful squire, Monsieur Pompée. Is Monsieur Pompée still in your service?—Why, yes, there he is now, dear Monsieur Pompée! Will you tell me that I don't know him either?"

The squire and the young woman looked at each other in speechless amazement.

"Oh! yes, that astonishes you, my gallant viscount," Cauvignac continued; "but dare to say that it was not you whom I met on the road to Saint-Martin de Cubzac, a fourth of a league from the hostelry of Master Biscarros."

"I do not deny the meeting, monsieur."

"What did I say?"

"But that was the time when I was disguised."

"Nay, nay, you are disguised now. I quite understand that, as the description of the Vicomte de Cambes has been given out all through Guyenne, you deemed it more prudent, in order to avoid suspicion, to adopt, for the moment, this costume, which, to do you justice, my fair sir, is extremely becoming to you."

"Monsieur," said the viscountess, with an anxiety which she tried in vain to conceal, "except that your conversation contains a word or two of sense now and then, I should think you mad."

"I will not pay you the same compliment, for it seems to me a most judicious thing to disguise one's self when one is conspiring."

The young woman gazed at Cauvignac with increasing uneasiness.

"Indeed, monsieur," she said, "it seems to me that I have seen you somewhere; but I cannot remember where."

"The first time, as I have told you, was on the banks of the Dordogne."

"And the second?"

"The second was at Chantilly."

"On the day of the hunt?"

"Even so."

"In that case, monsieur, I have nothing to fear, for you are one of us."

"Why so?"

"Because you were at Chantilly."

"Permit me to observe that that is no reason."

"It seems to me to be."

"There were too many there to be sure that they were all friends."

"Beware, monsieur, or you will force me to form a strange opinion of you."

"Oh! form whatever opinion you choose; I am not sensitive."

"But, when all is said, what do you desire?"

"To do the honors of the inn, if you have no objection."

"I am deeply grateful to you, monsieur, but I do not require your services. I am expecting a friend."

"Very good; dismount, and while you are waiting, we will talk."

"What am I to do, madame?" interposed Pompée.

"Dismount, engage a room, and order supper," said Cauvignac.

"Monsieur," rejoined the viscountess, "if I mistake not, it is for me to give orders to my servant."

"That depends upon circumstances, viscount. I command at Jaulnay, and have fifty men at my beck and call. Pompée; do as I bid you."

Pompée lowered his crest and entered the inn.

"Do you presume to arrest me, monsieur?" demanded the young woman.

"Perhaps."

"What do you mean by perhaps?"

"It will depend upon the conversation we are about to have. Pray take the trouble to dismount, viscount; so! that's right. Now accept my arm; the inn people will take your horse to the stable."

"I obey, monsieur; for, as you say, you are the stronger. I have no means of resisting, but I tell you now that the person I am expecting will soon be here, and that he is an officer of the king."

"Very well, viscount; you will do me the honor to present me to him, and I shall be charmed to make his acquaintance."

The viscountess realized that resistance was useless at present, and she led the way into the inn, making a sign to her strange interlocutor that he was at liberty to follow her if he chose.

Cauvignac escorted her to the door of the room bespoken by Pompée, and was about to follow her in, when Ferguzon ran quickly up the stairs and whispered to him:—

"Captain, a carriage with three horses, a young man, masked, inside, and two servants at the doors."

"Good!" said Cauvignac; "it is probably the gentleman expected."

"Ah! do we expect a gentleman?"

"Yes, and I will go down to meet him. Do you remain in this corridor; don't lose sight of the door; let everybody in, but see that nobody goes out."

"Very well, captain."

A travelling-carriage had stopped at the door of the inn, escorted by four men of Cauvignac's company, who joined it a quarter of a league outside the town, and had not since parted company with it.

A young gentleman, dressed in blue velvet, and wrapped in a great furred cloak, was lying rather than sitting inside the carriage. From the time that the four men surrounded his vehicle he had plied them with questions; but, finding that he could obtain no answer, despite his persistence, he seemed to have resigned himself to wait, and simply raised his head from time to time to see if somebody had not come up from whom he could demand an explanation of the strange conduct of these people in his regard.

It was impossible, however, to make a just estimate of the impression produced upon the young traveller by this episode, as one of the black satin masks, called *loups*, which were very much in vogue at that time, hid half of his face. Those portions which could be seen, however,—that is to say, the upper part of his forehead, and his mouth and chin,—denoted youth, beauty, and intelligence. His teeth were small and white, and a pair of bright eyes shone through the holes in the mask.

Two tall footmen, pale and trembling, although each held a blunderbuss across his knee, sat as if glued to their saddles at either door of the carriage.

The whole scene would have made an excellent picture of brigands stopping travellers on the highway, except for the bright daylight, the inn, the smiling features of Cauvignac, and the imperturbability of the pretended thieves.

At sight of Cauvignac, who, as we have said, when notified by Ferguzon, made his appearance at the door, the young man uttered a little shriek of surprise, and hastily put his hand to his face, as if to make sure that his mask was in place; finding that it was, he recovered his tranquillity.

Swift as the movement was, it did not escape Cauvignac. He gazed at the traveller with the eye of a man skilful in tracing resemblances even upon the most disguised features, and the next moment started, in spite of himself, apparently as much surprised as the young gentleman in blue. He recovered himself, however, and said, removing his hat with a grace that was peculiar to him:—

"Welcome, fair lady."

The traveller's eyes shone with surprise through the holes in his mask.

"Where are you going in this guise, pray?" continued Cauvignac.

"Where am I going?" replied the traveller, taking no notice of Cauvignac's salutation,—"where am I going? You ought to know better than I, as it seems that I am not at liberty to continue my journey. I am going where you take me."

"Permit me to remark," continued Cauvignac, with a greater show of politeness than ever, "that that does not answer my question, fair lady! Your arrest is only momentary. When we have talked together a few moments upon certain matters in which we are mutually interested, with our hearts and our faces laid bare, you may resume your journey unmolested."

"Pardon me," rejoined the traveller, "but before going any farther, let us rectify an error. You pretend to take me for a woman, although you can see from my dress that I am a man."

"You know the Latin proverb: *Ne nimium crede colori,*—the wise man doesn't judge by appearances. Now I make some pretensions to wisdom, and the consequence is that, under this deceitful costume, I have recognized—"

"What?" demanded the traveller, impatiently.

"Why, I have already told you,—a woman!"

"Well, if I am a woman, why do you stop me?"

"*Peste!* Because, in times like these, women are more dangerous than men; indeed, the war in which we are engaged might, properly speaking, be called the war of women. The queen and Madame de Condé are the two belligerent powers. They have taken for lieutenant-generals Mademoiselle de Chevreuse, Madame de Montbazon, Madame de Longueville—and yourself. Mademoiselle de Chevreuse is Monsieur le Coadjuteur's general, Madame de Montbazon is Monsieur de Beaufort's, Madame de Longueville Monsieur de La Rochefoucauld's, and you—you have every appearance of being Monsieur le Duc d'Épernon's."

"You are mad, monsieur," said the young traveller, shrugging his shoulders.

"I should not be inclined to believe you, fair lady, were it not for the fact that a handsome youth paid me the same compliment a moment since."

"Perhaps he was a woman whom you persisted in calling a man."

"Even so. I recognized my fine gentleman from having seen him on a certain evening early in May, prowling around Master Biscarros' inn, and I was not to be taken in by his petticoats and his wigs and his little soft voice, any more than I am taken in by your gray felt, and your fancy boots; and I said to him: 'My young friend, take what name you choose, wear what costume you choose, assume what voice you choose, you will be the Vicomte de Cambes none the less. '"

"The Vicomte de Cambes!" cried the traveller.

"Ah! the name seems to make an impression upon you. Do you happen to know him?"

"A very young man, almost a child?"

"Seventeen or eighteen years old, at most."

"Very fair?"

"Very fair."

"Large blue eyes?"

"Very large, very blue."

"Is he here?"

"He is here."

"And you say that he is—"

"Disguised as a woman, the rascal,—as you are as a man, slyboots."

"Why is he here, pray?" cried the young man, vehemently, and with evident distress, which increased perceptibly as Cauvignac assumed a more serious tone, and became more sparing of his words.

"Why," he replied, enunciating every syllable with great distinctness, "he claims to have an appointment with one of his friends."

"One of his friends?"

"Yes."

"A gentleman?"

"Probably."

"A baron?"

"Perhaps."

"And his name is—"

Cauvignac's brow contracted beneath a weighty thought which then first presented itself to his mind, and caused a perceptible commotion in his brain.

"Oho!" he muttered, "that would be a pretty kettle offish."

"And his name?" the traveller repeated.

"Wait a moment," said Cauvignac; "wait a moment—his name ends in *olles.*"

"Monsieur de Canolles!" cried the traveller, whose lips became deathly pale, making a ghastly contrast with the black silk mask.

"That's the name! Monsieur de Canolles," said Cauvignac, following, upon the visible portions of the young man's face and in the convulsive movement of his whole body, the revolution which was taking place in his mind. "Do you know Monsieur de Canolles, too? In God's name, do you know everybody?"

"A truce to jesting," faltered the young man, who was trembling all over, and seemed on the point of fainting.

"Where is this lady?"

"In that room yonder; look, the third window from this,—where the yellow curtains are."

"I want to see her!" cried the traveller.

"Oho! have I made a mistake, and can it be that you are this Monsieur de Canolles whom she expects? Or, rather, isn't this Monsieur de Canolles, this gallant cavalier just trotting up, followed by a lackey who looks to me like a consummate idiot?"

The young traveller jumped forward so precipitately to look through the glass in the front of the carriage that he broke it with his head.

"'T is he! 'tis he!" he cried, utterly regardless of the fact that the blood was flowing from a slight wound. "Oh! the villain! he is here to meet her; I am undone!"

"Ah! didn't I say that you were a woman?"

"They meet here by appointment," the young man continued, wringing his hands. "Oh! I will have my revenge!"

Cauvignac would have indulged in some further pleasantry; but the young man made an imperious gesture with one hand, while with the other he tore off his mask, and the pale, threatening face of Nanon was revealed to Cauvignac's impassive gaze.

VII

"Good-day to you, little sister," said Cauvignac, offering the young woman his hand with imperturbable phlegm.

"Good-day! So you recognized me, did you?"

"The instant I laid my eyes on you. It wasn't enough to hide your face; you should have covered up that charming dimple, and your pearly teeth. When you wish to disguise yourself, coquette, cover your whole face! but you were not careful—*et fugit ad salices*—"

"Enough!" said Nanon, imperiously; "let us talk seriously."

"I ask nothing better; only by talking seriously can business be properly transacted."

"You say that the Vicomtesse de Cambes is here?"

"In person."

"And that Monsieur de Canolles is entering the inn at this moment?"

"Not yet; he dismounts and throws his rein to his servant. Ah! he has been seen yonder also. See, the window with the yellow curtains opens, and the viscountess puts out her head. Ah! she gives a little shriek of delight. Monsieur de Canolles darts into the house; get out of sight, little sister, or all will be lost."

Nanon threw herself back, convulsively pressing Cauvignac's hand, as he gazed at her with an air of paternal compassion.

"And I was going to Paris to join him!" cried Nanon. "I risked everything for the sake of seeing him again!"

"Ah! such a sacrifice, little sister, and for an ingrate, into the bargain! Upon my word, you might bestow your favors to better purpose."

"What will they say to each other, now they are together? What will they do?"

'Faith, dear Nanon, you embarrass me sorely by putting such a question to me; they will—*pardieu!* they will love each other dearly, I suppose."

"Oh! that shall not be!" cried Nanon, frantically gnawing at her nails, which shone like polished ivory.

"On the contrary, I fancy that it will be," rejoined Cauvignac. "Ferguzon has orders to let no one come out, but not to keep anybody out. At this moment, in all probability, the viscountess and Baron de Canolles are exchanging all sorts of endearing terms, each more charming than the last. *Peste!* dear Nanon, you are too late."

"Do you think so?" retorted the young woman with an indefinable expression of irony and malignant cunning; "do you think so? Very good; just come in and sit beside me, you wretched diplomatist."

Cauvignac obeyed.

"Bertrand," said Nanon to one of her retainers, "tell the coachman to turn quietly about, and draw up under the clump of trees we left at the right as we entered the village.—Won't that be a safe place to talk?" she asked Cauvignac.

"There could be no better. But permit me to take a few precautions on my own account."

"Go on."

Cauvignac made signs to four of his men, who were strutting about the inn, buzzing and puffing like hornets in the sun, to follow him.

"You do well to take those men," said Nanon, "and if you follow my advice you will take six rather than four; there may be work cut out for them."

"Good!" said Cauvignac; "work of that kind is what I want."

"Then you will be content," said Nanon.

The coachman turned the carriage, and drove away, with Nanon, red with the flame of her thoughts, and Cauvignac, apparently calm and cold, but ready, nevertheless, to lend an attentive ear to his sister's suggestions.

Meanwhile, Canolles, attracted by the joyous cry uttered by Madame de Cambes when she caught sight of him, had darted into the inn, and to the viscountess's room, without noticing Ferguzon, whom he passed in the corridor, but who made no objection to his entering, as he had received no instructions concerning him.

"Ah! monsieur," cried Madame de Cambes, "come in quickly; I have been so impatient for you to come!"

"Those words would make me the happiest man in the world, madame, if your pallor and your evident distress did not tell me as plainly as words could do that you were not expecting me for myself alone."

"Yes, monsieur, you are right," said Claire with her charming smile, "and I desire to lay myself under still greater obligation to you."

"How so?"

"By begging you to save me from some peril, I know not what, which threatens me."

"Peril?"

"Yes. Wait."

She went to the door, and threw the bolt.

"I have been recognized," she said, returning to Canolles.

"By whom?"

"By a man whose name I do not know, but whose face and voice are familiar to me. It seems as if I heard his voice the evening that you, in this very room, received the order to repair at once to Mantes. It seems also as if I had seen his face at the hunting party at Chantilly, the day that I took Madame de Condé's place."

"Whom do you take the man to be?"

"An agent of Monsieur le Duc d'Épernon, and therefore an enemy."

"The devil!" exclaimed Canolles. "You say that he recognized you?"

"Yes; he called me by name, although he insisted that I was a man. There are officers of the king's party all over the country hereabout; I am known to belong to the party of the princes, and it may be that they proposed to make trouble for me. But you are here, and I no longer have any fear. You are an officer yourself, and belong to the same party that they do, so you will be my safeguard."

"Alas!" said Canolles, "I greatly fear that I can offer you no other defence or protection than that of my sword."

"How is that?"

"Because from this moment I cease to belong to the king's party."

"Do you mean what you say?" cried Claire, delighted beyond measure.

"I promised myself that I would forward my resignation from the place where I next met you. I have met you, and my resignation will be forwarded from Jaulnay."

"Oh! free! free! you are free! you can embrace the cause of justice and loyalty; you can join the party of the princes, that is to say, of all the nobility. Oh! I knew that you were too noble-hearted not to come to it at last."

Canolles kissed with transport the hand Claire offered him.

"How did it come about?" she continued. "Tell me every detail."

"Oh! it's not a long story. I wrote Monsieur de Mazarin to inform him of what had taken place. When I arrived at Mantes, I was ordered to wait upon him; he called me a poor fool, I called him a poor fool; he laughed, I lost my temper; he raised his voice, I bade him go to the devil. I returned to my hôtel; I was waiting until he thought fit to consign me to the Bastille; he was waiting until prudence should bid me begone from Mantes. After twenty-four hours prudence bade me take that course. And even that I owe to you, for I thought of what you promised me, and that you might be waiting for me. So it was that I threw away all responsibility, all thought of party, and with my hands free, and almost without preference, I remembered one thing only, that I loved you, madame, and that at last I might tell you so, aloud and boldly."

"So you have thrown away your rank for me, you are disgraced, ruined, all for my sake! Dear Monsieur de Canolles, how can I ever pay my debt? How can I prove my gratitude to you?"

With a smile and a tear which gave him back a hundred times more than he had lost, Madame de Cambes brought Canolles to her feet.

"Ah! madame," said he, "from this moment I am rich and happy; for I am to be always with you, I am never to leave you more, I shall be happy in the privilege of seeing you, and rich in your love."

"There is no further obstacle, then?"

"No."

"You belong to me absolutely, and, while keeping your heart, I may offer your arm to Madame la Princesse?"

"You may."

"You have sent your resignation, do you say?"

"Not yet; I wished to see you first; but, as I told you, now that I have seen you again, I propose to write it here, instantly. I preferred to wait until I could do it in obedience to your orders."

"Write, then, before anything else! If you do not write, you will be looked upon as a turncoat; indeed, you must wait, before taking any decisive step, until your resignation is accepted."

"Dear little diplomatist, have no fear that they will not accept it, and very gladly. My bungling at Chantilly will spare them any great regret. Did they not tell me," laughed Canolles, "that I was a poor fool?"

"Yes; but we will make up to you for any opinion they may entertain, never fear. Your affair at Chantilly will be more thoroughly appreciated at Bordeaux than at Paris, I assure you. But write, baron, write, so that we may leave this place! for I confess that I am not at ease by any means in this inn."

"Are you speaking of the past; is it the memory of another time that terrifies you so?" said Canolles, gazing fondly about the room.

"No. I am speaking of the present, and you do not enter into my fears to-day."

"Whom do you fear, pray? What have you to fear?"

"*Mon Dieu!* who knows?"

At that moment, as if to justify the viscountess's apprehension, three blows were struck upon the door with appalling solemnity.

Claire and Canolles ceased their conversation and exchanged an anxious, questioning glance.

"In the king's name!" said a voice outside. "Open!"

The next moment the fragile door was shattered. Canolles attempted to seize his sword, but a man had already stepped between his sword and him.

"What does this mean?" he demanded.

"You are Monsieur le Baron de Canolles, are you not?"

"I am."

"Captain in the Navailles regiment?"

"Yes."

"Sent upon a confidential mission by the Duc d'Épernon?"

Canolles nodded his head.

"In that case, in the names of the king, and her Majesty the Queen Regent, I arrest you."

"Your warrant?"

"Here it is."

"But, monsieur," said Canolles, handing back the paper after he had glanced over it rapidly, "it seems to me that I know you."

"Know me! *Parbleu!* Wasn't it in the same village where I arrest you to-day, that I brought you an order from Monsieur le Duc d'Épernon to betake yourself to the court? Your fortune was in that commission, my young gentleman. You have missed it; so much the worse for you!"

Claire turned pale, and fell weeping upon a chair; she had recognized the impertinent questioner.

"Monsieur de Mazarin is taking his revenge," muttered Canolles.

"Come, monsieur, we must be off," said Cauvignac.

Claire did not stir. Canolles, undecided as to the course he should pursue, seemed near going mad. The catastrophe was so overpowering and unexpected that he bent beneath its weight; he bowed his head and resigned himself.

Moreover, at that period the words "In the king's name!" had not lost their magic effect, and no one dared resist them.

"Where are you taking me, monsieur?" he said.

"Are you forbidden to afford me the poor consolation of knowing where I am going?"

"No, monsieur, I will tell you. We are to escort you to Île-Saint Georges."

"Adieu, madame," said Canolles, bowing respectfully to Madame de Cambes; "adieu!"

"Well, well," said Cauvignac to himself, "things aren't so far advanced as I thought. I will tell Nanon; it will please her immensely."

"Four men to escort the captain!" he cried, stepping to the door. "Forward, four men!"

"And where am I to be taken?" cried Madame de Cambes, holding out her arms toward the prisoner. "If the baron is guilty, I am still more guilty than he."

"You, madame," replied Cauvignac, "are free, and may go where you choose." And he left the room with the baron.

Madame de Cambes rose, with a gleam of hope, and prepared to leave the inn at once, before contrary orders should be issued.

"Free!" said she. "In that case I can watch over him; I will go at once."

Darting to the window, she was in time to see Canolles in the midst of his escort, and to exchange a farewell wave of the hand with him. Then she called Pompée, who, hoping for a halt of two or three days, had established himself in the best room he could find, and bade him make ready for immediate departure.

VIII

It was an even more melancholy journey for Canolles than he had anticipated. The most carefully guarded prisoner has a false feeling of freedom in the saddle, but the saddle was soon succeeded by a carriage, a leathern affair, the shape of which and its capacity for jolting are still retained in Touraine. Furthermore, Canolles' knees were interlocked with those of a man with the beak of an eagle, whose hand rested lovingly on the butt of a pistol. Sometimes, at night, for he slept during the day, he hoped to be able to elude the vigilance of this new Argus; but beside the eagle's beak were two great owl's-eyes, round, flaming, and most excellently adapted for nocturnal observations, so that, turn which way he would, Canolles would always see those two round eyes gleaming in that direction.

While he slept, one of the two eyes also slept, but only one. Nature had endowed this man with the faculty of sleeping with one eye open.

Two days and two nights Canolles passed in gloomy reflections; for the fortress of Île Saint-Georges — an inoffensive fortress enough, by the way — assumed terrifying proportions in the prisoner's eyes, as fear and remorse sank more deeply into his heart.

Remorse, because he realized that his mission to Madame la Princesse was a confidential mission, which he had made the most of to further his own interests, and that he had committed a terrible indiscretion on that occasion. At Chantilly, Madame de Condé was simply a fugitive. At Bordeaux, Madame de Condé was a rebel princess. Fear, because he knew by tradition the appalling vengeance of which Anne of Austria, in her wrath, was capable.

There was another source of perhaps even keener remorse than that we have mentioned. There was, somewhere in the world, a young woman, a beautiful, clever young woman, who had used her great influence solely to put him forward; a woman who, through her love for him, had again and again imperilled her position, her future, her fortune; and that woman, not only the most charming of mistresses, but the most devoted of friends, he had brutally abandoned, without excuse, at a time when her thoughts were busy with him, and instead of revenging herself upon him she had persistently bestowed additional tokens of her favor upon him; and her voice, instead of sounding reproachfully in his ears, had never lost the caressing sweetness of an almost regal favor. It is true that that favor had come to him at an inauspicious moment, at a moment when Canolles would certainly have preferred disgrace; but was that Nanon's fault? Nanon had looked upon that mission to his Majesty as a method of augmenting the fortune and worldly position of the man with whom her mind was constantly filled.

All those who have loved two women at once,—and I ask pardon of my lady-readers, but this phenomenon, which they find it so hard to understand, because they never have but one love, is very common among us men,—all those who have loved two women at once, I say, will understand that as Canolles reflected more and more deeply, Nanon recovered more and more of the influence over his mind which he thought she had lost forever. The harsh asperities of character which wound one in the constant contact of daily intercourse, and cause momentary irritation, are forgotten in absence; while, on the other hand, certain sweeter memories resume their former intensity with solitude. Fair and lost to him, kind and ill-treated,—in such guise did Nanon now appear to Canolles.

The fact was that Canolles searched his own heart ingenuously, and not with the bad grace of those accused persons who are forced to a general confession. What had Nanon done to him that he should abandon her? What had Madame de Cambes done that he should follow her? What was there so fascinating and lovable in the little cavalier of the Golden Calf? Was Madame de Cambes so vastly superior to Nanon? Are golden locks so much to be preferred to black that one should be a perjured ingrate to his mistress, and a traitor to his king, all for the sake of exchanging black locks for golden? And yet, oh, pitiable human nature! Canolles brought all these eminently sensible arguments to bear upon himself, but Canolles was not convinced. The heart is full of such mysteries, which bring happiness to lovers and despair to philosophers. All this did not prevent Canolles from hating himself, and berating his own folly soundly.

"I am going to be punished," he said, thinking that the punishment effaces the crime; "I am going to be punished, and so much the better. I suppose I shall have to do with some very rough-spoken, very insolent, very brutal captain, who will read to me, from the supreme height of his dignity as jailer-in-chief, an order from Monsieur de Mazarin, who will point out a dungeon for me, and will send me to forgather with the rats and toads fifteen feet underground, while I might have lived in the light, and flourished in the sun's rays, in the arms of a woman who loved me, whom I loved, and whom it may be that I still love. Cursed little viscount! why need you have served as envelope to such a fascinating viscountess? But is there anywhere in all the world a viscountess who is worth what this particular one is likely to cost me? For it's not simply the governor, and the dungeon fifteen feet under ground; if they think me a traitor, they won't leave matters half-investigated; they will pick a quarrel with me about that Chantilly affair, which I could not pay too heavy a penalty for, if it had been more fruitful of results for me; but it has brought me in just three kisses upon her hand. Triple idiot, when I had the power, not to use it! Poor fool! as Monsieur de Mazarin says, — to be a traitor, and not collect the pay for his treason! Who will pay me now?"

Canolles shrugged his shoulders contemptuously in reply to this mental question.

The man with the round eyes, clear-sighted as he was, could not understand this pantomime, and gazed at him in amazement.

"If they question me," Canolles continued, "I'll not answer; for what answer can I make? That I was not fond of Monsieur de Mazarin? In that case I was under no obligation to enter his service. That I did love Madame de Cambes? A fine reason that to give a queen and a first minister! So I won't reply at all. But these judges are very sensitive fellows; when they ask questions they like to be answered. There are brutal wedges in these provincial jails; they'll shatter my slender knees, of which I was so proud, and send me back to my rats and my toads a perfect wreck. I shall be bandy-legged all my life, like Monsieur le Prince de Conti, and that would make me extremely ugly, even supposing that his Majesty would cover me with his wing, which he will take good care not to do."

Besides the governor and the rats and toads and wedges, there were certain scaffolds whereon rebels were beheaded, certain gallows whereon traitors were hanged, and certain drill grounds where deserters were shot. But all this was of small consequence to a well-favored youth like Canolles, in comparison with bandy legs.

He resolved, therefore, to keep his mind clear and to question his companion upon the subject.

The round eyes, the eagle's beak, and the frowning expression of that personage gave him but slight encouragement to accost him. However, no matter how stolid a man's face may be, it must soften a little at times, and Canolles took advantage of an instant when a grimace resembling a smile passed across the features of the subaltern who watched him so sharply.

"Monsieur!" said he.

"Monsieur?" was the reply.

"Excuse me if I take you away from your reflections."

"Make no excuses, monsieur, for I never reflect."

"The devil! you are surely endowed with a fortunate mental organization, monsieur."

"And therefore I never complain."

"Ah, well, you're not like me in that; for I am very much inclined to complain."

"Of what, monsieur?"

"Because I was arrested just when I was least expecting it, to be taken I don't know where."

"Oh! yes, monsieur, you do know, for you were told."

"So I was. We are going to Île Saint-Georges, aren't we?"

"Precisely."

"Do you think I shall remain there long?"

"I have no idea, monsieur; but from the way in which you were recommended, I think it's likely."

"Oho! Is it a very forbidding place, this Île Saint-Georges?"

"Don't you know the fortress?"

"On the inside, no; I have never been inside."

"It's not very attractive, monsieur; and, aside from the governor's apartments, which have been newly furnished and are very pleasant, as I am informed, it's rather a gloomy abode."

"Very good. Do you suppose they will question me?"

"It's the custom."

"And suppose I don't answer?"

"Suppose you don't answer?"

"Yes."

"The devil! in that case there's the torture, you know."

"Ordinary?"

"Ordinary or extraordinary, according to the charge. What is the charge against you, monsieur?"

"Why," said Canolles, "I am much afraid that I am accused of offences against the State."

"Oho! in that case you will enjoy the extraordinary torture. Ten pots—"

"What's that? ten pots?"

"Yes."

"What do you mean?"

"I mean that you will have the ten pots of water poured down your throat."

"So the torture by water is in vogue at Île Saint-Georges, is it?"

"*Dame!* monsieur, you understand that on the Garonne—"

"To be sure, where the water is right at hand. How many pailfuls in the ten pots?"

"Three to three and a half."

"I shall swell up in that case."

"A little. But if you take the precaution to arrange matters with the jailer—"

"What then?"

"You will have an easy time of it."

"In what does the service that the jailer has it in his power to render me consist, I beg to know?"

"He can give you oil to drink."

"Is oil a specific?"

"Of sovereign efficacy."

"Do you think so?"

"I speak from experience. I have drunk (*bu*)—"

"You have drunk?"

"Pardon me; I meant to say, I have seen (*vu*). The habit of talking with Gascons makes me pronounce *v* like *b* sometimes, and *vice versa*."

"You were saying," said Canolles, unable to repress a smile, notwithstanding the gravity of the conversation,—"you were saying that you had seen—?"

"Yes, monsieur, I have seen a man drink the ten pots of water with great facility, thanks to the oil which he had taken to put the canals in proper condition. To be sure, he swelled up, as they all do; but with a good fire they disinflated him without much damage. That is the essential thing in the second part of the operation. Be sure and remember these words: *to heat without burning.*"

"I understand," said Canolles. "Mayhap monsieur was the executioner?"

"No, monsieur," replied his interlocutor, with courtesy seasoned with modesty.

"His assistant, perhaps?"

"No, monsieur; an onlooker, simply."

"Ah! and monsieur's name is—?"

"Barrabas."

"A fine name, an old name, too; made famous in the Scriptures."

"In the Passion, monsieur."

"That's what I meant; but from habit I used the other expression."

"Monsieur prefers to say 'the Scriptures.' Is monsieur a Huguenot?"

"Yes, but a very ignorant Huguenot. Would you believe that I know hardly three thousand verses of the Psalms?"

"Indeed, it is very little."

"I succeeded better in remembering the music. There has been much hanging and burning in my family."

"I hope that no such fate is in store for monsieur."

"No, there is a much more tolerant spirit to-day; they will submerge me probably, nothing more."

Barrabas began to laugh.

Canolles' heart leaped for joy; he had won over his keeper. If this jailer *ad interim* should become his permanent jailer, he stood a fair chance to obtain the oil; he determined, therefore, to take up the conversation where he had left it.

"Monsieur Barrabas," said he, "are we destined to be soon separated, or shall you do me the honor to continue to bear me company?"

"Monsieur, when we arrive at Île Saint-Georges, I shall be obliged, I deeply regret to say, to leave you; I must return to our company."

"Indeed; do you belong to a company of archers?"

"No, monsieur, to a company of soldiers."

"Levied by the minister?"

"No, monsieur, by Captain Cauvignac, the same man who had the honor of arresting you."

"Are you in the king's service?"

"I think so, monsieur."

"What the devil do you mean by that? Are you not sure?"

"One is sure of nothing in this world."

"Well, if you are in doubt there is one thing that you should do, in order to set your doubts at rest."

"What is that?"

"Let me go."

"Impossible, monsieur."

"But I will pay you handsomely for your kindness."

"With what?"

"*Pardieu!* with money,"

"Monsieur has none."

"I have no money?"

"No."

Canolles hastily felt in his pockets.

"Upon my word, my purse has disappeared," he said. "Who has taken my purse?"

"I, monsieur," replied Barrabas with a low bow.

"Why did you do it?"

"So that monsieur could not corrupt me."

Canolles stared at the honest keeper in open-mouthed admiration, and as the argument seemed to admit of no reply, he made none.

The result was that the travellers relapsed into silence, and the journey, as it drew near its close, resumed the depressing characteristics which marked its beginning.

IX

Day was breaking when the clumsy vehicle reached the village nearest to its island destination. Canolles, feeling that it had ceased to move, passed his head through the little loophole intended to furnish air to those who were free, and conveniently arranged to shut it off from prisoners.

A pretty little village, consisting of some hundred houses grouped about a church on a hillside, and overlooked by a château, was sharply outlined in the clear morning air, gilded by the first rays of the sun, which put to flight the thin, gauzy patches of vapor.

Just then the wagon started on up the incline, and the coachman left the box and walked beside the vehicle.

"My friend," said Canolles, "are you of this province?"

"Yes, monsieur, I am from Libourne."

"In that case you should know this village. What is yonder white house, and those pretty cottages?"

"The château, monsieur," was the reply, "is the manor house of Cambes, and the village is one of its dependencies."

Canolles started back, and his face instantly changed from the deepest red to deathly white.

"Monsieur," interposed Barrabas, whose round eye nothing escaped, "did you hurt yourself against the window?"

"No—thanks," said Canolles, and continued his examination of the peasant. "To whom does the property belong?" he asked.

"The Vicomtesse de Cambes."

"A young widow?"

"Very beautiful and very rich."

"And, consequently, much sought after?"

"Of course; a handsome dowry and a handsome woman; with that combination one doesn't lack suitors."

"Of good reputation?"

"Yes, but a furious partisan of the princes."

"I think I have heard so."

"A demon, monsieur, a downright demon!"

"An angel!" murmured Canolles, whose thoughts, whenever they recurred to Claire, recurred to her with transports of adoration, — "an angel!"

"Does she live here some of the time?" he inquired, raising his voice.

"Rarely, monsieur; but she did live here for a long while. Her husband left her here, and as long as she remained, her presence was a blessing to the whole countryside. Now she is said to be with the princess."

The carriage, having reached the top of the hill, was ready to go down again on the other side; the driver made a motion with his hand to ask permission to resume his place upon the box, and Canolles, who feared that he might arouse suspicion by continuing his questions, drew his head back into the lumbering vehicle, which started down hill at a slow trot, its most rapid gait.

After a quarter of an hour, during which time Canolles, still under the eye of Barrabas, was absorbed in gloomy reflection, the wagon halted again.

"Do we stop here for breakfast?" Canolles asked.

"We stop here altogether, monsieur. We have reached our destination. Yonder is Île Saint-Georges. We have only the river to cross now."

"True," muttered Canolles; "so near and yet so far!"

"Monsieur, some one is coming to meet us," said Barrabas; "be good enough to prepare to alight."

The second of Canolles' keepers, who was sitting on the box beside the driver, climbed down and unlocked the door, to which he had the key.

Canolles removed his eyes from the little white château, upon which he had kept them fixed, to the fortress which was to be his abode. He saw in the first place, on the other side of a swiftly flowing arm of the river, a ferry-boat, and beside it a guard of eight men and a sergeant. Behind them were the outworks of the citadel.

"Ah!" said Canolles to himself, "I am expected, it seems, and due precautions are taken. — Are those my new guards?" he asked Barrabas, aloud.

"I would be glad to answer monsieur's question intelligently; but really I have no idea."

At that moment, after exchanging signals with the sentinel on duty at the entrance to the fortress, the eight soldiers and the sergeant entered the ferry-boat, crossed the Garonne, and stepped ashore just as Canolles stepped to the ground.

Immediately the sergeant, seeing an officer, approached him and gave the military salute.

"Have I the honor of addressing Monsieur le Baron de Canolles, captain in the Navailles regiment?" he asked.

"Himself," replied Canolles, marvelling at the man's politeness.

The sergeant turned to his men, ordered them to present arms, and pointed with the end of his pike to the boat. Canolles took his place between his two guards, the eight men and the sergeant embarked after him, and the boat moved away from the shore, while Canolles cast a last glance at Cambes, which was just passing out of sight behind some rising ground.

The island was almost covered with scarps, counter-scarps, glaces, and bastions; a small fort in reasonably good condition overlooked all these outworks. The entrance was through an arched gateway, in front of which a sentinel was pacing back and forth.

"*Qui vive?*" he cried.

The little troop halted, the sergeant walked up to the sentinel, and said a few words to him.

"To arms!" cried the sentinel.

Immediately a score of men, who composed the picket, issued from a guard-house, and hastily drew up in line in front of the gateway.

"Come, monsieur," said the sergeant to Canolles. The drum began to beat.

"What does this mean?" said the young man to himself.

He walked toward the fort, quite at a loss to understand what was going on; for all these preparations resembled military honors paid to a superior much more than precautionary measures concerning a prisoner.

Nor was this all. Canolles did not notice that, just as he stepped from the carriage, a window in the governor's apartments was thrown open, and an officer stationed thereat watched attentively the movements of the boat and the reception given to the prisoner and his two keepers.

This officer, when Canolles stepped from the boat upon the island, hastily left the window, and hurried down to meet him.

"Aha!" said Canolles, as his eye fell upon him, "here comes the commandant to inspect his new boarder."

"I should say, monsieur," said Barrabas, "judging from appearances, that you'll not be left to languish a week in the anteroom like some people; you will be entered on the books at once."

"So much the better!" said Canolles.

Meanwhile the officer was drawing near. Canolles assumed the haughty, dignified attitude of a persecuted man.

A few steps from Canolles the officer removed his hat.

"Have I the honor of addressing Monsieur le Baron de Canolles?" he asked.

"Monsieur," the prisoner replied, "I am truly overwhelmed by your courtesy. Yes, I am Baron de Canolles; treat me, I beg you, as one officer might treat another, and assign me as comfortable quarters as possible."

"Monsieur," said the officer, "the place is not in the best of condition, but, as if in anticipation of your wishes, all possible improvements have been made."

"Whom should I thank for such unusual attention?" Canolles asked with a smile.

"The king, monsieur, who does well all that he does."

"To be sure, monsieur, to be sure. God forbid that I should slander his Majesty, especially on this occasion; I should not be sorry, however, to obtain certain information."

"If you so desire, monsieur, I am at your service; but I will take the liberty of reminding you that the garrison is waiting to make your acquaintance."

"*Peste!*" muttered Canolles, "a whole garrison to make the acquaintance of a prisoner who is to be shut up! Here's a deal of ceremony, I should say."

He added, aloud:—

"I am at your service, monsieur, and ready to follow you wherever you choose to take me."

"Permit me then to walk in advance to do the honors."

Canolles followed him, congratulating himself upon having fallen into the hands of so courteous a gentleman.

"I fancy you will be let off with the ordinary question, only four pots of water," Barrabas whispered in his ear.

"So much the better," said Canolles. "I shall swell up only half as much."

When they reached the court-yard of the citadel, Canolles found part of the garrison under arms. Thereupon the officer who escorted him drew his sword and saluted him.

"*Mon Dieu!* how tedious!" muttered Canolles.

At the same instant a drum beat under an archway near by. Canolles turned, and a second file of soldiers issued from the archway and took up a position behind the first.

The officer thereupon handed Canolles two keys.

"What does this mean?" the baron demanded; "what are you doing?"

"We are going through with the customary formalities in accordance with the most rigorous laws of military etiquette."

"For whom do you take me, in God's name?" exclaimed Canolles, amazed beyond expression.

"Why, for who you are, — for Monsieur le Baron de Canolles, Governor of Île Saint-Georges."

A cloud passed before Canolles' eyes, and he was near falling.

"I shall have the honor in a moment," continued the officer, "of turning over to Monsieur le Gouverneur his commission, which arrived this morning, accompanied by a letter announcing monsieur's arrival for to-day."

Canolles glanced at Barrabas, whose round eyes were fixed upon him with an expression of speechless amazement impossible to describe.

"So I am Governor of Île Saint-Georges?" faltered Canolles.

"Yes, monsieur, and his Majesty has made us very happy by his choice."

"You are sure that there's no mistake?"

"If you will deign to go with me to your apartments, monsieur, you will find there your commission."

Canolles, completely staggered by a dénouement so utterly different from that which he anticipated, followed the officer without a word, amid the beating of drums, soldiers presenting arms, and all the inhabitants of the fortress, who made the air resound with acclamations. Pale and excited, he saluted to right and left, and questioned Barrabas with dismayed glance.

At last he was introduced into a salon furnished with some pretensions to elegance, from the windows of which he noticed first of all that he could see the château de Cambes; and there he read his commission, drawn up in proper form, signed by the queen, and countersigned by the Duc d'Épernon.

At that sight Canolles' legs altogether failed him, and he fell helplessly upon a chair.

After all the fanfares and presenting arms and noisy demonstrations of respect in the military fashion, and after the first feeling of surprise which these demonstrations produced in him, Canolles was anxious to know just what to think with reference to the office the queen had bestowed upon him, and raised his eyes which for some time had been fastened upon the floor.

He then saw standing in front of him, no less thunderstruck than himself, his former keeper, become his very humble servant.

"Ah! is it you, Master Barrabas?" said he.

"Myself, Monsieur le Gouverneur."

"Will you explain what has happened? for I have all the difficulty in the world not to take it for a dream."

"I will explain to you, monsieur, that when I talked about the extraordinary question and the ten pots of water I thought, on my honor, that I was gilding the pill."

"You mean to say that you were convinced—?"

"That I was bringing you here to be broken on the wheel, monsieur."

"Thanks!" said Canolles, shuddering in spite of himself. "But have you any opinion now as to what has happened?"

"Yes, monsieur."

"Do me the favor to tell me what it is, monsieur."

"It is this, monsieur. The queen must have realized what a difficult mission it was that she intrusted to you. As soon as the first angry outburst had spent itself, she must have repented, and as you are not a repulsive fellow, all things considered, her gracious Majesty has thought fit to reward you because she had punished you too severely."

"Impossible!" said Canolles.

"Impossible, you think?"

"Improbable, at least."

"Improbable?"

"Yes."

"In that case, monsieur, it only remains for me to offer you my very humble respects. You can be as happy as a king at Île Saint-Georges,— excellent wine, abundance of game, and fresh fish at every tide, brought by boats from Bordeaux and by the women of Saint-Georges. Ah, monsieur, this is a miraculous ending!"

"Very good; I will try to follow your advice. Take this order signed by myself, and go to the paymaster, who will give you ten pistoles. I would give them to you myself, but since you took all my money as a measure of precaution—"

"And I did well, monsieur," cried Barrabas; "for if you had succeeded in corrupting me you would have fled, and if you had fled you would naturally have sacrificed the elevated position which you have now attained, and I should never have forgiven myself."

"Very cleverly argued, Master Barrabas. I have already noticed that you are a past master in logic. But take this paper as a token of my appreciation of your eloquence. The ancients, you know, represented Eloquence with chains of gold issuing from her mouth."

"Monsieur," rejoined Barrabas, "if I dared I would remark that I think it useless to call upon the paymaster—"

"What! you refuse?" cried Canolles.

"No, God forbid! I have no false pride, thank Heaven! But I can see certain strings, which look to me much like purse-strings, protruding from a box on your chimney-piece."

"You are evidently a connoisseur in strings, Master Barrabas," said Canolles. "We will see if your previsions are correct."

There was a casket of old faience, incrusted with silver, upon the chimney-piece. Canolles raised the lid, and found within, a purse, and in the purse a thousand pistoles with this little note:—

"For the privy purse of Monsieur le Gouverneur of Île Saint-Georges."

"*Corbleu!*" said Canolles, blushing; "the queen does things very well."

Instinctively the thought of Buckingham came into his mind. Perhaps the queen had seen the handsome features of the young captain from behind some curtain; perhaps a tender interest in him led her to extend her protecting influence over him. Perhaps—We must remember that Canolles was a Gascon.

Unfortunately, the queen was twenty years older than in Buckingham's time.

Whatever the explanation, wherever the purse came from, Canolles put his hand in it and took out ten pistoles, which he handed to Barrabas, who left the room with a profusion of most respectful reverences.

X

When Barrabas had gone, Canolles summoned the officer, and requested him to act as his guide in the inspection he proposed to make of his new dominions.

The officer at once placed himself at his command.

At the door he found a sort of staff composed of the other principal functionaries of the citadel. Escorted by them, talking with them, and listening to descriptions of all the half-moons, casemates, cellars, and attics, the morning wore away, and about eleven o'clock he returned to his apartments, having made a thorough inspection. His escort disappeared, and Canolles was left alone with the officer whose acquaintance he had first made.

"Now," said that officer, drawing near him with an air of mystery, "there remains but a single apartment and a single person for Monsieur le Gouverneur to see."

"I beg your pardon?" said Canolles.

"That person's apartment is yonder," said the officer, pointing to a door which Canolles had not yet opened.

"Ah! it is yonder, is it?"

"Yes."

"And the person too?

"Yes."

"Very well. Pardon me, I beg, but I am greatly fatigued, having travelled night and day, and my head's not very clear this morning; so pray explain your meaning a little more fully."

"Well, Monsieur le Gouverneur," rejoined the officer, with a most knowing smile, "the apartment—"

"—of the person—" said Canolles.

"—who awaits you, is yonder. You understand now, don't you?"

Canolles started, as if he were returning from the land of dreams.

"Yes, yes. Very good," said he; "and I may go in?"

"To be sure, as you are expected."

"Here goes, then!" said Canolles; and with his heart beating fit to burst its walls, hardly able to see, his fears and his desires inextricably confused in his mind, he opened the door and saw behind the hangings, with laughing face and sparkling eyes, Nanon de Lartigues, who cried out with joy, as she threw her arms around the young man's neck.

Canolles stood like a statue, with his arms hanging at his sides, and lifeless eye.

"You?" he faltered.

"I!" said she, redoubling her smiles and kisses.

The remembrance of the wrong he had done her passed through Canolles' mind, and as he divined instantly that he owed to this faithful friend his latest good-fortune, he was utterly crushed by the combined weight of remorse and gratitude.

"Ah!" said he; "you were at hand to save me while I was throwing myself away like a madman; you were watching over me; you are my guardian angel."

"Don't call me your angel, for I am a very devil," said Nanon; "but I appear only at opportune times, you will admit."

"You are right, dear friend; in good sooth, I believe that you have saved me from the scaffold."

"I think so too. Ah! baron, how could you, shrewd and far-sighted as you are, ever allow yourself to be taken in by those conceited jades of princesses?"

Canolles blushed to the whites of his eyes; but Nanon had adopted the plan of not noticing his embarrassment.

"In truth," said he, "I don't know. I can't understand myself."

"Oh, they are very cunning! Ah, messieurs, you choose to make war on women! What's this I have heard? They showed you, in place of the younger princess, a maid of honor, a chambermaid, a log of wood—what was it?"

Canolles felt the fever rising from his trembling fingers to his confused brain.

"I thought it was the princess," he said; "I didn't know her."

"Who was it, pray?"

"A maid of honor, I think."

"Ah, my poor boy! it's that traitor Mazarin's fault. What the devil! when a man is sent upon a delicate mission like that, they should give him a portrait. If you had had or seen a portrait of Madame la Princesse, you would certainly have recognized her. But let us say no more about it. Do you know that that awful Mazarin, on the pretext that you had betrayed the king, wanted to throw you to the toads?"

"I suspected as much."

"But I said: 'Let's throw him to the Nanons.' Did I do well? Tell me!"

Preoccupied as he was with the memory of the viscountess, and although he wore the viscountess's portrait upon his heart, Canolles could not resist the bewitching tenderness, the charming wit that sparkled in the loveliest eyes in the world; he stooped and pressed his lips upon the pretty hand which was offered him.

"And you came here to await me?"

"I went to Paris to find you, and bring you here. I carried your commission with me. The separation seemed very long and tedious to me, for Monsieur d'Épernon alone fell with his full weight upon my monotonous life. I learned of your discomfiture. By the way, I had forgotten to tell you; you are my brother, you know."

"I thought so from reading your letter."

"Yes, somebody betrayed us. The letter I wrote you fell into bad hands. The duke arrived in a rage. I told him your name, and that you were my brother, poor Canolles; and we are now united by the most legitimate bond. You are almost my husband, my poor boy."

Canolles yielded to her incredible powers of fascination. Having kissed her white hands he kissed her black eyes. The ghost of Madame de Cambes should have taken flight, veiling her eyes in sorrow.

"After that," continued Nanon, "I laid my plans, and provided for everything. I made of Monsieur d'Épernon your patron, or rather your friend. I turned aside the wrath of Mazarin. Lastly, I selected Saint-Georges as a place of retirement, because, dear boy, you know, they are forever wanting to stone me. Dear Canolles, you are the only soul in the whole world who loves me ever so little. Come, tell me that you love me!"

And the captivating siren, throwing her arms about the young man's neck, gazed ardently into his eyes, as if she would read to the very depths of his heart.

Canolles felt in his heart, which Nanon was seeking to read, that he could not remain insensible to such boundless devotion. A secret presentiment told him that there was something more than love in Nanon's feeling for him, that there was generosity too, and that she not only loved him, but forgave him.

He made a motion of his head which answered her question; for he would not have dared to say with his lips that he loved her, although at the bottom of his heart all his memories pleaded in her favor.

"And so I made choice of Île Saint-Georges," she continued, "as a safe place for my money, my jewelry, and my person. 'What other than the man I love,' I said to myself, 'can defend my life? What other than my master can guard my treasures?' Everything is in your hands, my own love,—my life and my wealth. Will you keep a jealous watch over it all? Will you be a faithful friend and faithful guardian?"

At that moment a bugle rang out in the court-yard, and awoke a sympathetic vibration in Canolles' heart. He had before him love, more eloquent than it had ever been; a hundred yards away was war,—war, which inflames and intoxicates the imagination.

"Yes, Nanon, yes!" he cried. "Your person and your treasure are safe in my hands, and I would die, I swear it, to save you from the slightest danger."

"Thanks, my noble knight," said she; "I am as sure of your courage as of your nobleness of heart. Alas!" she added with a smile, "I would I were as sure of your love."

"Oh!" murmured Canolles, "you may be sure—"

"Very well, very well," said Nanon, "love is proved by deeds, not by oaths; by what you do, monsieur, we will judge of your love."

Throwing the loveliest arms in the world around Canolles' neck, she laid her head against his throbbing breast.

"Now, he must forget," she said to herself, "and he will forget—"

XI

On the day that Canolles was arrested at Jaulnay, under the eyes of Madame de Cambes, she set out with Pompée to join Madame la Princesse, who was in the neighborhood of Coutras.

The worthy squire's first care was to try and prove to his mistress that the failure of Cauvignac's band to hold the fair traveller to ransom, or to commit any act of violence in her regard, was to be attributed to his resolute bearing, and his experience in the art of war. To be sure, Madame de Cambes was less easily convinced than Pompée hoped would be the case, and called his attention to the fact that for something more than an hour he had entirely disappeared; but Pompée explained to her that during that time he was hiding in a corridor, where he had prepared everything for the viscountess's flight, having a ladder in readiness; but he was compelled to maintain an unequal struggle with two frantic soldiers, who tried to take the ladder away from him; the which he did, of course, with his well-known indomitable courage.

This conversation naturally led Pompée to bestow a warm eulogium upon the soldiers of his day, who were savage as lions in face of the enemy, as they had proved at the siege of Montauban and the battle of Corbie; but gentle and courteous to their compatriots,—qualities of which the soldiers of that day could hardly boast, it must be confessed.

The fact is that, without suspecting it, Pompée narrowly escaped a great danger, that of being kidnapped. As he was strutting about, as usual, with gleaming eyes, puffed-out chest, and the general appearance of a Nimrod, he fell under Cauvignac's eye; but, thanks to subsequent events; thanks to the two hundred pistoles he had received from Nanon to molest no one save Baron de Canolles; and thanks to the philosophical reflection that jealousy is the most magnificent of passions, and must be treated with respect when one finds it in his path, the dear brother passed Pompée disdainfully by, and allowed Madame de Cambes to continue her journey to Bordeaux. Indeed, in Nanon's eyes Bordeaux was very near Canolles. She would have been glad to have the viscountess in Peru or Greenland or the Indies.

On the other hand, when Nanon reflected that henceforth she would have her dear Canolles all to herself within four strong walls, and that excellent fortifications, inaccessible to the king's soldiers, made a prisoner of Madame de Cambes to all intent, her heart swelled with the unspeakable joy which none but children and lovers know on this earth.

We have seen how her dream was realized, and Nanon and Canolles were united at Île Saint-Georges.

Madame de Cambes pursued her journey sadly and fearfully. Notwithstanding his boasting, Pompée was very far from reassuring her, and she was terrified beyond measure to see a considerable party of mounted-men approaching along a cross-road, toward evening of the day that she left Jaulnay.

They were the same gentlemen returning from the famous burial of the Duc de La Rochefoucauld, which afforded Monsieur le Prince de Marsillac an opportunity, under the pretext of rendering due honor to his father's memory, to get together all the nobility of France and Picardy, who hated Mazarin even more than they loved the princess. But Madame de Cambes and Pompée were struck by the fact that some of these horsemen carried an arm in a sling; others had a leg hanging limp and swathed in bandages; several had bloody bandages around their heads. It was necessary to look very closely at these cruelly maltreated gentlemen to recognize in them the active, spruce cavaliers who hunted the stag in the park at Chantilly.

But fear has keen eyes; and Pompée and Madame de Cambes recognized some familiar faces under the bloody bandages.

"*Peste!* madame," said Pompée, "the funeral procession must have travelled over very rough roads. I should say that most of these gentlemen had had a fall! see how they've been curried."

"That's just what I was looking at," said Claire.

"It reminds me of the return from Corbie," said Pompée, proudly; "but on that occasion I was not among the gallant fellows who returned, but among those who were brought back."

"But aren't these gentlemen commanded by any one?" Claire asked, in some anxiety as to the success of an enterprise which seemed to have had such inauspicious results. "Have they no leader? Has their leader been slain, that we do not see him? Pray look!"

"Madame," replied Pompée, rising majestically in his stirrups, "nothing is easier than to distinguish a leader among the people he commands. Ordinarily, on the march, the officer rides in the centre, with his staff; in action, he rides behind or on the flank of his troop. Cast your eyes at the different points that I mention and you can judge for yourself."

"I can see nothing, Pompée; but I think that some one is following us. Pray look back—"

"Hm! no, madame," said Pompée, clearing his throat, but omitting to turn his head lest he might really see some one. "No, there is nobody. But, stay, may that not be the leader with that red plume? No. That gilded sword? No. That piebald horse like Madame de Turenne's? No. It's a strange thing; there's no danger, and the commanding officer might venture to show himself; it isn't here as it was at Corbie—"

"You are mistaken, Master Pompée," said a harsh, mocking voice behind the poor squire, who nearly lost his seat in his fright; "you are mistaken, it's much worse than at Corbie."

Claire quickly turned her head, and saw within five feet of her a horseman of medium stature, dressed with an affectation of simplicity, who was looking at her with a pair of small, gleaming eyes, as deep set as a ferret's. "With his thick, black hair, his thin, twitching lips, his bilious pallor, and his frowning brow, this gentleman had a depressing effect even in broad daylight; at night his appearance would perhaps have inspired fear.

"Monsieur le Prince de Marsillac!" cried Claire, deeply moved. "Ah! well met, monsieur."

"Say Monsieur le Duc de La Rochefoucauld, madame; for now that the duke my father is dead I have succeeded to that name, under which all the actions of my life, good or bad, are to be set down."

"You are returning?" said Claire, with some hesitation.

"We are returning beaten, madame."

"Beaten! great Heaven!"

"I say that we are returning beaten, madame, because I am naturally little inclined to boast, and I tell the truth to myself as well as to others; otherwise I might claim that we are returning victorious; but, in point of fact, we are beaten because our design upon Saumur failed. I arrived too late; we have lost that important place, which Jarzé has surrendered. Henceforth, assuming that Madame la Princesse has Bordeaux, which has been promised her, the war will be concentrated in Guyenne."

"But, monsieur," said Claire, "if, as I understand you to say, the capitulation of Saumur took place without a blow, how does it happen that all these gentleman are wounded?"

"Because," said La Rochefoucauld, with pride, which he could not conceal, despite his power over himself, "we fell in with some royal troops."

"And you fought with them?" demanded Madame de Cambes, eagerly.

"*Mon Dieu!* yes, madame."

"So the first French blood has already been spilled by Frenchmen!" murmured the viscountess. "And you, Monsieur le Duc, were the one to set the example?"

"I was, madame."

"You, so calm and cool and shrewd!"

"When one upholds an unjust cause against me it sometimes happens that I become very unreasonable because I am so earnest in my support of what is reasonable."

"You are not wounded, I trust?"

"No, I was more fortunate this time than at Lignes and Paris. Indeed, I thought that I had had my fill of civil war, and was done with it forever; but I was mistaken. What would you have? Man always forms his plans without consulting his passions, the true architects of his life, which give an entirely different shape to the structure, when they do not overturn it altogether."

Madame de Cambes smiled, for she remembered that Monsieur de La Rochefoucauld had said that for Madame de Longueville's lovely eyes he had made war on kings, and would make war on the gods.

This smile did not escape the duke, and he gave the viscountess no time to follow up the thought which gave it birth.

"Allow me to offer you my congratulations, madame," he continued, "for you are, in truth, a very model of valor."

"Why so?"

"Good lack! to travel thus alone, or with a single attendant, like a Clorinda or a Bradamante! Oh! by the way, I have heard of your admirable conduct at Chantilly. They tell me that you fooled a poor devil of a royal officer to perfection. An easy victory, was it not?" added the duke, with the smile and the look which, upon his face, meant so much.

"How so?" Claire asked with emotion.

"I say easy," continued the duke, "because he did not fight on equal terms with you. There was one thing, however, that impressed me particularly in the version that was given me of that episode," — and the duke fixed his little eyes upon the viscountess more sharply than ever.

There was no way for Madame de Cambes to retreat with honor, so she prepared to make as vigorous a defence as possible.

"Tell me what it was that struck you so forcibly, Monsieur le Duc," said she.

"It was the very great skill, madame, with which you played that little comic part; in fact, if I am to believe what I hear, the officer had already seen your squire and yourself."

These last words, although uttered with the studied indifference of a man of tact, did not fail to produce a deep impression upon Madame de Cambes.

"He had seen me, monsieur, do you say?"

"One moment, madame; let us understand each other; it's not I who say it, but that indefinite personage called 'they' to whose power kings are as submissive as the lowest of their subjects."

"Where had he seen me, may I ask?"

"*They say* that it was on the way from Libourne to Chantilly, at a village called Jaulnay; but the interview was cut short, as the gentleman received an order from Monsieur d'Épernon to start at once for Mantes."

"But if this gentleman had seen me before, Monsieur le Duc, how could he have failed to recognize me?"

"Ah! the famous *they* of whom I spoke just now, and who have an answer for every question, would say that the thing was possible, as the interview took place in the dark."

"Really, Monsieur le Duc," said the viscountess, in dismay, "I am at a loss to understand what you mean by that."

"In that case," rejoined the duke, with assumed good-nature, "I must have been ill-informed; and then, what does a mere momentary encounter amount to, after all? It is true, madame," he added gallantly, "that your face and figure are calculated to leave a deep impression, even after an interview lasting only an instant."

"But that would not be possible," the viscountess retorted, "if, as you yourself say, the interview took place in the dark."

"Very true, and you parry cleverly, madame. I must be the one who is mistaken, then, unless the young man had noticed you even before the interview at Jaulnay, which in that case would not be precisely a meeting."

"What would it be, then? Be careful of your words, Monsieur le Duc."

"As you see, I am hesitating; our dear French language is so poor that I seek in vain for a word to express my thought. It would be what is called, in Italian, an *appuntamento*; in English, an *assignation*."

"If I am not mistaken, Monsieur le Duc," said Claire, "those two words are translated in French by *rendez-vous?*"

"Go to!" exclaimed the duke; "here I have said a foolish thing in two foreign languages, and lo! I stumble upon a person who understands them both! Pardon me, madame; it seems that Italian and English are as poor as French."

Claire pressed her hand to her heart to breathe more freely; she was suffocating. One thing was made clear to her mind which she had always suspected; namely, that Monsieur de La Rochefoucauld had for her been unfaithful to Madame de Longueville, in thought and in desire at least, and that it was a feeling of jealousy which led him to speak as he had been speaking. In fact, two years before, the Prince de Marsillac had paid court to her as assiduously as was consistent with his crafty nature, and his constant indecision and timidity, which made him the most vindictive of foes, when he was not the most grateful of friends. So it was that the viscountess preferred not to break a lance with the man who held public and private affairs in the hollow of his hand.

"Do you know, Monsieur le Duc," said she, "that you are an invaluable man, especially under circumstances like the present; and that Monsieur de Mazarin, much as he prides himself upon his police, is no better served in that regard than yourself?"

"If I knew nothing, madame," retorted Monsieur de la Rochefoucauld, "I should resemble that dear statesman too closely, and should have no reason for making war upon him. And so I try to keep myself posted on everything."

"Even the secrets of your allies, if they have any?"

"You used a word then which might be construed to your disadvantage, if it should be overheard, — 'secrets.' So that journey and that meeting were secrets, were they?"

"Let us understand each other, Monsieur le Duc, for you are no more than half right. The meeting was an accident. The journey was a secret, yes, and a woman's secret too, for it was known to none but Madame la Princesse and myself."

The duke smiled. This sturdy defence made him sharpen up his own wits.

"And to Lenet," he said, "and Richon, and Madame de Tourville, to say nothing of a certain Vicomte de Cambes, whose name I heard for the first time in connection with this matter. To be sure, as he is your brother, you might tell me that the secret was all in the family."

Claire began to laugh, to avoid irritating the duke, whose smile was beginning to show signs of vanishing.

"Do you know one thing, duke?" said she.

"No, tell it me; and if it is a secret, madame, I promise to be as discreet as yourself, and tell it to no one but my staff."

"Do as you please about that; I ask nothing better, although I thereby run the risk of making an enemy of a great princess, whose hatred would be no pleasant thing to incur."

The duke blushed imperceptibly.

"Well, what is this secret?" said he.

"Do you know whom Madame la Princesse selected for my companion in the journey I was asked to undertake?"

"No,"

"Yourself."

"Indeed! I remember that Madame la Princesse asked me if I could act as escort to a person returning from Libourne to Paris."

"And you refused?"

"I was unavoidably detained in Poitou by important business."

"Yes, you had to receive couriers from Madame de Longueville."

La Rochefoucauld gazed earnestly at the viscountess, as if to search the lowest depths of her heart before the trace of her words had disappeared, and said, riding closer to her side: "Do you reproach me for it?"

"Not at all; your heart is so well disposed in that place, Monsieur le Duc, that you have a right to expect compliments rather than reproaches."

"Ah!" said the duke, with an involuntary sigh; "would to God I had made that journey with you!"

"Why so?"

"Because then I should not have gone to Saumur," he replied, in a tone which indicated that he had another response ready, which he did not dare, or did not choose, to make.

"Richon must have told him everything," thought Claire.

"However, I do not repine at my private ill-fortune, since it has resulted to the public good."

"What do you mean, monsieur? I do not understand you."

"I mean that if I had been with you, you would not have fallen in with the officer, who happened, so clear it is that Heaven is on our side, to be the same one sent by Mazarin to Chantilly."

"Ah! Monsieur le Duc," said Claire, in a voice choked by the memory of the harrowing scene so recently enacted, "do not jest concerning that unfortunate officer!"

"Why? Is his person sacred?"

"Now, yes; for to noble hearts great misfortunes are no less sanctified than great good-fortune. That officer may be dead at this hour, monsieur, and he will have paid for his error, or his devotion, with his life."

"Dead with love?" queried the duke.

"Let us speak seriously, monsieur; you are well aware that if I give my heart away it will not be to people whom I meet on the high-road. I tell you that the unhappy man was arrested this very day by order of Monsieur de Mazarin."

"Arrested!" exclaimed the duke. "How do you know that?—still by accident?"

"*Mon Dieu*, yes! I was passing through Jaulnay—Do you know Jaulnay, monsieur?"

"Perfectly; I received a sword-cut in the shoulder there. You were passing through Jaulnay. Why, wasn't that the village where, as the story goes—?"

"Let us have done with the story, Monsieur le Duc," replied Claire, blushing. "I was passing through Jaulnay, as I tell you, when I saw a party of armed men halting with a prisoner in their midst; the prisoner was he."

"He, do you say? Ah! madame, take care, you said *he!*"

"The officer, I mean. *Mon Dieu!* Monsieur le Duc, how deep you are! A truce to your subtleties, and if you have no pity for the poor fellow—"

"Pity! I!" cried the duke. "In God's name, madame, have I time to have pity, especially for people I do not know?"

Claire cast a sidelong glance at La Rochefoucauld's pale face, and his thin lips curled by a joyless smile, and she shuddered involuntarily.

"Madame," he continued, "I would be glad to have the honor of escorting you farther; but I must throw a garrison into Montrond, so forgive me if I leave you. Twenty gentlemen, more fortunate than I, will look to your safety until you have joined Madame la Princesse, to whom I beg you to present my respects."

"Are you not going to Bordeaux?" Claire asked.

"No; just now I am on my way to Turenne to join Monsieur de Bouillon. We are engaged in a contest of courtesy to see which shall not be general; he's a doughty antagonist, but I am determined to get the better of him, and remain his lieutenant."

Upon that the duke ceremoniously saluted the viscountess and rode slowly away in the direction taken by his little band of horsemen. Claire followed him with her eyes, murmuring:—

"His pity! I invoked his pity! He spoke the truth; he has no time to feel pity."

A group of horsemen left the main body and came toward her, while the rest rode into the woods near by.

Behind them, with his reins over his horse's neck, La Rochefoucauld rode dreamily along, the man of the false look and the white hands, who wrote at the head of his memoirs this sentence, which sounds strangely enough in the mouth of a moral philosopher:—

"I think that one should content himself with making a show of compassion, but should be careful to have none. It is a passion which serves no useful purpose within a well-constituted mind, which serves only to weaken the heart, and which should be left to the common people, who, as they never do anything by reason, need to have passion in order to do anything."

Two days later Madame de Cambes was in attendance upon Madame la Princesse.

XII

Many, many times had Madame de Cambes instinctively reflected upon what might be the result of a hatred like Monsieur de La Rochefoucauld's; but feeling strong in her youth, her beauty, her wealth, and her high favor, she did not realize that that hatred, supposing it to exist, was likely to have a baleful effect upon her life.

But when Madame de Cambes knew beyond question that she occupied a sufficient place in his thoughts to lead him to take the trouble to find out all that he knew, she lost no time in broaching the subject to Madame la Princesse.

"Madame," said she, in reply to the compliments with which she was overwhelmed, "do not congratulate me overmuch upon the address which I am said to have exhibited upon that occasion; for there are those who claim that the officer, our dupe, knew the real state of the case as to the true and the false Princesse de Condé."

But as this supposition deprived Madame la Princesse of all credit for her part in the execution of the stratagem, she naturally refused to listen to it.

"Yes, yes, my dear Claire," said she; "now that our gentleman finds that we deceived him, he would be glad to pretend that he favored our plans; unfortunately, it's a little late to make that claim, as he has been disgraced for his fiasco. *à propos*, I am told that you fell in with Monsieur de La Rochefoucauld on your way hither."

"Yes, madame."

"What news did he tell you?"

"That he was going to Turenne, to come to terms with Monsieur de Bouillon."

"There is a struggle between them, I know, as to which of the two shall be generalissimo of our armies, both making a show of declining the honor. The fact is that when we make peace, the man who has made himself most feared as a rebel will have to pay the heaviest price for his return to favor. But I have a plan of Madame de Tourville's to bring them to terms."

"Oho!" said the viscountess, smiling at that name; "your Highness is reconciled, I judge, to your counsellor in ordinary."

"I was driven to it; she joined us at Montrond, carrying her roll of papers with a gravity which made Lenet and myself almost die of laughing.

"'Although your Highness,' she said, 'pays no attention to these reflections of mine, the fruit of many laborious nights' work, I bring my contribution to the general welfare.'"

"Was it a veritable harangue?"

"Under three heads."

"And your Highness replied to it?"

"Not I; I left that to Lenet. 'Madame,' said he, 'we have never doubted your zeal, still less your extensive knowledge; they are both so invaluable to us that Madame la Princesse and I have regretted your absence every day.' In a word, he said a multitude of such pleasant things to her that he won her heart, and she ended by giving him her plan."

"Which is—?"

"To appoint neither Monsieur de Bouillon nor Monsieur de La Rochefoucauld generalissimo, but Monsieur de Turenne."

"Well," said Claire, "it seems to me that the counsellor counselled wisely then, at all events; what do you say to it, Monsieur Lenet?"

"I say that Madame la Vicomtesse is right, and that she brings one more judicious voice to our deliberations," replied Lenet, who entered the room at that moment with a roll of paper, and with as serious an expression as Madame de Tourville's face could have worn. "Unfortunately, Monsieur de Turenne cannot leave the army of the North, and our plan provides for his marching upon Paris when Mazarin and the queen march upon Bordeaux."

"You will notice, my dear girl, that Lenet is the man of impossibilities. In fact, neither Monsieur de Bouillon, nor Monsieur de La Rochefoucauld, nor Monsieur de Turenne is our generalissimo, but Lenet!—What has your Excellency there,—a proclamation?"

"Yes, madame."

"Madame de Tourville's, of course?"

"Of course, madame; except for a few necessary changes, in her own words,—the style of the chancellor's office, you know."

"Nonsense!" said the princess, laughing; "let us not attach too much importance to the letter: if the spirit is there, that is all we need."

"It is there, madame."

"And where is Monsieur de Bouillon to sign?"

"On the same line with Monsieur de La Rochefoucauld."

"But you do not tell me where Monsieur de La Rochefoucauld will sign."

"Immediately below Monsieur le Duc d'Enghien."

"Monsieur le Duc d'Enghien should not sign such a document. A child!—think of it, Lenet."

"I have thought of it, madame. When the king dies, the dauphin succeeds him, though it be but for a single day. Why should it not be with the house of Condé as with the house of France?"

"But what will Monsieur de La Rochefoucauld say? What will Monsieur de Bouillon say?"

"The first has said, madame, and went away after he had said; the second will know nothing about it until it is done, and consequently will say what he pleases; it matters little."

"There is the cause of the duke's coolness to you, Claire."

"Let him be cool, madame," said Lenet; "he will warm up at the first gun Maréchal de la Meilleraie fires upon us. These gentlemen long to fight: very well, let them fight."

"Be careful not to irritate them too far, Lenet," said the princess; "we have only them."

"And they have only your name; just let them try to fight on their own account, and you will see how long they will hold out; give and take."

Madame de Tourville had entered the room a few seconds before, and the radiant expression of her countenance had given place to an anxious expression, which was deepened by the last words of her rival, the councillor.

She stepped forward hastily.

"Is the plan I laid before your Highness," she said, "so unfortunate as not to meet the approval of Monsieur Lenet?"

"On the contrary, madame," Lenet replied with a bow, "I have carefully retained the larger part of your draft; the only difference is that, instead of being signed in chief by the Duc de Bouillon or the Duc de La Rochefoucauld, the proclamation will be signed by Monseigneur le Duc d'Enghien; the names of those gentlemen will come after the prince's name."

"You will compromise the young prince, monsieur."

"It is only just that he should be compromised, madame, since the troops are fighting for him."

"But the Bordelais love the Duc de Bouillon, they adore the Duc de La Rochefoucauld, and they do not know the Duc d'Enghien."

"You are wrong," said Lenet, as usual taking a paper from that pocket whose enormous capacity had amazed Madame la Princesse, "for here is a letter from the President of the Parliament of Bordeaux, in which he begs me to have the young duke sign the proclamation."

"Oh! a fig for the Parliaments, Lenet!" cried the princess; "it's not worth while to escape from the power of Monsieur de Mazarin if we are to fall into the power of the Parliaments."

"Does your Highness wish to enter Bordeaux?"

"To be sure."

"Very good; then that is the *sine qua non*; they will not burn a match for any other than Monsieur le Duc d'Enghien."

Madame de Tourville bit her lips.

"And so," said the princess, "you induced us to fly from Chantilly, you caused us to travel a hundred and fifty leagues, to expose us at the last to insult from the Bordelais?"

"What you style an insult, madame, is an honor. Indeed, what could be more flattering to Madame la Princesse de Condé than to be assured that it is she who is made welcome at Bordeaux, and not these others?"

"You say that the Bordelais will not receive the two dukes?"

"They will receive your Highness only."

"What can I do alone?"

"What! *Mon Dieu!*—go in, to be sure; and as you go in leave the gates open so that the others may enter behind you."

"We cannot do without them."

"That is my opinion, and a fortnight hence it will be the opinion of the Parliament. Bordeaux repulses your army, which it fears, and within a fortnight it will call upon it for defence. You will then have the twofold merit of having done twice what the Bordelais requested you to do; and when that is so, have no fear; they will face death for you from the first man to the last."

"Is Bordeaux threatened?" asked Madame de Tourville.

"Very seriously threatened," Lenet replied; "that is why it is of such pressing importance to effect a lodgment there. So long as we are not there, Bordeaux can, without compromising its honor, refuse to open its gates to us; but when we are once there, Bordeaux cannot, without dishonoring itself, drive us outside its walls."

"Who is threatening Bordeaux, pray?"

"The king, the queen, Monsieur de Mazarin. The royal forces are levying recruits; our enemies are getting into position. Île Saint-Georges, which is but three leagues from the city, has received a re-enforcement of troops, a fresh supply of ammunition, and a new governor. The Bordelais propose to try and take the island, and will naturally be beaten back, as they will have to do with the king's best troops. Having been well and duly whipped, as becomes peaceable citizens who undertake to mimic soldiers, they will cry out loudly for the Ducs de Bouillon and de La Rochefoucauld. Then, madame, you, who hold those two dukes in your hand, will make your own terms with the Parliament."

"But would it not be better to try and win this new governor over to our side, before the Bordelais have undergone a defeat, which may discourage them?"

"If you are in Bordeaux when this defeat is sustained, you have nothing to fear. As for winning over the governor, it's an impossibility."

"An impossibility! Why so?"

"Because he is a personal enemy of your Highness."

"A personal enemy?"

"Yes."

"Pray what is the cause of his enmity?"

"He will never forgive your Highness the mystification of which he was the victim at Chantilly. Oh! Monsieur de Mazarin is no such fool as you think him, mesdames, although I wear myself out by constant efforts to convince you of your error! He has proved it by sending to Île Saint-Georges, that is to say, the most advantageous position in the province—whom do you guess?"

"I have already told you that I cannot imagine who it can be."

"Well, it's the officer at whom you laughed so much, and who, with inconceivable stupidity, allowed your Highness to escape from Chantilly."

"Monsieur de Canolles?" cried Claire.

"Yes."

"Monsieur de Canolles governor of Île Saint-Georges?"

"Himself."

"Impossible! He was arrested before my very eyes!"

"True. But he has a powerful protector, no doubt, and his disgrace is changed to favor."

"And you fancied him dead ere this, my poor Claire," said Madame la Princesse, laughingly.

"Are you quite sure?" asked the viscountess, amazed beyond measure.

As usual, Lenet put his hand into the famous pocket and produced a paper.

"Here is a letter from Richon," he said, "giving me all the details of the new governor's installation, and expressing his regret that your Highness did not station him at Île Saint-Georges."

"Madame la Princesse station Monsieur Richon at Île Saint-Georges!" exclaimed Madame de Tourville, with a smile of triumph. "Pray, do we dispose of governor-ships of his Majesty's fortresses?"

"We can dispose of one, madame," Lenet replied, "and that is enough."

"Of what one, I pray to know?"

Madame de Tourville shuddered as she saw Lenet put his hand in his pocket.

"Monsieur d'Épernon's signature in blank!" cried the princess. "True; I had forgotten it."

"Bah! what does that amount to?" said Madame de Tourville, disdainfully. "A scrap of paper, nothing more."

"That scrap of paper, madame," said Lenet, "is the appointment we need as a counterpoise to the one recently made. It is a counterpoise to Île

Saint-Georges; in fine, it is our salvation, for it means some place on the Dordogne, as Saint-Georges is on the Garonne."

"You are sure," said Claire, who had heard nothing for the last five minutes, and whose mind had remained stationary at the intelligence announced by Lenet and confirmed by Richon; "you are sure, monsieur, that it is the same Monsieur de Canolles who was arrested at Jaulnay, who is now governor of Île Saint-Georges?"

"I am sure of it, madame."

"Monsieur de Mazarin has a peculiar way," she continued, "of escorting his governors to their governments."

"True," said the princess, "and there certainly is something behind all this."

"To be sure there is," said Lenet; "there is Mademoiselle Nanon de Lartigues."

"Nanon de Lartigues!" cried Claire, stung to the heart by a terrible memory.

"That courtesan!" said the princess, with the utmost contempt.

"Yes, madame," said Lenet, "that courtesan, whom your Highness refused to see, when she solicited the honor of being presented to you, and whom the queen, less punctilious than yourself in matters of etiquette, did receive; which caused her to make answer to your chamberlain that it was possible that Madame la Princesse de Condé was a more exalted personage than Anne of Austria, but that Anne of Austria most assuredly had more prudence than the Princesse de Condé."

"Your memory is failing, Lenet, or else you wish to spare my feelings," cried the princess. "The insolent creature was not content to say 'more prudence,' she said 'more sense,' as well."

"Possibly," said Lenet, with a smile. "I stepped into the antechamber at that moment, and did not hear the end of the sentence."

"But I was listening at the door," said Madame la Princesse, "and I heard the whole of it."

"At all events you understand, madame, that it is a woman who will wage relentless war upon you. The queen would have sent soldiers to fight against you; Nanon will send insidious enemies, whom you must unearth and crush."

"Perhaps," said Madame de Tourville, sourly, to Lenet, "if you had been in her Highness's place you would have received her with reverential awe?"

"No, madame," said Lenet, "I would have received her with a smile, and would have bought her."

"Oh well, if it's a question of buying her, there is still time."

"Certainly there is still time; but at this time she would probably be too dear for our resources."

"How much is she worth?" the princess asked.

"Five hundred thousand livres before the war."

"But to-day?"

"A million."

"Why, for that price I could buy Monsieur de Mazarin!"

"'Tis possible," said Lenet; "things that have already been sold and resold are apt to grow cheaper."

"But, if we can't buy her, we must take her!" said Madame de Tourville, still in favor of violent measures.

"You would render her Highness an inestimable service, madame, could you attain that object; but it would be difficult of attainment, as we have absolutely no idea where she is. But let us leave that for the present; let us first of all effect an entrance into Bordeaux, then we will find a way into Île Saint-Georges."

"No, no!" cried Claire; "no, we will effect an entrance at Île Saint-Georges first!"

This exclamation, evidently from the heart, caused the other women to turn toward the viscountess, while Lenet gazed at her as earnestly as Monsieur de La Rochefoucauld could have done, but with a kindlier interest.

"Why, you are mad!" said the princess; "you have heard Lenet say that the place is impregnable!"

"That may be," said Claire, "but I think that we can take it."

"Have you a plan?" said Madame de Tourville, with the air of one who fears the erection of an altar in opposition to her own.

"Perhaps," said Claire.

"But," laughed the princess, "if Île Saint-Georges is held at so high a figure as Lenet says, perhaps we are not rich enough to buy it."

"We will not buy it," said Claire, "but we will have it all the same."

"By force, then," said Madame de Tourville; "my dear friend, you are coming around to my plan."

"That's it," said the princess. "We will send Richon to besiege Saint-Georges; he is of the province, he knows the locality, and if any man can take this fortress which you deem of such importance, he is the man."

"Before resorting to that means," said Claire, "let me try the experiment, madame. If I fail, then you can do as you think best."

"What!" said the amazed princess, "you will go to Île Saint-Georges?"

"I will."

"Alone?"

"With Pompée."

"You have no fear?"

"I will go as a flag of truce, if your Highness will deign to intrust me with your instructions."

"Upon my word! this is a novelty!" cried Madame de Tourville; "for my own part I should say that diplomatists do not spring up like this, and that one must have gone through a long course of study of that science, which Monsieur de Tourville, one of the greatest diplomatists, as he was one of the greatest soldiers of his time, declared to be the most difficult of all sciences."

"However ill-informed I may be," said Claire, "I will make the trial, nevertheless, if Madame la Princesse is pleased to allow me to do so."

"Certainly Madame la Princesse will allow you to do it," said Lenet, with a significant glance at Madame de Condé; "indeed, I am convinced that if there is any person on earth who can succeed in such a negotiation, you are that person."

"Pray what can madame do that another cannot do?"

"She will simply drive a bargain with Monsieur de Canolles, which a man could not do without getting himself thrown out of the window."

"A man if you please!" retorted Madame de Tourville; "but a woman?"

"If a woman is to go to Île Saint-Georges," said Lenet, "it is quite as well, indeed much better, that it should be madame rather than any other, because it is her idea."

At that moment a messenger entered, bringing a letter from the Parliament of Bordeaux.

"Ah!" cried the princess, "the reply to my request, I presume."

The two women drew near, impelled by a common sentiment of curiosity and interest. Lenet remained where he stood, as phlegmatic as always, knowing beforehand, in all probability, what the letter contained.

The princess read it with avidity.

"They ask me to come, they summon me, they expect me!" she cried.

"Ah!" ejaculated Madame de Tourville, triumphantly.

"But the dukes, madame, and the army?" queried Lenet.

"They say nothing of them."

"Then we are left destitute," said Madame de Tourville.

"No," said the princess; "for, thanks to the Duc d'Épernon's blank signature, I shall have Vayres, which commands the Dordogne."

"And I," said Claire, "shall have Saint-Georges, which is the key of the Garonne."

"And I," said Lenet, "shall have the dukes and the army,—that is, if you give me time."